KATARINA THE KILLER

TRENT ST. GERMAIN

Black Rose Writing | Texas

ISBN: 978-1-68433-089-8
PUBLISHED BY BLACK ROSE WRITING
www.blackrosewriting.com

Printed in the United States of America
Suggested retail price $20.95

Katarina the Killer is printed in Constantia

To old houses and darkened forests at twilight:
how you've both inspired me over the years ...

KATARINA THE KILLER

PROLOGUE

Ten Points Plantation, north of Monroe, Louisiana – 1821

"To know the secret means you cannot live as a mere mortal," the smaller man said. He moved swiftly; his strength defied his diminutive frame. He opened his mouth, revealed elongated, sharp canine teeth, and tore into the taller man's neck.

"Please!" the younger, much younger, man protested. He wished he had never wanted to know the secret. Too late for that!

Theodore Ogden, Senior empathized with the droopy Spanish moss that swayed sadly in a nearby oak tree. It looked as weak and helpless as Ted felt, as he lost a battle against a tinier man; the blood and will to fight absorbed from his body. Ted surrendered and draped the smaller but stronger man's arm; the moss hung at the mercy of an old but firm branch.

Ted knew this was the way it had to be, but he hesitated no less when the time arrived.

He hadn't known *when* it would arrive. Ted was ambushed just after nightfall, as he stepped outside the large two-story house at Ten Points, his new home. He was about to light a pipe under the fall of a clear autumn night, when he was overtaken by the brute strength of the smaller man who fed on him with a fierce hunger—one clearly not satiated in some time.

After a few seconds, the pain faded. After a few minutes, Ted no longer wanted to resist; no longer owned his will.

The smaller man with the curly brown hair pulled himself from Ted and stared him over with dark, almond-shaped eyes. He grabbed a silk handkerchief from the front pocket of a frock overcoat and dabbed at Ted's neck wound as if he were some fragile, wounded bird carefully scooped from the ground. Ted felt a gentle press of the handkerchief.

And he felt those dark eyes on him.

"We must wait," the other man said to Ted, with a slight accent that didn't belong in north Louisiana, or any of the southern territories, for that matter.

He looked European, maybe Spaniard. The nose was thin and long, but the face sculpted and attractive, though different than most of those Ted normally saw. Even in the darkness, Ted could see the ivory, brittle complexion restore to an olive glow. After another moment passed, he turned from Ted and glanced past the oak tree and that gray, piteous Spanish moss. He looked to an expertly-crafted well of gray stones and mortar jutted from the ground. "You are much too close," he said, eyes off Ted and pointed to the stone well. Then he moved those eyes to the house. "You built too closely."

"I don't understand," Ted said. He was unsteady on his feet; woozy and confused. Built *what* too closely? Did he refer to the house? Was that it?

"Yes, the house," the other man replied, as though he read Ted's mind. "This house must be destroyed. Burn it."

"Wha—?"

"You *must*... It is much too close." He licked away blood from the corners of his mouth, each curl of the plump lips displayed sharp canines.

"Too close?"

"The Tenth of the Ten Points. The well. The entrance and the exit. It is your secret. To pass to the generations that come after you. Only *your* generations. If the family line is broken, then it ends there. But first, you must destroy this house and build another farther away. You can stay here on the property, but the next house must be farther away."

"Can I—?" Ted began, unsure how to ask. It wasn't their first encounter, and tonight he longed for more of the knowledge promised a few meetings back.

"Can you *what?*" the other man asked.

"A son? Can I still? You didn't—?" *Everything was to change after this night.* No one had to tell him that much. But before there was no going back he must know!

"You are still *half*-alive, Mister Ogden. You can sire as many sons, or even daughters, as you so please."

"Then you won't kill me? You'll allow me to live and prosper?"

"Indeed. But you must destroy this house of yours and build anew. No matter how weak you feel at this very moment, your lifeline is extended. One day it will make sense. I must wait a little longer before I close the wound on your neck. You will feel differently than you did on this morning when you arise tomorrow."

"How so?"

"You will know when the time arrives. You are a wealthy man with many resources, Mister Ogden." The darkened eyes moved back to the stone well. "You can build an even grander house farther away on the property. Come morning your strength will return; you will begin plans to destroy this house."

"But I'm to be married soon. I—" The words rolled away into the thick but cooler air that blew in past sunset.

"Then give your bride a castle. Build her one. Postpone matrimony, if you must."

"The Tenth of the Ten Points? Is that what this place is?"

"I will explain it to you, now that you are what you are." His voice was as strong as the rest of him. It drowned out the chirps of the crickets, who came to life throughout the grounds, as the hour past sunset crept in from the east.

"What *am* I?"

"You are a hybrid!" The Man from Another Place said, pulling him closer. His fierce brown eyes seared into Ted's weary blue ones under the glow of the moonlight. "And *I* am Demetrio!"

1

Chicago – November 2015

"Why are you doing this? He's been gone for seven years. Can't you face the fact that your brother is *dead?*"

The pragmatic tone of his ex-wife brought a flinch from Remy Van Buren, an exertion of power he had not granted her since their divorce. After a beat, he resumed packing his suitcase. It sat on the edge of his bed in his downtown condominium. Why he had even let her inside his place, and into his bedroom, was beyond him.

"Won't you hear me out?" Melissa Van Buren asked. Her voice rose, but his back stayed turned to her. Remy's stubborn refusal of retort was one of the wedges to force them apart and into divorce court two years earlier.

That and his refusal to let go of his twin brother Jimmy's disappearance in West Hollywood seven years earlier.

"Damn it, Remy, think about the children!" Melissa shouted. Anything to make him turn around and look at her.

It worked. "You know that I *always* think of the children," he said quietly, refusing to yell back and engage in a full-blown argument. He was in no mood, but the mention of the children brought an immediate reaction. "Please don't suggest otherwise."

"Then let this wait, for God's sake," Melissa said, moving closer. "Abby's Thanksgiving play is next week, and Ricky's school has holiday stuff around the same time. This thing with your brother won't change anytime soon. *It never does.*"

"They've seen him! This is the most concrete lead we've had in years!" Remy's strong jaw tensed, and his dark eyes grew larger, as a fleeting look of hope Melissa had seen too often the past seven years crept to the surface.

The sculpted face and even more sculpted body that had first attracted Melissa to her ex-husband a decade ago was now too familiar and a trifle annoying. Especially when maintaining her own fitness was a challenge after giving birth and staying busy with their son and daughter.

Remy's identical twin brother, Jimmy Van Buren, had been a mirror image. Jimmy used his aesthetic attributes to try a career as an actor and model on the West Coast.

It had failed miserably before he fell off the Earth. In fact, Jimmy Van Buren's fledgling career sank to soft-core porn movies and escorting within a few years of his California arrival. Remy's and Jimmy's parents tried to sweep it under the rug.

Remy didn't pass judgment on his brother's proclivities or career choices. He traveled to California in the early stages of the investigation into his brother's disappearance, tracked down and talked to people in the B-movie industry, and Jimmy's friends, in search of any clues that could lead him to his brother—or give him closure. None ever had. Remy's stubbornness hadn't sat well with his wife or the LAPD detectives, whose bruised feelings weren't the source of worry and fear keeping Remy awake some nights ... all these years later.

"Remy," Melissa began, hands up. They came back down. One came up to her shoulder and played with a strand of chestnut hair. "These so-called sightings happen every so often, and all you do is get your hopes up and then get depressed all over again when it never goes anywhere."

"It's different this time," he said, turning back to his half-packed suitcase. He threw in more clothes. "Multiple sightings. All in different parts of one state. This hasn't happened in a long time. I have this *feeling*. I've always felt this connection to Jimmy. My gut tells me—"

"I know, I know," she said. Her eyes rolled before she could stop them. She was glad he had turned away from her again. "It's the twin thing."

The twin thing.

Yes, he thought to himself, that's *exactly* what it is. But Melissa didn't understand. She couldn't. She was an only child. She had grown up without any siblings, much less one that had grown in the womb beside her—two parts of a whole that split early after conception.

Remington and James. Or, as everyone came to know them, Remy and Jimmy. The nicknames were just another part of the 'twin thing'.

The 'twin thing' still told him Jimmy was out there somewhere. Or was it only his wishful thinking?

One night, seven months ago, Remy awoke in a cold sweat. He had clutched his neck in a horrified gasp. *Something* had happened to Jimmy. He wasn't sure what it was, but it was something harmful, painful; something bad. Now that there was a clue where to look, he had to go there and try to find out.

"As I was saying," he continued, irritated by her interruption. "I have this *feeling*." His face sank as the words came out. "Oh dear God, Melissa, it's a different feeling though ..."

One thing Melissa appreciated about her ex-husband was that he rarely raised his voice or flew into a rage, even at his worst. His mild temper was a stark contrast to that of his hot-headed, conceited brother. Jimmy Van Buren had never met a mirror he didn't like and screwed anything with a pulse. Even though Remy's exhaustive efforts to find his missing scoundrel of a brother contributed to the decay of their marriage, she couldn't begrudge him in the long run. He loved his brother and would go to the end of the Earth to find him.

What concerned her now was how the latest reignited search would affect the holidays with their seven-year-old daughter and five-year-old son. She had taken great care since the divorce, they both had, to acclimate the children to the current arrangement. Remy often took the children on weekends, when his busy schedule as a general practitioner at one of the Windy City's busiest hospitals didn't interfere. His career as a physician was another excusable distraction from his family, and it had been another of those wedges between Melissa and him.

Another dead-end search for Jimmy Van Buren could wait a month or two, Melissa thought.

She placed a gentle hand on his shoulder. "Remy, are you *sure* this can't wait?" she asked, her tone softer.

She knew yelling and carrying on would do no good. Even though they were no longer married, the look of sadness on his face made her want to hold and comfort him. She looked over his shoulder at the double bed and wondered how many other women he had shared it with since their divorce. She quickly put away the thought. It was *his* bed to do with, and with whom, as he pleased. The one they had shared during their marriage was the one she still slept in alone, in the house they once shared in the suburbs of Skokie. The final part of their divorce settlement was Melissa's insistence she buy out his half of their home.

"I know how you feel about him, Remy, but I have to think about Abby and Ricky, too. I'll be the one who has to explain this to them."

He paused again as he closed the suitcase. "My flight leaves in less than three hours," he said. "I have to get to the airport soon. Please tell the kids I'll call them. Tell them I love them and give them a kiss for me. *Please.*"

She nodded as she looked down. There was no point to keep at him. "Can I at least drive you to the airport?" she asked. "I can call the sitter and ask her to stay at the house with the kids for an extra hour."

Melissa had stopped on her way home from her nutritionist job at another hospital with which Remy wasn't affiliated. Her arrival was unexpected, but no surprise, after Remy realized why she was there.

It had hard to miss, if you were in Chicago and within earshot of a TV. Melissa was at work earlier that evening when she glanced over at a flat-screen on a hospital wall and saw Remy behind a podium at a news conference. He wasn't announcing some major breakthrough in the world of medicine. That would have been a welcome change. Instead, he was addressing the sensational missing-persons case surrounding his notorious brother. Remy told the media he would go to Louisiana to bulldoze past police—yet again—and follow new leads. Within a couple of hours, the gale force of a juicy local news item blew up the ranks to the national cable networks.

Jimmy Van Buren. An extremely handsome man who failed in Hollywood and then vanished, leaving no trace. Every so often if there was a sighting, the media would jump on it. First, the tabloid-type shows, and then the local Chicago stations, since Jimmy Van Buren hailed from there. It was almost like the Black Dahlia case from the 1940s—only there was no severed body to be found and exploited.

Nobody cared about them when they were alive and needy, but let a beautiful, struggling person fall into a dark abyss, and then they were a sensation to be shared—these days on social media—where they finally achieved the notoriety they had craved but never relished in life.

And, of course, any Jimmy Van Buren news item was accompanied by an over-the-shoulder graphic of some old modeling photo of Jimmy in a speedo, or some other form of half-nakedness.

"No, it's fine," Remy declined politely. "I'll take a cab."

"Okay then, if you insist," she replied. "Remy, just promise me you'll be careful."

Remy nodded quietly and then turned away as a memory from his childhood grabbed at him. He and Jimmy were nine years old and fighting over a basketball, of all things. The brothers had always gotten along and shared equally much of the time, but not that day. Both wanted the same thing at the same time, and neither would compromise—or play together. Each wanted to shoot hoops solo, at the goal posted above the garage door of their suburban childhood home in Skokie. The same home where their parents still lived, only about a mile from the other house Melissa received in the divorce.

The commotion and melee finally ended when Gerard Van Buren, the boys' father, walked outside, armed with a Phillips screwdriver. He grabbed the basketball from one of the boys and stabbed a hole into it. *There!* It was now deflated and no good to either of them.

The brothers' pursuit of the same things ended some years later. Remy was an honors student. Jimmy was a star athlete, though his brother didn't lack in that department either. But Remy had the grades, the athleticism, and the looks all rolled into one. As high school ended, Remy received a scholarship to Northwestern, and from there, medical school at Johns Hopkins. The pride of his parents.

Jimmy was only left with his good looks and little else. Remy still loved his brother, but Jimmy resented him. The closeness they shared early in their lives slowly eroded into estrangement. Jimmy pushed Remy away, and after a successful catalog modeling gig in Chicago, decided to try his luck in Los Angeles.

Then when they were both twenty-nine years old—Jimmy down on his luck, not exactly setting Hollywood on fire; Remy barely out of medical school, marrying, and starting a family sooner than he would have really liked—Jimmy vanished. He was last seen leaving a West Hollywood gay bar one night. It was a place detectives later learned he frequented, allowing well-to-do older men to buy him drinks—and buy *him*. Gerard and Maria Van Buren refused to believe it or talk about it. Their father Gerard, an upstanding upper middle-class Republican as he was; their mother Maria, who had come from a strict Catholic upbringing in an Italian home.

Remy sensed all the allegations surrounding his brother were grounded in fact. Instead of passing judgement, or worse, living in denial, he went to the West Coast for his own answers.

The looks Remy had received and the heads that turned when he walked into that bar one night! One old queen even dropped and shattered his beer mug, thinking the hot beefcake stud himself, Jimmy Van Buren, was back from the dead. Many of the different people who knew his brother, that he tracked down on his own and interrogated, told him as much. That they believed his brother was *dead*.

Remy refused to accept it. Not until he saw a body. Some of the men at the gay bar Jimmy hustled at didn't speak too highly of his brother. Jimmy was straight and only gay-for-pay. According to one tale, a man took Jimmy back to his place but wouldn't pay up when Jimmy refused to let the man kiss him on the lips. That man ended up with a broken nose, but, out of embarrassment, he refused to press charges.

All the stories Remy heard about his brother, scandalous or not, ended the same way.

Everyone believed Jimmy was dead.

Remy didn't care what they thought. He would hold on as long as he could, until solid evidence proved him wrong.

But then there was that horrible feeling that shot through him seven months ago and pulled him from his sleep in the wee hours of the morning. Cold sweat had run down his chest, as he sat up in bed and clutched his own throat. Then he put both hands around his neck to make sure his head was still attached. Something was amiss. Something was *different* now.

Jimmy?

Remy had to find out what it was. And then the new reports surfaced about his brother.

Jimmy had been sighted first in New Orleans and then in north Louisiana after that.

Bayou Country. A world away from the skyscrapers, suburbs, and chilly late autumn of Chicago.

North Louisiana was where Dr. Remy Van Buren would begin.

2

Ten Points Plantation, north of Monroe, Louisiana – November 2015

She sat in the dark that evening in a leather chair. She twirled her long, blonde hair in the fingers of her left hand, as she watched the report on "America's trusted and most balanced news source."

So the cable network claimed, though many who leaned to one particular political spectrum often disagreed.

"He was an extremely handsome wannabe actor and sometime model who friends say was willing to do whatever it took to become famous."

The equally blonde commentator wore a smirk on her heavily made-up face as she delivered the story to viewers across America. The dramatic enunciations and pauses were in just the right places, as she read from the teleprompter.

The leather chair creaked a bit in the dark, as the other blonde, the viewer, found herself mesmerized by the television report and the woman who delivered it.

"What a bimbo," she muttered to herself. She could remember a time before twenty-four hour news networks. A time before TV. A time before radio ... or daily newspapers.

"It's a story with the makings of a Hollywood mystery written all over it... Jimmy Van Buren was only twenty-nine years old when he was last seen at a well-known gay bar in West Hollywood seven years ago. People who know him say he had fallen on hard times and resorted to prostitution after his acting career failed. Sadly, his only claim to fame

was a, err hmmm, large supporting role in a late-night cable soft core adult movie titled Lays of Our Lives. *Hey, America, what can I say, that was the name of it. You really can't make this stuff up. Anyway, on a more serious note, Jimmy Van Buren's identical twin brother, Doctor Remy Van Buren, a successful general practitioner in Chicago, has renewed the search for his missing brother after reported sightings in Louisiana. Doctor Remy Van Buren held a news conference today. Here's what he had to say."*

A man with a well-sculpted face, a chin with a familiar cleft, and thick wavy brown hair stood at a podium. Identical to Jimmy Van Buren, only he wore a more conservative gray designer suit and a solemn expression as he read from a prepared statement.

"For more than seven years my family has sought answers and hoped beyond hope that we would have some closure in the disappearance of my twin brother, Jimmy," Remy Van Buren said, as he occasionally glanced down at a piece of paper in his right hand at the bottom of the screen. *"In the early days after he went missing, we had great faith that he would be found alive and with a simple explanation of where he had been. As time went on, we began to accept the fact that it wasn't likely to happen. But now, we have new hope. Numerous sources have reported sightings of my brother in Louisiana, in both the New Orleans metropolitan area, as well as near the city of Monroe in north Louisiana. Investigators in both areas have been contacted, and I plan to travel there myself to seek answers and hopefully bring my brother home. Let this be known: I will leave no stone unturned and will help follow every lead there is until I know where my brother is and have satisfactory answers as to what happened to him."*

"How interesting," the blonde in the leather chair said. A slight difference in Remy Van Buren's speech patterns and mannerisms from those of his lookalike were also intriguing.

"So similar. Yet so opposite," she said to herself. A light cackle escaped. Her English was fluent and intelligible, but her thick Scandinavian accent clung like a persistent cough. This, despite the fact she had left her native Sweden long, *long* ago.

The overhead lights in the study of the great house at Ten Points, a one hundred ninety-seven-year-old former cotton plantation, came on, as a woman with long wavy, raven hair stepped into the room.

"Who's in here?" she called out. The husky voice exuded authority; commanded subordination. "Show yourself!"

The leather chair spun around over at the desk, and Katarina Castille did as she was told—but by *her* choice.

"Hello, *whore*," Katarina greeted, with a smile for her old enemy. But a flash of white teeth didn't exude endearment.

"Oh my God, it can't—" Flannery Lanehart said. The surprise deflated the strong voice, as Katarina knew it would. *"How?"*

"Let's not get into specifics, *whore*. Just be clear that I'm free, and I have been for quite some time. The fact that all of your family is not dead *yet* just goes to show how ... merciful I can be."

"How did you get into this house? Why are you in here watching the TV?" Flannery said. Her senses returned, but her face remained fallen from the shock of her resurrected nemesis. "Damn it, Katarina, whatever you're here for ... deal with *me!* But leave my family out of this!"

Katarina smiled again. "Did you really think that demon husband of yours would leave me buried under the water? He only put me there to make you feel safe. I have been walking around dry for some time. It's a good thing Conrad let me out, given what you and your family ... your *nephew* ... eventually did to him."

Flannery looked away at one of the oak walls of the study—a room inside the large home prone to much senseless violence and cruelty over the years.

"Of course he did," Flannery said. Conrad had always made those in his circle his unwitting fools. It had been his specialty.

"Your demon husband lost his head and is no longer here to protect you. Or try to destroy you. Then again, he must be around somewhere. He is not as easy to destroy as you are, is he?"

"Conrad is alive and well, I'm sure of it," Flannery said. "It was only the body *hosting* him that was—that was killed. I'm sure he's moved on and found another to inhabit by now. Hopefully one far away from here."

"I haven't made it a point to keep in touch. Perhaps I can find him on Facebook sometime and add him as a friend," Katarina said. She rocked playfully in the chair and twirled her hair again, this time with her right index finger. "Do you know how cold Lake Pontchartrain gets in the winter time? He *did* leave me down there for a while."

Flannery kept a hard stare on the wall.

"I once told you that you were an intelligent woman," Katarina said, as she stood from the chair and walked to the other side of the desk.

Katarina looked the same as always, thin but not emaciated. Her makeup was flawless, her lipstick bright red, and the ivory skin of her dead face gave her blue eyes a harsh glow underneath the lights of the study.

A beautiful woman.

More like a beautiful shell holding an ugly, blackened heart that hadn't known a pulse since the seventeenth century.

"I was wrong," Katarina continued. "Only an imbecile would trust Conrad the demon. Did you not think he would turn on you? Idiot *whore*. Frank was dumb as well. Speaking of Frank, my issue with you was that you moved into my territory and stole my husband. *Not* that I was ever in love with Frank."

Flannery turned back to Katarina. "I don't care about your feelings and opinions," she said. "What have you come here to do? If you were here to kill everybody, it seems as though you would have come like a thief in the night and taken us by surprise."

Katarina laughed aloud. "Despite the fact you are one of the damned, you still quote phrases from the Bible. Good for you. There are verses about *whores* in there as well. Can you tell me some of those?"

"'Suffer not a witch to live'?"

"I'm not a witch, whore."

"Your name calling got old before you went away. Just tell me what the hell it is you want."

"*Went away?* Is that what you call it?" Katarina asked, insulted. "More like left for *destroyed*. No thanks to you. I did not exactly go on a cruise to the Caribbean."

It had been more than five years since Katarina and two of her goons attacked Flannery in a New Orleans office building. They bit her neck, drained her of her blood, all of it, and turned her into one of the living dead—as they were. All retribution for Flannery's affair with U.S. Senator Frank Castille, Katarina's husband—mostly Flannery's refusal to end the relationship. Katarina had one of her two associates snap Frank's neck before they attacked Flannery. The three later locked Flannery inside a trunk with Frank's body and made plans to bury the two of them together. To leave a conscious, undead Flannery underground with Frank's rotting corpse. Those plans backfired when Frank's demonic friend Conrad burst in, destroyed the two undead men, tied up Katarina with a silver chain, and rescued Flannery.

Conrad sealed the wooden trunk with Katarina and Frank Castille's bodies inside an anchored concrete burial vault and sent it to the bottom of Lake Pontchartrain.

Frank Castille had turned to Conrad for power, wealth, and a more fruitful political future—when his unholy union with Katarina failed to produce the desired results. Little did the Senator know Conrad only used him for access to Flannery. She was Conrad's key to Ten Points, his home in his previous, mortal life as Theodore Ogden, Junior—the one-time master of the estate who shot and killed himself in the downstairs study in the year 1872.

The same study where Katarina and Flannery now stood. Conrad was gone, again, but the two women remained.

"How is life among the dead?" Katarina said teasingly. "Getting enough blood? You look a little pale tonight. Especially the last couple of minutes."

"Enough small talk," Flannery said. She stepped closer, ready for battle. "Tell me what it is you want, what you came here for … and bring it on."

"Not so fast," Katarina said, in a demure tone riddled with pretense. "I need you to do something for me," she said, batting her eyes. "I need a favor from the *whore*."

Flannery's emerald green eyes gave the same deadly glow as Katarina's under the lights. "You have got to be joking. Me do something for you? Never."

Katarina stopped fluttering her lashes, made a face, and then scrunched her smooth, unwrinkled face as she pretended to mull things over.

"Hmm, then I suppose I will have to take your brother Marcus, cut off a finger each time you refuse, and mail them to you one by one. If you insist on still being a stubborn whore after I've mailed you all ten of his fingers and then killed him, well, little nephew Travis will be next ... oh *wait* ..." Her smile returned a third time. "Not Travis. I can hit you harder than that. Perhaps your *mother*..."

Flannery kept a poker face. "My mother died when I was a girl."

Katarina laughed out loud again. "Oh come now, Flannery, it is me you are talking to. I know all about the black housekeeper Maximilian Lanehart raped. That is where you came from. Foolish whore. You think I have not been watching? That woman who died when you were a little girl was no more your mother than she was mine."

"I can't—"

"Your real mother Izzy is a clairvoyant, yes, but even with all her psychic ability she will never see me when I come for her."

Katarina had her in her grasp the moment Marcus's name slipped from her lips, but Flannery couldn't let the bitch see a successful strike. "What is this favor you want?" she asked, in a continued, conscious effort to look and sound neutral.

"For starters, I need room and board. There are no decent hostels within the area," she said, with a smile and a wink.

"There are plenty of hotels and *cemeteries* around us ... Take your pick."

"I do not exactly travel with a credit card," Katarina lied.

She had credit cards and a state identification card. She hadn't come straight to Ten Points after her retrieval from a watery grave. Conrad passed her a dead person's social security number once she was back on dry land. The one she had obtained years ago from an unscrupulous modeling agent in New York was no good since Katarina Castille—along with her husband—was officially listed as a missing person. It had taken a variety of disguises for her to prowl unnoticed—and hunt and drink— after being front-page news in the Big Easy.

"Do you think you'll feel safe, if I know where it is you sleep?" Flannery asked her.

"You will not harm me," Katarina said, her expression now serious.

"What makes you so sure of that?" Flannery asked, not budging.

Katarina ignored the question. "There are plenty of empty rooms in this large house. Many of which haven't been entered in years. No one ever goes to the third floor. Put me there somewhere. No one will ever know I am there."

"Until you get hungry and decide to prowl in the night."

"You are in no position to pass judgment. Scattered any dead ducks across the front yard lately? And what was that business with the horse? Or was that another one of *us* you helped bring into the lineage? I suppose you weren't directly responsible for what happened at the stables. Does it disappoint you that you were never able to properly mentor your sister-in-law in our ways and teach her better etiquette before Conrad destroyed her?"

"Tilda wasn't the one who killed the horse. *That* was Rochelle Dubois, and just how the hell long have you been around to know all of this?"

"Long enough to sit idly by, as you Southerners say, and learn the players. I'm three hundred forty-seven years old. Time is on my side. I can be patient. I notice some of the players did not make it to this act. Like your older brother Geoffrey, for instance. He and I could have been a wonderful match. It is difficult to impress me, but I rather admired his enthusiasm. Even if he only got in one good kill before—"

"Again, what makes you so sure I won't stake you in your sleep?" Flannery was in no mood to reminisce. "Why would I trust some revenge-minded bloodsucker in the same house as my family members?"

"Because you can't afford *not* to," Katarina told her. She paused a moment and then continued. "Plus, there is something here I need. Perhaps if you help me, I can one day give *you* access to the secret I know about ... Ten Points." Another impish smile surfaced.

"I can't imagine you would have anything that I need," Flannery replied. "And how do you know so much about Ten Points and the land?"

"All in good time," she insisted, not ready to show her hand.

"Will you at least give me a hint?"

Katarina smiled. "It is here on the property. And I am the only one who can lead you to it. You and your family's survival is in my hands, Flannery Lanehart. You haven't much of a choice."

Flannery tried to keep up the front, but the defeat left her weak and concerned for the others inside the house. There was no choice. Damn it. "Shall I show you to your room?"

"I know the way," Katarina replied. "I thought it would be more—how shall I put it—*mannerly* to have your blessing, but I have already been living on the top floor of this house for the past eight months. I could have killed everybody here countless times. Your mother needs to go in for, what do they say, a tune-up on her gift. It is amazing how well-hidden you can remain in a great house such as this, isn't it ... *whore?*"

3

The great house at Ten Points was dark, as everyone was retired for the night. Cracking sounds popped here and there—if you were awake and unable to sleep—as the nearly two-hundred-year-old, fifty-seven room home settled after a day's activity. Travis Lanehart had been told as a boy by D'Lynn that it was the walls talking and telling stories of all the days past. It scared young Travis at the time, but now, at seventeen, he did not buy into such nonsense.

These days Travis took in all the sounds and could differentiate them. If he strained his ears the right way on a sleepless night he could hear the tick-tock of the large grandfather clock in the foyer, all the way down the hall and the grand staircase from his upstairs bedroom. He had always preferred the room at the end of the second-floor hallway. It was his private den and world away from the rest of the Laneharts, a dysfunctional family unit that had dwindled and changed ranks the past seven months.

Tonight it was another kind of sound that called to the seventeen year old and beckoned him from the sanctity of a warm bed. The room was a blacked-out macabre and Goth façade that included Rob Zombie movie posters, a black light, a lava lamp that glowed red, and his pet tarantula Harry, safely secured in an aquarium over near the desk where he kept his graphic novels.

Something—or *someone*—summoned him away from all of it.

Travis pulled back the covers of his double bed, winced at the chill that struck him as he climbed out and placed his feet on to the cool carpet below. The Louisiana weather was unpredictable year-round but especially during the late fall and winter months. A mild temperature one night; a cold snap the next. Tonight's was the latter. D'Lynn, the longtime live-in housekeeper at Ten Points, never neglected to turn down the thermostat to an ungodly number before she turned in every evening. This was especially true on the nights of a toasty fire in the living room fireplace, as this one had been.

Travis pulled on a pair of sneakers and a black leather jacket, his color of choice, and went to the bedroom door. He slowly opened and closed it behind him, creeping down the long hallway—also carpeted, as most of the upstairs rooms had been during various renovations through the previous century. Travis and his lanky, thin frame moved quietly along the cushion of the carpet, the thick oak walls disguising his presence from the sleeping ones in the rooms around him. He made his way down the wooden, winding staircase. A dimmed crystal chandelier that hung over the foyer and the welcoming glow of the cream marble foyer floor below guided him to the bottom of the stairs. At the first floor, he went for the front door of the great house. He opened and closed it behind him with the same care as his bedroom door a full minute earlier.

Travis blended into the night outside. His dyed jet-black hair and clothing camouflaged him underneath the dark sky. Pale skin and the twinkle of a nose and ear piercings weren't visible under a crescent moon. The night was clear, the air drier than normal, and despite the November cold, a few surviving crickets chirped disjointed melodies across the spacious front yard of the estate. It was otherwise still and quiet through the maze of oak trees that lined the driveway to the house. Travis descended the curved granite steps at the side of the front porch. Once his sneakers hit the St. Augustine grass, he sprinted to the northeast corner of the house. Off in the distance, past more oak trees and a wide clearing, lay the entrance into the woods.

Travis paused as he looked ahead and then took off in another jog. He knew the grounds, so navigation wasn't difficult despite limited moonlight. An echoed hoot of an owl somewhere in the distance greeted him as the blackened silhouettes of trees moved closer. The ebony blanket of the forest comforted Travis more than any variegated nature walk during the daylight.

But why? How could he be so fearless and comforted by what he couldn't see when there was that surreal night seven months earlier, when he was dragged through those same woods by ...

Travis willed away the thought as the clearing ended, and the forest began. The woods he had used as a shortcut to Zeke Colson's house on that night last spring.

It never left his memory no matter how badly he wanted it gone.

Then it occurred to him that he didn't know why he was there. What was it that lured him out of a warm bed to a place that suddenly evoked a trauma he didn't want to face?

Then he knew.

"Travis." It whispered somewhere just inside the forest, behind one of the trees. "Here. Over here, Travis."

"Wh—what?" he said aloud, uncertain it was real. It was too low and quiet to be recognized. It wasn't loud enough to reveal a gender.

"Over here," it called out again, in a high hiss that gave no identifiable clues. "Come closer, Travis. *Over here.*"

Travis crept farther into the forest. He was surrounded by trees, as any remaining moonlight dissipated. The darkness enveloped and cloaked him, yet he felt vulnerable.

He found his voice again and got the words out. "Where are you? *Who* are you?"

Out of nowhere, a strong hand grabbed his shoulder from behind. Travis turned with a shriek.

"I'm *right here,* you little bastard!" Conrad said, an evil grin across his pale face. The perfectly white teeth from last spring were dark and rotten. His head was reattached to his body—sutures visible across the neck, where Travis had decapitated him in the living room of Ten Points that night last April.

"Oh God, no, please leave me alone!" Travis cried aloud, as Conrad pulled him closer.

What had been brown eyes were dead, glazed over, and sunken into his skull. Pupils, irises, and all were the same milky color. The skin on a once-handsome face was scaly, as it had shed along the cheeks and jawline.

"Why did you do this to me? Why didn't you *obey me* as I ordered?" Conrad shouted, shaking him. The thick and wavy hair was matted and grave-dirty. It rattled in clumps as it clung to a rotting scalp. The white dress shirt and dark slacks he wore the night of his decapitation were darkened, soiled, and baggy against a withering, bony body. *"I'm going to fucking kill you, you little son of a bitch."*

The large hands closed around and throttled Travis's throat, causing him to cough and gasp for air.

"Please!" Travis begged, barely able to utter the words. He knew pleas were of no use. He was more than a quarter-mile away from the main house where everyone slept behind thick walls.

Who the hell had put the monster back together? *Why?*

Conrad laughed aloud and pressed the boy's throat harder. A chunk of rotten flesh popped loose and hung from a dead chin. "You will *never* escape me now," he said. *"You belong to me ..."*

"Oh God, get the hell away from me!" Travis exclaimed, screaming himself awake. He sat up in his bed in a cold sweat. He panted loudly for a full minute before he could calm himself.

It was only a nightmare, oh thank God. He was back in his room, inside the house, where no one could harm him. He was safe.

Was he? He had killed the host but not the demon himself. Conrad was still out there. Perhaps plotting revenge. The worry stayed in the back of Travis's mind. He was sure it weighed on his Uncle Marcus as well. If Conrad ever came back, locked doors and thick walls wouldn't bar him.

If Conrad ever came back. Sometimes it felt like only a matter of *when* he came back. Conrad was the spirit of Theodore Ogden, Junior— the master of the estate more than one hundred forty years ago. When he had returned last spring, he was hell-bent on picking up where he left off. He ingratiated himself into the Lanehart family circle. The bisexual incubus roped in Geoffrey, Travis's stepfather, with promises of wealth and eternal life on Earth; had a sexual relationship with Tilda, Travis's mother, with Geoffrey's blessing; and, then, was determined to make

Travis's Uncle Marcus *his.* Conrad was convinced Marcus was the reincarnation of his cousin, Adam Ogden, and a secret, incestuous love forbidden in the post-Civil War era could resume in the present day.

Conrad had almost choked the life from Marcus in the living room downstairs, determined to make him one of the eternal living dead, when Travis ran him through with a replica Civil War sword and then, without further thought, took off his head. The sword may not have been authentic, but the blade was razor sharp and did its job as it sliced through flesh and bone that early April morning.

"Uncle Marcus, I think we need to get a priest to come and exorcise the house or somethin'," Travis said to Marcus downstairs the next morning, over breakfast at their own corner of a long mahogany dining room table.

"What are you talking about?" Marcus asked, looking from his iPad where he read the news from different sites he followed. The thirty-seven year old had been left to take over the estate and serve as guardian of Travis and his ten-year-old sister Maxine.

Marcus's brother Geoffrey, sister-in-law Tilda, and nephew Bobby were all still official missing persons, though Marcus, Travis, and Flannery really knew what had happened last spring.

They were the only ones.

Deputy Wes Washer also witnessed Geoffrey and Bobby turn into dust as the dawn sun struck them. But Wes's old high school crush Flannery intervened and erased his conscious memory of the events that morning—by way of her teeth.

Despite Flannery's drinking from Wes, and his amnesia of the details, something lurked in the man's subconscious. He went around town and rambled about the Devil and evil spirits, though he wasn't sure why. He was also in his Reverend father's Baptist church every Sunday and Wednesday, where he repented and rededicated his life to the Lord so often even the most fanatical of the Bible-beaters in the sizeable congregration had developed grave concern over the deputy's sanity—or lack thereof.

"Conrad," Travis said. The mention disturbed Marcus and brought a fitful fidget in his seat. "I had a nightmare last night," Travis continued, despite any discomfort he caused his uncle. "He was in the woods and tried to kill me. Somebody sewed his head back—"

"Travis, we shouldn't talk about that," Marcus said. He reached for his coffee cup, then pulled his hand away without picking it up. His eyes darted around the room and back to the tablet. "M—Maxine could walk in here any second. She doesn't need to hear any of this."

"We need a priest to come in here and sprinkle holy water or somethin'," Travis continued, with a soft tread.

"Absolutely *not*," Marcus said. He pretended to read something on the tablet to avoid eye contact. "Ridiculous. No way. Not a chance."

Marcus wasn't a religious man, not for years. The events of last spring made him even less of a follower, if that were possible. He had come home to Ten Points from San Diego for his father's funeral, still saddened and without closure over the unsolved disappearance of his partner Landon Smithfield the year before. While home, he had rekindled a romance with his old childhood friend, Zeke Colson, only to lose Zeke days later when Geoffrey, at a jealous Conrad's bidding, killed Zeke.

A few stray bones identified as those of Ezekiel Colson's turned up in the woods later that summer, the woods between Ten Points and Zeke's house—the same woods of Travis's nightmare.

Zeke's remains got a proper burial; laid to rest beside his parents in a nearby cemetery. Even in ultraconservative north Louisiana, the gay veterinarian was well-respected and loved by his community. It was evidenced by the standing-room only funeral service that came three months after his death. No definitive conclusions about Zeke's cause of death could be drawn, since the medical examiner had so little to work with.

But Marcus knew.

Goddamn you both, Conrad and Geoffrey, he thought often, during the empty days. If there was any justice, a toasty, special corner of Hell hosted Geoffrey Lanehart and his demonic protégé these days.

But Marcus never felt certain of it.

"But if we—" Travis began again.

Marcus pounded his fist on the table; eyes hard and up at his nephew. "I said *no*, now drop it!" he shouted.

"Okay, sorry. Jeez," Travis muttered, with an annoyed face at his uncle. He stared down into a half-empty bowl of Raisin Bran. The small silver stud in his right nostril twinkled as it caught a ray of sunlight through the dining room window. "I miss Bobby," he said, eyes in his cereal bowl.

Marcus looked up from the tablet and softened. "You miss all of them," he said.

Travis's face turned sad, and he shook his head. "I don't miss Geoff. *Ever.*"

Marcus reached out and touched his arm. "I don't miss Geoff either. Not after what he did to—" He pulled his hand away and quietened.

"You can't say his name?" Travis asked.

No, but I can sure think about him every waking hour of the day, Marcus thought. He changed the subject. "D'Lynn offered to make waffles, and I can't believe you're eating that instead. Maybe Maxine went with her to the kitchen for some."

Travis shrugged. "I don't like waffles."

"Well, finish your cereal so you aren't late for school," Marcus said.

Ten-year-old Maxine entered the dining room, carrying a pink book bag. A blue dress matched the blue ribbon in her hair. The chubby little girl's red eyeglasses were a mismatch, but the frames were her favorite. D'Lynn, the closest thing left to a maternal figure, had obviously helped with her hair. Flannery was never seen after sunrise. When she was around, she took little interest in any children, even nieces and nephews.

"There you are," Marcus said. "Have you had breakfast yet?"

"Not hungry," Maxine said, as she stood by the table. Something was in her left hand, but from where Marcus sat he couldn't make out what she clutched at her side with such determination.

"No, no, you have to eat. Breakfast is the most important meal of the day. I'm done with mine. Let's go get you some cereal or something. Maybe there's time to talk D'Lynn into those waffles."

When Marcus stood and got a closer look, he saw a doll in a choke-grip at Maxine's left side. It looked like an old rag doll from generations back.

Or even a couple of centuries.

"What is that? I've never seen that before. Where did you get that?" he asked.

"She left it in my room," Maxine said. She shrugged and stared back at her uncle, as if he should understand.

"She?"

"The pretty blonde lady," she said.

"What pretty blonde lady?"

"The one who talks to me sometimes. She sounds like she's not from around here. I think it's the angel version of Mommy."

"Oh great," Travis said. He stirred his spoon through an empty puddle of milk. "Maxine has a new friend ... and she isn't real ..."

"Is too!" Maxine shouted, with a mean look for her older brother.

"Okay, okay enough," Marcus said to them.

There were old relics from days past up on the third floor of the house, even though the adults told Maxine never to go up there alone. Marcus decided she must have wandered up anyway and found the doll in an old trunk or the like.

In no mood to further scold after his words with Travis, Marcus placed a gentle hand on Maxine's arm and walked with her toward the kitchen. "Come on, let's go see if D'Lynn or Tarva can fix you something to eat before you're late for school."

4

Flannery blended into a patch of cypress trees at the edge of a yard that night. An SUV she didn't recognize held her back from the quaint log house she had fixated on for the past forty-five minutes. Her mouth was partially open, her cuspids half-sprouted, and her body ached from a lack of what it craved. There were other places she could hunt, but determination won as she stood frozen by a tree. Her black blouse and dark pants concealed her in the thicket about fifty yards from the house.

Her emerald green eyes occasionally moved to a silver Ford Explorer, which had become a source of annoyance.

"Leave," she hissed, with an odd hope her words would summon the SUV's absent driver.

It was easy to summon those she had fed on. But in all her ignorance and rush to satisfy herself, she had never tried mind control on someone until after the bite. There was no one to consult; no teacher to tell her if it was possible to manipulate someone beforehand. The tricks she knew she learned on her own. Katarina created her and left her behind like a wayward, junkie mother, never teaching her a damn thing.

That brought her thoughts to Katarina. Flannery also bore anxiety over allowing Katarina to squat at Ten Points, but she had no choice. There was no doubt the sadistic bitch would follow through on her threats to kill Marcus and Izzy should there be any noncompliance. Besides, Katarina had been there for months. It was impossible to try and control her.

But where is she feeding? Flannery thought, eyes on the log house and strange SUV but her head elsewhere.

Nobody at Ten Points had shown symptoms of bites or attacks. Flannery would have immediately known—the signs were unmistakable.

There were no reports of strange attacks in Monroe or the surrounding area; no reports of people killed or missing under strange circumstances. Except for Geoffrey, Tilda, and Bobby, but Flannery knew the truth behind that.

A muffled murmur of voices came from inside the house. The words grew clearer as the door creaked open. Light from inside the home crept on to a lonely corner of the porch.

A medium-built woman with long, flawless blonde hair—hair that rivaled Katarina's—stepped on to the porch. "I'll see you at church on Wednesday," she called back into the house before she closed the door behind her. Flannery recognized the voice and the smile as the other woman walked down the front steps toward the SUV.

Flannery's eyes were those of an enraged feral cat as the Explorer pulled away. Clementine LeMonde. The bitch!

Flannery and Clementine's history went back to high school. Clementine hated Flannery nearly twenty years later. The apple of Clementine's eye, Wes Washer, had always longed for Flannery—and he still did. Only in high school, Flannery was extremely popular, ignored Wes, dated football players, and was one of the best dancers on the drill team. Outside of beautiful natural blonde locks, the rest of Clementine was as flat and plain as a north Louisiana soybean field. She was somewhat intellectual, but unathletic, uncoordinated, and lacking any of Flannery's natural beauty and poise. Clementine put popularity aspirations aside—begrudgingly, at first—and was groomed by her mother and home economics teachers to be a perfect Christian housewife.

Unfortunately, Clementine never sought out other eligible bachelors within the church. All these years later she still threw her energy toward Wes. Failure persisted, and Flannery's reappearance in the community earned occasional dirty looks and unspoken resentment from Clementine.

With good reason, since it was Wes's house Flannery stood in the shadows of this night. Her blood lust intensified as Clementine drove away.

Flannery moved beyond the trees, into the driveway, and closed her eyes.

Come to me, Wes ...

Sometimes it took a few minutes. She was never sure if he heard immediately and tried to resist, or if she wasn't as tuned-in as she hoped. Tonight she was hungry, impatient, and pushed hard.

Come to me. Now!

About fifteen seconds later, the front door slowly opened, as if weights were attached. Flannery saw Wes's silhouette block the light inside the house as the gape of the open door grew. He finally made a space large enough to slide through and exited to the porch. He looked dazed, as he stepped into the chilly night air with only a T-shirt and jogging pants.

As anxious as she was to feed, Flannery was planted in one spot, as he made his way down the steps toward her.

Always make them come to you, she told herself. She wasn't sure if it was something she had invented, an undead instinct. No matter how hungry she was, or how far away they were, she *never* rushed to them. They came to her.

Tonight's feed was a needy one. She had held off. She was starving.

Flannery pierced Wes with those feline eyes and said nothing. There was no need to say anything because he knew what to do. He was under her control—and had been for months. She often waited until she couldn't take it anymore before she appeared outside his house.

Just a little, not a lot, she always told herself. Wes Washer was human, and if she took too much blood there would be consequences. She didn't share his affection for her, but she did care for his well-being. Small amounts of his blood here and there were also the only way to stay under the radar. She certainly couldn't cruise the Ouachita River late at night and pick off homeless people and drinking college kids near bridges or levees. *That* would cause community-wide panic; leave her vulnerable to exposure. This was much cleaner and neater.

As Wes arrived, she extended her arms and drew him to her in an embrace. He gave her a drunken, dizzy smile, as she affectionately ran her hands through his thin, sandy blond hair. Some of his color was back from a few days ago; he didn't look as pale as he sometimes did. It concerned her that she could turn him into an anemia case, but right now there was no suitable alternative.

"Flannery," he whispered. He gazed upon her lovingly, with a slightly pudgy face. Tiny freckles dotted his short nose under the moonlight.

She nodded, with a small smile and opened her mouth wide. Her canine teeth had grown twice their size since his arrival.

Hypnotized, there was no show of panic or anxiety as she closed in on his throat. With quick and precise laps of her tongue, Flannery licked and slurped up any blood that oozed past her lips. She had mastered how to take it without leaving any tell-tale drops or stains on Wes's clothing. He owned an obscene stock of Fruit of the Loom T-shirts, the white cotton fabric so bright it often hurt her eyes.

Wes would not remember any of this later. *He must not.*

When she finished, she held an index finger over the puncture wounds, and a bright yellow light glowed from underneath her finger. She pulled away after a few seconds and saw only a red mark and faint signs of the puncture wounds. Clementine was at Wes's house before she arrived. Let the deputy's coworkers at the sheriff's office think Clementine had delivered a hickey to Wes. As well as the people at his father Wilkins Washer's church—where it could create a small scandal.

Flannery was amused by potential embarrassment and humiliation for Clementine, as she walked Wes to his front door.

When they reached the entrance, Wes turned with another woozy smile. "Do you want to come inside, Flannery?" he asked. He leaned in to kiss her on the lips, but she pulled away before the landing.

"I must go," she said slowly. "Look at me," she continued, with a hard stare. "You won't remember I was ever here. *Look into my eyes.* The only person who came to visit you tonight was Clementine LeMonde. That's all you remember. Do you understand? Look at me, Wes. Tell me you understand."

"Yes, only Clementine," he said, sleepy, as his eyes locked with hers.

She gave him a 'goodnight' nod. "Go get some sleep, Wes."

"G'night," he said. He opened the door, moving backwards into the house without taking his eyes off her.

Flannery sighed in the darkness of the porch. She could only humor his puppy dog behavior for so long each time this happened. As always, he tried to steal a kiss at the end. As always, she rejected the effort. Thankfully, he wasn't in his conscious mind, couldn't remember later, and there were never any injured feelings.

She descended the front steps, walked down the driveway, and soaked in the feel of the night around her. In her previous life, she would have needed a jacket, maybe even a coat. But the cold had developed a new feel over the past five years. She could wear short sleeves, or she could run nude through the woods—though the latter was not her thing. The thirty-five-degree temperatures brought no effect as they had during her days of mortality—days she missed more often.

Everything had a different feel than from before. Sound, touch, smells, and the rest of her senses. Right now, it was the way the gravel and pebbles of the driveway felt underneath her plain pair of sneakers. She took off at a brisker pace, once she was sure Wes was tucked away inside.

The rush never got old. It was something she had discovered by accident, not long after Katarina turned her into one of the living dead. A gift she embraced in this unholy servitude she endured, for however long lay ahead.

As Flannery increased speed, the cool air took on a new sensation as the wings enveloped her. First her legs, next her arms, and then her body, head, and face disappeared as she felt herself leave the ground— like a jet leaving a tarmac. Once she took off, there was the transformation into what Conrad once told her looked like a large, black flying cape. She could never see what it was; she could only see ahead. She could will a destination for herself and go there with little effort. The thing, "The Cape", as she came to call it, would flap across the night sky and do the work for her.

Sometimes it was her escape, and on many nights, especially those nights she knew she must leave Wes alone and let him recover, she would fly undetected for hours across the skies of north Louisiana. She would unwind, think, and found it to be as close to peace as she would ever come again.

Just as Flannery took to the air on this night, a flash of blinding headlights shot around the curve in the driveway. The speeding car came with no warning, no sound, and it barely missed her as she left the ground. The blare of the car's horn gave Flannery a start, as she went up and over the trees, making a hasty exit from Wes's property.

It was as if The Cape knew to usher her from danger. As if it were a built-in defense mechanism; its uncanny ability never explained.

Who was that? she thought. She assumed she was at a much greater altitude, as the air around her grew colder.

But still—there was unease. Someone had seen her in flight. *Who?*

Marcus had caught a glimpse of The Cape more than five years earlier, on the night their father Maximilian Lanehart disinherited, disowned, and ordered them off Ten Points. She was fueled by anger and rage that night. Being seen by Marcus was a clumsy mistake she couldn't explain away when he finally confronted her last spring.

She could not afford to be so careless again.

Flannery was certain whoever it was would report the strange sighting to Wes, since they were obviously there to see him. Did Clementine forget something and return—or was it someone else?

She would have to find out.

5

"What is it that you expect from me?" Katarina asked, in her thick accent. She sat at a vanity and applied fresh polish to her fingernails. "Have you not already had two mothers in your lifetime? Well, three—if you count that elderly maid downstairs. I have no desire to be the next one."

"Do you have any room to call somebody *old?*" Flannery asked, before she could stop herself.

Katarina released a dry cackle. "Ha! Good one, whore."

Flannery glanced about the room and tried to hide awe at Katarina's transformation of a long-abandoned, dusty room on the third floor of the house into a private boudoir. The old wooden vanity from long ago was cleaned and polished, accompanied by an antique armchair. There was a cozy bed in a corner, safely tucked away from a well-shuttered window. One of their kind could never be too safe, when it came to the potential of even a small amount of sunlight.

The bedroom was lit by strategically-placed candles in holders from days past. Flannery wasn't sure which of the third-floor rooms were wired for electricity. The room Tilda had briefly stayed in after her *turn* was, but Flannery never ventured much on the top floor.

Katarina's room was only about fifty steps away from where Tilda Lanehart and Rochelle Dubois had been stashed during their short tenures as the undead. Rochelle was still out there somewhere, Flannery guessed, though she never heard from the rambunctious and obnoxious woman after the night of Maximilian Lanehart's funeral. For all Flannery knew, Conrad could have destroyed Rochelle that night.

"You *made* me, and you never showed me what I could do ... or what I can't do. I didn't know I could fly until I found out by accident," Flannery said.

Katarina scoffed and blew at a set of red nails to dry them quicker. She wiggled her fingers and admired them. "I am supposed to give you a tutorial? Is that what I am hearing?" she asked, turning her attention to the other hand.

"Yes!" Flannery replied. "Don't you owe me at least that much?"

"I owe you nothing," Katarina said, keeping her eyes on her hand. She applied polish to the other set of nails. "You took what was mine; you paid the price. I *still* make you pay. Let us not forget who is in the power position here."

"Trust me," Flannery said. "I know all too well."

"How is your deputy friend these days?" Katarina asked. She cocked an eye toward Flannery. "You're such a considerate little monster. You never take from anywhere else. You do know you could fly far away from here in the night? Take what you want. And then be back here by sunrise. Yet you go only to this man."

"It's too much to stalk and hunt people. I wait until I have to," Flannery said and looked away. "It's always been that way."

Katarina gave a condescending smile and shook her head disapprovingly. "I don't believe you. Conrad would have never allowed it while you were with him. You killed plenty in New Orleans. And other places. I know you must have. Yet you are afraid to do it here. Maybe your family brings out this side of you? Emotions. *Compassion*. So human of you, Flannery."

"There is nothing human left in me," Flannery said, with loathing and quiet fury. "*You* took care of that."

"You are what you are," Katarina said. She lost interest in her fingernails and gave Flannery her undivided attention. "Do you think Tilda Lanehart wanted to become what you made her? You cannot deny you are any different than I am."

"Oh but I *am*," Flannery said defiantly. "We are nothing alike."

"Do not fool yourself, Flannery Lanehart. Do you think I love who I am? I make the best of it. Do you think I wanted this? Why do you think I created you? Yes, I wanted you to suffer for what you did with Frank after I told you to stop. This was the quickest and easiest way to make you suffer. A natural and final death would have been over with so, so quickly. Frank was the lucky one."

Flannery was angrier. "I loved Frank."

Katarina smirked and shook her head again as she went back to her nails. "Then that was your weakness and your misfortune. Frank was a follower; not a leader. Why else would he first come to me, then to Conrad? A self-made man he was not."

"That wasn't for you to decide."

Katarina let out another "ha" and looked at Flannery as if she were a moron. "But it *was*, my little adulterous whore friend. He sold himself into servitude to me, and then to Conrad. Betraying me by trying to serve another master warranted his execution. You were the proverbial straw. I also had to deal with you when you took what was *not* yours."

"As you keep pointing out," Flannery said, and gave up. "I get it." With a look of worry, she changed the subject. "Somebody saw me tonight." Flannery wasn't sure why she confided in Katarina about anything, but here it went.

Katarina stopped with her nails again and looked back over at her. "Someone saw you where? Doing what?"

"When I flew away from Wes's house … I was hit by somebody's headlights when they came up the driveway."

"They saw you transform and fly?"

"Yeah, not sure about the transformation part, but they definitely saw me fly."

"Did you see who it was? The car? You must kill them."

"Kill them?"

Katarina rolled her eyes and looked at her again as if she were stupid. "Is there an echo in here?"

"I couldn't see what kind of car. I was too blinded by the flash of lights. High beams. I don't think they could see my face anymore."

"But you do not know that for sure. They could know who you are. They could come looking for you here. *I* could be in danger." Katarina was perturbed. And a little paranoid. "I was a fashion model and then a senator's wife who went missing. Do you know how important it is that I stay underground—for at least a few generations?"

"Yes, and how you managed to become a supermodel and a U.S. Senator's wife all under the cover of night is something I'll never understand."

"You fool! Listen to me. You've put us both in danger. You must find out who saw you, and you *must* deal with them."

"I don't think—"

"You *must!* Because Flannery Lanehart, if you don't, and this comes back to me in any way, I will start with your brother, and then—"

"Okay, okay!" She had no desire to hear more threats. "I'll try and figure it out. Maybe whoever it was is still there."

"Good," Katarina said, settled somewhat. "You should find out."

"But what if they didn't see anything? Why is it necessary to kill them?"

"You are so very new to all of this," Katarina said. "Whatever is left of the heart you ever had will harden over time. A day will come where you never remember anymore what it was like before this. You won't concern yourself with the feelings of others."

"And you created me ... *this* ... yet won't teach me the ways?" Flannery said. "Or even answer simple questions?"

Katarina stood and pointed a finger at Flannery. "I never said I wouldn't teach you. I only said I have no desire to become your next maternal figure. Do not take any of this as a sign of kindness on my part. Just because I show you what you need to know does not make me, what do they say, your new *BFF*. I won't hesitate to destroy you or anyone else in this house in a moment if I suspect my existence is threatened."

"Fair enough," Flannery said. "So what else can I do besides turn into some black cloak thing and fly around?"

"You do not decide the order of the lessons I teach you, or the questions I answer," Katarina said sternly. "*I* decide."

"What do we cover first then?" Flannery asked, afraid to let her guard down.

Katarina nodded. "Let us go on a little night flight, shall we?"

A moment later, two black capes ascended from the beneath the oak trees in front of Ten Points and took to the night sky.

Within minutes, they hovered over Wes's driveway.

"No one is here except Wes," Flannery said, though her vision was limited. "The other car is gone." All she could see next to her was a flowing black wave of what looked to be a fine fabric. Katarina wasn't visible, but Flannery could feel a scowl of disapproval.

Without a word, Katarina guided her westward. Flannery wasn't sure where they headed but assumed it was part of the lesson Katarina promised.

Within minutes they landed on the banks of the Ouachita River, across a levee from Forsythe Park in Monroe. The tall, grassy levee held vigilant guard over the park and surrounding Garden District neighborhood during the rainy season. The river itself separated Monroe from its sister city, West Monroe.

Moments after they touched down, Katarina was back in her normal form. Flannery knew she was too, when she saw the wide open space around her. She looked down; her arms and legs were returned to her.

"Why are we here?" Flannery asked, as they walked an uncertain path, close to the river's bank.

The night was quiet; there was an eerie stillness to the crisp air. A yellow hue from the street lights yards away gave humans a blurry, obstructed view of a narrow road that wound through a picnic and recreation area. But Flannery and Katarina saw yards and yards ahead of even that. This was a popular spot for joggers—but anyone who dared to do it here after dark usually did it as part of a group. But even none of those were out tonight.

The long levee to their left guarded the park and the neighborhood, and it also shielded Flannery and Katarina from Riverside Drive, which ran parallel on the other side. Traffic was sparse, but there were still drivers out. Flannery heard the occasional hum of a car. Thankfully, no boaters were out on the river to their right. Ahead of them, even farther away, sat the shapes of a couple of abandoned picnic tables.

"Shhh," Katarina shushed, looking back with a frown. "Patience."

They continued their slow stroll near the water in silence until they came upon a patch of woods. The narrow road came to an end and led to a bicycling and jogging trail that disappeared into the cluster of trees.

Flannery heard a clumsy rustling inside the brush. Who was there? Had Katarina set her up for an ambush?

If it were an ambush, Katarina began the possible charade well. "Who is in there?" she barked toward the trees. Her voice was strong, but her accent set her far apart from the locals and made her easily identifiable if there was about to be trouble. The noise and dulled snaps of limbs and twigs came closer to them. It was either a large animal—or an average-sized person. "Show yourself to me!"

Flannery stood behind her, wary of what could emerge.

Katarina looked over her shoulder. "Flannery Lanehart, don't be such a pussy," she snarled, like a disapproving father whose son was scared to catch a fly ball. "*You* are supposed to be more frightening than anything that is in there!"

Loud and uneven steps, followed by a crunch of dead, dry leaves, emerged from the woods. Finally, a middle-aged man with a liquor bottle wrapped in a brown paper bag stumbled out into the open with a wheezy exhale. He was dirty, disheveled; he wore old clothes. His thin and wispy gray hair stuck out everywhere. Large bags ballooned beneath bloodshot eyes.

"They'll take it if I come out here," he said hoarsely, plenty drunk as he waved the bottle around. "Gotta stay hid in there."

"Come," Katarina said to him, with a smile. She stood her ground and led him to her with a direct stare.

"Pretty lady," he said, walking toward her. "I might let you have some of this here stuff. I saved a while for a couple a'bottles. Keeps ya warm on a cool night. Who's that other pretty one behind you? Two pretty ladies walkin' alone at night. Y'all want company?"

Katarina reached back, grabbed Flannery by the arm with extravagant force, and moved her to the front. "*Kill him,*" she hissed, in a whisper only Flannery could hear.

Katarina placed her chin on Flannery's shoulder in a goading, coaching manner from behind. She smiled and kept her eyes on the drunken homeless man as she egged Flannery on.

"Oh Katarina, not this guy. He isn't bothering anybody—"

"You imbecile," Katarina whispered, her lips next to Flannery's right ear. "Do as I say. Would you rather go back to Ten Points and wake up D'Lynn and kill her instead? Because *that* is what will happen—what I will make you do—if you do not follow my orders, whore."

It was a setup, but not the kind Flannery had first suspected. She couldn't bear to do what she was being told to do, but there was no choice. It had been *so long* since she had killed a harmless bystander for feeding purposes. Not since her New Orleans days. But she knew Katarina would indeed carry out the threat against D'Lynn if she didn't obey.

"Katarina, please. Can't we go somewhere else—find some rapist or robber? This guy isn't hurting anybody."

"Do it!"

Flannery threw out her *make them come to you* rule and anxiously moved forward. She hoped the glow of her eyes or a display of fangs would cause the poor man to drop dead of a heart attack. She felt the canine teeth start to grow and knew the only way to keep everyone at Ten Points safe was to do as the evil bitch commanded. In the beginning, with Conrad, back in New Orleans, it hadn't felt so wrong. When she was hungry, Conrad had whispered into her ear, feeding her excuses; ways to rationalize a kill. Over time it became easier and more natural.

Now—in the months that followed her homecoming at Ten Points and drinking exclusively from Wes Washer—shards of a remaining conscience reemerged, telling her there were other ways to satiate the blood lust.

The doomed derelict gave a wide, drunken grin and revealed dirty teeth that were snaggled in some areas; gapped and gone in others.

"Well, since you're not shy you get the first sip," he slurred, unwittingly spelling out his doom. He extended his bottle to Flannery.

She knocked it out of his hand with a loud feline-like hiss. She went for this throat without any further hesitation. The opened bottle of whiskey fell out of his hands. Liquor spilled into the patchy grass and dirt. Much more soaked into the brown paper bag.

"Ahhh!" the man screamed loudly. In a quick and unforeseen show of strength and lucidity, he shoved Flannery off him.

He gave her a pitiful and wounded look, shock and betrayal across his unshaven face. Blood ran in a steady stream from his neck. The dirty flannel shirt protecting him from the chilly night absorbed some of it and turned dark at the collar.

Flannery was surprised he was so strong. Before he could see her reaction she lunged, grabbed a handful of his oily hair, pulled his head closer, and resumed the feast. She closed her eyes; tried not to think about what she did as some of the blood poured back out of her mouth and cascaded down her chin.

Flannery felt a forceful yank from behind and was shoved aside. "My turn," Katarina said, cutting in, fangs erect.

Katarina latched on to him like a tick. She devoured the blood at a much faster pace than Flannery ever had with anyone. The slurps and guttural growls of a half-starved predator echoed across the river. She came up for air once, and looked over at Flannery, her blue eyes large and frenzied by the wave of murderous nourishment.

"*This* is how it's done, whore!" Katarina exclaimed with wild laughter, as if they were sorority girls in a drinking game. She went back at him. He was no longer conscious.

Flannery took two steps back. She watched, she hoped he was dead. At that moment she hated Katarina almost as much as the night she had her goons kill Frank. She wished she had something sharp so that she could sneak up on Katarina and pierce her through the heart. Finish the bitch off. No reprieves from that equally loathsome bastard Conrad would be able to save Katarina this time. But a wave of paralysis and a strange sense of obedience overcame her.

The man lay lifeless on the ground underneath Katarina. The bottle of whiskey was beside him, mostly empty. The bottle's neck jutted out of the wet paper bag.

Katarina stood and wiped blood from her chin. She licked it from her fingers and stared at Flannery with a victorious grin. "You did as I told you. Good job."

Flannery stared back but said nothing. With a wave of her tongue inside her closed mouth, she could feel her canines had returned to their normal size.

"For your obedience, I will reward you with some information," Katarina said. Some of her words sounded slurred; there was a higher tilt to her voice. "But first, we must move him back to the woods. They will find him and blame an animal for this."

"We *are* animals," Flannery corrected her.

Katarina giggled and stumbled as she moved around the body. She looked over to Flannery with a strange expression and giggled a bit more.

"Okay, let's move him," Flannery said flatly. She felt like nothing more than Katarina's slave.

Katarina's giggles continued, as one of them grabbed the man's arms and the other took him by the legs. They moved toward the trees with the body.

"Oh, the look on your face when I told you to kill him," Katarina said, in her giggle fit, as if it were all a naughty prank.

Flannery was accustomed only to bitchy laughs and cackles from Katarina. Nothing as jovial and ongoing as this. Katarina nearly dropped her end of the body as they scooted toward the trees with it. She regained her composure, but Flannery noticed by the time they made it to the woods she was the one doing most of the work. What the hell had come over Katarina?

As they positioned the body against a tree in a sitting position, Flannery recognized an old feeling. A light head buzz. Something she would have felt once upon a time after a couple of drinks.

The whiskey. The homeless man's blood alcohol level was likely through the roof, and Katarina did most of the feeding. She was drunk. It was apparent when they came back out of the woods, and she wobbled with her steps. Flannery was hardly affected.

This could be my chance, she thought to herself. If only there was a way. Something unseen stopped her—prevented her from moving in and attacking her undead accessory in murder.

"You know what I like about you, whore?" Katarina asked with a slur, as she put her arm around Flannery, buddy-like.

"I don't really care," Flannery replied. She wanted to reach over and twist the bitch's arm off her body. But she couldn't. Why?

"You are stubborn. You *liiike* to put up resistance and have your way!" Katarina said loudly, with a snort and an umpteenth giggle. "I don't like it when you do that with me, but it is a good, what do they say, *quality* to have with others."

"You are drunk from that guy's blood and make no absolutely sense," Flannery said. If only there was a sharp object around. *If only*. It could be quick and easy. Katarina's defenses were down. How could she be so dumb? An opportunity such as this might never present itself again.

But even if there *were* a sharp object around ... she *couldn't*. What the hell was happening? Why these feelings? She loathed Katarina. Why wouldn't it be simple to just destroy her and be done?

Katarina jerked her arm away from Flannery and looked over. Her eyes instantly narrowed and were more lucid. The merriment vanished. "I know what you are thinking," she said. "If you continue to think it, I swear I will go into the old woman's room and snap her neck when we return to the house. Then I will stake you myself."

"I would be a fool *not* to think about it," Flannery said.

"*All* you can do is think about it," Katarina said. "You cannot destroy your own Maker, whore. That's one bit of information I give you now."

They flew back to Ten Points. Flannery led the way this time. Katarina was as unsteady in the air as she had been on her feet. She drifted aimlessly through the sky. The black flowing shape flapped this way and that; a giant, disoriented bat.

Flannery tried to obey and put the thoughts of destroying Katarina out of her mind. Had she been able to get inside Flannery's head when she put her arm around her? *Maybe.* Surely she couldn't see inside Flannery's head when they weren't touching. Or could she?

They landed in a discreet, nondescript area behind the house and slipped inside a back entrance. Flannery guided Katarina up the stairs and around a corner to the other staircase to the third floor. Thankfully, Katarina was light on her feet. Practice, Flannery supposed. After all, Katarina had hidden in the house for the better part of a year. Being undetectable shouldn't be difficult, even in drunkenness.

They entered Katarina's lair, where the blonde kicked off a pair of blue flats and fell across her bed. She obviously wanted to pass out and take slumber before sunrise. But there were a few hours before daylight. Flannery had more questions.

"So I couldn't destroy you even if I wanted to. Will you now tell me something I need to know about myself?" Flannery asked.

She stood over near the vanity and stared at Katarina, who was lying on her side, her back to Flannery.

Katarina groaned but didn't answer.

She made me kill that guy for sport and nothing else, Flannery thought. *The bitch. I could open of those shutters on the window. Just a little. The light would slip in come sunrise and destroy her.*

She wanted to go to the window, but her feet wouldn't take her there. Was it in her own head, or did Katarina tell the truth?

Katarina didn't stir. She wasn't touching Flannery. She could no longer hear her thoughts. *That had to be it.* She could only read Flannery's mind when they touched.

Flannery found herself more confident and considered other ways she—or someone else—could destroy Katarina.

There were no sharp objects in the room. Not even a fingernail file in sight. Flannery eyed the vanity. Makeup, a hairbrush, and a bottle of red fingernail polish. She tiptoed closer and slowly slid a drawer open as quietly as she could and peered inside.

A short dagger! She reached inside for it and paused. The silver blade couldn't have been more than eight inches long. But it was *silver,* something their kind could not tolerate. She had learned all about the allergy of silver her first night as one of them. Conrad used a silver chain to restrain Katarina and take her captive after he rescued Flannery that night. She could still remember the agonizing screams five years ago as the chain burned into Katarina's pale dead flesh. The touch of silver was akin to a mortal's hand on a hot stovetop.

The thick metal crossguard between the blade and handle was emblazoned with the letter "D." What the "D" stood for she wasn't sure. Katarina could have taken it from someone with that initial.

The handle was wrapped in a black material, leather maybe. She cautiously tapped a fingertip on the handle before she grasped it and picked it up.

Flannery crept to the bed where Katarina looked to be asleep and stood over her with the dagger. Her feet moved this time. Maybe it *was* all in her head? One quick stab through the back, through the heart, and out the other side. It could be done in a matter of seconds, and the silver would ensure Katarina's destruction. She would be out of Flannery's life and out of this world forever.

Flannery raised her right hand and prepared to bring down the dagger and stab her sleeping bitch of a Maker, but a sudden paralysis in mid-air froze her; left her unable to carry out the act.

She couldn't do it. Katarina was right. There was a resistance, a force she couldn't explain to herself or anyone else. What was it that caused her to be so beholden to someone who had destroyed her life?

Defeated, Flannery was back at the vanity. She replaced the dagger inside the drawer. Then two other things she had neglected to see inside the drawer caught her eye.

There was what appeared to be a business card and a folded slip of paper beside it. Flannery reached in and picked up the card. It was a golden color with a distinctive black-lettered font. She read it, frowned, and then reread the unfamiliar name.

Alexander Lanehart, Esquire. Who was Alexander Lanehart? A relative? She had never heard of him. How was he involved with Katarina? The card looked new, not something stashed away in an antique drawer for decades. She would have to ask Marcus later if he knew of any Alexander in the family. She certainly didn't. She quickly memorized the phone number on the card.

She replaced the card and picked up the slip of folded paper. It was fresh and white, not yellowed or frayed, as old paper would be.

She unfolded it and was further confused.

In clear block letters, handwritten in pencil, was the word VAMPIRE.

"Vampire? What's a vampire?" she asked herself, as she folded the piece of paper and replaced it inside the drawer.

She had two new questions, and even if she figured out a way to destroy Katarina, it would have to wait. Katarina could be the only one to give Flannery answers.

6

A knock at the door stirred Wes Washer awake. He stumbled out of his bedroom and down the hallway. He squinted as a bright flash of light through a window pierced his eyes. He felt a trifle dizzy, even weak; he hoped he wasn't coming down with something. Two other deputies at work had colds. Transporting the occasional criminal could leave a squad car a cesspool of germs. The last thing he remembered from last night was going to bed shortly after Clementine LeMonde dropped by with a batch of cookies. He wished some nice and pretty woman from the church he really wanted to settle down with would drop by with cookies.

Wes parted with groggy thoughts of gooey chocolate chip-goodness and the malaise of perpetual bachelorhood when the clock on the living room wall told him it was past ten o'clock in the morning. His green eyes shot open; he flew into a panic.

"Oh darn it, how long did I sleep? I'm gonna be late for work," he said to himself.

Another loud knock on the front door jarred his thoughts, and he realized why he had awoken in the first place.

Wes made his way past the hand-me-down furniture that decorated the small living room and reached up and unlatched the bolt on the front door.

As soon as he opened the door he let out a loud yelp and tried to slam it shut.

Dr. Remy Van Buren blocked the attempt. "What the hell is the matter with you?" he asked, bewildered and holding the door open.

"The Devil! It's you! You're the Devil!" Wes yelled, then put one hand over his mouth. He pointed at Remy with the other.

Remy shook his head. He had come across nothing but strange people since his arrival in north Louisiana a day earlier. There was now this man, who not only acted like an oddball but also had what appeared to be a large hickey on the left side of his neck.

The latter was none of his concern. "I'm Remy Van Buren, I've come here from Chicago, and I can assure you I'm *not* the Devil," he said. "Are you Deputy Wes Washer?"

"How do you know my name?" Wes asked. He moved his hand away from his mouth and looked on the other man with suspicion. "Only the Devil would know somethin' like that. Or God, and I *know* you ain't Him."

"What is this fixation you have with the Devil?" Remy frowned. "I just need to ask you a few questions about a call you went on last spring. If you don't mind. Then I'll be on my way, okay?"

"What call?" Wes asked, tight-lipped as he looked Remy over. Perhaps for horns, the other man assumed.

"The one at the old plantation north of town. I came here to ask you about it last night, but you were apparently asleep. The lights were off, and no one ever came to the door."

What a strange night it had been. More odd than this fellow. Remy was startled and not sure what he had seen when he had pulled up the driveway in his rental car. Some dark, blackish thing that looked like a giant cape or a flying tarp had blown in front of him halfway up the driveway. He had blinked, and it was gone just as quickly. It alarmed him so that he had to bring the car to a complete stop and collect his thoughts.

But Remy was back today. There was no need to mention the unexplained encounter to Wes. The deputy didn't appear too tightly wrapped. Some wild story could further agitate him.

"Well, I don't talk about my official business with strangers," Wes said, with fabricated gruffness. "You can obtain a copy of the report if you go down to the sheriff's office and pay fifty cents. They'll print you out a copy."

Remy became impatient. "I've already been there. They sent me to you. And I don't have to pay fifty cents to read anything. You do know that affidavits can be read online, don't you? But since this happened right around the time Geoff Lanehart and his wife and son went missing, your call to the house still seems fresh on the sheriff's mind."

"You look just like that guy," Wes said. "How do I know you're not here playin' some kinda practical joke?"

Remy's annoyed mood was stolen by Wes's unwitting bait. "*What guy?* He looks just like me, you said?"

"Oh, I know it's you, don't try to pull my leg," Wes said, now the annoyed one. "You're friends with Geoff Lanehart, or you *were*. Nobody knows anymore if he's dead or where he is."

"So Geoff Lanehart was friends with a guy who looks just like me?" Remy asked. Progress! "Was he at the house when you went there that morning?"

"I don't know. I don't recall seein' him there then. I just saw him the night I had to go to Ten Points and check about the dead animals. And there was the night after that when Mister Maximilian Lanehart, God rest his soul, was laid to rest."

"Dead animals?" Remy asked. "I only know that you responded to a domestic disturbance at the house last spring, but what is this dead animals thing?"

"Travis Lanehart is a child of Satan and made some kind of sacrifice with ducks and a raccoon in the front yard," Wes said matter-of-factly, brow raised. "Geoff and Tilda said they'd handle it, but who knows, that might be why they're missin'. Travis is a Devil worshipper, so he probably worked some of his black magic and made them all disappear. I ain't able to prove none of that, but that's the direction I keep tellin' our detectives to go in."

"Travis Lanehart?" Remy said, making a mental note. "Who is he?"

"Geoff and Tilda's son. The one who's still around. Now you have to go because I am late for work!"

Wes tried to close the door, but Remy stopped him again. "Wait," he said.

"I am *late!*" Wes exclaimed curtly, with a frown. He had finally gotten off nights the month before and wasn't about to let anything jeopardize his cushier day shift.

"You're right," Remy said. He had all the information he needed from Wes. For now. "I'm sorry to keep you. I'm here looking for information about my brother Jimmy Van Buren, and it sounds like he was acquainted with Geoff Lanehart. Thank you for your time."

As he turned to leave, Wes stepped out on to the front porch. "Hey wait a minute," he called.

Remy turned back to face him. "Yeah?"

"That guy who looks like you. His name ain't Jimmy. It was, um, *Conrad,* I think?"

"You're sure about that?" Remy asked.

"Yeah, I'm sure," Wes replied. "And now that I've had a look at you, well, you look a little older than him."

Remy nodded, not put off by the last part. Jimmy had been the vain one. If his brother was alive, there was also a chance he would use an alias.

"Thank you for your time, Deputy Washer," Remy said, as he left.

Remy drove out to U.S. 165, the main highway, and turned north. He had Googled and read all about Ten Points, its history, the Ogden family who built it, and the evolution of the Ogden family tree to the Laneharts who had been there ever since. The same photographic memory that helped him graduate near the top of his class at Johns Hopkins served him well the night before when he studied up on Ten Points. He felt a search for Jimmy would take him to the former cotton plantation. So he had done the homework.

Remy followed the rental car's GPS and made a left turn off the highway on to another road that led him where he needed to go. He knew he would recognize the grand house when it came into view. About two miles in, there it was, at the end of a long driveway, partially hidden by an array of large oak trees, many there longer than the 198-year-old estate.

The great house of Ten Points was a three-story medley of Greek Revival and Italianate Styles of days past. Cypress logs that were cut and cured for several years underwater were used in the construction of the mansion; the Corinthian columns were visible from the south end of the driveway. Remy read Theodore Ogden Senior spared no expense on architects and carpenters. There had no doubt been plenty of free slave labor as well.

Remy wondered how many of the fifty-seven rooms were still used. A Google image search even showed photos from inside the house. It seemed a trifle extravagant for one small, dwindling family. Most of the surviving antebellum homes from the Old South served as museums and tourist stops. That had not happened at Ten Points, though its cotton empire of the past was long gone. As a northerner, Remy wondered what kind of atonement, if any, the family had made for the past sin of slavery. It seemed a valid question but not one he would dare ask.

He reached the house and parked the car. He stepped out and absorbed the close-up view no photo could give someone, when they had studied a subject but finally came upon it in the flesh. Or, in this case, wood and brick and mortar. He stared up and down the three stories before he snapped to his senses and walked up the curved granite steps to the front porch. He had never traveled in the southern states; it felt as if he had been planted into a movie. When he made it to the front door, Remy shook off the fantastical and romantic indulgence and rang the bell.

It took a moment, but a thin woman who looked to be in her late twenties or early thirties with closely-cropped blonde hair answered the door. Her amber eyes widened at the sight of Remy, a flirtatious smile pulled at her plump lips.

"Hey there," she said, a twang in her voice, showing slightly bucked teeth. "Can I help you?"

Remy was dressed conservatively—polo shirt and slacks—yet her eyes wandered up and down.

Not even subtle. He paid it no further mind. "Yes, is there a Marcus Lanehart at home, or someone else I can speak with? I'm Doctor Remington Van Buren. I've traveled from Chicago."

"Sure," she said, stepping aside without reservation. "Chicago, huh?

That's a real long way to come for a visit. Come on in."

"Thanks," he said. He walked inside to the foyer. Awe returned; he soaked in more of what he had seen online but never in person. It looked smaller than the photos, but still, more impressive as he stood in the middle of it. "Quite a place you have here," he added, his eyes everywhere but on his hostess.

"Yeah, it's a lot of work sometimes, but I like a *challenge,*" she said, hoping he caught the innuendo. Remy did, but he was too enamored with the house. "I'm Tarva, by the way," she added. "I work here. You probably think I live here, but I don't. I might one day though, if I take D'Lynn's place. She's the head housekeeper. I'm her assistant. But that don't mean I don't have a lot of work to do. I—"

"I see," he interrupted, with a polite nod. He brought his dark brown eyes back to hers. "So ... may I please speak to Mister Lanehart, *or* somebody in charge of the house?"

A younger man who looked to be in his late twenties, with black hair and a matching Stetson, strolled into the foyer from an adjoining hallway. Despite holding a fried chicken drumstick, he was lean, fit, and slightly muscular, with a sleeveless gray shirt tucked into tight, faded jeans.

Tarva frowned. "D.C., what are you doin' in here?" she asked, in a scolding tone. "You know you ain't supposed to be walkin' around on a marble floor in them boots. D'Lynn and me waxed it yesterday, and you're just gonna track it all up." She glared at the well-traveled leather cowboy boots.

"Oh hell, these boots are clean and I walked all gentle-like in here," D.C. said. He took a bite off the drumstick and stared at Remy. "Who are you?" he asked, pointedly but not rudely.

"I'm Doctor Remington Van Buren. I'm here to see the head of the house," Remy said. He looked to Tarva and hoped she would take the hint to go find the person he needed to speak with.

"I'm D.C. Cunningham," said the other man. He held out his right hand. Remy accepted the handshake, grateful D.C. Cunningham must be left-handed, since his left hand looked greasy from the chicken. "Well, Dwight Charles is my name, but I go by my initials 'cuz I don't like my name."

"Well, Remington is mine, but I go by Remy. *So*, is Mister Lanehart—?"

"You ain't even supposed to be in here," Tarva said to D.C., diverted and annoyed.

"I help with the maintenance and stables and ground stuff," D.C. told Remy, ignoring Tarva.

Remy wasn't sure why these two insisted on oral presentations of their resumes. "A house like this must need a lot of maintenance from time to time. Very fascinating. I wonder if I could have a quick tour—" he began.

"Maybe Marcus can give you a tour after you talk to him," Tarva said.

"Marcus ain't here," D.C. told her.

"Marcus ain't here?" Tarva asked. "Well, where the heck is he?"

D.C. rolled his blue eyes, perturbed. "Same place as always," he said.

"Oh, gotcha," Tarva said, as if she knew. "Is D'Lynn in the kitchen?"

"Yeah, and she said I could have some of her chicken," D.C. said, back to a grin. He opened the front door. "Nice to meet you, Remy. See ya later, Tarva," he called, as he stepped outside and closed the door behind him.

"He's a mess," Tarva said. "He better not've left that doorknob all greasy with his chicken hands. And there better not be any scuff marks on these floors."

"So the floor is marble, you said?" Remy asked, as he looked across the room at the shiny, cream-colored floor. He noticed a wider doorway led to a carpeted living room.

"Yeah, it is," Tarva replied, with another smile. "Let me go see if I can find D'Lynn. Wait right here."

Remy stood and looked around, the winding wooden staircase between the entrances to the downstairs hallway and the living room caught his interest. With discretion, he tiptoed over for a peek at the living room. He saw leather armchairs, a green velvet antique sofa, and other elaborate furniture. A gray-haired man in a designer suit, painted in oil, stared down from a large gilded frame on the mahogany wall above the fireplace. Maximilian Lanehart. Remy recognized the face from his research.

"Tarva, I'm gonna put these vases out in the livin' room, and then I'll speak with the young man."

Another woman's voice approached from the hallway. Tarva came into the foyer first, and behind her, a short, slightly round older woman with graying hair carried a tray of glass vases. The older woman screamed as if she saw the Devil himself; she dropped the silver tray. Vases shattered across the clean marble. Shards of glass scurried across the glossy white of the floor.

"Oh my God!" D'Lynn cried, in her thick country accent. She clutched her chest. Tarva ran to her. "It's *him!* The evil! *The evil has returned!*"

"D'Lynn, get a-hold of yourself! What's the matter?" Tarva asked. She grabbed D'Lynn by the arm and tried to calm her. "He came here to see Marcus."

"Well, *of course* he did!" D'Lynn continued. She pulled her arm away from Tarva and stumbled over to a wooden chair beside a small table, suddenly out of breath. "Oh dear God in Heaven, I thought you had left. Where is Geoffrey? What did you do with Tilda? Where is little Bobby?"

Confused, Remy moved closer to D'Lynn, but she screamed again. It was wavered and not as loud. She stuck out a hand, determined to keep him at a distance.

"You stay far away from me!" she warned him. "I know good and well you bein' here and them disappearin' at the same time ain't no coincidence. *Ohhh!*" She started to cry.

"D'Lynn you have got to calm down," Tarva said to her. "Who is this man? Why are you actin' this way? You know the police said that Geoffrey and Tilda ran away. They found some of the clothes they dropped out in the yard."

"Ma'am, I will go. I didn't mean to upset you in any way. I am just here to find out information about my brother is all," Remy said, as apologetically as he could. He looked to Tarva for help.

D'Lynn continued to clutch at her chest. "Oh my heart! Tarva, I think I need one of my nitroglycerin pills. I might be about to have a heart attack if I ain't already."

Tarva panicked. "D'Lynn, I don't even know where you keep those *or* what those are!"

"Please," Remy cut in. "I'm a doctor. I'm not a cardiologist, just a general practitioner, but if you'll let me, I can maybe be of assistance here."

"I don't want him touchin' me," D'Lynn said to Tarva. She looked on Remy with distrust. "He's evil."

"But D'Lynn, he said he's a doctor. Let him help," Tarva argued, as she patted the older woman's short, chubby arm and tried to assuage the hysteria. "I'll be right here. I won't let him do nothin' to hurt you."

D'Lynn stared down Remy with stubborn eyes and released a sniffle. "Okay, okay. But you never said you were a doctor when you were here before."

"I've never been here before," Remy said, throwing his hands up in exasperation.

"You're a liar!" D'Lynn charged, worked up again. Tarva tugged at her again, to try and quieten her.

"I'm looking for my brother Jimmy. Was he here? Is *that* who you think I am?"

"I don't know any Jimmy," D'Lynn said.

Remy recalled what Wes had told him. "Conrad," he said. "Did he tell you his name was *Conrad?*"

"Yes! It's you!" she exclaimed. "But you look like you got a few years older in just a few months."

"D'Lynn," Tarva said in a low voice, shushing her.

"I'm Doctor Remy Van Buren. Jimmy Van Buren is my twin brother. He's been missing for seven years. I think he was here, calling himself Conrad. That's why I'm here. I've looked for him all these years. *God...*" Remy paced around the room, aggravated at the screaming, bellowing woman.

"Your twin?" D'Lynn asked, a little calmer.

"*Yes!*" Remy shouted. As soon as it came out he regretted raising his voice. "I mean yes," he said, gentler. "I didn't mean to yell at you. I'm sorry."

"Tarva, go get me some water," D'Lynn said. "Okay, if you're not *him,* then I guess it'll be all right for you to take a look and make sure I ain't about to die."

"I don't have my medical bag with me, but I can do a basic examination," he said. "Just tell me the symptoms, and we can go from there and call an ambulance if we need to."

He went over, slow and cautious, afraid D'Lynn could go on the attack again.

"No, it's okay," she assured him. Tarva rushed in with a glass of water. "I believe you now."

7

D.C. Cunningham shook his head and frowned, when he pulled the silver GMC pick-up into the driveway two miles from Ten Points. One of the estate's silver Bentleys was parked outside. D.C. always knew the first place to look anytime Marcus disappeared from Ten Points for any length of time. Had it not been for Doctor Remy Van Buren back at the house, D.C. probably would have left it alone. The same scene as always was about to play out.

He put the truck in park, stepped out, and walked up to the front door of the one-story brick house. Even though he had been through this several times, he was never sure whether to knock or ring the doorbell.

What the hell difference did it make, D.C. thought, as he pulled back the screen door and rapped his knuckles on the wooden door. He counted to five in his head before he knocked a second time. He pressed his ear to the door for any sounds of movement inside the house.

He pulled his head back, as Marcus pulled open the door. "What are you doin'?" D.C. asked.

"Nothing," Marcus replied, unapologetic. "Go on back to the house. Shouldn't you be helping Buddy with something?"

D.C. gave a loving brush across Marcus's cheek with the back of his hand, and then let it rest on Marcus's shoulder. "Come on. I'll drive you home. We can come back and get the car later."

Marcus took a step back. "I'll drive myself home later. Just leave me be."

"Marcus, why do you keep doin' this to yourself? It's no good for you. For *us*…"

"I don't want to talk about it," Marcus said. He turned and walked back into the house.

D.C. followed him inside. "We *do* need to talk about it, Marcus. Zeke is gone. He ain't ever comin' back. You went and bought this house to try to keep him alive, and you just keep comin' over here. You sit and stare at the walls like you expect him to pop out and announce he's done come back to Earth."

"Don't say things like that," Marcus said, though he knew D.C. could be correct. "You're in his house. It's not even right for you to be in here."

"I'm in what *used to be* his house," D.C. said, his voice jumping a tad higher and louder, as it tended to do when he was excited. "It ain't been *his* house in about seven months, and it's been *your* house for about two months now. And I know that 'cuz I'm over here every fuckin' seven or ten days talkin' you down from a pity party and draggin' your ass back to Ten Points."

"You don't understand," Marcus said. He looked at the other man as if he were young and dumb—a sore point with D.C. "I never told you that you had to do any of that. You can feel free to leave, and to leave me the hell alone, any time."

D.C. grabbed him by the shoulders and gave him a gentle kiss on the lips. Then he released him and went on a tirade again.

"Damn it! Can't you see that I love you, and I don't wanna leave you the hell alone? You just need to find a healthier way to honor Zeke than to linger around over here durin' your free time."

"You shouldn't say things like that," Marcus said. "I don't love you, D.C. Not the way you want me to. I'm not ready for any of that."

"Are you in here drinkin'?" D.C. asked, changing the subject. He knew how Marcus felt about him. It wasn't the first time he had heard it. His blue eyes wandered the room for a liquor bottle. "I swear that was whiskey I just tasted on your breath."

"What if it was?"

"Damn, man, it's barely lunchtime. I know it's five o'clock somewhere an' all, but do you think that's gonna help? Now you're gettin' drunk when you come over here? What if Maxine needs help with her math homework later or somethin'?"

"I'm not drunk," Marcus said. "I had one drink. Just *one.*"

"I'm not tryin' to put a label on you, Marcus. Or my brand. I'll wait however long you want me to wait."

"You're young. You should be out dating other people. You should go have fun with your friends. You waste your time with me, D.C."

"What if I *want* to waste my time on you?" he said more playfully, as he smiled and gave Marcus a light nudge. "Have you seen the other choices in this town?" he said, as he moved in closer and gave him another kiss.

D.C. did have a point. Monroe was not exactly thriving with a robust gay community or strong LGBT coalition. A majority of the gay men he had come across in the area had strange attitudes and hang-ups about things. Many of them smoked cigarettes and preferred to hang out at the bar and sleep around with one another with little or no attachment. The ones who tried to make a difference and bring change to the community were outnumbered by barflies. It was a world away from the environment of southern California and the kind of atmosphere to keep Marcus at home—or at Zeke's house—the lion's share of the time.

But he wasn't dumb. D.C. came from a lower-class family in Union Parish. Marcus wasn't convinced the twelve-year age difference—and his newfound status in town—didn't make him more of a sugar daddy-catch in D.C.'s eyes.

Trust did not come easily for Marcus Lanehart.

So far, the otherwise clean-cut twenty-five-year-old D.C. had unknowingly passed all the secret tests Marcus had volleyed his way in the past three months. They hooked up about a week after D.C. was hired by Buddy, the head groundskeeper at Ten Points. Marcus had let it go as a one-time thing until D.C. latched on afterward.

As of late, D.C. used the *love* word, something Marcus didn't want to hear. It had only been seven months since Zeke Colson was killed by Marcus's brother Geoffrey—the circumstances of which still weren't clear, since Geoffrey too was dead.

Or Geoffrey was destroyed, *or* whatever you call it when someone who's already dead but animated and living on human blood is wiped out. It was too much for Marcus to process at times, hence the purchase of Zeke's house and the copious amount of time spent there.

Before the brief reunion with Zeke last spring, Marcus had been bereaved—was *still* bereaved—over the disappearance of his partner Landon Smithfield in San Diego two years ago. No sign or clue of what had happened to Landon ever surfaced, something Marcus slowly accepted would never materialize and give him closure. Adding an involvement with D.C. to the mix was another complication he didn't need. It was a moment of loneliness and weakness to which he had succumbed, but D.C. wanted more and wasn't shy about it.

"Time with me is time you won't get back at the end of your life," he said to D.C..

But D.C. was stubborn; he never budged. "Don't sell it all so short," he said, pulling Marcus close.

Marcus pulled away. "Not here. Not *ever* here," he said sternly.

D.C. let out a heavy and frustrated exhale. "Well, goddamn it then," he said angrily and moved for the door. "I forgot there's a goddamn ghost watchin' us in here."

"D.C., please—"

"I'll be back at Ten Points. Just stay here and get drunk or whatever the hell it is you plan to do. I guess call me before you try to drive later. Lord knows we don't want some scandal with a fancy-ass Ten Points luxury car gettin' wrapped around a tree. Or pulled over and busted by the po-po."

Marcus laughed but not because anything D.C. said was funny. It was the weary laugh of a man exhausted by the persistence of another. "Waste of time. I try to make this easy for you."

"Well, the main reason I wasted my time and drove over here is to tell you there's some guy back at the house lookin' for you. Some doctor." D.C. forgot his frustrations with Marcus and grinned. "Super hot. I felt a little threatened at first, but after I figured out he was straight, I knew he wasn't one of your Cali friends here to visit."

"A doctor? From where? Did he say what he wanted?"

"I left before he said much. He talked mostly to Tarva. Boy, she gave him the eye, too, but she didn't get nowhere. He wasn't wearin' any ring, but I know he ain't *family* 'cuz, well, I just know ..."

For someone who had never traveled much or lived in a major metropolitan area, D.C.'s gift of 'gaydar' always impressed Marcus. He could sniff out a closet case a mile away—or answer the 'is he or isn't he?' question after only a couple of minutes of observation of any man just about anywhere.

"Is he still there?" Marcus asked. "You're sure you don't know what he wanted?"

"Maybe you should call D'Lynn and ask her. I assume that's who he ended up talkin' to."

"Later," Marcus said. "He can come back later. I'm not in the mood today. I wonder if he was an M.D. or a Ph.D.?"

It could have always been someone from some historical society there to inquire about the house. There was always interest from potential buyers who eyed it as a promising tourist investment. But the thought of Ten Points employees at the mercy of a new employer, especially someone like D'Lynn who had been there for decades, didn't go over well with Marcus.

"I don't know, Marcus," D.C. said, still burnt. He also didn't know the difference between a Ph.D. and an M.D. "You're askin' the wrong person. I'm takin' off. I guess I'll see you later."

"Maybe," Marcus said, with no heed to D.C.'s disgusted grunt. The younger man stormed out without another word.

Instead, Marcus looked at the average sofa, the small coffee table, and the simple dry-wall around him in Zeke's living room. There was an armchair in one corner and a recliner in the other. It all looked the same way it did when Zeke lived there. *When Zeke was alive.*

The bank had seized the house after Zeke's death. An auction was about to be held to sell it and its contents, until Marcus stepped up and swiftly bought the property.

He couldn't let go yet. It wasn't time. He couldn't bear the thought of someone else discarding Zeke's things; someone else who never knew the trusty and beloved veterinarian moving in. The memory of Zeke in the house he had lived in and grown up in would be erased if some stranger moved in.

Marcus walked over to a cabinet and pulled out a photo album. Zeke never did social media, other than a Facebook page for his business. All his personal photos were in the album. A picture of him working at his veterinary practice, and then one near the back of the album that made Marcus pause.

It was a two-decades-old picture of Marcus and Zeke near the tailgate of a long-gone pickup truck of Zeke's, a red plastic cup in each of their hands. Probably beer. They weren't even legal adults yet.

"We probably thought we were pullin' one over on your Mom and Dad," Marcus said aloud, though no one was there to hear him. He grinned at the photo and shook his head.

Zeke's parents would have had something to say about it, but Maximilian Lanehart was probably off somewhere on that particular day in the late 1990's putting business, Geoff, or other things, ahead of Marcus.

Ezekiel Colson, DVM. He was also the staunch gay Republican. If only there was a chance to see him behind the wheel of the blue Ford F-250 again, with conservative talk radio blaring out of the speakers. Marcus could put his own disgruntlement with certain right-wingers aside and endure it. Then he wondered if their different ideas on things would have even allowed them to work as a couple.

Marcus closed the album. It had been seven months since he walked back into Zeke's life, and shortly thereafter, lost him again.

Permanently.

"But not if you have anything to say about it," he said. He closed his eyes and tried to imagine him there. If only it were possible. Zeke had promised him it would be.

"I'll find my way back ... however I can—whatever it takes! I swear on everything I believe in I'll find my way back to you! ..."

He could still hear it in his head. Their last meeting in the field. Some days it was a drug-induced dream, but there were the other days Marcus believed it had happened. Other events of the surreal night had sufficed as truth. He had somehow left his body that night, encountered Zeke in the field and, later, Flannery in the woods as she went to tell

Tilda what she had learned about Geoffrey's and Conrad's plans for young Bobby.

Zeke couldn't have said what he said in the field if it was never to happen. *Could he?*

Some of Zeke's remains were found in the woods. An arm and a leg bone were identified as his. They were interred beside his parents in a nearby cemetery. It was final. There was no way he could or would ever come back.

"It was a dream!" Marcus spat, back over at the glass decanter of bourbon in the corner of Zeke's living room. "*My* dream. That evil son of a bitch drugged me and forced me to dream those things so I would be tortured. *That's* what happened!"

Conrad would've fed you dreams to make you forget about Zeke if this were his doing, another voice told him.

Marcus poured more whiskey into a glass. Then he indulged himself with another splash after he was done with that. And then another.

As the afternoon progressed, he invented reasons to fill and raise the glass.

Sometime later he awoke face-down on the sofa. A half-empty glass was still on the coffee table. The living room TV blared loudly. At first it wasn't clear how much later it was. The room had darkened, and the clock on the wall said five-fifteen.

Shit. A.M. or P.M.?

The light outside was dim. It was difficult to tell. But the news was on the television, with the local evening team. *P.M.,* thank God. He was still out too late. Everyone at Ten Points was probably worried. But it wasn't as if he were gone an entire night, which would have caused alarm back at the house.

Travis and Maxine were more prone to panic these days. They had been home at least two hours after school without a word from him. He needed to let them know he was okay. D'Lynn or Tarva would serve dinner soon. Both women would get nosy.

There were no texts or missed calls on his phone; he was assured he wasn't missed. Not yet. No missed calls also told him D.C. was still pissed off and blowing off steam somewhere.

Marcus sat up on the couch, with a grimace; his head pounded—not terribly but just enough for an aspirin. How much had he drunk? His mouth was dry, and he desperately needed water. He went to the kitchen, where he kept bottled water stocked in the refrigerator.

All for the house I don't even live in. He gulped down half a bottle while he stood with the refrigerator door open.

The yellow light shined out into the darkened room and mocked him.

He told it to shut up and closed the fridge. He went back to the living room, foggy and unsteady. He poured a little more bourbon and guzzled it down. Then another for the road.

Hair of the dog. Or maybe he would start again.

His sensible side said driving the Bentley back to Ten Points was foolish. He closed one eye and strained the other one wide to focus on the road. He caught himself in a swerve and nearly ran into a ditch halfway home. He hoped just to get there under the radar of any police or deputies out on a rural patrol. Thankfully, he encountered no other cars along the two-mile stretch.

Hair of the dog be damned. He wasn't done yet and wanted another drink.

Marcus parked the car in the driveway, hoped no one had heard him pull up, and sneaked into his own house. The foyer was empty when he tiptoed through the front door. No noise came from the living room.

Marcus stayed as quiet and light as he could on unsteady feet, pulled an unopened bottle of whiskey from the living room liquor cabinet and grabbed a glass. He went back across the foyer in a half-jog. He went down the hallway, into the study, and quietly closed the door behind him. If anybody looked for him, he would pretend he was bogged down with work and other matters. He could try to look occupied. Nobody would ever suspect a thing.

What Marcus didn't realize was that Tarva caught a glance of him, as he darted into the study. She came downstairs ahead of Remy when she saw him from the entrance of the hallway. Tarva and Remy had put D'Lynn to bed for the evening after it was determined she only suffered from a panic attack.

"Thank you for stayin' here all afternoon and lookin' after her," Tarva said to Remy, as he reached the bottom of the stairs behind her. She turned away from the hall and to the doctor. "You should really stay and have some supper with us." Tarva hoped her cooking could charm him since nothing else did the trick.

"That's so kind, and thank you for the offer, but I feel like I've already intruded enough on everyone's time. If my brother was here, I'm just curious why he went by another name, and why he's caused so much distress for this family. It makes no sense."

Tarva put on a look of concern. "You've had such a rough go of it," she said, finding an excuse to put her hand on his sinewy forearm. Upstairs it had been a hand on a muscular shoulder when she expressed relief over his prognosis for D'Lynn.

"We all have our problems in life, however big or small," he said, with a faint smile.

She put on an air of enlightenment. "Oh, what a smart and brave man you are," she sighed. She stared into his dark brown eyes a beat too long for his liking; he looked away.

"Well, I must be going," he said. "Please let Mister Lanehart know I'll come back tomorrow. I hate I missed him today. I would like to also check on D'Lynn and make sure she's better."

"I think Marcus is home now," Tarva said, with a nod. Perhaps *he* could talk the hunky doctor into supper. Oh but she hoped desperately the doctor wasn't on Marcus's team! "I just saw him go in the study and close the door when we came downstairs."

"The study?" Remy asked.

"Yeah, right down the hallway there," Tarva said. "I need to check on my stew in the kitchen. If you go knock on the door, I'm sure he'll let you in. Third door on the right."

"Thanks," Remy said. He waited for Tarva to leave before he followed the directions down the hallway. He arrived at the study, knocked on the closed door, and waited.

After no reply, he lightly rapped his knuckles on the antique door again. "Marcus Lanehart, are you in there?" he called out, frowning since it felt awkward.

A few seconds later, the door creaked open. The color drained from Marcus's face as he stood eye to eye with Remy. He shook his head, frowned, and backed away a few steps.

"No, no, it can't be," Marcus said, in a near whisper. There was puffiness around his hazel eyes. Eyes so bloodshot Remy thought they were demonic, demented.

He delved in gently and warily. "Are you okay? Your housekeeper said—"

Remy didn't get the rest of the sentence out. The hard punch to his jaw knocked him to the floor inside the study. He felt a pop and wondered if his jaw was broken. Marcus shut and locked the door behind them.

Before Remy had time to process anything, Marcus was on top of him on the floor, punching him across the face repeatedly. Remy could smell the stench of booze coming off Marcus as he did his best to block the punches. For someone who wasn't large, the man was fueled by alcohol and strengthened by an adrenaline rush like he had never seen.

"You son of a bitch! Where the fuck is he? Where the fuck is he? *Where the fuck is he, you son of a bitch!*" Marcus yelled the same thing, over and over. He left Remy on the floor as he jumped to his feet, went over to the desk, angrily pulled a drawer nearly out of its slats, and rifled through it.

Remy stumbled to his own feet and rubbed his sore jaw. What the hell was this?

"*Please!*" Remy pleaded. He held out a hand for mercy and backed away. Marcus pulled something out of the drawer, but Remy couldn't see what it was. He tried to find the door to leave. Before he could reach it, Marcus rushed back over. He shoved Remy's hand away from the doorknob and blocked his exit.

"*Where ... is ... he?*" Marcus yelled again.

Someone started pounding on the door from the other side.

It was Tarva. "Marcus! What's going on in there? Marcus? Doctor Van Buren? Are you okay?"

Marcus ignored her. "*Where is he?*" he repeated. His face trembled with rage and grew more deranged.

"Where is *who?*" Remy asked, terrified. *What the hell kind of crimes had Jimmy committed in this house?*

"Landon. You made him disappear. Then you made Geoff kill Zeke. And you came into my dreams ... but you had to drug me to cause all that!"

An unexpected physical attack, the stench of a river of booze, and the flurry of strangers' names disoriented Remy. "Oh my God, *please*. I have no idea what you're talking abou—"

"Liar! *Incubus!*" Marcus cried out.

Remy only saw a flash of the large, sharp letter opener as Marcus drove it into him.

8

"Daddy up in Heaven must be so proud of his three little angels. You kill poor defenseless homeless men down by the river, your brother Geoff kills his brother's boyfriend, and your other brother Marcus tries to kill doctors who look like demons from his past."

"Just be quiet, Katarina," Flannery said. "If I had seen him first, I might have reacted badly as well. I knew nothing about the man whose body Conrad took, or that he had a twin brother who would show up here looking for him."

They were on the third floor in Katarina's lair. A few hours had passed since the commotion downstairs. Katarina sat at her vanity, brushing her hair. Flannery stood over near a corner.

"It was quite hard to stay up here and not go downstairs for a look," Katarina said, before a mischievous smirk. "Why am I lying? Of course I sneaked down for a look. I have my ways to spy without being seen."

Flannery said nothing.

"You had a taste of the wounded doctor before the ambulance arrived. When that skinny blonde housekeeper helped the authorities take your brother away, you had a few seconds alone with him."

"I'm not saying I did ... not saying I *didn't* ..."

"Do not insult my intelligence. You know it is not a question with me. I know what you did. I'm just curious what the whore has planned for the doctor."

Flannery wasn't ready to share those plans. "I do hope you're careful when you slip out of here and wander around the house. While others are still awake and about."

Katarina stared back at Flannery through the mirror. "Yes, you *should* because you are the one with something to lose if I'm ever seen."

"I'm a little tired of your threats. They're getting old. And you tricked me last night. You made me help you kill that poor man. You passed out drunk on his blood before you gave me any other information ... like you said you would."

"Patience, whore," Katarina growled. "Last night was a test. And you should be happy to know it was a test that you passed with flying colors. Ha, no pun intended on the flying part."

"What test?" Flannery asked. She moved closer.

"You could have easily destroyed me. You did not."

"Don't think I didn't consider it. Besides you told me I couldn't."

Katarina laughed. "I'm sure you are not so dumb that you couldn't get someone else to try and do it for you. Don't worry. You will have more opportunities in the future. But even then, you may have trouble allowing someone else to harm me."

"You think? I let Conrad toss you overboard that yacht."

"Conrad is no mortal. That was different. I am your Maker. No matter how strong the urge, you *cannot* destroy me. That's why you couldn't send me to the bottom of the lake yourself—or bear to look inside the vault before he threw me over."

It made sense. Flannery decided to take it further. "While you were drunk and passed out on the bed over there, I found something interesting inside the drawer of your vanity."

Katarina gave a hard glare through the mirror. "That is not yours to dig through!"

"Au contraire. You're a squatter in my house."

"Your *brother's* house," Katarina hissed. "Your father left none of this to you. His disinherited whore of a daughter."

"Well, either way, Marcus is only in charge by default, and it's not really your property either. So, let's cut to the chase. Who the hell is Alexander Lanehart, and what is a vampire?"

Their eyes locked through the mirror a full minute when Flannery saw another smile form at the corner of Katarina's mouth. "If you want to know who Alexander Lanehart is so badly, then why have you not called the number on the card?"

"I did. It's not a working phone number. I even did an internet search and couldn't find anything relevant."

The smile crawled from its corner and leapt across. "Maybe none of it is real."

"Don't play games with me."

"Do not snoop through my things. But since I left you hanging last night, I will answer one of those questions."

After one question was answered, Flannery returned downstairs. She heard voices from the living room. She found an emotional D'Lynn with Tarva and Travis. Travis's girlfriend Regan, a pretty black girl with long dark curly hair, who looked about Travis's age, was in the room with them. Regan stayed mostly quiet while the others carried on.

"I'm not a woman who takes liquor, but I sure need some brandy for my nerves," D'Lynn said to Tarva, who poured some into a snifter for her. "Make it a double."

"D'Lynn, you need to go right back to bed after you have this brandy," Tarva said, trying to sound authoritative. But the others didn't find it convincing. She poured just a tad more than the standard amount of brandy for D'Lynn and handed it to her.

"Be careful, D'Lynn. Uncle Marcus's boozin' made him go bat-shit crazy," Travis said, with a short pout. "Will he have to go to prison if that doctor who looks like Conrad dies?"

"Don't say such things!" D'Lynn scolded. A whine in her otherwise syrupy voice hinted a crying jag could be imminent.

"The doctor who looks like Conrad *won't* die," Flannery said, walking into the room. "He was only stabbed in the arm. Marcus won't go to prison. I'll make sure of that."

"Flannery." D'Lynn took a nervous gulp of brandy. "Were you here when it happened?"

Flannery looked sourly at D'Lynn. They both knew why, but no one else in the room did. "Yes, I was with him until the ambulance arrived," Flannery said, her voice as cold as the rest of her.

Flannery glanced over to Tarva, who got antsy and turned away.

Tarva wasn't quite sure what it was or why, but something about Flannery had always given her the heebie-jeebies.

Flannery continued. "Tarva was helping with Marcus, so I stayed with the doctor." *And I licked up some of his blood and used my magic finger to ease the depth of the wound and make it less serious and more superficial. Then I coaxed him with my eyes. So ... he will never remember any of it.*

The truth was Flannery had arisen from the basement the very moment Marcus plunged the letter opener into Remy Van Buren's upper arm.

Tarva was in the hallway, where she beat on the door to the study, and screamed for Marcus to open it. Flannery moved in front of Tarva and busted down the door before she thought about it.

"How on Earth did you do that?" an exasperated Tarva had asked.

"Never mind!" Flannery snapped at her. She saw the disoriented doctor, clutching his bloodied arm. The shock of the familiar face fazed her a few seconds, but she knew it wasn't Conrad. Unfortunately, D'Lynn and Marcus had not. "Call an ambulance," she ordered Tarva. Flannery ignored the doctor a moment and went to Marcus. "Marcus? What have you done? *Marcus!*"

An unresponsive Marcus sat on the floor beside Remy, frozen, the bloody letter opener in his hand. Flannery grabbed it, tried not to let the blood on it distract her, and turned her attention to Remy.

The doctor held tightly to his bleeding left arm, the color drained from his face as he stared absently at Marcus and then back to Flannery, whom he had never seen before.

"He stabbed me," Remy told her, shaking his head. "Oh my God, what did my brother *do* to you people?"

"You look just like him," Flannery said to Remy, before she could stop herself.

She turned back to Marcus. "Let's get you up," she said to her brother. But Marcus wouldn't move.

Tarva ran into the study. She held a smartphone and frantically shrieked at a 911 dispatcher.

"Yes, yes, he's conscious!" Tarva screamed, looking down at Remy on the floor and running around the room. "Bleedin'? *Bleedin'?*" She looked over to Remy again. *"Are you bleedin'?"* she asked, panting like an overheated dog in the summer.

"Tarva, hand me the goddamn phone and let me do the talking!" Flannery demanded, ready to slap the hysteria out of her. "You're making it worse. I need you to try to get Marcus off the floor. Put him in a chair or something. I can't get him to respond."

"What makes you think *I* can?" Tarva cried out, pulling at her closely-cropped hair with shaky hands on each side of her head. "Oh my gosh, there's just been too much excitement around here today."

A short while later, as Tarva helped a sheriff's deputy escort Marcus out of the study, Flannery turned to Remy.

"What did Marcus tell you?" she asked, staring into his dark eyes. Eyes that reminded her so much of Conrad's. Only there was no malice or threat in these eyes.

"Huh?" Remy asked, still in shock and unable to fully process what had happened.

He instinctively held pressure to his arm with a hand towel someone had brought him. He couldn't remember who. A light blue towel partially soaked with his blood.

Flannery took the towel away and helped him loosen his grip.

"I—I don't ..." he began.

"Shhh," she quieted him, then put her lips to the bloody wound on his arm.

It was strange at first, but when she pulled away and looked deeply into his eyes again, he accepted it as natural.

Flannery was curious about the resemblance to Conrad but didn't let Remy see it. Despite Marcus's afternoon of boozing, Flannery could see why her brother had lost his senses at the sight of this man.

Remy looked a few years older, so if he was a twin she guessed Conrad had slowed the aging process a bit when he possessed the other brother. But Conrad had been a fan of moisturizers and skin pampering. None of it would have lasted long term. Conrad was already making plans last spring to take over the body of little Bobby Lanehart when the child came of age.

Geoffrey Lanehart had sold his own developmentally-disabled child to the demon. The little boy had been damaged goods—in Geoffrey's eyes.

"I had a nightmare about Conrad just a couple of nights ago. I wonder if it was some kind of omen about this twin brother?" Travis wondered aloud, bringing Flannery back to the present.

"What kind of nightmare?" D'Lynn asked, interested as well.

Flannery gave Travis a wide-eyed glare that screamed *Shut your damned mouth!*

"Oh nothing," he said, put off by the look from his aunt. "You know how that asshole, sorry, I mean, *that guy*, creeped some of us out. I just dreamed he stopped back by for a visit."

Flannery nodded her approval at his cover. She and Marcus and Travis were the only ones who knew—or remembered—that Travis was the one who had beheaded Conrad. Or, as it now appeared, Travis had actually decapitated Dr. Remy Van Buren's brother.

"I thought it was *him* at first when I saw the doctor earlier today. I nearly had a heart attack!" D'Lynn exclaimed, clutching her chest again for effect. "Ain't that right, Tarva?"

"She's right. She did," Tarva agreed, with raised brows. She was calmer than earlier. "I thought I was gonna have to whop her upside the head to get her to settle down."

"Well, I'm glad you didn't do that!" said the older woman, with a frown.

Tarva gave a buck-toothed grin. "Oh, D'Lynn, I'm just joshin'. I could never hit you. But you know one time my Aunt Felicia was screamin' and carryin' on after seein' a rattlesnake in the backyard. She couldn't calm down at all. Well, she was so worked up that she couldn't tell my Uncle Roy where it was so he could go kill it. She was wavin' her arms all around and havin' such a fit. Finally, my Aunt Trudy—she was my Mama's other sister—whacked her up side the head real good. Ain't that somethin'? But anyway, it calmed her down, and they were finally able to go find—"

"Well, that *is* somethin'," D'Lynn quickly agreed, to put an end to Tarva's story.

Flannery rolled her eyes at the two women and didn't care if they saw. "It isn't clear yet what's wrong with Marcus. He was in a kind of catatonic state when they took him out of here. He was conscious but unresponsive. Completely shut down. He's under observation at the hospital."

"Is Uncle Marcus gonna go to jail after that?" Travis asked again.

"I already said he's *not!*" Flannery snapped impatiently. Children were not her forte, even the older ones. "Don't you *ever* listen?"

Travis wanted to strike back but held his tongue. "Well, I just don't want to get sent off to a foster home," he said instead.

"You won't go to a foster home," Flannery said, calmer, as she reeled herself back in. The boy was understandably worried. "There are plenty of us who can petition for temporary custody of you and Maxine, or whatever is necessary, until Marcus's situation is handled," she said, looking to D'Lynn and Tarva. She would let one of them volunteer for that burden.

"No offense, Aunt Flannery, but you're kind of a bitch, so I don't know if I want you to be my new Mom," Travis said. There was also the little matter of her being dead, but he was convinced she didn't know about his discovery of that incredible fact.

Flannery raised a brow but let it slide. Despite her distaste for children, even the older ones, she had to admire the multi-pierced, Goth-dressed kid. He had tried to save Zeke and the rest of Ten Points but was thwarted by Conrad. Travis killed what he believed to be Conrad, as the demonic monster tried to strangle Marcus to death. Flannery also had to commend the teenager for openly dating outside his race, for the way it must have riled Geoffrey, Tilda, and Maximilian. Her hatred for the three of them lived on despite their deaths.

"Well, you could always come stay in the guest room at my house," Regan said, with a shy and demure smile.

"Oh Regan, your Mama would shit a brick if you ever brought up that idea to her," Travis replied. "She wouldn't piss on me if I was on fire."

"One day I'm gonna drag you back to that kitchen and wash your mouth out with some Ajax," Tarva chided him. "Where'd you learn to talk like that all the time?"

Travis let out a sarcastic chuckle. "Have you ever listened to the other people who live in this house?"

D'Lynn sat back in the armchair and took a large sip of brandy. Normally a nondrinker, the strength of it brought a slight cough as she slid her eyes shut. The brandy did nothing to ease her heavy head, and she sighed and reopened her eyes. "So many horrible things have happened in this house," she said.

"Yes," Flannery said, with a tinge of resentment. *Like old-bitty housekeepers who help their rich, rapist masters keep daughters and mothers apart for years.* "Let's talk about some of them."

"Well, there's Geoff, Tilda, and Bobby. We may never know what happened to them," Tarva chimed in. Flannery and Travis gave each other another glance.

"Mister Lanehart—God rest his sweet soul—just fell over dead out in the backyard behind the house. They said it was a heart attack. He was fine right before that," D'Lynn said, referring to Maximilian.

Yes, what a sweet soul he had. Just more than three decades before his sweet soul left the Earth, he raped my mother in the study down the hallway, and that's why I'm here to grace you all with my undead presence tonight, Flannery wanted to add. Instead, she said, "Well, the idea of a curse or anything like that is a bunch of silly nonsense. Any house that's been around as long as this one has its share of tragedy."

A loud knock at the front door turned their attention toward the foyer.

D'Lynn waved it away as if it were a fly in the room. "Tarva, hon, can you please go see who it is? If it's some reporter from the *News-Star* or KNOE, make 'em go away."

Tarva went to the door while D'Lynn stood and poured herself a little more brandy. The large amount Tarva had poured was down the chute in four big gulps. The older woman would either settle her nerves or get drunk trying.

"Sister!" The voice that greeted Tarva at the front door echoed through the foyer and into the living room. Flannery cringed and stood a little straighter. Tarva showed Reverend Wilkins Washer and Clementine LeMonde into the living room.

The two bestowed warm, sympathetic looks upon D'Lynn and Tarva. Their expressions were cooler but civil for Travis and Regan. They barely kept their disdain in check when it was Flannery's turn to be acknowledged.

The Reverend carried more heft around his middle than normal. He had probably just come from a sumptuous, deep-fried meal at a follower's house, Flannery surmised, since gluttony wasn't a sin in the Deep South.

Flannery offered a false smile everyone could see through. "Why Reverend Washer and Clementine LeMonde," she said, her voice creeping up to a slight drawl. She moved closer to make them more uncomfortable. "We are always so happy to see you here at Ten Points, and it is always a comfort to know you are here for us in our times of need."

"Oh? Are you living here again?" Clementine asked, with a contemptuous stare down her short nose. "I didn't realize you moved back in."

"Why yes," Flannery said. "I hate that you never want to get together and catch up on old times. If you did, maybe you would have known that."

Clementine put on her own fallacious smile. "Old times?" she asked.

"Yes, well, I mean, we were such good friends in high school and all."

Clementine replied with a curt 'no we were not' chortle. She turned her attention to D'Lynn, who was back in her chair. "Oh D'Lynn, I am so sorry to hear about Marcus. I hope he'll be okay."

The Reverend grumbled when he heard Marcus's name. "We are really here to just see how you are, sister," he said to D'Lynn. "And, you too, of course," he added, with a smile for Tarva.

"D'Lynn, is that alcohol you're drinkin'?" Clementine asked, with a naughty giggle. "Oh my, you shouldn't be doing that!" she added, with a wag of an index finger. "Why don't I take that from you, hon?"

"It's just a little brandy to settle my nerves," D'Lynn said, with a guilty look.

"You know, my Uncle Billy never drank brandy, but he sure liked some whiskey," Tarva began, deciding it was story time. "He lived with my Grandpaw and Grandmaw because his wife got tired of all his drinkin' and kicked him out. Can you blame her? Well, anyway, Grandpaw and Grandmaw were Baptists, so they didn't let Uncle Billy bring whiskey in their house either. So Uncle Billy would sneak off to my Grandpaw's shed and get all drunk in the evenin' time. Well, Grandpaw went to get a box down from a shelf one day and found all these empty bottles, and—"

"Tarva, I think Brother Washer and I could use some coffee," Clementine interrupted, letting an eye roll slip. "That might also do better by D'Lynn than the Devil's drink she's got in her hand."

"She wants to calm her nerves, so I don't think coffee is what she needs either," Flannery said.

Everyone's attention was caught again by the opening and closing of the front door in the foyer. A bereft D.C. then appeared in the living room. He still wore his gray sleeveless T-shirt, worn jeans, and boots from earlier, but his Stetson was gone. His mess of brown hair was pressed flat from the hat most of the day.

"*Sodomite,*" the Reverend whispered. It was under his breath but loud enough so that Flannery and Travis heard.

"I parked the car Marcus was drivin' back in its correct spot," D.C. blurted out loudly to D'Lynn. "I'm about to go to the hospital and see if they'll tell me anything."

"Unless you're a family member they won't tell you anything," Flannery said to him.

"The car Marcus was *driving?*" Clementine asked, like a prosecutor demanding readback from a court reporter during a cross-examination. "Was Marcus out driving tonight in his condition? Is that what I'm hearing?"

"I'm sure you will only hear what you want to hear," Flannery said, before she could stop herself. She also entertained a fantasy of introducing Clementine to Katarina sometime.

"I think it would be a wonderful idea if we were all to join and have prayer together over this tragedy—and the interference of Satan in this household," Reverend Washer suggested.

"I'll pass," Flannery said, unfazed by the wide-eyed response that followed.

"Flannery," D'Lynn gasped, with a hand to her chest. "You shouldn't say such things."

"Why not?" she asked daringly.

"Perhaps we can pray for you too, Flannery," Clementine said sweetly. "Would that be okay?"

"Go fuck yourself, you mealy-mouthed cow," Flannery said to her. The fun was over. "Maybe you should pray that Wes will one day want your maidenly old ass. You've waited long enough."

"You shouldn't say such things!" Reverend Washer shouted at her. His puffy jowls shook and turned crimson.

"Why I *never!*" Clementine squealed, as if she might cry.

"I *know,*" Flannery replied. "Maybe if you *did* you would finally get somewhere with Wes. How many years have you wasted trying all the other ways?"

"Flannery, please!" D'Lynn interjected. She was out of her chair. "These are our guests. From the church at that. You can't behave this way."

Travis turned away to laugh but was admonished by Regan's elbow.

"Where is Maxine?" Flannery asked. "Maybe I should go check on her." Even the company of children would be better than this.

"Perhaps you should," the Reverend agreed, with a frown. "Though I have my doubts whether impressionable children should be allowed around someone as prone to vulgarity and wickedness as you are."

"We all have our dark side, good Reverend," Flannery said. "I'm sure there are plenty of things about *you* that you wouldn't want any of us to know about. Excuse me."

D'Lynn turned to Reverend Washer and Clementine once Flannery was out of the room. "I'm so sorry. She's worried about her brother and beside herself. She just *don't* know what she's sayin.'"

"I always tried to do everything I could to win her over, but Flannery has hated me ever since we were girls," Clementine said, in the most pitiful tone she could muster. "I guess that's the way it'll always be."

"She is a lost sheep, and she enjoys reveling in it," the Reverend said, with a clasp of pudgy hands. He continued dramatically, in drawn-out enunciations, as if a pulpit had materialized in the Ten Points living room. "She bleats loudly in the field of darkness, to draw attention to herself, yet wanders aimlessly and refuses to be guided by the Good Shepherd. Such a shame. Such a pity."

Travis quickly faked a cough to cover the start of laughter. "I'll go see if Flannery needs any help with Maxine." He was barely able to hack out the words with a straight face before he left with Regan.

"That boy is going down the same wayward path as his sinful aunt and uncle," the Reverend said to D'Lynn. "There is still time to save him from a life of serving Satan."

"Oh, Reverend, my nerves! I just don't know if I can handle anymore tonight!" D'Lynn cried out.

Tarva came back in with a silver tray weighed down with an urn of coffee, china, and condiments. "Did I miss anything?" she asked.

"Well, I can't just stay around here and not do nothin'," D.C. announced, feeling left out. "Maybe the people at the hospital won't say anything to anybody who's not family, but what if Marcus comes to his senses and asks for me? They'll have to let me see him then."

Reverend Washer groaned. Tarva smiled and batted her eyes at D.C. as if he had just said the most romantic thing ever. Clementine pursed her thin lips and rolled her eyes again. D'Lynn anxiously twiddled her thumbs and wished she had more brandy instead of coffee.

"Well, I'm goin'," D.C. repeated, as if he waited for somebody to stop him. He paused a moment and then exited. He knew all about Reverend Wilkins Washer anyway. Marcus had told him the old man was a bigot and a homophobe.

D.C. walked outside into the chilly night air and pulled his jacket back on as he descended the steps at the end of the porch. He would drive to the hospital and hang around the lobby near the nurse's station. If Marcus did not come to or ask for him in a couple of hours, he would return home for the night. It was worth a try.

He reached for the driver's door of his pickup, when a small but strong hand came out of nowhere, landed on his shoulder, and yanked him back with the force of a funnel cloud.

All D.C. saw was a flash of long blonde hair as the woman shoved him harshly against the side of the pickup truck, enough to break a rib, and knocked the wind out of him. It was too late. There was no time to process the ache in his body before she was on his throat. He felt the long, sharp teeth stab into the left side of his neck.

"Oh God!" he yelped, but a quick hand went over his mouth to shut him up.

Oddly, it hurt less after a few seconds. Soon, he closed his eyes. An unusual rush of pleasure and ecstasy swept over. That—*not Marcus*—was his final memory as his strength, blood, and, finally, his life, slipped from him.

9

"We've come to take Travis and Maxine to their new homes," the woman in the black dress and dark sunglasses announced, handing a mortified D'Lynn a piece of paper to cement the claim. She was plain of feature, no makeup, and her blonde hair was pulled tightly into a round schoolmarm bun behind her head. She was accompanied by an overweight older man in a dark suit, also clad in shades. The sunglasses obscured his eyes but couldn't hide a fleshy, pudgy face. He stood silently; his companion did the talking.

"Oh please don't take my babies away," D'Lynn cried. She sniffled and looked with helplessness at a document she was handed, then back to the blonde woman. "Tarva and me can handle this until Marcus gets better. Travis and Maxine are both looked after real good here in this house. They go to school. They have plenty of food and clothes."

"It is *not* enough!" the strange but familiar woman snapped. "Now please have the children brought downstairs. There's no need to make any of this more difficult than it has to be."

"Oh, I guess I ain't got no choice," D'Lynn said, pitiful and defeated.

A crying Tarva came down the stairs with a sobbing Maxine. Tarva carried the girl's small suitcase for her.

As Maxine looked around, she noticed everyone wore black. Tarva, D'Lynn, the mean woman, and the scary old fat man.

"Where is the boy? Travis? *Where is he?*" the mean woman barked at D'Lynn and Tarva. "Bring him down here. At once!"

Tarva let out a sniffle of her own and nodded.

Maxine screamed as she looked up the staircase.

"Oh, poor Travis!" D'Lynn bellowed, as she broke into more sobs. "He had to die so young. Why? Why? Oh, so many horrible things in this house!"

A procession of pallbearers walked slowly in formation down the stairs, carrying a wooden coffin.

Maxine cried out. "No! *Travis!*"

A trace of menace was in the mean woman's chuckle as she stared down a short nose at Maxine. "That's right, Maxine. First your Mommy and Daddy and your brother Bobby. Now your Uncle Marcus and big brother Travis are gone. Forever. You don't have anybody but us now. We're your new family, Maxine."

"I don't want to go!" she cried, as the scary man grabbed her by the arms. "D'Lynn, Tarva, please don't let them take me away!"

The two women cried and shook their heads in hopelessness, as the mean woman and scary man dragged her out the front door. There was nothing D'Lynn and Tarva could do to stop them.

At the foot of the granite porch steps, near a black limousine in the driveway, was another older man, larger in girth and perched in a mobility scooter.

He too wore black, even a black beret on top of his head, and opened his mouth in a wide yellow smile. "It's time to come with us, little Miss Lanehart ..."

"No!" Maxine screamed again, awake and sitting up in her bed. Her breathing was heavy and labored, but it slowed and calmed as it became clearer it was a dream. She was relieved. Then the thought of it frightened her all over again, and she began to cry as she settled back on the pillow.

Travis was alive but not old enough to be her guardian. Her Uncle Marcus was gone away. Everybody else was dead. Tarva and D'Lynn weren't her real family. It occurred to her that everything in the dream was a possibility, and somebody could come and take her away.

"I don't wanna go away," she sobbed. She felt the weight of the bed shift, as someone took a seat on the edge of it.

Maxine stopped crying; her eyes widened. *Who was there?* Normally she would have been frightened to know someone lurked nearby, in the dark, but a sense of safety washed over her. It comforted her.

A gentle hand stroked her hair. Maxine turned and, though most of the room was pitch black, the beautiful blonde woman and the loving smile on a ghostly, waxen face fell into focus.

"Oh my little baby, no one will take you away from here," the pretty lady said. She spoke with a strange accent, but her voice was soothing, and Maxine always understood every word she said.

Maxine started to cry more. She sat up and clung to the woman, the way she did the floaties at the country club swimming pool when the water was too deep. The pretty lady wrapped her arms around Maxine and rocked her gently back and forth.

"Shhh," she shushed and gave her a kiss on the top of the head. "Mommy is here now. Nobody will take my little Edela away from me. Never *never* again ..." She began to softly sing a lullaby, in some foreign language Maxine couldn't understand.

It relaxed Maxine; it made her happy when the pretty lady called her *Edela*. She had no idea who Edela was, if was even a name, or what it meant, but it always made her feel peaceful. Even though she never knew the words to the songs the pretty lady sang, the lyrics made her feel good; they often helped her go back to sleep.

When school ended the next day, Maxine went to the same Ten Points silver Bentley in the parent line outside only to find Travis in the driver's seat. He was a little taken aback to see her wide smile when she got into the car and saw it was him.

"What are you smilin' about?" he asked.

"I'm just so happy to see you!" she said brightly. She feared she would never see him again after the nightmare from the night before.

He looked at her and wondered if she was feeling okay. "Well, I can't believe they made me come pick you up in this old *grandpaw* car," he said. "D'Lynn says the school won't let you leave with somebody in a strange car, so I couldn't drive mine. Tarva is too busy washing the curtains and hanging them back up, so I had to come pick you up."

"Can we go home now?" Maxine asked. "I should get started on my homework."

"No, it's Wednesday," Travis said. The darkwave music on the XM radio partially drowned him out. "I have to drop you off for your piano lesson."

Maxine made a face. "Can't I skip today? I don't feel like that today."

"I thought you liked takin' piano lessons," he said.

She shrugged and wouldn't say anything else.

"Well, don't you?" he asked. He looked over at her but then quickly moved his blue eyes back toward the road.

She stared out the window and said nothing else until he dropped her off outside the home of Percy Stratworth.

Percy was the last surviving member of the Stratworths, which had been one of the more prominent and wealthy north Monroe families in decades past. Percy had been an only child. He never married or had any children of his own. He was now in his sixties and so extremely obese that he needed a mobility scooter to carry his expanded girth around the crumbling house. No one expected him to take a bride and produce heirs at this late, sedentary stage of life. Travis had once joked that Percy probably hadn't seen his own dick in twenty years, but Marcus quickly quieted him out of fear that Maxine or D'Lynn might be around and shouldn't hear him say such things.

"Well, look at you," Percy said, greeting her at the door, seated in the scooter. The same blue beret as always adorned his bald head. A fluffy orange cat, burdened with a weight problem of its own, rested lethargically on his lap. "Come in, little Miss Lanehart. There's no need to linger outside."

With hesitation, Maxine stepped into the large house, which in past generations had been the scene of social gatherings, extravagant parties, and home to a larger family. Now it was a musty relic of disrepair, falling apart and filled with old junk and rustic heirlooms.

And an old man from whom Maxine wanted to be away.

A large grand piano in the corner of the spacious living room was used by Percy to supplement his income. He had been a concert pianist in his teens and twenties and traveled the country for performances. In those days, he was the subject of praise and awe. Then, as he grew older, he evolved to a bitter piano bar player in a local lounge. He ate too much when his fingers weren't tickling the ivories and lamented to anyone with a sympathetic ear that his career never reached its potential. Being at the mercy of drunken, obnoxious patrons who even cussed and admonished him if he didn't play the same old stupid shit they repeatedly requested placed a bigger and angrier chip on his shoulder as the years passed.

Percy blamed his father, who thought being a pianist was an unmanly occupation. He hated the overbearing old man, who was long dead. He rarely spoke of his father, unless a few drinks were in him. If it hadn't been for the encouragement of his dear, sweet mother—God rest her soul—he would've never accomplished all he had.

"Oh, that's so terrible that your Daddy wasn't more understandin'," his good friend D'Lynn told him over coffee one day.

It was one of those rare days Percy mentioned his father while sober. D'Lynn had befriended him after she saw him play at Reverend Wilkins Washer's church during Sunday morning services. The Reverend introduced the two of them, perhaps hoping for a love connection, but D'Lynn wasn't interested in anything beyond friendship with Percy.

The feeling was mutual.

When D'Lynn learned Percy sometimes taught piano lessons to children after school, she prodded Marcus to allow Maxine to drop by the old Stratworth house on Wednesdays. Maxine seemed interested at the time, so Marcus saw no reason to object. This had not been long after Geoffrey, Tilda, and Bobby vanished, so Marcus saw it as an opportunity for his niece to have an extracurricular activity to take her mind off things.

But Maxine noticed there were never any other children at Percy Stratworth's house—at least not on Wednesdays. She was the only one.

"Let's go to the living room, Maxine. I want you to start with what we played last week at the end of our lesson," he said, as he moved the scooter through the entrance hall. It made a humming sound that irritated Maxine. "I do hope you've practiced at home."

They passed through an arched doorway with yellow and peeling paint, as they made their way into the living room. Percy slowed down the scooter and looked back with a grin. His teeth matched the frayed paint. Maxine lingered behind. "Why don't you walk ahead of me, Maxine?" he suggested, giving the fat orange cat a stroke behind the ears.

Maxine looked at him strangely but obliged. She quietly stepped ahead and led the way into the dusty living room. She grew a little queasy as she felt Percy's gaze on her.

Old, worn furniture filled the living room, much of it as in need of fixing as the rest of the house. Piles of old newspapers and magazines in uneven, sloppy stacks circled a well-used chair. A metal cage dangled and jostled over in the corner; the parrot inside squawked and annoyed Maxine, more so than the hum of Percy's scooter. The big blue-purple bird never talked or did anything like she had seen parrots on TV do. More old newspapers with weird spots and a cluster of blue and purple feathers on top adorned the floor underneath the shaky cage. Maxine always thought there was a funny smell. She was glad the bothersome parrot and its cage were in an opposite corner from the piano.

"Oh but hon, Percy is an artist and a genius," D'Lynn explained once, when Maxine complained about the unkempt house. "They're what you call a little bit different and eccentric. If everybody acted the same way all the time, then the world'd be a borin' place!"

At ten years old, Maxine wasn't sure what *eccentric* meant, but she was sure *eccentric* wasn't why Percy and his unkempt house caused a knot in her stomach. There was another reason. It was the strange things he made her do that brought dread when Wednesday neared, and, sometimes, bad dreams on the nights that followed.

As they neared the piano, Maxine heard something fall off Percy's lap and roll underneath the wooden piano bench.

"Oh for tarnation's sake," he said, in a manner so exaggerated it came across as rehearsed even to a child. "I've dropped my pen on the floor. Would you be a good little girl and crawl underneath the bench and fetch it for me?"

She looked back at him as if she wanted to say no but was afraid of explicit insubordination.

"Please, just crawl under the bench and get me my pen," he said, soberer, as his stained grin sank.

Maxine got down on her knees and crawled underneath the bench, a bit self-conscious as she felt the awkward position cause her skirt to ride up.

She flinched and nearly hit her head on the bench when she heard a camera shutter sound effect from a smartphone.

"Oh, silly me," he said from the scooter behind her. "I meant to turn that on silent..."

She quickly crawled backwards from the beneath the bench. As she turned to hand him his pen, she saw him quickly hide the phone away.

"I was just taking a picture of Mozart here," he said, speaking of the large cat on his lap. The feline's eyes were half-open green slits. Overweight and sedentary like his master, the neutered tom was resigned and oblivious to anything but food and rest.

Maxine knew Percy Stratworth was lying, the same way he had lied the week before. And the week before that. She fought back tears for the next hour and tried not to think about the ache of her stomach as she sat at the piano and felt the burn of the creepy man's leer.

10

The suppertime gathering at Ten Points was smaller than of days past, but the long mahogany dining table was the same size, Travis noted. On that evening it was just D'Lynn, Tarva, and Maxine seated around him at one end of the table. The two women sat quietly; little did they speak. The clangs of spoons interrupted bits of conversation here and there.

Downcast, Maxine glared into her bowl of beef stew.

Marcus was still catatonic and unresponsive and at a nearby mental hospital for further evaluation. That was what the women had told Travis earlier in the evening, outside Maxine's earshot. As for Flannery, she never showed up at mealtime. It may have been a mystery to the others at the table, but Travis knew why.

He was certain D'Lynn had no clue what Flannery was, and there was no way Tarva had any inkling. Neither of the women likely knew such a thing existed. Travis hadn't until last spring, when he eavesdropped and learned three of the residents of Ten Points walked only at night. Two of them were his own parents. Well, Geoffrey was his father in name only, but for all intents and purposes he lost both his parents when they were destroyed during the early-morning hours one Monday last spring.

Maxine never mentioned Flannery's absence if she noticed it at all. She certainly never asked about it. Maxine was the one who had called police the morning the others were destroyed. She heard commotion from upstairs but to this day had never asked Travis the cause of it. As far as Travis knew, Maxine had seen nothing of what happened downstairs. If she had, it was like Flannery's mealtime absence. She never discussed it. Travis was almost afraid to ask Maxine what exactly she knew. The way she moped around much of late concerned him. He assumed Maxine was sad in her own way about the past year, but the frightened look on her face when he had dropped her off at her piano lesson also set off an alarm. He wondered if something else was on her mind. He suddenly felt guilty for how he had verbally wiped the smile off her face when she had gotten into the car at school earlier that day.

But, like most teenagers, it didn't take long for Travis to turn his thoughts to himself and his own plans. "I was thinkin' maybe I could take Regan to Tinseltown for a movie after I'm done with my supper," he said to D'Lynn.

"No sir, you will not," she replied. She stirred the stew in her bowl with a spoon, but he had yet to see her take a bite. "It's a school night. Y'all can go on a date when it's the weekend."

He nodded without argument or backtalk. After D'Lynn's anxiety spell the previous day, the last thing he wanted was to work her into a tizzy and cause a heart attack. If she died, there would only be three left at the table, and as much as he didn't miss his bastard of a stepfather, the dwindling number of people at mealtime made it sullen and lonesome. Tarva had always gone home in the past and never remained at the house for supper. These days she stayed and ate every evening before she left for the day. D'Lynn had rarely joined the family at the dinner table before last spring. Travis assumed Tarva and D'Lynn did it out of pity, so he and his sister wouldn't have to eat alone.

"Maxine, how was your piano lesson today?" Tarva asked with a smile, to break the awkward silence.

Maxine glanced up, startled. She bolted from her seat and ran out of the room.

"What's got into her?" Tarva asked, a bit hurt her simple question repelled Maxine as it had.

"She didn't even wanna go today," Travis said, curious about his sister again. "I'm not sure why. That old Percy is kinda weird."

"Percy is such a poor, misunderstood man," D'Lynn said, stirring the stew with a slow and drowsy rhythm not unlike her thick, north Louisiana accent. "The child can't stand him for some reason."

"Um, because he's a creep?" Travis reiterated, earning a scowl of rebuke from the older housekeeper.

"Well, I figured talkin' about her piano lessons would help take her mind off Marcus and all the other stuff goin' on around here," Tarva said, pulling apart a piece of cornbread to nibble on. Tarva spoke with a thick accent as well, only faster, especially when she was excited. "D'Lynn, did you hear about the homeless guy they found dead in the woods at the bike trail by the river? It was right across the levee from Forsythe Park!"

"No, but don't say anything about it if Maxine comes back in here," D'Lynn warned her. She sat up more in her chair. "But before she does, what did you hear?"

"They found him propped up against a tree in them woods where the bike trail starts. There was a hole or some kinda puncture wounds in his neck. They said some of his blood might've been drained. Like he got bit by an animal or somethin'. They think that's what happened."

A chill hit Travis's spine. What kind of animal bit people on the neck inside Monroe city limits? *An animal that used to be human, that's what.*

"You don't say!" D'Lynn exclaimed. "How strange! It's like them ducks and that raccoon from out front last spring ... *Oooh!*" she suddenly bellowed. The morbid twist of her face wrinkled it more than normal. "And like Angel's Glory down at the stables!" She dropped her spoon in the bowl and put a hand over her mouth until she calmed. "But I didn't see anything about a dead homeless guy in the *News-Star* or on KNOE or KTVE news."

"I don't think it's been on TV or in the papers," Tarva said. She kept going, between chews of cornbread. "I heard it from my cousin's boyfriend's sister. Delia Larsen. She lives over there in the Garden District close to where it happened. Sometimes she goes walkin' on those trails for exercise."

"Did she see anything strange? Oh my," D'Lynn replied. She couldn't decide whether to pick up her spoon and try to eat again or leave it alone.

Tarva shrugged. "I don't know, but I bet Delia will find somewhere new to go for those walks of hers. She's always been kind of a scaredy cat."

"Well, what could've done such a thing to that poor guy? A coyote or somethin'?" D'Lynn asked. "I *still* don't know what got hold of them ducks and that raccoon. It was right after Marcus got here last spring. And then Zeke Colson showed up. *Oh!*" D'Lynn made herself sad with her mention of the late Zeke Colson.

"Speaking of poor men in the woods, oh that *poor* Doctor Colson. We'll never know what happened to him. How he ended up in those woods out yonder," Tarva said. Her large brown eyes went to the dining room window, to the direction of the forest out past the house.

I know. *That bastard Geoffrey is what happened to Zeke*, Travis thought. He struggled to keep a poker face in the presence of the ladies.

"Are you sure nobody did no exaggeratin' about the guy on the bike trail?" D'Lynn asked, moving from the dismal topic of Zeke Colson. "It could have been some homeless guy who died of a heart attack and got picked on by animals before they found him."

Travis no longer had an appetite. Like D'Lynn before him, he plopped his spoon to a rest inside his half-eaten bowl of stew. The women looked over, Tarva now embarrassed. "Oh gosh, maybe we shouldn't talk about stuff like that with Travis tryin' to eat. Me and my big mouth."

Travis stared back and nodded, but the reason he lost his appetite was because he *knew* what had happened on the bike trail. He was sure Flannery was involved. Who else? Were there other dead people who walked at night in the area? Another chill struck. What if there was a whole underground community of the undead—hidden away in town, or out in the woods? Kind of like a cult. Was Flannery a part of it? Travis knew he would have to do some subtle digging without triggering suspicion from his aunt. But how?

"Have you ever cleaned in Travis's room?" D'Lynn asked Tarva, as if Travis weren't at the table. "All those scary, bloody posters on the wall. Those morbid comic books he looks at. I doubt we're even fazin' him with talk about dead bodies gettin' eat on by animals."

"I'm too scared to go in his room. I heard there was a big hairy spider in a cage in there," Tarva said.

"There is," D'Lynn replied. "But he keeps it locked away in an aquarium. Not a cage. Thank the Good Lord for that. That scary-lookin' booger would probably be able to get out of a cage and run around in the house somewhere."

"Oh don't say stuff like that!" Tarva hollered. She followed the outburst with an overdramatic shudder. "I still can't even watch that movie *Arachnophobia* with the lights off. Then there was that other old movie with William Shatner and the town getting overrun and bit and killed by them there tarantulas. Scarred my brain for life! I'd just up and die if that thing got loose in here!"

Hello, don't mind me or my pets. Travis shook his head at them.

"Oh I know. If Reverend Washer only knew the half of it," D'Lynn said. "But that was Geoff and Tilda's doin'," she added and looked over at Travis. "No offense, hon, I just don't think we're botherin' you by talkin' about dead bodies is all I'm tryin' to get at."

"None taken at all," Travis said, with an indignant grin. "I can step to the other room if you two wanna finish talking shit about me."

"Watch that dirty mouth at the table, young man," D'Lynn scolded.

"Y'all ain't even touchin' your supper," Tarva said. "And if I keep sittin' here eatin' cornbread I won't be able to fit in my jeans. Why don't I clear up these dishes?"

"I'll put on a pot of coffee," D'Lynn said. "I guess we could go to the livin' room."

Half an hour later the three of them were in the living room when the doorbell rang. "I'll get it," Travis said, since he was the only one not sipping coffee.

Travis's face fell as soon as it met the face on the other side of the door. Blue eyes widened as he stared incredulously, speechless at the man staring back at him.

The events of that horrifying night seven months ago rushed back—dragged him back—like a fast and unexpected punch to the stomach.

Conrad jerked the boy's head forward so that they were nose to nose and their eyes were only an inch apart. "Look into my eyes. Don't look away from me," he said, as Travis trembled even more. "Look inside, Travis..."

"Oh God, no!" Travis screamed, as he indeed looked inside—against

his will. "Don't make me. Please! Oh God, make it stop!" He saw agony, torture, wailing, the gnashing of teeth, rivers of blood, death, and much more. All the dark things of the world magnified by a thousand. He cried out, and his head began to pound, but he couldn't take his eyes away from Conrad's no matter how badly he wanted to do so.

"Don't you fucking look away, you little bastard," Conrad whispered, smiling wide as he continued to subject the boy to a sadistic mental slide show. "We're almost done. Remember, this hurts Daddy much more than it hurts you."

"Please! Oh God, I'll do anything! Make it stop!" Travis hyperventilated madly and felt himself become sick as Conrad finally shoved him away. He stumbled over to a small trash can in the room and began to vomit.

"Oh God," Travis finally said, finally finding words. He clutched the front door as if he feared being dragged outside ... by *it*. "You can't be ..."

"I can't be *who?*" Remy Van Buren asked. His eyes remained locked with Travis's. The eyes were familiar, dark, but different at the same time. The face had no readable expression. "Who do you think I am?"

Travis also found his senses and invented a quick cover. "Um, I just heard some guy got stabbed here," he said, nodding to the sling Remy wore to support his injured left arm.

Other than the sling, Remy looked recovered from his ordeal. Marcus's punching attack hadn't left any major bruises or swelling, though Remy couldn't understand how.

Travis slowly stood aside to allow him into the house. "Yes, I mean, I know all about what happened to you—"

"And? That's *all?*" Remy was unconvinced. From the piercings, dyed-black hair, and matching wardrobe, Remy knew it was the Lanehart kid Wes Washer had warned him about. Remy took the 'child of Satan' nonsense with a grain of salt, but he knew from the boy's nonconformist appearance he set himself apart from the rest of the conservative majority.

Travis cooled and cleared his throat as he evicted Conrad from his head. "My uncle stabbed you. I'm just amazed you're not hurt any worse, man."

"I had a few stitches; the wound wasn't deep..." Remy's speech drifted and his eyes moved away from Travis to something—or someone— behind Travis.

Travis turned and saw Flannery in the foyer. She had just come from the hallway, from the basement downstairs. Travis knew it was from there she had just emerged, after a day of slumber. He never let on to her that he knew she stashed herself there during daylight hours. But he did. He also suspected she had reversed some of the damage to Remy's arm. Travis had seen the letter opener. It was as big and as potentially lethal as a knife.

Travis watched the long, sober stare Flannery laid into Remy's stupefied one. The doctor was transfixed, full lips slightly parted. He looked back at Flannery, as though he were in lust. *How well did they know one another?* It would have been more entertaining observation for Travis, if it weren't for one of them being a near-copy of Conrad.

Without a word to her nephew or Remy, Flannery turned and walked to the living room to join D'Lynn and Tarva.

"*Flannery,*" Remy whispered, as he watched her go.

"Pardon?" Travis asked.

Remy ignored Travis. The doctor moved past him toward the living room. "I must go after..." Remy said, as his voice trailed away. "*Um...*" Her eyes were longer fixed on his. Remy paused, snapped back, and looked to Travis. He had control again. "Let's have a little chat later. I have a feeling you know something you would like to talk to me about," he said. Before he could see his words gave Travis a discomforting jolt, the fog returned. Remy continued to the living room.

"Sure, come on in," Travis said sardonically. He stayed behind and let the cool night breeze blow through the open door, whip his face, and prepare him for whatever awaited.

What would he say if Remy peppered him with questions about Conrad—or whatever the name was of the dead brother? Marcus wasn't there to intervene or help him concoct a clever cover story. God only knew what Marcus had said to Remy before he drove the letter opener into him. Marcus was drunk and out of his mind. Something incriminating could have slipped out.

Travis closed the front door before anymore cold air came into the house. He went toward the living room, where he could hear D'Lynn's delighted cries over Remy.

Another thought occurred to Travis. He turned back and bolted up the stairs before anyone could see him or summon him to the living room.

In the living room, D'Lynn carried on. "Oh, I'm so happy you're able to walk and talk," she said to Remy. She remained seated in an armchair. Unlike their first meeting, she now fussed over Remy as if he were a new member of the family. "It could have all been so much worse!"

"I'm sore and needed a few stitches, but that's all," Remy replied. "I'm a doctor, and it beats me how minor it turned out to be. I specifically remember Mister Lanehart taking the letter opener and—"

"*Oh!*" D'Lynn cried, a hand up in protest as she squeezed her small eyes shut. She shook her head, looked away, and then back to Remy. "I can't bear to think about all that stuff. You must believe how out of character that kinda behavior is for Marcus. He ain't never done nothin' like that before."

"She's right," Tarva said. "He's been the glue that's held this here house together since all that mess last spring."

"Tell me about that *mess* from last spring," Remy said, eager to get down to business. "I would love to hear more about it."

Flannery was perched in a corner, a silent, predatory feline ready to pounce—and guide the conversation elsewhere—if one of the other women said too much.

"Well, Wes Washer came to the house that mornin'," Tarva began, going into story mode. "Whatever brought him here happened before I came to work. I just remember the rug in here bein' gone, which was strange. I got to work and there was Wes Washer, havin' a drink of Scotch over there at the bar. Wes's daddy is a preacher, and Wes is in church every time the doors are open, so it was real weird to see him have a drink, and in the mornin' at that!"

"The rug?" Remy asked. "Why was the rug missing?" He felt the need to track down Wes Washer and speak with him again. Their conversation the day before had been too rushed, with Wes's frustration over being late for work.

"It's the same rug that's here now," Flannery said, moving from the corner and taking over. She stepped closer to the trio. "We have them taken out and professionally cleaned every few months. Isn't that right, D'Lynn?"

Remy turned to Flannery. A small smile formed as he stared into the bright green eyes. "I see," he said. His smile grew larger. Her mouth remained a straight line.

Tarva noticed how entranced Remy was with Flannery and tried in earnest to keep her disappointment under the surface.

"Yes, yes," D'Lynn said, with a thoughtful frown. She went along with Flannery's blatant lie about the rug, though she wasn't sure why a fib was necessary.

The green and blue Persian rug that covered a large portion of the wooden living room floor was not the same one from last spring. The old, similar one was gone *because Marcus told D'Lynn somebody spilled red wine on it the night of Maximilian Lanehart's funeral.* D'Lynn wasn't sure why Flannery didn't just say that, but something told her to leave it alone.

"I wonder why the deputy was in your living room having a drink during the morning time?" Remy asked. He broke his gaze on Flannery and turned to the other two women.

"Well, Wes worked the night shift back then. He was probably just off work," Flannery said, directing his attention back to her. "The morning was probably like evening for him," she added, a feeling she knew well. "He's a friend of ours. There's nothing unusual about him spending time here at the house. We've known Wes for years. Wes and Marcus and I all grew up and went to school together."

"I see," Remy said, with yet another smile for her. "And this was also around the time Geoffrey Lanehart and his wife and son disappeared?"

"I don't see what one has to do with the other," Flannery said. She gave him another hard stare, hoping it would dissuade a line of questions.

Remy's face went blank, the lips parted again, and Flannery could have sworn she saw a bulge grow in his pants as he watched her. The dark eyes were the same color and shape as Conrad's, but they looked on her so much differently than Conrad's ever had. *Lustfully.* Remy wanted her sexually; Conrad never had. Remy stirred a dormant longing in her as well, but she kept the cards up high. There were other more important things to think about—as well as people to protect.

Tarva felt her resolve fade as the eye play between Remy and Flannery aggravated her. "So, Doctor Van Buren, would you like some coffee or anything? A drink?" she interrupted, with a false grin, hoping to divert his gaze.

"Yes, you mentioned Scotch at your bar over there. If it's no trouble, I think I'll have one of those, if you don't mind," he said, though his eyes remained on Flannery. "It's been a strange two days. I think I could actually use a drink."

"You seem to be making a full recovery, Doctor Van Buren," Flannery said, as she forced a warmer expression. She remembered the taste of his blood and wasn't sure if she wanted more of that—or if she would seek something else. "You aren't on any medication, are you? I hope a drink won't interfere with anything."

"I'm not on any medication, and I *am* a doctor. It will be fine. Like I said, it wasn't much of a wound. I'm sore, but it only took six stitches to close it. I guess I was lucky," he said.

"Amazing," Flannery said. *Lucky indeed, thanks to me.*

"But enough about me," Remy said. He accepted a glass of Scotch from Tarva and gave her a courteous nod. "Thank you, Tarva." He looked to D'Lynn. "The real reason I stopped by was to check on you," Remy continued, though it was only a half-truth. "How are you feeling today?"

"Much better but worried about Marcus," D'Lynn said. "I hope you'll forgive the way I acted when I first saw you yesterday. And I really hope you'll forgive Marcus, too. He's a good boy. Like I said a minute ago, he ain't normally like that."

"Marcus is thirty-seven years old. He's no boy," Flannery corrected.

Remy noticed the chill between Flannery and D'Lynn. "Try not to worry so much," he said to D'Lynn. "No more anxiety attacks. Doctor's orders."

D'Lynn offered a short smile. "Thank you for bein' so understandin'."

"Of course, and everything that happened between the two of us yesterday is forgotten," he said to her. The older woman's hysterics when she first laid eyes on him were already a distant memory.

Remy took a final gulp of the Scotch. Attentive servant that she was, Tarva was at his side to take the empty glass. "Another?" she asked, eager to accommodate.

"No, thank you," he replied, his voice a touch deeper as the warm whiskey slid down his throat. He looked to the others. "I must be going. I have a lot of digging to do when it comes to my brother. Would it be okay if I stopped by tomorrow? The boy, Travis. I have some questions I would like to ask him, but I don't see him anywhere around."

"Oh, what's your hurry?" D'Lynn said, standing from the armchair. "We have leftover stew and cornbread in the kitchen if you'd like to stay and have some supper."

Remy smiled at her. "That's very kind of you, but I'm not that hungry."

"Well, you have to eat!" D'Lynn insisted, refusing to take 'no' for an answer. "I'll at least fix you a plate to take with you if you can't stay."

Remy nodded. "Sure, if you insist," he said.

"D'Lynn, why don't you just stay in here," Tarva suggested, determined to score points any way she could. "I can go fix the plate for him."

"Oh nonsense," D'Lynn said, waving away the notion. "I can do it."

D'Lynn took three steps from the chair before she gave a loud gasp, clutched her chest, and collapsed to the floor.

11

Travis waded through high grass at the edge of the clearing as he reached the woods at the edge of Ten Points. He pointed the flashlight straight ahead and hoped no one back at the house had heard him sneak out. He carried a shovel in his other hand. He knew what he was there to do, unsure if it would bring peace of mind or nightmares later.

He looked back over his shoulder at the house before he entered the forest. Like a dollhouse from where he stood ... dots of light from tiny windows penetrated the black of night. The smallness of it from far away made him feel less disobedient for sneaking out. Yes, he should have waited for Dr. Remy Van Buren to leave, but once he escaped to his bedroom back at the house he found himself restless, needing answers.

Travis walked into the woods, shining the flashlight here and there. Sounds of wild animals scattered deeper throughout the forest didn't deter him. The beam of the flashlight spotted one of them, a fox or maybe even a squirrel. Frightened by the foreign light in its eyes, it shot off into the darkness like a bullet, before Travis could get a closer look.

He knew the spot he sought so well he probably could have found it without the flashlight. Once there, he set down the shovel, took off his jacket, and got to work.

He used his feet to clear away leaves then walked on tiptoes to press the ground and figure out how soft it was. Travis wasn't sure if it was his paranoid imagination, or if the ground in this one spot felt a trifle off from the surrounding area. It seemed mushier and easier to break with the shovel. As if it were a fresh grave; not one months old.

He dug for a few minutes and found it easy. Yes, the soil was indeed softer. He wondered if putting rocks on top of the spot would have been wiser. While it would have prevented animal activity, it could have also welcomed unwanted attention. He decided with all the leaves and twigs and other manifestations he had cleared away the grave was untouched and undisturbed, no matter how effortless it was to dig here again.

The grave. The final resting place of Jimmy Van Buren, the man who now had a name. Before it had only been Conrad; that made it less burdensome. But the body belonged to a real person who had a real brother who had real questions.

His identical twin brother.

Travis couldn't think about that part of it. About five feet in, he felt the shovel bump something hard. He was there. Why was he doing this again? He knew he had to look inside to assure himself the secret he shared with his Uncle Marcus remained safe.

But Uncle Marcus was not there to help him this time.

The old green and navy blue Persian rug that once covered the living room floor at Ten Points was dark and soiled. Faint shades of the original colors were still visible but dulled by dirty stains of moist earth. Travis climbed down into the hole and carefully unfolded the grimy rug. It was a tough chore. Months of being compacted in a tight underground space left the rug stubborn and worn into place. It had been tightly rolled, the body inside, before burial.

Travis realized the only way he would succeed at pulling it open would be to climb out, dig a larger perimeter, and make more space.

He commenced digging for ten or fifteen more minutes until he was satisfied.

He's in here. A body. Probably all rotted and withered away. What am I about to see? Nervousness and overexertion caused his hands to shake. The inside of his mouth was parched and dry, as he pried open the rug and prayed his hand wouldn't land on a piece of loose, half-rotted flesh or dry bone.

Travis strained his arms and his back as he hunched inside the grave and pulled at the rug. He held the butt of the flashlight between his teeth so both his hands were free to work. It made the light unsteady, and it bobbed this way and that. The thought of what the remains must look like by now frightened Travis—it wouldn't be like the movies—but he knew he must see evidence.

But he saw *nothing.*

Travis freed a hand and took the flashlight from his mouth. "What the hell," he said. He stuck the flashlight under one arm and grunted as he gave the large rug one final tug and pulled it the rest of the way open.

The body wasn't there.

He took the flashlight back into his hand and shined it everywhere inside the rug. Dirty and brown and frayed, but no sign of flesh, bone, or human decomposition anywhere. He and Marcus had placed the body *in* the rug, along with the decapitated head, and buried it there. Where was it, and who the hell had taken it? Did Marcus move it without Travis's knowledge? No, Marcus couldn't have. He would have told Travis.

"Oh my God, oh my God," Travis moaned, as he tried to roll the rug back to the way it had been. He did a mediocre and sloppy job but climbed out of the hole and threw dirt back in.

This was the grave of a retired rug and nothing else.

Once the hole was filled, he slapped the surface haphazardly with the shovel. His panic made it a careless effort, when it came to leaving the ground looking untouched. He thought about scattering dead leaves so it would appear as undisturbed as before, but he was too upset and decided to leave it to nature. His legs were weak; he felt he might be sick. He was so overcome he didn't notice all the caked and wet dirt he wore on his clothes and shoes.

Somebody was fucking with him. That was it. Marcus didn't move the body. *Somebody else did. He must find out who it was!* Maybe, just maybe, Remy had already found his brother's body. Maybe the doctor was messing with everybody at the house to get a confession so he could go to the police. That was it. Yes! The doctor was behind *all* of this!

"I have to beat that son of a bitch at his own game," Travis said, just as the furious crunches of dead leaves dozens of yards away stole his breath.

Someone ran through the woods. *This* was a person, not an animal.

He could tell by the sound of the steps. They got closer.

Someone in the woods ran toward him.

"Who's there? I've got a fuckin' gun!" he lied. "Stay back, or I'll shoot!" Frantic, he reached for the flashlight and shined it in front of him.

The bright white beam hit a pretty—but strangely familiar and frighteningly pale—face of a young woman. She held up a defensive arm to shield herself. She wore an odd black dress with long sleeves. Outside of a hooped, petticoat-style mini-skirt around her middle, the top half of her unusual outfit looked to be Victorian.

She slowed down with haphazard moves as the light blinded her. She could have been late teens or early twenties in age, Travis guessed. It was hard to tell.

"Get that damn light out of my eyes, man!" she snapped, before tripping and falling with a hoarse scream.

Travis moved the light off her face and ran over to see if she was okay. "What the hell?" he said. He helped her to her feet and took a closer look at her strange outfit. She had short hair dyed as black as his; their blue eyes were a perfect match.

"Who the hell are you, and why are you running through the woods late at night?" Travis asked. "And what kind of outfit is that? Halloween was last month."

She brushed off leaves and dirt. Her face was as ghostly white as his. She looked him over and then made a wary turn to glance over her shoulder, as if someone was on her tail.

"You look similar, but you're not one of them," she said, staring back at him and his dirty clothes. He wore his usual. A black T-shirt, black jeans, and a pair of black leather shoes that were likely ruined.

"What? I don't understand."

"And what's up with the shovel?" she asked. "Why are you out here with that, man? Are you plannin' on hittin' somebody with that thing? You look dirty as hell."

"Answer some of my questions, and *maybe* I'll answer some of yours," he said.

"I have to go!" she said. She took off in a hurry, in another direction, wasting no time for chit-chat.

"Wait," Travis called out. He tried to follow but nearly tripped and fell himself. "Wait up. Don't go!"

"I can't!" she called back, from a distance away. The flashlight's beam would never find her. "He's after me."

"*Who's* after you?" Travis called out, but it was pointless.

The young woman's pace was quick for someone who ran amongst the trees without a flashlight. The footsteps faded way into darkness.

Travis stared off into the vast black for a full minute before he turned and headed back toward the house.

12

When Travis reached the corner of the house, he saw the flashing red lights of the ambulance, its siren silenced as it sped off down the driveway. He dropped the shovel in the yard and took off for the steps to the porch. He nearly knocked down Tarva and Flannery in the foyer as he burst through the front door.

"What happened? Oh God, did somebody else get hurt?" Travis asked, as he braced himself for more bad news.

Tarva cried and was hysterical; Flannery, icy calm.

"It's D'Lynn," Tarva sobbed, wiping at her eyes as they dripped mascara. "We think she had a heart attack or somethin'," she said, high pitch and rapid fire. "She grabbed her chest and fell out cold. She wasn't breathin', but thank God Doctor Van Buren was here to get her goin' again."

"Will she die?" Travis asked, frantic. So much loss in the house over the past year. Please!—no more.

Tarva continued to cry. She had no answer.

Flannery stood a few feet away from Tarva, arms folded. "She won't die," she said to Travis. Flannery tried to be reassuring, but he could tell it was forced. "She'll be fine."

"Can you guarantee that?" Travis asked, feeling as if he too might cry.

"After that episode yesterday we should've had her checked out at the hospital," Tarva said. "I thought she was about to have a heart attack then."

"Nobody knew this would happen," Flannery said, in her frozen mannequin stance.

"We should go to the hospital," Travis said. "Where is the doctor?"

"He rode with her in the ambulance," Tarva said. "Oh gosh, if it wasn't for him bein' here she'd probably be dead now," she repeated.

"She's not dead," Flannery reminded them with a complacent tone.

Travis stared at his aunt. *Do you even give a shit about anybody but yourself, you cold bitch?* he thought. He wondered if she could read his mind and know how much he hated her right now. Maybe she could only read the thoughts of those she drank from, he decided. Maybe *she* needed to die. But she was already dead. She should be destroyed. Was her presence a threat to all of them? Marcus had protected her all these months, but Travis was not so inclined. His aunt creeped him out; he didn't give a shit whether she knew or not.

Flannery caught the breeze of hostility. "Something you want to get off your chest, Travis?" she asked, with a hint of a smile.

"Yeah," he said defiantly, locking his eyes with hers. "But this isn't the time."

"Then feel free to come find me when it *is* the proper time," Flannery said. The invitation for a chat sounded more like a dare.

The wheels turned as he stared at her. Maybe *she* stole the body. She and Conrad had a strange and twisted relationship. They were supposedly married, though not by law. Maybe she had some hidden agenda with the corpse. Some illicit, dark ritual her kind—the *dead kind*—practiced. Besides Marcus, Flannery was the only person who knew there was a corpse to be stolen, as far as Travis knew.

Flannery sensed Travis was suspicious about something, but she wasn't sure of what. There was no way he could think she caused D'Lynn's heart attack. That was nature, *not* her. D'Lynn was an overweight sixty-nine-year-old woman prone to dizzy spells and other health scares. This wasn't a unique situation.

Flannery had known for some time that Travis knew her secret. It was never openly discussed; she was certain Marcus had never told him. But after the events of last spring, and the way she always caught his peculiar stares, well, it was obvious he knew. She guessed it was after he learned about Geoffrey and Tilda. Maybe he even knew Flannery was the one who birthed his mother, Tilda, into the kingdom of the undead. So many open secrets. The Lanehart way. Sweep it under the rug and never discuss it. Then it wouldn't be real.

Another oddity struck Flannery as she studied her nephew. "Why are your clothes and shoes so filthy?" she asked. "You look like you were outside rolling around in the dirt."

He hadn't a suitable answer. "Where is Maxine?" he asked, changing the subject. "I haven't seen her since she ran out of the room at supper time."

"She's upstairs doin' her homework," Tarva said, still wiping her eyes with a tissue. "I checked on her just a few minutes ago. She don't know about D'Lynn. I couldn't tell her."

"How the hell could Maxine miss an ambulance outside?" Travis asked with astonishment. If the siren had ever screeched, he wondered how he had missed it from the woods.

"If you two want to go to the hospital I can stay here with Maxine," Flannery said.

"That sounds like a great idea!" Tarva agreed, before Travis could object.

Travis was wary of leaving Maxine alone with Flannery—and she sensed his hesitation.

"Don't worry, Travis," Flannery said, her eyes on him like lasers. "Maxine is safe here with me."

"Of course she is," Tarva said, ignorant of the silent battle between the other two. "I really hope D'Lynn is gonna be okay. I'm so worried."

"I'll go take a shower and change my clothes before we leave," Travis said.

"Yeah, why are you so filthy?" Tarva asked.

"I would still like to know the answer to that," Flannery added.

Travis ignored both women and went upstairs.

Once they arrived at the hospital, Travis and Tarva were met by Remy in the waiting room.

"It may be a case of angina rather than an actual heart attack," he told them. "Either way it's very serious, and they're keeping her here for more tests."

"Oh," Tarva sighed., clutching her own chest. She rested her other hand on Remy's good shoulder. "Does that mean she's gonna be okay?"

"It's too soon to say anything. But it looks like they have her stabilized," Remy said. He entertained her hand gesture but hoped she wasn't using D'Lynn's predicament as another excuse to get touchy-feely. "Even if it's angina, it could very well be an indicator of an impending heart attack."

"Thanks for bein' there, Doctor Van Buren," Travis said begrudgingly, as he now found himself eye-locked with the doctor. Travis knew Remy tried to read him. *What the hell does he know?*

"Yes, I'm glad I was there," Remy replied soberly, as he watched Travis.

"D'Lynn is such a busybody around that house," Tarva said, again ignorant of Travis in another stare down. "I guess this is gonna slow her down some."

"I would think so," Remy said, finally moving off Travis. "She will need to stay off her feet for a while."

"Can we see her?" Tarva asked.

"It's late. I don't think they will let you see her tonight," Remy said.

"Oh, Doctor Van Buren, for somebody who's from out of town, you've sure seen a lot of this hospital in the last couple of days!" Tarva said, squeezing his shoulder.

"Please. Call me Remy," he said. "There's no need for *doctor this* and *doctor that.*"

A nurse walked into the waiting area. "Doctor Van Buren?" she asked.

Remy turned to her. "Yes?"

"She would like to see you. Come with me, and I can take you to her room," the nurse said.

"She doesn't wanna see Tarva or me?" Travis asked.

Tarva nudged him with her elbow. "You heard what he said. It's late and past visitin' hours. They're only lettin' him go in there 'cuz he's a doctor. We can see her tomorrow."

Remy returned about ten minutes later with a strange look on his face.

"What happened? What did she tell you?" Tarva asked, her hands clasped and off Remy this time around.

"She made me an offer to move into Ten Points temporarily and keep an eye on her when she's out of the hospital," Remy said. He exhaled at the inconvenience he had failed to refuse.

Travis couldn't hide his objection. "Don't you have to go home to Chicago?" he asked, wondering where D'Lynn's head was. Why would she suggest such a thing? The thought of Remy Van Buren snooping around Ten Points at all hours was another unwelcome burden.

"I can delay my departure a few days," Remy said, the dark eyes back on Travis. "D'Lynn asked me to stay for two weeks, but I'm not sure I can promise her that much time. I do have a family back in Chicago. I'm no cardiologist, but I can offer her my assistance ... as I investigate my brother's activities here in town."

"Maybe your brother left here and went somewhere else," Travis said. "Maybe that's where you should look."

"I have a feeling there are still some answers here I don't have," Remy said sharply. "Thanks for your concern though."

Travis refused to break eye contact. He willed himself not to do it. He knew dodgy eyes were a sign of dishonesty. "You bet," he said, not relishing the challenge ahead.

13

"My nephew has become a problem," Flannery said.

She paced Katarina's room on the third floor. She wasn't sure why she sought counsel from someone she detested and wished destroyed, but there was no one else who would understand. This was one of the few times she wished Tilda Lanehart or Rochelle Dubois were still around. Even they would be better sounding boards than this monstrous bitch.

"Oh?" Katarina replied, unconcerned.

"He knows what I am," Flannery said.

"Then kill him," Katarina answered matter-of-factly.

"I—I really have thought about it," Flannery confessed. She couldn't believe her own words. Blood lust had made her murderous in the past, yes, but she had never considered killing a family member to cover her tracks. "He isn't even a blood relative anyway," she continued, as if that made it more palatable.

"What difference does it make?" Katarina asked. "It doesn't matter how he's related to you. He's a threat. You must eliminate him."

"Maybe there's another way," Flannery said. "I erase Wes's memory every time I drink from him. Maybe I could do something similar with Travis."

"Pussy," Katarina muttered, her face a white glow in a mirror. She was seated at her vanity, this time playing with her makeup, as she glared through the mirror at Flannery behind her.

"I don't enjoy killing people as much as you do. I guess you should give me a few hundred years. I don't like him very much, but I don't hate him. He *did* get rid of Conrad."

"Idiot. Conrad is not gone. He's still around somewhere. Conrad cannot be destroyed as you or I can be. Which is why you should kill the boy."

"Well, no matter *where* Conrad is, he's out of our lives right now. I can thank my nephew for that."

Katarina put down a tube of lipstick and stood and walked over to her. "Your nephew created even more problems for you when he cut off Jimmy Van Buren's head," she said. "He forever ended any possibility of Remy Van Buren finding his brother alive. Conrad was only set free to go and possess somebody else. We don't know where he is or when he will strike again. All we have is a dead human your nephew killed."

"*Conrad* ended the life of Jimmy Van Buren," Flannery argued. "I think he even slowed down the aging process with the body. Remy is Jimmy's twin, but he looks a little older. Jimmy must have already been dead all the years Conrad was in that body. I never saw, never heard a peep from Jimmy Van Buren during my years with Conrad."

"That is ridiculous," Katarina said. "If Conrad used magic he could have created a body without Jimmy. I say Jimmy Van Buren was still alive up until the point your nephew cut off his head with that sword. He may have been, what do they call it, *dormant* while Conrad was inside his body, but he never died until last spring."

"Maybe Conrad's powers aren't strong enough to create a body." She gave Katarina a wicked grin. "But they were strong enough to push a concrete vault over the edge of a yacht."

"If you weren't already dead I would kill you for your part in that," Katarina said. "You were just as much to blame as your demon friend for putting me in that water. Even if you could not do it yourself."

"Yes, you already killed me. You in the water *was* revenge for that."

Katarina laughed at her. "Touche, whore. And then Conrad double-crossed you when he set me free. Enough with memory lane. What are we going to do about your nephew? If you are too chickenshit to kill him, I will happily do the job for you."

"I need to figure out what Travis knows, and what he's hiding. He came back to the house earlier tonight with filthy clothes. His shoes were caked with dirt. I have to find out what he's up to."

"Strange," Katarina commented, looking away.

"I suspect he was out somewhere digging around. I found a shovel out in the yard when he and Tarva went to the hospital. Remy's presence here makes him nervous. He knows where Conrad's body is. It's obviously something to do with that."

"You mean *Jimmy's* body...?"

"Whatever. The body must be nearby. I wonder why he's out digging? Maybe the body was stashed somewhere above ground and he got antsy and finally buried it so Remy couldn't find it. Like I said, I need to find out what he's up to."

"A rotting corpse would have been buried long before tonight," Katarina said, discounting the theory. "It would be foolish to keep it somewhere it could easily be found."

"Why would he be out with a shovel unless he buried it—or moved it to a new spot?" Flannery asked. "But if it was already buried in a safe area, it wouldn't make any sense for him to dig it up."

Katarina did another aside glance and stayed silent.

"Do you know something I don't?" Flannery asked, suspicious of her Maker.

"Of course not," Katarina said. "I now see your logic for keeping Travis alive until you have answers."

"I will figure out a way to get the information out of him," Flannery said. "But right now I have to find out the latest about D'Lynn."

"Yes, the poor housekeeper," Katarina said, with a smirk. "It would be terrible if she died before you make your peace with her."

"She hid the truth about Izzy from me my entire life. I don't have any plans to make peace with her. We can be civil and live under one roof, but she will never be the same to me after what she did."

"So judgmental." Katarina shook her head with a 'tsk-tsk-tsk'. "Yet you stole my husband and expected me to have mercy on you."

Flannery gave her another bitchy smile. "I didn't steal your husband. He chose *me*. Let's not revise history."

"Are you pleased now ... to have a name for what I made you?"

Katarina always had to remind Flannery of what she had *made her* whenever Frank Castille's name came up. Typical scorned woman, Flannery thought. Or perhaps outdone, since Katarina claimed to have never loved Frank.

"A *vampire?* Well, Katarina, I won't organize any vampire pride parades soon."

Katarina frowned and waved her away. "A vampire you are. Go check on your nanny or housekeeper or whatever she is to you."

"What are your plans for the evening?" Flannery asked, as she went for the door.

Katarina shrugged with a wide, mischievous grin. "I will play things by ear and see where the night takes me," she said.

Once Flannery was gone and the door was closed, Katarina folded her arms and stared into the emptiness across the candlelit room. She stood and paced a few seconds before she checked the time on the small clock she kept on the vanity. She slowly slid open the drawer and pulled out the business card. She looked it over a moment as she contemplated things.

Alexander Lanehart, Esquire.

"Not tonight," she said to herself. She placed the card back inside the drawer and closed it. She was irritated Flannery had seen it. She would have to keep any questions to herself.

It wasn't time yet.

With Flannery gone, Katarina slipped out of the room and into the drab, lonely third-floor hallway never used anymore. At least not by humans. Such an isolated squander in a large house, but it was perfect for her clandestine quarters.

Katarina walked three doors down, pulled a skeleton key from her pocket, and unlocked the old oak door in front of her. A light hum and the dotted green and yellow lights of a machine at a far wall greeted her as she carefully and quietly slid into the darkened room.

There was no overhead light or lamp around in the old space. She lit two candles and left one in a holder on a table. She carried the free candle with her to the other end of the room to bring *it* into view.

It was completely covered with a sheet on an old bed. The white sheet took shape, became visible, amongst shadows and flickers of candlelight. An outline of the human form left no mystery as to what lay in repose on the antique bed. An array of tubes went from underneath the sheet to a gold-colored machine the size of a small refrigerator. It ran on a battery that hadn't needed changing or recharging in quite some time.

"*Soon*," Katarina said, staring at the bed and the obscured body.

She then turned toward the wall a few feet away from the foot of the bed.

The wall was solid, for there was no full moon tonight.

Once she assured herself one other secret even Flannery was unaware of remained safe, Katarina slipped out of the house. There was a matter related to a sliver of conversation she had overheard downstairs earlier; it called for her undivided attention.

Just because Flannery was hesitant to deal with things that needed permanent solutions didn't mean her Maker wasn't.

14

At nearly midnight that evening, a taxi dropped Remy off in the Ten Points driveway. With all the events of the evening, his rental car was still there. D'Lynn had extended an invitation for him to board at Ten Points for the next two weeks. That, coupled with being stabbed the night before, was all a trifle overwhelming. But he knew he must take D'Lynn up on her offer if he were to find the answers he sought about his brother.

When it came to Marcus's attack, it still puzzled him to think how someone with so much rage could go after him with such force and leave only a minor injury. He was alive and outside of an arm sling, some soreness, and a few stitches, was virtually unharmed. If it had been poor, drunken aim on Marcus's part, then he was thankful for that.

Remy stood beside his rented Nissan Sentra. He couldn't bring himself to climb inside and drive to the hotel and gather his things. He turned and faced the house; it was mostly dark and asleep. Mostly. Dim light dotted a few windows. Travis and Tarva left the hospital long before Remy; they were inside and likely asleep by now.

The night was still, quiet, and cold. Yet something called to him, prevented him from getting into the car and going back to the hotel.

Now I'm hearing voices in my head. Then he dismissed the idea of anything bizarre or crazy. Whatever he heard felt normal. The longing, the need to go inside the house. Someone called him there. He moved away from the car and walked up the steps to the porch. Before he realized it, he was at the large wooden front double doors of the mansion.

Come to me, it said. He listened.

Without a knock, he found the doors unlocked and walked inside. The foyer light was turned down low, the rest of downstairs dark, but he had no trouble finding the downstairs hallway, where, by instinct, he opened the first door on the right. Inside were the stairs leading to the basement.

He was slow as he descended the small, narrow staircase. Only faint light here as well, to take him where he needed to go. Where he *must* go. He had never been here before, yet he knew the way. As he reached the bottom step, a damp and musty odor dissolved to a sweeter aroma. As Remy's feet touched down on the cement floor, the new and more inviting smell drew him through a tiny corridor to yet another door.

He reached for the knob and opened it.

There she stood.

In a ruffled white negligee, Flannery greeted him, with an expression neither warm nor off-putting. He moved closer, drawn by her ... to her. He was entranced by the emerald-green eyes and the large breasts he could almost see through the thin fabric of the negligee. Flannery's shapely, ivory-colored thighs were partially exposed; he felt the heat emanate from his own body as his desire for hers strengthened; his pulse raced, hair prickled, and his body throbbed from his toes to his ears.

"I'm glad you feel better, Remy," Flannery said, finally breaking the silence. There was a jolt as she reached out and put a hand on his arm. It was cold, *unnatural,* but he didn't—couldn't—recoil, just the opposite. Flannery pulled the Velcro loose on his arm sling and removed it. "And I'm glad you're moving in."

He nodded, without questions about how *she* would know of D'Lynn's proposal. It didn't matter. He tried to speak but could not. He only wanted to be with her.

Remy reached out with his newly freed arm, then the other, and put his hands around her waist.

Without further provocation, Flannery unbuttoned his shirt. When she reached the bottom button, she slipped the shirt off his rock-hard body and let it fall to the floor. *Like Conrad in every way,* it occurred to her, but she hid her thoughts as she ran her fingers along the bandage that covered his shoulder wound. She slowly began to pull at it, tug it loose, and remove it. He didn't resist

Can I do this? Is this possible? It wasn't the first time she had wondered about sex while dead. But it was the first time—at last—where she would find out one way or another whether it was a possibility.

She put her lips to his shoulder and gently kissed the wound, as she reached down and stroked his erection through the fabric of his pants. She heard heavier exhales and felt the bulge grow even larger as she continued to move the palm of her hand up and down and over it. She moved her mouth from his shoulder and put her lips to his.

"Can I?" she asked, as she pulled back. She spoke to no one. Remy reached, took her face in his hands, and returned a deep and passionate kiss to answer the question for her.

Flannery allowed it; allowed it all. She knew it was foolish to surrender control, as he slid down the negligee, cupped her breasts in his hands before devouring them with his lips and tongue. She began to moan, at first surprising herself, then refusing to think about it.

"Oh my God," Flannery said, taken aback. She opened her eyes, as she ran her hands up and down the muscular body, reacquainting herself with an old urge. Despite her arousal, her teeth behaved; they stayed normal. Yes, it was possible. She could be stimulated without any adverse reaction.

So it seemed.

But I am a vampire, she thought, as Remy continued at her breasts, as he expertly moved hands and fingers underneath the negligee and removed it from her cold body.

Being a vampire meant she could take back control at any time. That would have to be how she rationalized this, what she decided. But the more her control waned, the more she found herself wanting to be dominated. Remy's hands went up her thighs, to areas that had gone untouched and without pleasure in years.

"Remy, *I want you inside me,*" she heard herself say to him, as he further stimulated her. She had forgotten the excitement and sensation of touch down there.

"I want you, too," he whispered. His mouth moved to her ear. His pants were already down around his ankles, and she could feel the large hardness against her. Without warning, he picked her up off her feet, and she instinctively wrapped her legs around his waist as he straddled her against the wall and slowly slid himself inside her.

"Yes, oh yes, Remy, just like that, ohhh—"

At first he went slowly, back and forth, and then the thrusts grew in speed, and the moans became louder from both of them. It was then the cuspids started to grow inside Flannery's mouth, but she was too far gone to do anything about it. She had had his blood before he had gone to the hospital, and even though she gave him latitude, he would not be the aggressor when this ended.

I'm alive. She knew it was ridiculous to think such a thing; his body had grown warmer, incredibly hot, and she realized it was only his heat she consumed. By now, she and Remy were on the floor, and that was where he finished first; a loud cry as he came inside of her and soon after brought her to an intense climax she had not expected to ever feel again.

He lay on top of her, inhaling and exhaling in heaves, as she lay underneath him, startled that she had achieved orgasm. As she felt Remy's warmth subside, and his breathing slow, she saw three of his six stitches had popped, and out it had come. Two drops of blood; they were as warm as he had been as they fell down on to Flannery's shoulder.

Without any hesitance, Flannery took to the wound of his upper arm like a nursing pup. She used her lips and her tongue to cleanse and close it.

Remy had no choice—he *knew* he had no choice—and allowed it. He closed his eyes and let out another post-ejaculatory sigh. Flannery was in charge; he was hers.

I am a vampire. It shot through her mind again, as if the word had been there all along the last five-and-a-half years. It was the one question Katarina had answered for her and, in some satisfactory way, it pleased her to now have a name for what she was.

Flannery suddenly felt dead again and shoved him off her, like a feline turning against the tom who had just inseminated her.

Remy was lost as he fell over to the other side of the basement floor. He was hers; he felt no dejection from her immediate detachment.

15

Two days later, D'Lynn was released from the hospital and returned to Ten Points. Remy also turned in his hotel key and moved his things into an empty guest room next door to hers.

But theirs weren't the only arrivals at Ten Points on a cool and rainy November evening.

The doorbell rang after dusk, as if whoever was there showed up by appointment underneath thick and angry clouds that ushered nightfall, and at last gave way to a rainstorm they had teased most of the afternoon.

Clang-clang-clang, demanded the doorbell, as Flannery emerged from the basement and into the hallway. D'Lynn was indisposed, Tarva God knew where, so Flannery answered it herself. She flung open the double doors and was face to face with Clementine LeMonde.

Clementine wore what looked to be nurse's scrubs. With her, an orderly—and an expressionless Marcus seated at their waists in a wheelchair.

"I don't understand," Flannery said. She looked first to Clementine, and then to Marcus, a listless, unblinking blank slate. He wore a navy robe with what appeared to be his hospital gown underneath. The orderly stood behind him with firm hands to the wheelchair.

Clementine was animated enough for everyone. Now that the three of them were shielded from the rain by the roof of the porch, she closed a large umbrella and, with a brisk snap, held it at her side as she spoke. "He's been released from the Eastlake Sanitarium," Clementine announced curtly. She referenced the old east Ouachita Parish mental hospital that still bore an archaic name from a bygone era. "They were out of bed space. I've been hired as his sitter."

"By *whom?*" Flannery asked, her brows up. Who the hell made the household decisions at Ten Points these days?

"Oh Clementine, you brought Marcus home!" beamed Tarva, who appeared behind Flannery. "Is he sayin' anything?" she asked. Tarva butted ahead of Flannery and knelt at Marcus's side. His hazel eyes were fixed. He didn't notice anything—or anyone around him.

"You approved this?" Flannery asked Tarva. "I don't think it was your call."

"D'Lynn did," Tarva said. "She told me to have Marcus's room ready. I just got done. Sorry I didn't hear the bell in time."

"The last time I checked D'Lynn wasn't the one in charge here either," Flannery said. "Was she making calls to Eastlake from her own hospital bed?"

"I don't know where or when D'Lynn decided all this, but who's supposed to be in charge these days?" Tarva asked. "You? *Travis?* We're runnin' out of adults in this here house."

"I'll get him settled this evening, but Henry here will stay with him tonight," Clementine said, nodding toward the orderly and smiling as she spoke. "But not to worry, Flannery, I'll be back in the morning to relieve Henry."

Henry, an overweight twentysomething black man in a white uniform, was as devoid of emotion as Marcus. He was planted behind the wheelchair and looked straight ahead like an army private awaiting orders.

"You mean to tell me Eastlake couldn't find a way to keep him longer?" Flannery asked. "Marcus needs more than people around to slide a bedpan under him. He's had a mental break and needs psychiatric care."

"The doctor will make visits here twice a week," Clementine said. She never lost the smile. "Aren't you happy to see your brother, Flannery?"

"No," she replied.

"Flannery!" Tarva said in a discreet, wide-eyed whisper, as if no one else could hear. She stayed crouched at the wheelchair and made a dumb, protective cover of Marcus's ears. The movement of Tarva's hands around his face didn't even evoke a blink. "How can you say such a thing?"

"He's not even here," Flannery said, disturbed by the sight of him. "He's like a vegetable. I can't look at him like this."

"I guess it's good Remy is here. When he ain't helpin' D'Lynn maybe he can help look in on Marcus, too," Tarva suggested.

"Wait ... the doctor from Chicago is here?" Clementine asked. Her smile sank. "Isn't he the one Marcus attacked? Should they even be under the same roof?"

"No, they shouldn't," Flannery said. She stood with her arms crossed and frowned at all of them. "And don't be ridiculous, Tarva. Remy doesn't want to be anywhere near Marcus. D'Lynn knew better than to approve all this. She must have lost the blood flow to her brain when she had this spell of hers."

"You shouldn't talk about D'Lynn like that," Tarva said.

"It's chilly and wet out here," Clementine said, from the other side of the doorway, uninterested in any bickering amongst Flannery and Tarva. "May we please bring Marcus out of this cold rain and into *his* house?"

Flannery and Tarva stood aside and let them in. Tarva closed the doors once everyone was in the warm foyer. Clementine leaned the dripping umbrella against the door frame. She shot Henry the stern look of a drill sergeant and pointed to a rug, where they wiped their wet shoes.

Out of the corner of her eye, Flannery saw Remy come down the stairs. He no longer wore a sling and smiled upon seeing Flannery. Then the smile faded and wariness set in when he spotted the center of everyone's attention.

"He can't hurt you now," Tarva said, sensing Remy's apprehension. "I bet when he finally comes to he'll apologize for everything that ever happened."

"*If* he ever comes to," Flannery corrected her.

"It's his home. I'm only a guest," Remy said, as he joined them in the foyer. "Maybe I should reconsider D'Lynn's offer."

When it happened, Flannery seemed to be the only one who noticed. Remy's presence and the sound of his voice caused Marcus's hand to pull tighter to the arm of the wheelchair.

"Did you see that?" Flannery asked, staring at her brother.

"See what?" Clementine asked.

"His hand moved," Flannery said. Maybe he wasn't so absent after all.

"Oh maybe he's returnin' to normal!" Tarva cried out.

"I don't think so," Clementine said, with prudent dismissal. "His doctor says he had a complete psychotic break, and there's unlikely to be any change anytime soon."

"That's what I just said," Flannery told her. "It makes no sense that he's been released."

"With all due respect, Flannery, you should just be happy your brother's not in jail and up on charges," Clementine said to her. "Eastlake is overcrowded and couldn't hold him any longer. He's in good hands and will receive the best outpatient care possible."

"I wasn't aware you were a psychiatric nurse these days," Flannery said to her.

"I'm a nurse's aide and a professional sitter. I feel it's my Christian duty to help those who can't help themselves."

"Oh God ..." Flannery couldn't hold the scoff.

"I volunteer at Eastlake Sanitarium, and when Reverend Washer visited D'Lynn at the hospital, he recommended me to her." Clementine narrowed her eyes at Flannery. "He also thought just *maybe* I could bring some much-needed Divine Light into this house."

"I'm sure you will bring *something* ..."

"Excuse me?"

Flannery forced a smile. "Would you like me to show you to Marcus's room? There's obviously nothing I can do to stop this nonsense since everybody wants to make decisions around here without consulting me." Her eyes went to Tarva. "The last time I checked, I *am* still a Lanehart."

Tarva looked away sheepishly, again put off by the other woman. Remy also noticed something about Flannery bristled the housekeeper.

"I can even show you where his real clothes are," Flannery continued, back to Clementine. "Pajamas would be better for him than some terrible hospital gown. He's probably cold."

No matter what Clementine said, Flannery knew she had seen her brother's hand move. She wondered what else could stir Marcus back to reality. Once Clementine was gone Flannery decided she would send the orderly on an errand and have some alone time with her brother.

"He has the robe. 'Sides, I don't think Marcus even knows what's goin' on anyway," said Henry the orderly, who finally spoke up.

His air of cockiness made Flannery turn on her heels. "Um, *who* are you?" she asked. Her husky voice and hard stare made him go back a step.

"H—Henry," he replied nervously, losing whatever cool he had mustered. Something told him he had just made a grave error.

Flannery held on to the same artificial smile she had shown Clementine. "Henry, I'm Flannery Lanehart, Marcus's sister." She briefly switched her gaze back to Tarva. "I guess you could call me the *mistress* of the house since I'm the only female Lanehart left who resides here." Then back to Henry. "So whenever you're inside this house you won't share your opinion on my brother or any other subject unless it's solicited. Is that understood?"

"Mistress *is* something you're no stranger to," Clementine said, under her breath.

Flannery ignored the jab. *For now.* The bitch would pay for that later.

Henry fidgeted and put his hands back on the wheelchair so no one could see them tremble. "Yes ma'am. I'm so sorry, Miss Lanehart. I can take him upstairs now, if ya like."

"Please! Let's not get off on the wrong foot, Henry. Call me Flannery, and you'll have to carry him. There aren't any elevators around. You're a big boy, Henry. Marcus is maybe a hundred and seventy-five soaking wet. I think you can handle the job."

Henry swept Marcus from the wheelchair and carried him up the stairs. It would have been an amusing scene had it not been for Marcus's catatonic state and the fact Flannery had to entertain Clementine as the newest house guest.

Remy relaxed a little more. He picked up the wheelchair and followed everyone up the stairs. "Once you have him upstairs, I can examine and help with him if you like. D'Lynn is settled in her room and won't need me for a while," he said.

Clementine turned toward Remy. "I really *don't* think—"

"Are you sure you're comfortable with that?" Flannery cut in. She spoke to Remy but watched Clementine out of the corner of an eye. "If you don't have any problem with it, then I don't."

"Well, I won't lie and say I'm not a little ... *uneasy* ... but he seems harmless now," Remy replied.

"Marcus attacked *him*," Clementine hissed under her breath to Flannery, as they continued up the stairs. "That man's presence could agitate Marcus."

"If it does, then wouldn't that be a good sign?" Flannery asked her. "It would mean Marcus is waking up and might be okay."

Clementine wasn't swayed. "I think it's a bad idea. Marcus is in a delicate place right now."

"He's a *Lanehart*," Flannery corrected. "We're tough. Marcus has been through a lot of loss in the past couple of years, and it all caught up to him. Besides, if he jumps out of that wheelchair and goes on another rampage there are four of us here to hold him down. Maybe then that foolish doctor will see he was released from Eastlake way too soon."

"Doctor Fortier is *not* foolish. I told you the sanitarium is overcrowded. There are more urgent cases."

"I didn't know there were so many crazies running around Ouachita Parish."

When they got upstairs, Remy set down the wheelchair so Henry could place Marcus back into it.

"Should you carry wheelchairs around so soon?" Flannery asked Remy, after the fact. "I would hate for you to lose more stitches," she said.

Her reference to their time in the basement earned her another smile from him.

"I'm good," he said, as he paused and stared at her with a longing Flannery hadn't intended to elicit, especially in front of others.

Clementine caught wind of the exchange and nondescriptly studied the two of them, as Henry adjusted Marcus back into the wheelchair.

"It's the third door on the left," Flannery said, directing Henry. Clementine stepped ahead of them and opened the door for the orderly.

In his seven months back at Ten Points, Marcus had never made his accommodations grand ones. There they stood in the same bedroom the middle Lanehart child had made his during his childhood and teenage years. Old grunge posters and other signs a teenage boy once lived there in the 1990's were long gone from what was now the room of a thirty-seven-year-old man. Besides the traditional bedroom furniture, there was only a stuffed armchair, a desk and chair, and a bookshelf. The latter bore a meager but impressive collection Marcus kept to himself and away from the study downstairs.

On the wall, a lone oil portrait of a long road that wound amidst rows of oak trees—not unlike the driveway leading to Ten Points. Only this road led to nowhere.

"Let's set him up in the chair for now," Clementine suggested. "He shouldn't have to be in bed all the time."

Tarva showed up in the doorway behind them. "Oh look, he's back in his room," she said, with her usual sunny disposition. She pushed ahead of them and knelt before Marcus again.

"This could be a little overwhelming for him. All of us in here at once," Flannery said, irritated by Tarva's treating Marcus like a new pet project.

Clementine shrugged. "He doesn't know what's going on. He has no idea any of us are here." She looked back at Remy. "But I *still* have my reservations about ..."

"I'm not so sure he's unaware of what's going on. Not anymore. He moved his hand earlier. I *know* what I saw," Flannery insisted.

"Having familiar things and people around him could help bring him back to life, don't you think?" Tarva asked, standing and moving back to the others.

"Doctor Fortier doesn't seem to think so," Clementine said.

"Well, Doctor Van Buren, um *Remy*, I meant..."—Tarva corrected herself with a giggle— "...you see him. What do you think?"

Remy had stayed back near the doorway. He smiled nervously. "I'm no psychiatrist," he said. "It wouldn't be ethical of me to second-guess the diagnosis of one."

"We only want your opinion. I don't think it would be overstepping," Flannery said to Remy. "Maybe you should have a look at him."

"I really don't think—" Clementine began. She was the next to kneel at the chair, as if to shield Marcus.

"Why so hesitant?" Flannery asked. "Just let Remy have a look. He won't step on Doctor Fortier's toes."

Remy moved in closer to Marcus. "When was the last time this Doctor Fortier met with Marcus?" he asked Clementine.

"Today, before Marcus left Eastlake. Everything checked out okay with him, at least physically, so he was cleared to come home," Clementine said. She talked fast, and her eyes showed alarm at Remy's being so close.

He knelt and peered into Marcus's eyes. "His pupils look normal. I can't see anything unusual. Does he respond to any kind of stimuli at all?"

Clementine shook her head. "No. He's been in a stupor ever since, well, since he stabbed you."

Remy stood. "When is Doctor Fortier supposed to come here to the house?"

"Tomorrow ... I think," Clementine said. "Now if you'll all step out a while, Henry and I should get Marcus changed into the pajamas."

"You should be able to find somethin' over there," Tarva said. She pointed to a wooden chest of drawers on the other side of the room.

"Maybe I spoke out of turn earlier," Flannery said, as she schemed to be alone with her brother later. "Maybe Marcus *could* get better care here at Ten Points."

Everyone filed out, Remy the last to go. He turned back to Clementine, who still knelt at the chair beside Marcus. "I would like to speak with Doctor Fortier when he stops in tomorrow. If that's okay."

Clementine nodded and Remy left. She quickly grabbed a folded blanket from the end of the bed and threw it over Marcus's hand when she saw it start to move again.

"Henry," she said, not looking away from Marcus. Marcus's hazel eyes were losing their dormancy and shifted in her direction.

"Yeah, what's up?" Henry asked from across the room, his back to them as he dug through a dresser drawer.

"Never mind with the pajamas right now. Could you please go downstairs and ask Tarva for a glass of water?"

"Tarva?"

"The blonde woman with the short hair. The space cadet chatterbox. Water. Now, please."

"Okay, okay, I'm goin'," he said.

"Oh, and Henry?" she called to him, as he reached the door.

He turned back. "Yeah?"

"Flannery, the one with the long black hair ..."

"She ain't very nice," Henry said, with a frown. He was still sore from the reprimand downstairs.

Clementine kept her eyes on Marcus. "*That's* putting it mildly. Steer clear of her. And if she approaches you, be sure and let me know about any conversations you have with her after I leave tonight."

"Yes ma'am," he said, then left the room.

Clementine reached into one of the bags that had been brought in and pulled out a bottle of water she had kept there all along and a vial of pills. She removed a pill and quickly stashed the orange plastic bottle into the pocket of her scrubs. "I'll keep these with me," she said, as she twisted the cap off the plastic water bottle.

Marcus's eyes were off Clementine. They scanned the room. She could see a hand stir underneath the blanket, as if it were alive on its own.

Clementine used her fingers to pry open Marcus's mouth and shove the pill in. She pressed the bottle up to his lips and poured in some water to wash it down. Marcus instinctively swallowed with a soft gulp and then blinked hard.

"There now, take your medicine," she said soothingly. "We can't have you bouncing back to life just yet."

She stood and walked over to the bag and brandished the water bottle as she put it away. "We can't have Henry seeing this, when he comes back with a glass of water, now can we? I've never been able to control you while you were awake. It's time to get back inside your head,

Marcus."

Clementine knelt at the chair again. She took Marcus's face in both hands and gave him a soft kiss on the lips. His eyes grew large, and a hand reached from under the blanket and grabbed her wrist.

He gently removed Marcus's hand and replaced it underneath the blanket. "Don't fight me, Marcus. Clementine tried, and she didn't get very far either. You know I love you even more than I love Ten Points, and you knew I would find my way back to you somehow."

Marcus saw the form of a woman stand and float over to the full-length body mirror near the dresser, where yet another form reflected in the glass. It was no woman.

Theodore Ogden, Junior.

Conrad.

"One way or another, I always find my way home," Conrad said, the old, familiar voice emerging from Clementine LeMonde's lips.

16

"He looks even more out of it than he did when you brought him home," Flannery complained, perched by Marcus's side as he slouched in the armchair upstairs.

His eyes were narrow slits, and he had the appearance of a neglected and slumped department store mannequin. A mannequin with drool leaking out the side of its mouth.

Henry stood back a couple of yards and watched with caution. Worried he would catch a chill, Flannery pulled the blanket more securely around her brother. He had been changed into pajamas that matched the navy robe.

"Something isn't right," Flannery said, standing and shaking her head. She walked over to Henry, who was startled when she came almost nose-to-nose with him. "What did you do to my brother?" she asked, low but stern.

Enough to keep Henry on edge. "I—I gave him a sip of water from the kitchen. I swear that's all I did since Miss Clementine left," he stammered. "She put the pajamas on him and changed the diaper."

Flannery gave Henry a hard stare for a few seconds. His upper lip began to tremble, and the whites of his eyes bulged like overly poached eggs.

He finally exhaled as Flannery backed away. "I believe *you're* telling the truth, Henry. I need Clementine's phone number. Wait, no, not the phone. I would rather see her face-to-face. If I see her eyes I'll know whether she's lying to me or not. When I ask her if she knows why my brother has taken ten steps backward in the last hour."

"I don't know," Henry said, relieved she was a few feet away.

Flannery realized Clementine wouldn't be back until morning—when it would be impossible to see her. "Damn it, I *know* I saw his hand move earlier. There was something in his eyes, too, when you brought him upstairs. Are you sure you didn't notice the thing with his hand in the foyer? It's like nobody saw it but me."

"Mmm, don't know," Henry repeated, not sure what answer was satisfactory.

"I should bring Remy back in here," Flannery said, mostly thinking aloud.

"Mmmm, I don't know if—"

"Henry, why don't you take a break and go downstairs to the kitchen? I can stay with my brother, and you can grab a bite to eat. Tarva's been staying here at the house since our other housekeeper D'Lynn got sick. Tarva's nothing if not hospitable. She's probably still down in the kitchen and will gladly fix you something to eat. You must be hungry."

"Well, I ain't had no food since about four this afternoon," Henry said, rubbing his chin as he considered the offer.

"Oh, that settles it. Go on downstairs. Tarva can make you a sandwich or something."

"Are you sure, 'cuz Miss Clementine told me specifically—"

Flannery gave him a friendly wink. "Clementine doesn't have to know everything. I'll never tell."

Henry needed no further prodding. Once he was gone, Flannery turned to Marcus. She grabbed a tissue and wiped drool from the corner of his mouth before she stood and faced the door.

Remy, come to me. Marcus's bedroom, she summoned. She had taken his blood. More than once. He was hers. She would think about how to use that to her advantage over his Jimmy questions later, but now she needed him for something else.

In less than two minutes Remy was there. When she answered the door, he gave her a stare almost as blank as her brother's. He reached out and ran his hands through her hair and leaned in for a kiss.

"Not now, Remy," Flannery said, backing away. "Take another look at

Marcus. He's been drugged or something since we were here earlier. I'm sure of it. He's in even more of a stupor than before."

Once Remy stepped closer to Marcus and was no longer making eye contact with Flannery, his senses sharpened and his dumb smile faded. "Yeah, he does look different," the doctor said, down at eye level with Marcus. "Don't ask me why, but I'm not afraid of him attacking me anymore. Not at all."

"Well damn it, Remy, look at him. I would hope not."

"No, it isn't that. I mean even if he came to. I feel like ... I feel like he wants to tell me something."

Flannery came over and knelt alongside Remy. "What do you think he wants to tell you? He's frozen; he looks totally empty. I can't tell anything."

"I can't explain it. There's something else going on here. Maybe there's something he can tell me about Jimmy."

"Remy, I don't ..." Flannery began, then another thought struck her.

Katarina. Shit! Has she done something to stir the pot? she wondered, then put it away. She was certain Marcus knew nothing about Katarina's presence in the house.

Remy was suspicious. "You don't *what?*"

"Nothing." She wished he would look at her so she could divert him. "I have to speak with this Doctor Fortier myself and figure out what's going on with Marcus."

"Well, he should be here during the daytime tomorrow. Surely you can talk to him then?"

"I—I *can't.* I won't be around during the day tomorrow. I need you to do it for me."

"I don't mind helping you, I already told Clementine I wanted to talk to him, but why can't you be here as well? You seem so eager to see him."

She knew she couldn't concoct a good cover story on a whim. "I have obligations tomorrow that I can't get out of," she lied. It was vague, but she hoped it would do the trick. "I would like to be here, but I just can't."

"I see," he said. She couldn't tell whether he believed her or not. He hadn't given her more than two seconds of eye contact since she had rebuffed his kiss.

"Well, can you have a talk with him?"

"Sure," he said. He gave her a short smile as he stood to his feet. "I have to call home and check on a few things. Do you need anything else?"

He was likely telling the truth, but she was nervous he was off to check in with the sheriff's office or a private eye or whomever it was he reported to about his Jimmy investigation. "No," Flannery said.

"I'm not even sure why I came in here to begin with," he said, with another fleeting smile and a quick glance at her. "I just felt like ... well, never mind. Weird. I'll see you tomorrow, Flannery. Goodnight."

"'Night," she called after him, as he left.

Henry returned to Marcus's room shortly after Remy left. "I want you to find me if there's any change with him at all," Flannery instructed the orderly, as she stood and went to the door.

"This is a big house, ma'am. You got a cell phone or somethin' I can call you on?" Henry said. "I won't know where to look if I need to find you."

"I don't carry a phone," Flannery said. She paused and stared at him. "Look at me, Henry."

After a few seconds, the tension in the orderly's anxious face disappeared. A dotty grin washed over him as he obeyed her command. Without verbal orders, he stepped toward her until they were an inch apart.

Flannery placed her hands on his shoulders. She stood on her tiptoes before the taller man, opened her mouth, revealed the enlarged canine teeth, and went for the neck without any protest from Henry.

A few minutes later, as she used the glow of her index and middle fingers to close the open wound on Henry's neck, she brought him back to her eyes and gave him detailed instructions. "When you need me, just think to yourself, *Flannery, I need to see you,* and I will appear. You can only do this after nightfall and before dawn. Do you understand what I'm saying to you, Henry?"

The goofy grin returned. *"Yes'm,"* he said.

"You will immediately report to me anything you see Clementine do that's out of the ordinary. Is that clear, Henry?"

"Yes ma'am."

"When I snap my fingers, Henry, you won't remember anything that's just happened, but you will know to follow all of my instructions. *Do you understand?*"

"Mmm hmmm."

She snapped her fingers, and the orderly slid out of his daze and looked at her strangely. "Did you say something, ma'am?" he asked, confused.

Just as she wanted. "There was drool running out of my brother's mouth when you left to go downstairs," Flannery said. "I wiped it away. I hope you'll keep a closer eye on that. And change him on a regular basis. It will be humiliating enough for my brother if he comes to and realizes he's wearing a diaper."

"I'll take care of it, ma'am."

"Then I'll leave and let you get to it," Flannery said, distracted.

Someone else was calling her.

Flannery slipped out the front door of the house and took a quarter-mile walk down the Ten Points driveway. The cool night air bathed her colder skin after the rain. The shadows of the large oak trees hid her before the ascent. The Cape was camouflaged in the night sky. No one from the ground could see it on a moonless night. Flannery flew the four miles and landed a few dozen yards from a ramshackle wooden house that was slowly falling apart.

Her mother liked it there and refused to live anywhere else.

"What are you *doin'*?" Izzy scolded, the moment Flannery walked through the front door.

Izzy was a medium-sized black woman, moving into her late fifties, with hair like her daughter's, only hers bore the marks of gray that separated them by twenty years. They had been physically separated even longer than that. Flannery had only learned seven months earlier that Izzy—not Jessica Lanehart—was her biological mother.

A product of rape, Flannery was. A drunken Maximilian Lanehart had overpowered Izzy, a young Ten Points housekeeper, as she cleaned up after a holiday party back in 1979. Jessica Lanehart became pregnant around the same time. Izzy hid her own condition as best she could, but then there was a tornado one fateful night in the fall of 1980.

Thunder rattled the great house every few seconds. Then a frightful, powerful wind that sounded like a freight train pushed through, as it rattled and shattered windows, putting everyone on edge. Limbs, trees, and powerlines tumbled and blew across roads, the driveway, and the property, blocking exits. It also prevented an arrival of an ambulance and paramedics when the stress and fright forced Jessica Lanehart into labor. She screamed and yelled at everyone and struck wherever she could. When Izzy tried to help the cantankerous woman into bed, Jessica gave her a kick, sending her to the floor. Then Izzy's own pains began.

D'Lynn witnessed Izzy's water break as she stumbled down the stairs a short time later. She quickly ushered Izzy into the Ten Points basement, where she wouldn't be seen. That was where D'Lynn helped Izzy deliver Flannery.

Jessica Lanehart gave birth in her bedroom upstairs. A baby boy who was stillborn. Jessica was already passed out from a tremendous loss of blood. When Maximilian discovered Izzy had also given birth, he engineered the switch. Flannery was pale enough to pass as fully white, and her baby blue eyes turned the emerald green they still were by the time she was a year old. Jessica eventually figured out the truth, but by then Flannery was several years old—and Jessica eventually died anyway. A broken neck in a horse-riding accident caused by Maximilian but never proven. Following a bitter argument between the couple at the Ten Points stables, Jessica charged away on her mare. Maximilian fired off a gun to spook the horse and hopefully teach his disagreeable shrew of a wife a lesson. He had only hoped the horse would throw her and cause her to land on her bottom. Little did he know she would land on the other end instead.

D'Lynn took over mothering duties for Flannery, Marcus, and Geoffrey afterward. She had known for the past thirty-five years that Izzy was Flannery's biological mother. Flannery and Izzy were separated—Izzy threatened with physical harm if she ever came near Ten Points again or tried to claim Flannery as hers.

Maximilian was no longer alive to hate, so Flannery directed much of her resentment over the matter toward D'Lynn. Even though D'Lynn had begun to figure out what motivated Flannery's newfound hatred, there had never been any direct confrontation between them about it. Much of it was Flannery's own fear of a lack of self-control should an argument between them escalate. She had killed Tilda Lanehart in a fit of rage seven months earlier. D'Lynn was a senior citizen and not the volatile woman Tilda had been, but Flannery didn't trust herself. Thankfully, D'Lynn hadn't approached her about the dirty family secret in which she had played a role.

"I have no idea what you're talking about," Flannery said to her mother. "What do you mean?"

"You know good and well what I'm talkin' about," Izzy said, ready to shake her. "Givin' the Devil's disciple room and board!"

Despite all the missing years between them, Izzy had reclaimed her true maternal role in the past few months. There were no qualms about scolding her daughter when she felt it was necessary. Flannery had grown to love her; something she hadn't known was possible. She even backed down sometimes when her mother called her out on misbehavior.

It was not hard for Izzy to learn of any of her daughter's misdeeds because Izzy *knew* things. No one ever had to tell her. Her clairvoyance unsettled Flannery at times. The fact Flannery was dead also kept a thin sheet of ice over a relationship and prevented the full connection blood would have brought them in life.

"I don't have a choice. She's going to kill everybody in the house if I don't go along with her."

"How long is she plannin' to stay there? Stake the bitch in her sleep!"

"I—I can't do that..."

"Why the hell not?" Izzy looked heavenward and crossed herself, though she was Baptist by faith and not Catholic. "You've got me so worked up, I've gone to cussin'. Forgive me, Lord."

"She's my Maker. You wouldn't understand. It's complicated."

"Well, she's not *my* Maker! *I'll* do it! Give me somethin' sharp and show me the way to her room."

"Don't say things like that. I can't afford to have her come after you, too."

"And *Travis?* You're thinkin' about killin' your own nephew? Good God, girl, what's the matter with you?"

"I won't kill Travis. I *won't*. It was a passing thought. But he does know too much."

"*I* know too much!" Izzy exclaimed. "Am I on your hit list, too?"

"Of course not!" Flannery was insulted her mother would ask such a thing.

"Gotta be sure. You never know. That poor boy ain't goin' to harm you."

"I know, I know. I'll figure something else out. I can maybe do something to make him ... forget."

Izzy shook her head and looked to the ceiling again as she folded her arms. "I pray for you so many times every day."

"Isn't it a little late for that?"

"You walk and you talk. And you do things. You're not in the ground. At least not at night. I pray there's still a chance to make you a real live person again."

"There's not. Those are wasted prayers. You should move on to world peace or a cure for cancer."

"That Swedish ... *thing* ... ain't the only reason I called you here."

"What else then? Do you predict that D'Lynn will die soon?"

"Don't say that. I've told you that you must forgive her."

"I don't have to forgive her for anything at all. She kept us apart. If that bastard rapist of a father of mine can't be here to answer for any of it, I'll make damn sure somebody does."

"You chose to attack the homeless man over killin' D'Lynn," Izzy reminded her. "You *do* still love D'Lynn. That's why you carry this anger around."

Damn it, did she know everything? "I don't want to talk about her anymore. What's the other reason you called me here?"

"There's evil inside of Ten Points. And it's not *her*," Izzy said, referring to Katarina. "It's somethin' else. It hit me like a migraine this evenin'."

"Evil inside Ten Points," Flannery replied, with a huff, even if she knew it was true. "Here you go again. What's new? Marcus came home this evening. Is it something to do with that? That damn Clementine LeMonde came with him. She and some orderly are his sitters now. I swear, I couldn't stand that frumpy girl in high school, and she hated me, too, and now—"

"It's *her!*" Izzy hissed, grabbing Flannery by the shoulders. "Yes, it's Clementine ..."

"Clementine is a Bible beater who hangs out with Wilkins Washer and his bunch and fantasizes about being Wes's wife. Her idea of evil is a burnt batch of cookies."

Izzy shook her head and released Flannery. "There's somethin' not right. You have to watch her."

"Oh, I plan to watch her, but for different reasons," Flannery said. "I know I saw Marcus's hand move earlier, but nobody believed me. When I went back to his room later, it was almost like he had been drugged."

"You *did* see his hand move," Izzy agreed. "Yes, yes. I don't like what you did to the orderly, I don't, but you need eyes and ears for when you're not there, and he may be your best chance for help. You had to sway him. I get it."

"But Henry won't be there during the daytime. That's my only problem. I need somebody to keep an eye during the daytime. I think that's where Remy will come in."

"Be careful with him," Izzy said, a wary look on her face. "Naughty girl. I know about what happened in the basement."

"Oh for God's sake! Is there anything you *don't* pick up on with that weird psychic antenna of yours? Mother!"

She then noticed Izzy was smiling at her.

"What are you looking at me like that for?" Flannery asked, irritated. Yes, they had developed a relationship, but they still rarely smiled at one another.

"That's the first time you ever called me 'Mother'," Izzy said. She still wore the smile, but Flannery could see tears forming in her deep brown eyes.

17

When Flannery arose from the basement the next evening, she stepped into the foyer and saw Remy and Tarva helping D'Lynn down the stairs. Lucky for her, they didn't see her emerge from the door to the basement stairs. It was easy to make it appear she had been about the house and not a full corpse for the last twelve hours.

Ten Points sat in northern Louisiana, so it held an advantage over the old plantation homes of southern Louisiana, which rested too close to sea level for the thought of a basement. North Louisiana was different; the elevation was much higher, though floods were common. The basement at Ten Points had been underwater numerous times over the past two centuries. No one had ever bothered filling it in and doing away with it. Thankfully, for Flannery, it had stayed dry in the past year.

D'Lynn may or may not have known what Flannery *was*—that was never clear to Flannery. D'Lynn was a trifle disquieted around her of late, but Flannery preferred to think the revelation of the Izzy secret accounted for that.

Travis knew Flannery was dead, but Flannery had promised Izzy she wouldn't harm him. Deep down she didn't want to harm him. She *didn't*.

Marcus knew but pretended not to know. It was a topic they never discussed, but at times she could sense his knowledge. He would never tell and apparently couldn't do so now even if he felt the need. But he wouldn't. He allowed her to have the basement, without any questions, and kept it between the two of them.

Tarva was clueless.

Remy didn't know in his conscious mind.

She was a vampire. It was a word she was growing accustomed to, from within. She had never said it aloud again after she asked Katarina what it meant.

D'Lynn was in a feisty mood that evening. "I'm not some invalid. Y'all don't have to stand on each side and help me walk down the stairs," she fussed, at Tarva and Remy.

"Well, I can't believe you're comin' down to help with supper," Tarva said. "I told you I could handle it. You don't need to be exertin' yourself this way right now."

"If I stay in that bed one more minute I'll go crazy. If I'm gonna go, I'd rather be doin' somethin' useful for everybody when it happens," D'Lynn said.

"Don't talk like that!" Tarva cried, as if her superior might indeed keel over.

"I'll keep an eye on her and make she doesn't overdo it," Remy said. Then he caught sight of Flannery in the foyer and lost all interest in D'Lynn, practically handing her over to Tarva.

Flannery ignored Remy's smile—for now. She would talk to him later. She also felt another yearning he had proven he could satisfy. *Sexual desire.* As baffling and overwhelming as it was, it had awakened from its dormancy; the dam breeched and beyond repair. But any second encounters would have to wait until the house was asleep.

"Has anybody looked in on Marcus recently?" Flannery asked. She looked to Remy. "Did you speak with Doctor Fortier?"

"I did," he said. Flannery could feel him mentally undress her. *Not now!* "I won't use a bunch of medical jargon, but he basically repeated everything Clementine told us last night."

"Speakin' of Clementine, she's upstairs with Marcus," Tarva said. "He seemed okay when I stuck my head in this afternoon. Just sittin' back in the chair, not really doin' anything."

"I need to go up there," Flannery said, moving past them. The heat came off Remy like a furnace when she passed by them. *Soon, Remy, settle down.*

"There's nothin' you can do for poor Marcus," D'Lynn called after her.

Flannery turned back with a glare. She wished the old bitty would mind her own business. "Maybe I would just like to see my brother," she said, and continued up the stairs.

When she got to the second floor and the third door on the left, she walked in without as much as a knock.

Clementine sat in a chair with a book, a few feet away from Marcus, and met Flannery with a scowl. "What if I had been changing him? You can't just barge in here."

Flannery remained calm. "I can handle whatever I see when I walk in here. How is he today?"

Clementine shrugged and looked back down at the book. "The same. No change."

"Was Doctor Fortier here today?" She wanted to see if Remy's and Clementine's stories would match.

"Yes. He says there haven't been any changes."

"None? There's no sign he could be coming out of this ... *catatonia* ... anytime soon? That is what we should call it, right?"

"Yes, that's what it is, and no, he could be like this for a while. Or permanently."

Bitch, Conrad thought. Flannery had interrupted his alone time with Marcus, and his reading time. The book he had on the Old South and plantation life fascinated him, though he caught inaccuracies here and there amongst the pages. Perhaps *he* should write a book on the subject, since he had lived it. If only there was a desire to go backward in his life. The tome he held with Clementine's hands was authored by some two-bit historian born one hundred years after the Civil War.

"Then maybe he needs more long-term care. Maybe they should find a way to make room for him at Eastlake." Flannery no longer believed it but wanted to see what reaction she could stir. She went over and knelt by the chair where her immobilized brother sat. His eyes were open wider than the evening before, but he was still far gone. "I hoped his being here would cause a change, but I guess it won't happen." She glanced out of the corner of her eye at Clementine.

A more dismissive than conversational "hmmm" sound came from Clementine's direction. Flannery couldn't help but notice how engrossed

Clementine was in the book she read.

"What are you reading?" Flannery asked, trying to catch a peek at the cover. It looked to be an historical memoir. "Anything good?"

"It's nonfiction, so I doubt it's anything you would be interested in."

"This job of yours ..." Flannery began, as she stood and went to a window. She peered out into the darkness.

She heard the book close behind her. "What about it?"

"You have no other clients you sit with? All your time is devoted ... *here?*"

"Well, yes, I can't be other places when I'm here with Marcus all day."

"I guess if Marcus never gets better you'll practically be living here."

Clementine's arms crossed over in the chair. "Is that what this is really about? You want him to hurry and recover so I'll be out of your hair?"

"Don't be ridiculous," Flannery said, turning away from the window. "I want him to get better because he's my family, and I can't stand to see him this way. But having you no longer around would be an added benefit."

A smirk came. Clementine's lips curled in a strange way Flannery had never seen; a different air about her never there in the past. It troubled Flannery; she couldn't let Clementine see that.

"Well, Flannery, let's lay out all the cards here, shall we?"

That's something Clementine would never say, Flannery thought. *She's not the 'shall we' type.* "I'll be civil to you while you're here, Clementine, but let's not pretend we're friends. I know I goaded you in the living room with Reverend Washer the other night. I'll own my part in that. But we've never liked one another, and it will take too much of my energy to pretend otherwise," Flannery said.

"Well, your little comment about Wes and me was a bit telling." *Does she suspect something?* Conrad thought.

"Clementine, let me ask you something. Don't you think it's a little sad that you've spent all these years pining away for Wes? Aren't there some other nice single men at your church who are better suited for your time?"

"I think you're exaggerating this a bit, Flannery. Wes and I enjoy a special friendship. We both stayed behind and made lives here after school; we have that in common. I'm not pining away over anybody." *Clementine does lead a rather boring life,* Conrad agreed.

"But you were at his house—" Flannery began, then quickly shut her big mouth. *Idiot!*

Clementine's eyes narrowed. "I was *at* his house? And, Flannery, just how would you know that? Were you outside spying?" *Like I care, but she's so busted! The woman can never control herself or her words for very long.*

"What I meant to say was I assume you spend time at his house when you're both free from work." Weak, but it could do.

"Okay, sure. My book is more interesting than this conversation." Conrad picked up the book again. *Now leave me the hell alone. I will deal with you later though ... that's a promise.*

As if she had heard him, Flannery went for the door. "Please let me know if there are any changes with my brother."

Clementine's head nodded, her hand waved, as Flannery exited. Once she was gone, Conrad closed and set the book aside and chuckled.

Marcus sat frozen, no indication of anything amiss.

"I still can't make up my mind about her intelligence level." It was Conrad's voice, coming out of Clementine's mouth, speaking to no one. "I once took back all the times I ever called her stupid, but maybe I was wrong. She goes and gets all catty over dowdy Clementine. I guess even the undead can be a little insecure sometimes."

Conrad moved from his seat and knelt in front of Marcus. "What your sister doesn't know is that *I* know all about the little secret she's keeping upstairs on the third floor. She should be more worried about that instead of Clementine LeMonde's social life."

Conrad stood and went to the door. "Sit tight, Marcus. I'll be back to give you your medicine before Henry gets here. I would say 'don't go anywhere', but ... maybe it's too soon to make a joke like that? My apologies."

Conrad—as Clementine—left the room and went down the hallway to the second set of stairs that led to the third floor. There was no one around, and Henry wasn't due for another forty-five minutes. It would be quick anyway. Conrad knew what he must do on the top floor.

He knew which room was Katarina's and, taking a cue from Flannery, didn't bother to knock. Clementine's skirt rustled in careless fashion as he trotted in and closed the door behind him.

Katarina, sitting at her vanity and brushing her long blonde hair, looked up with a start at what she assumed was Clementine. "Where did you come from? How the hell did you get in here?"

Conrad gave a sweet country girl smile. "Why through the door, of course!" he said brightly, in Clementine's chirpy voice.

Katarina stood and came closer. Conrad kept a wide smile. "You should not be up here. You should have stayed with Marcus."

"This is *suuuuch* a fascinating house. I had to go explore a little. Why is some pretty lady up here all alone, brushing her hair in some dark and abandoned part of the house? Are you one of the Laneharts?"

Katarina gave her own cold smile. "No, I'm the last person you'll ever see. Your curiosity is your undoing, Clementine LeMonde. I'm about to do Flannery Lanehart—and probably a few other people—a huge favor and rid the world of you."

This would be even more fun than the exchange with Flannery. "Well, I declare! How do you know my name? I don't think I've ever seen you before. I guess you're not from around these parts, with that foreign accent and all."

Katarina moved even closer. "What is it they say? *Curiosity killed the cat,* is it? You should not have come up here."

Conrad decided to play along. "Oh, please don't hurt me!" he cried, with contrived fright. "I won't tell anybody I saw you up here, cross my heart and swear to God and all that."

"That time has passed, Clementine LeMonde. You can swear to God all you want when you meet with Him face to face!"

Katarina's teeth were exposed as she grabbed each of Clementine's shoulders.

"Oh my gosh, those teeth! What are you? *No!*" he screamed in Clementine's voice, as Katarina went for the neck.

Conrad gave Clementine a hearty laugh.

Katarina moved away from Clementine's neck with a peculiar stare.

"Wait a minute..."

The words were barely out before Conrad backhanded her so hard it sent Katarina backwards across the room and over and on to the bed. "A minute is a little too long, don't you think?"

Katarina sat up rubbing a sore cheek, in mild shock. "A human could never do that. *I do not understand.*"

She stood to her feet and within two seconds, Conrad—as Clementine—was at her side, with a clump of Katarina's hair in one hand and her arm behind her back with the other. "Look into my eyes, bitch," he said, making Clementine's eyes glow yellow. "Look into my eyes!"

"You have got to be fucking kidding me—"

Conrad pulled her arm more to quieten her. "Surprise!" He then released and shoved her back on to the mattress. The normal eyes returned as gales of his natural laughter burst free.

Katarina rubbed at her cheek, unamused. "I must say that is a very clever disguise, demon."

"Not my first choice, but it will keep me here. Marcus needs me," he said, as another Clementine smile surfaced.

Katarina stood from the bed and walked a little closer so that they were almost chin to chin. "I admire the bravado, but that will be the first and last time you ever hit me, demon bastard. I am not that whore you dragged around as your sidekick for five years."

"Now is that any way to speak about your good friend Flannery? I thought you two had warmed up to each other and let bygones be bygones. She *is* letting you squat here rent-free."

"The whore and I are only a means to an end for one another. She would not hesitate to see me destroyed, and vice-versa."

"Well, your relationship with Flannery is no concern of mine."

"The two of you were responsible for dumping me into Lake Pontchartrain, so you're still entangled whether you like it or not."

"Before you go making threats, Katarina, just remember it was little ole me who freed you from that watery grave."

"After you left me down there for a year!" she snarled, blue eyes bulging and bitter.

"Enough about Flannery. Let's talk about somebody else. The terms of my letting you out of the deep end of the pool, so to speak. Landon Smithfield. Did you go to San Diego and do as I asked you to do? I've wondered all this time if you stiffed me on our deal. I know he's out of the picture, but he didn't disappear until nearly two years ago. I released you from that vault more than *four* years ago. You took your sweet-ass time getting to the West Coast. He may be out of Marcus's life, but you *know* that's not enough to make me rest easy. I want *all* the details. It's been four long years, and I never heard from you again. This isn't like an overdue library book, my dear. Did you do as I asked? Did you kill him?"

Katarina's anger settled. She paused on Conrad with an empty look before she finally responded. "Marcus will never find him."

"That is *not* a satisfactory answer. Did you kill him as I asked you to do?"

"You wanted him gone from this world. He's no longer around." But she left it at that.

"He had better be. Because you know what will happen if he isn't ..."

"Again, demon, I am not Flannery Lanehart. Enough with the threats."

"And enough about Landon Smithfield. *For now.* Let's move on to Marcus and his present-day life. The little low-class stable boy he's been cavorting with since Ezekiel Colson's unfortunate demise. What have you done with D.C. Cunningham?"

"D.C. is under my control and will do whatever I want him to do," Katarina smiled. "He hasn't been to see Marcus once since he returned home. You're welcome, demon."

"Oh my, it's like a really bad deep-fried American version of *Upstairs Downstairs*," Conrad said, with an eye roll.

Katarina was stone-like. "I have my reasons for needing D.C. Cunningham around."

"Good. Keep him around *you.* And keep him away from Marcus."

"Or what?"

"I assume you have a purpose and a plan for D.C., considering what you've done with him. That's the only reason I will allow him continued existence. That and the fact Marcus is too busy grieving over Landon and Ezekiel to take D.C. seriously. Speaking of the good vet, has anyone ever told you the story of poor Zeke Colson?"

"I've been in this house for eight months. I know all about the veterinarian that you had Geoffrey kill."

"He got in my way. I suggest you keep D.C. on a leash so he doesn't become a similar problem."

"D.C. Cunningham is on a very tight leash, trust me."

Conrad brought up Clementine's left brow and shook her head. "I don't trust you at all. Let's not get carried away. But enough about that. Marcus and Flannery aren't the only things you've played puppet master with lately. *Take me down the hallway.*"

"Down the hallway?" Katarina asked innocently.

"Yes. To that other room."

"What are you talking about?" she asked, playing dumb.

"Don't lie to me. I can see it in your dead eyes. You've got the key in your pocket. Now *take* me there."

"Do you really want to put yourself through that? I mean—" Her eyes went up and down Clementine's body. "—you went from hot to *not*. Do you really need to be reminded of that?"

"Take me there now, Katarina. Don't make me tell you again. Next time it won't be verbal."

"Threats," she said, rigid and unblinking.

"Katarina!"

"So pushy and demanding. So grumpy. It must be time for Clementine's period, no? Okay, okay. Follow me, demon."

Quietly down the hall the hall they went, though the third floor was secluded and there was no real danger of being heard. When they reached the door, Katarina hesitated as she slid the skeleton key into the lock. She still wasn't sure why Conrad wanted a peek at what they were about to see.

"Turn the key. Open the door." This time it was Conrad in Clementine's voice, hushed but authoritative.

Katarina obeyed, and they went inside. She quickly closed the door behind them.

"What are those lights?" Conrad was referring to the blinking green and yellow lights of the machine near the bed. It was all he could see in the darkness.

Katarina lit candles. "There is no working overhead light in here," she explained.

The white sheet on the bed near a back wall was the first thing to come into focus for Conrad, as the yellow-orange glow of the candlelight gave a shape to their surroundings. He couldn't resist the urge to grab one of the candles and go toward the bed. Clementine's shadow loomed large in the glow on the wall of the old forgotten room. The entire bedroom took on a dreary, dim life as Katarina lit several more candles.

"It is a delicate situation," she said. "Wait for me before you touch anything over there."

"What is that machine? What is this?"

"And here I thought you knew everything."

"What is it, I said? And lift the sheet. I want to see."

"It might be hard for you to see it as it is—"

"Do it, damn you!"

Katarina came over. The room was depressing and dull but bright enough for a corpse to be visible. Her hand was on the sheet, but she hesitated, just as she had at the door.

"Why are you being so resistant and difficult? Lift the goddamn sheet," Clementine's voice ordered.

There was more at stake than Conrad's reaction, but Katarina couldn't tell him that. Taking a gamble, she yanked back the sheet, letting it rest at the waist of the corpse. She could have sworn she heard a gasp from Conrad. Her anxiety was gone; it pleased her to know she had gotten a rise out of the demon.

"The head," Conrad said. "How did you?"

"Who said it was *me?*" she replied, refusing to elaborate.

The body of Jimmy Van Buren, the body Conrad inhabited for seven years, lay before them, fully preserved. The definition of the chest, the six-pack abs, the muscular arms and shoulders—all of it was still there. A sleeping Ken doll.

It would have been perfect had it not been for two thin tubes from the square-shaped, golden machine humming near the bed. One tube went into the corpse's arm, delivering an intravenous fluid; the other traveled under the sheet, perhaps into the inner thigh, Conrad guessed.

Then there was that other grotesque imperfection. Thick, large, and ugly black stitches zig-zagged around the neck, where the head had been reattached. A vertical row of stitches also covered the initial gash Travis had delivered before the beheading.

Conrad admired the physical beauty below the shoulders but, with disgust, he grimaced at the suture job on the neck. A few dots of candlewax dripped on to Clementine's hand; it didn't faze Conrad.

"Cover it. Just pull the sheet back over it. I can't look at it. Why didn't you leave it buried?"

Katarina replaced the sheet and lost the smug and pleased look when she faced Conrad again. "I have my reasons," she said cryptically.

"Those tubes ... what are you pumping into him? *It*, I mean. Formaldehyde? *Embalming fluid?*"

"No. This will preserve the body much, much better." She gave another dramatic pause. "And perhaps allow it to be mobile again ... at some point."

"What? Mobile? *As what?* And you won't tell me why you're doing this? Or *who* is helping you?"

"All in good time, demon. Why hand away all the cookies so early?"

"Cookies, my ass. There is no way I can ever inhabit that body again. Some things are irreversible. No matter how much of that stuff you fill it with, that disgusting, disfigured neck will still be there, held together by those ugly stitches. Dead flesh can't repair itself."

"Mine can," Katarina replied, grinning at her own wit.

Conrad ignored her attempt at humor. "The head will never stay attached," he continued. "Young Bobby fed on the neck after that bastard Travis decapitated me with his sword."

Katarina stood in silence and grew sober again, as she contemplated whether she had divulged too much.

"You may not tell me anything now, Katarina, but you will in time. Remember. I can always find a way to put you back at the bottom of the lake with that greedy, Flannery-loving husband of yours. I'm sure he must be a floating pile of bones by now."

"Threats," she said again quietly.

"Don't make me regret releasing you. And you should either rebury or destroy that corpse before Jimmy Van Buren's nosy brother wanders up here."

"The body isn't for you," she finally said. "Your days inside of it have passed. Remy Van Buren is an almost exact duplicate of his brother Jimmy. Why not go and possess him?"

"Remy Van Buren doesn't need me for anything. That's the only way it would work. Jimmy Van Buren thought he was selling me his soul so he could become a famous, rich movie star and not have to hustle on Hollywood Boulevard and let nasty old trolls blow him for fifty dollars a pop."

Katarina stared quizzically at Conrad. "Clementine would have never asked a demon for help," she said. Another pause, and then her dead blue eyes did a dance. "Or *did* she?"

Conrad brought back the wide smile he had worn on Clementine's ordinary face when he entered Katarina's lair earlier. "Indeed, she did ..."

18

Travis came through the front door of the house and into the foyer just as Flannery reached the bottom of the stairs. They were face to face and alone. Something that almost never happened. Flannery took the cool indifference of her nephew as another sign he was aware of more than he let on.

Travis froze in his tracks for a beat, then tried to walk around Flannery and go up the stairs.

"Excuse me," he said.

She grabbed him by the arm. "Not so fast. I think it's time we have a little chat, Travis."

Travis tried to disguise his unease, but Flannery wasn't fooled. "What do we need to talk about?" he asked.

"Let's go to the study," she suggested.

"Let's talk right here." It was obvious he didn't want to be alone with her.

"Let's go to the study," Flannery repeated.

"Nothin' good ever happens in that room," Travis said.

"I won't hurt you." It was better to go ahead and finish the thought for him.

Flannery followed him down the hallway, and once they were inside the study, she closed the door. "See? I didn't lock it. You can walk out anytime," she said.

"What is it?" he asked. "Is something wrong with Uncle Marcus? D'Lynn? Oh God, one of them ain't dead, I hope."

"*Isn't* dead," she corrected. "And no, they're not. *I* am."

He didn't bother faking a reaction. "Why are you telling me this?" he asked.

"Let me present a theory, and please tell me if I'm correct. You found out about me the night Geoff and Conrad went on their little rampage?"

He looked away. "Yeah."

"Wow, so Geoff did rat me out. A prick 'til the end."

Travis looked back to her and put up a hand. "No, not exactly. I was eavesdropping from the top of the stairs. I heard them all down in the living room talkin' about it. And the conversation pretty much outed all of you."

"Who else have you told about this? D'Lynn? Tarva? Your little girlfriend ... Regan, isn't that her name?"

"Regan doesn't know. And if D'Lynn or Tarva know, then it ain't ... *isn't* from me."

"I'm certain Tarva doesn't know. I can't be sure about D'Lynn. Marcus knows but is in denial. He confronted me about something the night all the shit hit the fan but never talked about it again after that. He lets me sleep in the basement. He knows but doesn't *want* to know."

Travis laughed nervously. "The night the shit hit the fan? And exactly what night would that be? There are a few of those to choose from in this house."

Flannery's ice-cold glare shut down his laughter. "I suggest we keep more of it from hitting the fan," she said.

"How?"

"I want you to keep this little secret between us."

"That my aunt's a vampire? And my mom, stepdad, and little brother were, too? Sure, why not, I mean—"

"Where did you hear that *word?*" she interrupted, now in his face. "Where did you hear that? *How* did you find out about that?"

"What word? I'm confused ..."

"*Vampire!* That's a new word. I just learned that word. *Where* did you hear it?" She frightened him with rapid-fire questions out of nowhere but didn't care. *Damn it! Had Katarina gotten to Travis, too?*

"I don't remember," he said. "It just came out of my mouth. Like it was buried in my brain or somethin'."

"Think, Travis, *think!* It's important. You have to remember, and you have to tell me."

"Holy shit, Aunt Flannery, why are you so upset about this? You already know I'm not gonna say anything. Jesus, what the fuck—"

"Watch your dirty mouth," she scolded. "And you better be telling me the truth."

"Oh, so now you're gonna get on my ass for bad language? Like *you* have any room to talk. Oh my God ..."

"Where did you hear that word, Travis? Answer me!"

"I don't fucking know! Geez, can you please lay off?"

Then another possibility struck Flannery. Katarina could have orchestrated the entire thing to cause conflict.

That had to be it. Katarina had planted that word—*vampire*—around somewhere, maybe around the house on another scrap of paper. Travis could have seen it and gotten it into his subconscious.

No! Too incredible and ridiculous. Katarina would make herself vulnerable with such an act. But Travis had heard it somewhere.

It was time to move to another piece of the puzzle.

"Why were your clothes so filthy the other night?" Flannery asked Travis, as he turned to leave the room.

"What do you mean?" he asked, feigning ignorance as he turned back toward her.

"The night D'Lynn went to the hospital. Don't play games with me."

"What does that have to do with anything?" he asked defensively.

"Were you outside somewhere ... maybe the woods ... burying something?"

"No." It was mostly the truth. The only thing he *reburied* was a rug.

"Let's talk about where you buried Conrad's body last April."

Travis's pale face went a deeper white. "Let's not talk about that."

"Are you the one who buried the body?" she asked.

He shook his head and paced the room a minute before he answered her. "I mostly watched. It was Uncle Marcus. He did it, and now—now—the body ..."

"The body what?"

Travis clammed up. He couldn't trust her with the next bit of information.

Flannery sensed his distrust and grew impatient. "Finish the story, Travis. The body *what?*"

"Well," he began, his blue eyes going back and forth. He made it up as he went along. "I've always just thought of it as Conrad's body. Now we know who it was. Jimmy Van Buren. Remy's brother. And I feel bad about what I did."

"Yes, I'm sure you do," Flannery said, buying it. "Remy's also asking a lot of questions."

"He's been tryin' to get at me. I've managed to avoid him, but I don't know how much longer I can now that he's here in the house all the time."

A realization seized Flannery. Until that point she had seen Travis as the obstacle. Perhaps she had looked at the situation wrong. Maybe *Remy* was the problem.

"Leave Remy to me," she said to Travis. "I'll take care of it."

Travis's eyes grew large. "Take care of it ... *how?*"

Flannery went to the door to leave. "Don't worry about it. But I still intend to find out why your clothes were so dirty the other night. I know you're up to something. If you dug up that body and moved it, you'll have to tell me where. I don't like it when people keep things from me, Travis."

She left, and Travis waited a full two minutes before he sneaked out of the study, down the hall, into the foyer, and out the front door.

"Vampire?" he said to himself, as he walked down the steps of the front porch and into the yard. "Why did she freak out about me knowing that word?"

He paused as he saw the woods fall into focus off in the distance, across the clearing. Dark and menacing, but not over anything imagined as they would have been to most others. Did he want to go back there? *Why* was he headed in that direction? There were still questions, but he wasn't sure if it was there he would find the answers.

If anyone at the house knew where the body had been moved, they weren't talking. One of them couldn't. But why would Marcus have moved it?

Travis moved across the clearing, unsure what he would do when he arrived at the edge of the forest. A barrier of unseen clouds in the night sky shut out any trace of the moon; no one from the house would be able to see him, so he kept his pace slow and took time to collect his thoughts. When he reached the woods, he paused by a very tall and very old pine.

The girl in the strange, black Victorian-era top and hoop mini-skirt. Where the hell did she come from? Where was she running? Where did she live? She didn't look familiar. He had never seen her at school or around town. Was she part of a group of grave robbers? Did they have the body? *How* would they know where to find it? Was *she* in the woods watching when he and Marcus buried the body all those months ago? Maybe *she* was also one of the undead. An undead coven could hang out in the woods at night. Yes, it made sense, though Flannery would probably be their leader if that were the case.

No, no, none of it made sense. He rested his head against the pine. The redolence of pine sap masked the odor of moist dead leaves; everything else was quiet. He only heard his own breaths. There was a chill out, but the air was thick, as if rain was coming.

Travis turned on his flashlight for the first time and shined it through the band of trees. Nothing. He turned it back off and was ready to turn and go back when he heard the steps. Slower this time ... but angry stomps that were undeniably human. Had the beam of the flashlight disturbed someone?

He looked back through the trees, but left the flashlight turned off and at his side. It might be needed as a weapon. The steps came closer, and the urge to turn on the flashlight was gone. He was too frightened to turn it back on. The nightmare about Conrad from the week before still weighed on him, the events clear and easy to recollect; not fuzzy and half-forgotten as dreams often were only minutes after waking.

A crunch of twigs underneath feet only a few yards away tingled Travis's ears. He moved behind a tree to shield himself, took a deep breath, and clicked on the flashlight. He jumped around the corner of the tree and pointed the beam at the noise.

"*What?*" he said aloud with surprise. The shape of a man putting his arms up in surrender came toward him.

"Please, it hurts, the *light!* Take it away, please ... Who's there?"

Travis recognized the voice. "D.C.?"

"Travis, please get that light outta my eyes!" D.C. said, coming closer.

"Okay, okay. What are you doin' out here?" Travis asked, keeping the flashlight on but moving it off D.C.

D.C. reached him. He walked strangely, his shirt was halfway unbuttoned, and his face, arms, and chest looked pale as if he were sick. D.C. usually sported a natural tan, even in late fall, from working outside.

"I ain't sure," he said, in shallow breaths. He acted as if he were a bit drunk, though Travis couldn't smell any beer or booze rolling off him.

"Well, it's kinda hard to end up here by accident," Travis said, finding the explanation odd. "Where did you come from?"

D.C. looked at him and blinked a couple of times. "Huh?"

"Are you okay? You're acting kinda weird, man."

D.C. gave a hazy smile. "I'm sorry, Travis."

"Don't be sorry. But are you okay?"

D.C. shrugged but didn't say anything as they left the woods and walked back into the clearing.

"You need me or somebody to drive you home? You seem kinda drunk or somethin'."

"I'm sorry, Travis," he repeated.

Travis didn't acknowledge the weird apology. "I haven't seen you around the house much lately. Have you seen Uncle Marcus at all?"

"Marcus? No, he told me we were different and I was wastin' my time. No, I'm keepin' my distance from Marcus. He won't know I'm there anyhow."

"Well, that's kind of a surprise, man. You seemed so devoted to him. Especially when they first took him to the hospital. I think Uncle Marcus will come back to us. I don't think he'll stay like this forever."

D.C. didn't answer and walked clumsily alongside Travis. He acted forlorn and bothered as if something else distracted him; nothing to do with Marcus.

"Did you see anything strange while you were in the woods?" Travis asked.

"Strange? Like what?" D.C. asked, his words almost slurred. He stumbled every few steps.

Travis was ready to reach over and grab him in case he fell. "Like a girl in the woods. Dressed in weird clothes. Kinda like mine, but a little different. Like she was on her way to some steampunk costume party."

"No, I ain't seen nothin' like that."

"I figured. It's a longshot. I had to ask."

"I'm sorry, Travis," D.C. said, for the third time.

"Man, really, it's all good. There's no need to constantly apologize."

D.C. began to laugh. It started as a low giggle and then matured into a bellowing, crazy cackle that caused Travis to stop and stare at him.

"You're not okay, man. Are you fucked up on drugs or somethin'? You act all out of it, but I don't smell any beer or booze."

"I'm sorry, Travis," D.C. answered, unable to control his laughter.

"And why do you keep saying that? Sorry for *what?*"

The laughing fit halted as quickly as it had begun. D.C.'s goofy grin vanished, his face stiffened; he was serious, sober. He kept his eyes on Travis and stepped closer. "For *this,*" he said, flashing distended canines as he shoved Travis to the ground. D.C. then climbed on top of the boy and pinned him down.

"Oh my God, no!" Travis screamed. He wasn't strong enough to fight back.

Before Travis could protest or struggle further, D.C. went for his neck with the teeth.

19

"It's been a week. When are you coming home? The kids keep asking me, and I don't know what to tell them."

Melissa Van Buren's irritation was as apparent on the other end of the phone as if she were standing in the same room as Remy. She still attempted, he knew, to stay calm to avoid any kind of quarrel, but it wouldn't last much longer. Remy always recognized the signs of an imminent explosion.

"Soon," he told her. "Some unexpected things have come up here."

"Like what?" she asked. "Have these people seen Jimmy?"

These people, he thought.

Well, let's see, darling. One of these people *stabbed me with a letter opener. I still can't figure out how I got lucky enough to escape a more serious injury. Then I ended up having incredible sex with the said stabber's sister, whom I barely know, but she's the most mind-blowing woman I've ever had in my entire life—sorry, Melissa, that even includes you—and now I can't get her out of my head. She's always there. I don't know why. I can't ever stop thinking about her, and when we're in the same room, I lose it. She keeps me at bay and that makes me even more nuts. Oh, and I'm also boarding at the same house where I was stabbed, playing house-call doctor to the housekeeper, all while basically getting nowhere with why I originally came here. That about sums it up, my dear ex-wife.*

"So, you don't have any more information about Jimmy than when you arrived there?" Melissa asked again, terser, as if she had heard his final thought.

Flannery was on his mind again. Her essence, her lips, her breasts, her ...

Remy brought himself back. "Well, he was definitely here. There's no *maybe* about it," he managed to say.

"Where is he now? What did he do when he was there? What did he tell people? Where the hell has he been for seven years?"

"Honey, I don't know. It hasn't been easy getting answers out of anybody. I'm still working on it."

"Well, jeez, Remy, you were so gung-ho when you took off to go there. You sound like you're a little distracted now. Almost complacent."

"I have no idea what you mean," he lied.

"Thanksgiving is next week, Remy. Will you be home or not?" she asked.

"No, I—I won't be back for Thanksgiving ..."

"Damn it, Remy. The kids!" Here it went.

"I kind of got tied down to an obligation here," he said, not wanting to share details about D'Lynn and send Melissa on a tirade.

"You have obligations *here*," she replied. "What about the hospital? Your patients. Why don't you let the police handle this?"

He took a deep breath. So much for an argument, he thought. "The police decided it was a cold case and haven't really pursued it past a certain point. It's basically up to me."

"Where exactly are you? Who *are* these people who saw Jimmy?"

"Um, the Lanehart family. They live at Ten Points, north of Monroe. It was a cotton plantation back in the eighteen-hundreds. The house and some of the land is still here, and the descendants of the original family, the Laneharts, they still live here."

He could hear keyboard pecks on the other end as she did a Google search behind him. "Oh my God, that house is gorgeous. To die for," she said, her tone rigid but less angry as she softened more. She marveled over photos she found online and softened more. "Looks like something out of *Gone with the Wind*."

"Not quite the architectural style of Tara, but yeah, it feels very Old South and from some movie," he agreed.

"Oh my God!" she yelled out.

He almost jumped. "What!" he exclaimed, startled by her outburst.

"The article attached to this photo of the house. It's from some newspaper last spring. Three of the Lanehart family members went missing." She was skimming and talking at the same time. "A father, a wife, and their young son. What's *that* about? When was Jimmy there? Could he somehow be connected—?"

"I know all about the three disappearances," Remy said. "The police want to believe Geoffrey Lanehart ran away with his wife and youngest son, but it makes no sense to me that they left their other two kids behind. Sloppy police work. I'm trying to figure out if there's any connection to Jimmy and the three missing family members. From what I've gathered, he was seen here around that time. Nobody in the house is very forthcoming. One of them is now in a catatonic state. It's a long, confusing story."

He knew if he told her about the stabbing she would lose it, or maybe even be on the next flight down there. Despite their divorce, she still tried to play the role of the dutiful wife at times. Remy wouldn't tell her, just to be safe and ensure she stayed put in Chicago. The kids needed at least one parent around.

"Why are the police so lax about this?" she repeated. "What if this Geoffrey guy killed his wife and kid and ran away by himself? Or what if *Jimmy's* with him and involved somehow? For God's sake, all the stereotypes about the southern justice system must be true."

He knew he would have to question Wes again. "I'm not sure about that. There's at least one deputy who cares, but he's all superstitious or maybe fundamentalist and thinks the Devil is involved. From what I can gather, detectives investigated all of this when it happened, and they've had no new leads about where Geoffrey Lanehart and his family could be."

"*The Devil?* None of this makes any sense," Melissa said. "Jimmy was an outsider and hung around this family? I'm no detective, but even I know that's a little fishy."

"It is," he agreed. "I don't know what else to say or do except try to find out more."

"We've had no sign of Jimmy in seven years. Then he shows up hanging around rich people, pretending to be somebody else. It doesn't sound good, Remy. He was obviously hiding from all of us and living another life somewhere else. I know he's your brother, but it sounds shady. What if he murdered the man, the wife, and the boy? He was always the greedy and opportunistic type, and—"

"Melissa, please," Remy protested. "That's way too much conjecture. Let me try to get more facts and go one step at a time before we assume the worst." Jimmy was self-centered and fame-seeking, yes. Calling him greedy was a tad of a stretch. Jimmy had hustled to survive in Hollywood, but he hadn't shacked up with old rich women—or men—as far as Remy knew.

"I can't help it, Remy ..."

"The Laneharts and their staff are a tight group. I think if they suspected somebody of murder they would be hell-bent on tracking down Jimmy."

D'Lynn's ill reaction and accusations when she first saw him and confused him with his brother came to mind. Melissa would take that information and run with it, just as she would if she knew about the stabbing. *Better not to tell her.*

"Well, if they're all so close, then they've obviously banded together and decided not to tell you anything."

"If that's the case then I'll chisel away until I find the weak link in the house who *will* tell me the truth." He thought of Flannery again, though there was nothing weak about her.

"I can't believe you're missing Thanksgiving with the kids. I don't know what I'll tell them," she said again, before their phone conversation ended.

Once he was off the phone, Remy left the guest bedroom and went downstairs. Lucky for him, Flannery was in the living room. He felt the pull but tried not to make eye contact with her. He must stay focused. Any effort would be lost if he was caught up in her essence—or whatever the hell it was that stirred him whenever she was around.

Flannery looked up as he came in, with the warmest look she could muster, which still felt somewhat cool.

"I need to talk to you," he said, eyes moving everywhere but to her.

"What about?" she asked.

She must have some idea. "About my brother. About Jimmy. I can't—I can't get distracted tonight. I need you to tell me what happened when he was here. In this house."

"I don't really know anything about your brother," she lied.

Remy looked at her and then quickly diverted his eyes before they met hers. "When you say you don't *really* know, does that mean you *do* know something?"

She knew she had to give him something but needed to keep the details lean and not implicate anyone, especially herself. "He was here. He was a friend of Geoff's. He called himself Conrad. I suppose it could have been an alias. He seemed like a nice guy. Nothing suspicious." The lies kept coming. *Your brother is* dead, *Remy. He was dead long before his body ever walked into this house.* Those *are the facts!*

"What else?" Remy asked, looking at the floor. "I need to know!"

"Why won't you look at me?" Flannery asked. *Look at me, and I'll be able to end this conversation right now!*

Can't do it, can't do it, he thought. "You know the effect you have on me. Look—" his eyes were pointed at the floor. "—the only reason I'm even here in your house is because I need to know what my brother was doing here, *why* he was doing it, and *where* he could have gone after he left. This whole thing with D'Lynn just kind of happened and wasn't part of my plan. If I get any concrete information before the two weeks I promised her, well, then I'll have to break that promise and move on."

"Oh," she said, pretending to be disappointed at the possibility of his leaving. Or was she pretending? *Damn it, stop thinking and feeling like something you're not anymore.*

"I don't know what this is. *This* between us. But I have to remember why I came here."

"All I know is I never saw your brother again after the night of my father's funeral," she said. That much was true.

"Who else? D'Lynn knows nothing. I've asked her repeatedly while helping her around here. Marcus can't talk. Tarva claims she never had encounters with Jimmy. Your young niece knows nothing ..."

He paused and they both turned toward the foyer as the front door opened. From the distance of the living room they could see Travis walk into the house. Or, rather, stumble in.

"Travis. I need to talk to him," Remy said. "He's avoided me. Not anymore. Maybe he can tell me what the rest of you won't!"

Remy went to the foyer where Travis took clumsy steps toward the stairs. He was paler than normal; his expressionless face rivaled that of his catatonic uncle's.

"Travis, I need to talk ..." Remy began, moving toward him. Then he stopped when saw the boy's state. "Are you okay?"

"What's the matter?" Flannery asked, now in the foyer behind Remy.

"My God!" Remy said, grabbing an unresponsive Travis by the shoulders. Remy pulled him closer. "Look at this!"

There were four puncture wounds on the left side of the teenager's neck, dried caked blood down the side, and some blood that still appeared wet on the wounds. Travis gave Remy a lethargic glare but said nothing.

"He's been attacked!" Remy said. "Maybe some kind of animal, I don't know. Travis, what happened? Can you tell me what happened?"

Travis shook his head slowly and after a few seconds mumbled an "I don't know."

Flannery feigned cluelessness and worked up some false concern. "Does he have a fever? He's acting strange."

"You stay here with him," Remy said. "I need to examine him. My bag is upstairs. I'll go get it. Take him to the living room and put him in a chair or on the sofa."

Remy took off up the stairs, and Flannery took Travis's arm and walked him into the living room. "Can you hear me, Travis?" she whispered, her lips to his ear.

"I don't know," he repeated in a groggy voice. "Woods. *Woods.*"

"Were you in the woods?" She peered back through the doorway to make sure no one else was around. "Sit here ... stay quiet!"

"Yeah," he mumbled. "Woods."

"Got it," she replied. "No more. Stop talking about it."

Remy quickly returned with his medical bag. "What the hell kind of animal would leave puncture marks on his neck like that?"

Flannery shrugged. "Makes no sense at all. He seems kind of weak but okay."

Remy stared up at her and then quickly looked away. "You don't seem too concerned," he said.

"Well, of course I am!" Flannery said, faking offense this time. But he was correct. She needed to turn it up a notch and emote more. "It's just so—oh Remy, so many horrible things have happened in this house in the past year! It never ends!"

"Yes, horrible things most of you are evasive about. Things I *will* get to the bottom of," he said, his voice low as he studied Travis.

Flannery looked away as Remy sat on the sofa beside Travis.

Remy took supplies out of the bag then examined and cleaned the wound. "Travis, what happened? Tell me what happened to you outside."

"*Um,*" Travis began. Then he looked confused and stopped. The contrast of the boy's bone-colored skin to his jet-black T-shirt was alarming.

Remy put on his stethoscope and checked Travis's pulse. "Oh my," he said, then pulled out a blood pressure cuff.

"What?" Flannery asked, though she already knew the answer.

"His pulse. Just a second." Remy used a sphygmomanometer to check Travis's blood pressure. He inflated the cuff as he held the stethoscope at the crook of the boy's arm. After he was done, he shook his head. "He's lost some blood. His blood pressure and his pulse are a little weak, but I think he'll be okay. I think he's in shock from this attack. We need to take him to the hospital to be better checked out. I don't think he needs a blood transfusion, but I would rather have him examined at a hospital."

"Vampires," Travis muttered, eyes fluttering. "*Vampires ... vampires in the woods...*"

Flannery's eyes went large; she turned to hide her reaction from Remy. Thankfully, he still avoided eye contact with her.

"What is he saying?" Remy asked, his eyes on Travis. "Vampires? What does that mean?"

"I have no clue," Flannery said, staring off at the wall. "Vampire? I've never heard such a word. It sounds like another language. He's acting delirious ... feverish!"

"We need to take him to the hospital to be checked out," Remy repeated. "Let's get him to the car."

"No, no, let's just put him to bed. Maybe give him something to eat. He'll be fine," Flannery said.

"I think he needs tests. He can't even tell us what the hell happened to his neck. He may need a tetanus shot. Or God forbid, rabies shots. Let's hope not, for his sake."

She turned back to the sofa. "No, you can't take him to the hospital."

"Why the hell not, Flannery?" he asked. He spun around and looked into her eyes before he thought about it. Then he could not look away in time.

"Because I said he's going to be fine. *Trust me, Remy,*" she said, with a small smile.

Remy's concern and near-panic faded. He stood in slow motion from the sofa. "Okay, okay," he said, moving toward her. Leaning in, he gave her a light kiss on the lips. "You really don't think there's any need to go to the hospital?"

"I don't," she said. Their eyes remained locked. "Clean and dress the wound, and then we'll give him something to eat, and then we'll help him to bed. *Okay, Remy?*"

After the puncture wounds were treated, Remy and Flannery took Travis to the kitchen for some food and fruit juice. When they reached the foyer on their way upstairs, Flannery put her hand on Remy's shoulder and stood closely so he couldn't avoid eye contact.

"Take Travis to his room and put him to bed," she commanded. "His room is the last door on the left at the end of the upstairs hallway."

Remy gave her another smile. "Of course," he said. "Will you be here when I get back?"

She nodded; her hand glided seductively from his shoulder, down his arm. "If I'm not, then go to the basement and wait for me."

"Absolutely," Remy said, smile wider.

"Take great care with him. Make sure he's comfortable before you leave him alone up there. I must step outside a moment, but you go to the basement once you're back downstairs and wait for me there. Do you understand, Remy?"

He nodded and made his way up the stairs with Travis, who was dazed and oblivious to the exchange.

Flannery watched until they were out of sight, then headed to the front door and outside.

D.C. awaited her arrival at the far end of the porch. Travis's blood was still on one corner of his mouth, but the glow of the light on the porch showed some of his color was back. His sleeveless shirt was fully unbuttoned, smooth hard pecs and six-pack abs protruding.

With a neutral stride, Flannery moved toward D.C. When she reached him, she stopped and looked at him for a moment before she slapped him—hard!—across the face.

D.C. failed to flinch and offered a sarcastic eye roll. "Oh my, the mosquitoes sure are bitin' tonight. You think that hurts anymore?"

"You fucking idiot," she said to him. "Did Katarina teach you nothing? You can't even close a wound on somebody's neck? What the hell is the matter with you? The only smart thing you did was stop feeding before you killed him. The rest of it was sloppy."

"Well, I'm still hungry. Maybe now I can go have some of that hot boyfriend of yours," D.C. said. He rubbed his bare chest through his open shirt like an animal in heat. "Of course, I wouldn't mind havin' *more* than blood from him."

"I've already had his blood," Flannery reminded him. "That means Remy is off limits to you. Marcus is also off limits. Stay the hell away from my brother. You've forfeited anything that was ever between the two of you. Travis is under your control now. I don't care what you do with him."

D.C. made a repulsed face. "Travis *ain't* my type, and even if he was, I ain't no pedophile. Lord, don't insult me that way, woman."

"I didn't mean have sex with him, you hillbilly jackass. I meant control him and guide him in other ways, to keep him out of my hair. My brother must have truly been lonely and desperate to ever hook up with you. Outside of that pretty face and body, you're as dumb as a box of rocks."

"Well, excuse me for not aimin' as high as a married congressman," D.C. said, with another roll of his eyes.

Flannery was ready to hit him again. "He was a senator, you moron. A *U.S.* senator!"

"Either way, *whoop-tee-doo* and *lah-tee-dah*," D.C. said, spinning around in his cowboy boots and throwing one of his heels up in the air behind him. With his open shirt and exposed chest, he looked like a line-dancer wannabe at a country and western-themed gay bar.

"Are you done pretending we're two of the *Real Housewives* in a catfight? I have other more important things to do."

"Why? Is your stud inside waitin' on you?" D.C. asked, not ready to stop.

"Any business I have with Remy can wait. I need to see Katarina first. As in *now*. She's the only one who can get through to you and keep you under control."

"Well, *you're* the one who told her to send me out to the woods to attack Travis and make him forget stuff!" D.C. shouted.

"Shut the hell up before somebody hears you," she hissed, moving closer. "*That* is not to be repeated. *Ever.* And you did a shitty job making him forget anything because he was in there rambling and carrying on about vampires in the woods. In front of Remy. Thank God I reined him in! It's up to *you* to help me with that now because you drank his blood, and he's under your command."

"Why couldn't you just do it? I can't be expected to be any kind of expert at this yet," D.C. said. "But yeah, I think I can control him now. I'm convinced of that much."

"You better be because my whole reason behind this was to keep him from going rogue. My only other choice was to kill him. You better keep him in line, D.C., or that hot chest you like to show off may have a stake through it real soon."

"You Laneharts always think you're so much better than everybody else. Marcus always treated me like I was beneath him, well, when I was *beneath* him. Guess what? You Laneharts all sit on the pot the same way to take a dump as the rest of us do."

"Oh calm down, Mary," she said, turning to go back inside the house. "The good news is you don't have to worry about taking a shit anymore now that you're dead. And for the love of God, wipe that blood off the corner of your mouth."

20

Maxine tossed in her sleep as heavy rain moved in and started to spatter the pane of her bedroom window. Here and there, she cried out. The same scene from the last few nights played out the same way. Katarina heard the call. Within minutes, she appeared from a corner of the dark bedroom and went to Maxine. It was a situation that had become so common that she knew when to expect an outburst.

"My little Edela, what is the matter?" Katarina asked. She took a seat on the edge of the bed and settled a cold, maternal hand on the girl's back.

Maxine awoke and sprang into Katarina's arms. "He won't stop. He won't leave me alone," she mumbled.

Katarina raised a suspicious brow, as a shot of lightning brightened the room for a full two seconds. "*Who* won't leave you alone?"

"The bad man," she finally said, clutching tighter to Katarina.

"Who is the bad man, Edela? Tell Mommy who it is!"

"I *can't* ..." she sniffled.

"You must," Katarina whispered to her. The voice turned to a near growl. "Then *Moder* can make the bad man leave her little Edela alone."

"Will you stay here with me until I go back to sleep?" Maxine pulled back and looked up to her. Another lightning flash snapped a quick and pretty picture of Katarina. It gave Maxine comfort. Having her mommy there made her feel safe. Even if her mommy didn't look or sound the same anymore after spending time in Heaven.

"Yes, my little baby," Katarina replied, giving Maxine a kiss on the forehead. Heaven also gave people frosty-cold lips, Maxine decided. "But you need to tell me who causes you to have these bad dreams."

"Not right now," Maxine said. She pulled away more and put her head back on the pillow.

The lightning strikes outside subsided, so it wasn't hard for Katarina to hide her disappointment—and her impatience. "You will tell Mommy soon, yes?" she asked, in a sweeter voice.

Maxine nodded her head, and then, "Will you sing to me like you always do ... Mommy?"

Katarina was tempted to withhold lullaby requests until *Edela* disclosed the culprit's identity, but she couldn't bring herself to do it. "Of course, my little darling. Promise me you will go back to sleep and have happy dreams, yes?"

"I love you, Mommy," Maxine said, groggy as Katarina kept a hand on her. "Please don't ever leave me again."

"*Moder* loves her little Edela, too," Katarina said, stroking Maxine's hair. There was a crash of thunder outside. Maxine was wide awake and clung to her again. "I won't ever leave you. I will always protect my baby."

I won't ever let you slip away from me again now that I have you back, my darling Edela...

"You are spoiling our child, woman," Arfast Gerhardsson said to his wife one spring morning as she held up a ragdoll and smiled at him.

He was sitting at the table in their modest farm house. The smell of rain outside the open window cooled the feel of that summer in Sweden, but continuous rain greatly aggravated a usually even-tempered Arfast.

He cleaned thick field mud from a pair of work boots. They were the only boots he had until after the harvest, still ahead and looking bleaker with the excessive rain.

Yes, Arfast thought of new boots. But first he planned to use whatever money to be earned toward new shoes for his wife and daughter, and material his wife could use for new dresses.

"Now, now, Arfast," Katarina said, walking over and putting her arms around him from behind. She brought her head around and gave him a kiss on the cheek. "It is only a ragdoll. It will be here for Edela when she wakes up. I finished it last night. I used leftover scraps from a dress I made last winter."

"You make ragdolls for our daughter, and I'm worried whether we will have any food in another month," he said, with a grumble.

"She cannot see us worry like this. I want her to remain happy," Katarina said.

Arfast looked back at her with a smile. They were both in their late twenties, but with his blond whiskers and hardened blue eyes, he looked older. Katarina was the same picturesque beauty she had been when they married nearly a decade earlier. Long blonde hair, porcelain features, and a thin but voluptuous body that remained intact after the birth of their daughter seven years before.

Katarina never bore Arfast anymore children after Edela, and neither one of them was sure why. Arfast desired a son to help in the fields, but he never said this aloud to Katarina. She and Edela were his life and his heart; he knew never to regard his family members as a commodity, as some other men did.

Katarina never had to hear Arfast say it to know he wanted a son, but she too never spoke of it. A boy was expected. Whispers of family members and others in the village hadn't gone unheard. The way the couple had only one child, while others had multiple children. *Especially* the way Katarina doted on her only child Edela, when sons were the ones who deserved such prestige. Many Swedish mothers detached themselves from the girls in the family.

There was never any guarantee a child would survive; another reason many of Katarina's contemporaries refused to become overly attached to their daughters *or* sons.

"You are right. I'm sure Edela will like her new toy," he said, returning a kiss to his wife before he went back to his boots.

The other men on the surrounding farms and the nearby village would think it an odd and even emasculatory sight for a man such as Arfast to clean his own boots—and not order his wife to do it for him. Many of Arfast's peers shook their heads at the way he honored his wife. Their wives were no different than their other property. The women were there to clean the house, milk the cows, and give them children—more specifically, sons. This poor farmer Arfast Gerhardsson treated his wife as if she were a queen, when she had only borne him one daughter; obviously incapable of producing a son.

"Arfast, I have told you not to put those filthy boots on the table where we eat," Katarina lightly scolded, keeping her arms around him from behind. She looked over his shoulder where her chin was rested as she watched him clean the boots. "A woman's work in this house is never done."

"Well, well, if it so pleases you, I will do a woman's work and clean this table for you when I am done. Is that something that will make it better?" he teased, standing to his feet and picking her up off the floor by her sides. He squeezed her playfully and gave her a kiss on the lips.

"Arfast!" she giggled modestly. "You must stop. Edela could be awake and in here at any moment. She could see us."

"You are so beautiful I cannot resist. My Katarina. Pretty as the day we married. I cannot help myself."

"Now you embarrass me," she laughed, as he gave her another kiss. He then set her down. "Go back to your boots. I will make the breakfast. You have already been outside hard at work today, and you must have an appetite. I will wake Edela if she is not here at the table with you when I am finished. She sleeps too much."

"She is a growing child," Arfast said, waving his hand at Katarina. "She can sleep longer than us."

"Arfast," Katarina said. Concern creeped in as her husband retook his seat at the table. "What will happen if the rain does not stop?"

"Let us not think about it, Katarina," he said, though it was *all* he could think about. "The Lord will provide. We will make it one way or another."

She nodded. "We have potatoes, beans, some vegetables. Thanks to God, we have enough to last for a short while."

He refused to look up from his boots. "We will make it through the harvest season as well as the winter, Katarina. I promise you we will make it to the other side of this."

Katarina nodded again, as she gathered ingredients to cook

breakfast. Arfast was right, she knew. God would protect them and provide where they could not.

"Look who has decided to show herself to us!" Arfast exclaimed, switching to a brighter mood for his daughter, who stepped into the room.

Edela was a small girl for seven years old, with blonde hair like her parents. Hers was curly. She smiled at Arfast and then ran to put her arms around Katarina, who stopped preparing breakfast and returned the embrace.

"And look how happy she is to see us this morning," Katarina added, bending and giving her daughter a kiss on the cheek. "Good morning, my Edela. Look what *Moder* has for you."

Arfast set down his boots and smiled as he watched his wife present the ragdoll to the little girl. "I suppose she will have to give it a name as she has with the other ones," he said.

"If she so chooses," Katarina said.

"Thank you, Moder," Edela said, giving Katarina another hug. "She's beautiful."

"You are too kind, my sweet child," Katarina said.

Edela's bright morning smile made her mother forget about the bleak spatter of rain on the soggy ground and its steamy smells outside the open window. Edela carried the blue doll with her as she went over to Arfast. He stopped what he did with the boots and embraced the little girl as she took a seat on his lap.

Katarina admired the sight of them for a moment before she turned away to prepare breakfast.

It will be fine. Everything will work out. We've had hard times before, and we made it through, thanks to God above, she told herself, as she heard the giggles and laughter of her Edela behind her.

"You're quiet," she heard her Edela say.

"Huh—wh—what?"

It was a rainy November night in the twenty-first century. Katarina found herself back in the second-floor bedroom at Ten Points and no longer in late-seventeenth century Sweden.

"You're not talking," Maxine repeated. She was wide awake, looking on Katarina curiously. Mommy was barely visible in the darkness. "You're not ... singing."

Katarina had not permitted the thought of her handsome and beloved Arfast in years and felt an ache she forced away before she could dwell. That time was forever gone.

"Mommy has a lot on her mind," she said. "Go to sleep, my little Edela."

Fifteen minutes later when Katarina heard the deep, slumberous breathing, she knew the little girl was back to sleep. She bent down and gave her a final kiss on the forehead and exited the room.

The second-floor hallway was quiet and empty, as most of the house slept, but she realized she should have practiced more discretion when walking out of the bedroom. Eight months in the great house, and she acted like a regular resident—and that could prove dangerous.

What would happen if she did encounter someone from the house in the hallway while sneaking into and out of her Edela's bedroom?

Why kill them, of course!

But there would have to be a neat way to do it, or else there would be problems. Other than killing the drunken homeless man on the night out with Flannery, Katarina had been so careful to leave everything clean and precise. No bodies, no attacks (other than the one on D.C., but only she and Flannery knew about that) and no traces of anything to endanger her.

Flannery was suspicious of *how* Katarina sustained herself. D.C. was now in the circle, and even though he wasn't very bright, he too would start to ask questions.

Flannery and D.C. were her underlings. Katarina thought of them as she sneaked back up the stairs to the third floor. A dysfunctional kind of undead family where none of the three members liked one another. Hell, *dislike* was an understatement! The vampire trio *detested* one another. Yet they needed each other.

Momentarily, Katarina decided, mulling over her hatred of Flannery—the whore—as she reached the third floor. She wasn't sure what she wanted more—to let Flannery into the bigger circle, or to simply destroy her.

I created her. Can I destroy her? I can't trust Conrad to do it. I'm no fool. He will eventually reveal himself to her and play the two of us against one another.

Soon, she thought, she must decide.

21

Katarina met Flannery down near the duck pond, away from the house. It was a chilly, moonless night, but the rain had stopped. As far as the temperature went, neither of them felt the cold; their long sleeves did nothing but obscure pale flesh.

Katarina was dressed in blue business attire, as if she were about to assemble a board meeting. Flannery wore a causal dark cotton blouse and jeans.

In a contrast to her conservative look, Katarina arrived at the pond, snatched up a quacking duck, ripped off its head with her teeth, got a healthy dose of blood, and tossed the headless carcass into the water ten feet away, where it bobbed lifelessly. Other ducks went wild with their quacking, assembled around their fallen family member; the noise and flaps grew madder. Katarina turned and shot them all a fierce stare. They broke their melody of despair and scattered, many lifting off out of the water and out of sight. The headless carcass was left alone to float and bleed out. Some wild animal would come along and grab it when it drifted back closer to the bank.

"How did you do that?" Flannery asked, marveling at the way the ducks disbanded.

"Three hundred years of practice," Katarina said. She rubbed around her lips with her fingers and licked away stray blood until she was presentable again. "But I feel a lesson on duck hunting is not why you wanted to see me."

"D.C. is going to turn into another Rochelle Dubois if you don't get a handle on him," Flannery said. "He attacked Travis. He left the wound and sign of the attack clearly visible. Remy saw the marks on Travis's neck. I had to guide Remy in another direction to throw him off track."

"Nobody likes a snitch, Flannery."

"I'm not being a snitch. I'm *warning* you. D.C. Cunningham is a buffoon who will cause problems."

"Why couldn't you tell me this upstairs at the house? Why here?"

"Over there." Flannery pointed off into the distance. "The woods. Something is out there. Travis has been up to something, and he won't tell me the full story."

"Yes, I know he is," Katarina said. "D.C. followed him there tonight and then flew ahead when he saw where your little punk-freak nephew was going."

"D.C. can fly, too? Great."

"We can all fly, silly whore. But that is beside the point. You think I do not know all of this about your nephew and D.C.?"

"So, you say you know Travis is up to something in the woods. *What* is he up to?"

Katarina shrugged. "I presume it is something to do with that hidden body of Jimmy Van Buren's. The one Remy Van Buren would love to know about."

"The one Remy can *never* know about," Flannery reminded her. "And what exactly does D.C. know about it?"

"You would have to ask him that."

"Katarina, you can't let D.C. run rampant. He could put us in danger."

Katarina gave her a cold smile. "You put yourself in danger when you try to give me orders."

"He can't tell anybody I asked *you* to have *him* attack Travis. He practically blurted it out on a loudspeaker on the front porch earlier."

"You ask me to have a boy do a man's job," she said, then made a face. "Ugh, what a human thing to say. Besides, who would he tell? Nobody knows D.C. is one of us ... except you and I."

"He has a daytime job here. I can imagine our foreman Buddy has already tried to find out why D.C. hasn't shown up for work lately."

"Your foreman Buddy will assume he's, what do you call it, a *deadbeat.* Ha, no pun intended. Such overreaction and needless worry tonight."

"Okay, let's talk about the woods again," Flannery said, eyes in that direction. "I think if we go out there we can figure out where the body is."

"In these shoes?" Katarina said. She pointed down to stilettos planted in the wet grass. The shoes were draped by her silk pants. "Go to the woods and play detective by yourself. I had some duck stew. I am good for the night."

"You haven't survived on duck blood these past eight months," Flannery said, crossing her arms as she always did. "Other than our guy at the bike trail, no attacks in all that time. There aren't enough stray rats on the third floor of the house or critters in the woods to satisfy you. I'm curious how you've sustained yourself, Katarina. Will you ever tell me?"

The bigger circle. The whore isn't ready, Katarina thought. "Perhaps not. Or I may think about it." She smiled again.

"Okay, fine, you don't have to tell me. Maybe tell D.C. because he's the sloppy one. If there's a lesson on how to keep things neat, then *he's* the one you should share it with."

"What I will share is that I hope my dead and headless duck floats back this way so a coyote grabs it. It would be a shame to have your friend Wes out here tomorrow investigating more mutilated animals at Ten Points. You are not one who has room to talk about neat!"

Katarina started back to the house but paused and turned back. "I know everything D.C. does. I have a plan for him that I won't share with you. *Yet.* Let us leave it at that. There is no need for you to tattle to me about anything else."

Flannery watched her float through the grassy clearing toward the house. There was also no need to respond. Katarina relished having the last word.

Patience wasn't anything Flannery carried in large doses, so she did the next best thing she could to find answers.

"I can't read that one too good. Sometimes not at all," Izzy said, after Flannery touched down at her doorstep a few minutes later. "I had no idea she was in the house all that time, and I walked back in that house the night of your Daddy's wake. I even showed up on the porch after the funeral, and I still couldn't feel her there. It's always bits and pieces with her. Why are you so worried with all this? She killed and turned that poor D.C. fellow into one of you."

Izzy knew she had misspoken. She opened her mouth to try and backtrack.

Flannery cut her off. "It's okay, no offense taken," she insisted. "I know what you meant."

"The woods," Izzy said, as a chill came over her. Then something clicked. "It's somethin' to do with the woods. Oh, and Travis ..." Her dark eyes were larger.

"What? Tell me!" Flannery moved closer and put her hand on Izzy's arm.

Izzy shook her head. "It ain't clear. Somethin' related to the woods. D.C.'s attack on Travis kept Travis from findin' it. But it's only a matter of time until somebody does."

"Finds *what?*"

"It's too..." Izzy made aggravated signals and impatient gestures with her hands as she became frustrated with herself. "It's too ... *foggy*. I can't see everything."

"Is it the body?" Flannery heard herself say. Then she cringed at her own big mouth for the second time in as many days.

"You think I don't already know about that?"

"Well, I never know with you ..."

"No, it isn't about the body that was buried. It's somethin' else in the woods. Oh, I feel terrible and guilty sometimes. Knowin' all these shady things that you and the rest of the Laneharts are up to. And havin' Katarina get D.C. to attack Travis? Why, Flannery, *why* did you do that?"

"It was the lesser of two evils. Travis will be okay by tomorrow."

"Are you sure of that? *I'm* not sure of that!"

"Of course, I'm sure. Why wouldn't I be? Why aren't you?"

"I'll never understand."

"I have to go," Flannery said. Izzy had put another unsettling idea into her head. Had D.C.'s attack done something to Travis? Maybe she could leave before Izzy figured it out and made her feel guiltier. *Damn it, why did human emotions get the best of her ...*

"You just got here," Izzy said, as if she wanted to pour coffee and socialize.

"I'll be back to see you tomorrow," Flannery said. "Mother." She gave Izzy a small smile and touched her arm again, more affectionately, catching the older woman off guard.

"Where are you off to?" Izzy asked, with a grin of her own, touched by her daughter's rare show of affection.

Flannery opened the door to leave. "Don't worry. I'll be okay."

She wondered if she had been incredibly stupid to go to Izzy with all of this. Katarina knew things, too, and on top of her new fear over Travis, Flannery now worried she could have put her mother in danger.

A few minutes later, Flannery landed in the Ten Points clearing, away from the house and near the woods. She stared past the darkness, into the masses of trees, as her night vision brought into focus what it never could in her human years. All she could detect were occasional flutters and movements of wildlife. A few squirrels, one rabbit, and then nothing.

Flannery went on air to the edge of the trees, without a sound. A light breeze rustled limbs. Driblets of the earlier rainfall spilled from treetops, noisy and angry deluges to random spots of the forest floor.

Flannery wasn't sure where to look, or what to expect. Supposedly none of this was related to Conrad's—*Jimmy's*—buried body, but even if it were, she wasn't certain where to begin. Unsure if she could sniff out the dead and buried, the vast forest outweighed her patience. If *she* couldn't find a body, she knew Remy never would.

She needed to feed. Remy would be in the basement where she left him. He would have been there waiting a while by now, like the devoted servant she had made him. She could take some blood from him. Not a lot. Just enough. The blood from his stab wound was all she had ever taken—but enough to wield influence. It was time to drink again. This time in a more forthright way.

As she turned to leave, an intense red-orange-white flash of light deep into the woods caught her off guard. She spun back toward the trees.

"What the hell was that?" she said, going back in. It looked like a flare, but the hues were too bright. It faded as soon as it had come.

Flannery moved deeper into the woods and ignored the water droplets sprinkling down into her curly locks.

Something or someone *is close.* She felt a presence. Stealthy and quiet, she went toward the area where she had seen the bright light.

Flannery focused her sight, trying to pinpoint the exact location. She and Marcus had played in these woods as children, but that was long ago, and she couldn't remember the layout. Not that it would make a difference. The trees were different sizes and shapes all these years later. Some of the newer trees hadn't even been around back then. Nothing looked the same anymore.

Then she heard it. Someone ran. *Toward her.* Oh, this would be good. She could see the outline as a figure approached. Whoever it was *couldn't see her.* It was difficult to tell if it was a man or a woman. If only they knew what it was they ran toward!

Flannery felt powerful, confident. *Dangerous.* Unlike the night at the bike trail when she cowered behind Katarina. Instincts she had acquired in the past five years took over. She felt her canine teeth elongate. Whatever it was, *whoever* it was, they were *hers.* They took their final steps. She needed blood, and Remy slipped from her thoughts as she looked to a new target.

For the first time since several blood-deprived occasions in New Orleans, it was in her heart. The dead heart that no longer had a beat. *Murder.* She was hungry. She would kill whoever it was that came toward her.

This must be how Katarina feels all the time, Flannery thought. She went behind a tree where she could watch without being seen.

It ran. Yes, someone was about to regret a nighttime run through the woods. But not before they first answered a few questions.

It got closer. A woman, a young woman. Maybe she was still a teenager, Flannery thought. It was so hard to tell these days. But what was she wearing?

A Victorian-style top and a more progressive hoop mini-skirt. And was that black lipstick? The gifts of night vision. So many minor details could be picked up from afar.

Flannery sprang out and clotheslined the stranger when she came past the tree. The other woman, or girl, was on the ground. In an instant, Flannery was on top of her—fangs out for attack.

"Who are you?" Flannery demanded, as she pinned her down. "Why the hell are you out here in the dark, and *what* was that huge flash of light? Did you do that? Tell me. Before you die."

"Whoa, bitch. One question at a time," the young woman replied, out of breath but ready to fight back.

"Excuse me?" Flannery said. Nerves of steel! Who the hell did this little twit think she dealt with?

"Get the hell off me, man!" the other woman yelled, giving Flannery a hard shove that nearly did the trick.

"A strong one," Flannery replied, eyes wide, undeterred.

The other woman opened her mouth and revealed her own set of erect canines. "You think? *Now get the fuck off me!*" She shoved again with enough force to send Flannery flying backward into a tree.

"What the hell," Flannery said, scraping herself off the tree and brushing herself off. The impact would have broken the back of a human; it gave Flannery a tinge of pain that quickly evaporated.

"Sorry, but you're out of questions, man."

"I doubt that. Who are you?"

"Scarlett," she said. "But you have to answer a question for a question. Who the hell are you?"

"Flannery. Now tell me why you're out here on my family's property. You're a—um—a *vampire,* too?"

Scarlett gave a loud and husky laugh. Her bobbed, jet-black hair stayed in place as she shook her head every which way. Her small fingers protruded from cutoff silk gloves attached to the long sleeves of the silky black Victorian-style blouse. She wiggled them as she sprang to her feet with little effort.

"Oh hell no. I'm not a damn vampire. Don't insult me like that, man."

Flannery was too bewildered to point out to Scarlett that she was a woman and not a man. "But your teeth? Your strength?"

Scarlett was amused. She let her eyes wander, something that further riled Flannery.

"What was that bright light I saw off in the woods? Is that connected to you?"

Scarlett shrugged and pursed her lips into a demure smile.

"Why do you have those teeth and that strength if you're not one of the—" Flannery could barely spit it out. "—the, um, living dead?" Something inside her told her not to blurt out the 'v-word' again. If this odd young woman wasn't one of them, saying such a word could prove risky.

"I'm what you call a *hybrid*," Scarlett said, losing the attitude and looking warily behind her as she spoke to Flannery.

"A *what?*"

"Sorry, man, but our little 'Q and A' time is over. You want to know anymore then buy me dinner and some drinks. *Real* food and *real* alcohol. I've got a fake ID for the booze. I'm not much of a blood person. I mean, maybe sometimes, but not my choice, ya know."

"A *hybrid?* This is getting more confusing ..."

"For *you* maybe. Gotta run! Another time, Flannery. Dinner and drinks, man."

Scarlett took off through the woods, picking up speed and putting distance between them in only seconds. The sounds of her steps were gone within fifteen seconds. Flannery saw no one else chasing her and couldn't figure out why she ran as if pursued.

A hybrid? She had never heard of such. What did it mean?

She would pay Katarina another visit and seek answers.

But first, Flannery decided Remy had waited long enough.

Like the strange, blinding light in the forest, her desire to kill someone had come and gone.

22

A meaty aroma of frying sausage patties drifted into the dining from the kitchen. It made Travis queasy. He gulped orange juice and wore dark sunglasses. The juice tasted sour; it burnt his tongue. That wasn't the only burning sensation. The light from outside blazed through the white lace curtains of the window and dark lenses of his sunglasses. It hurt his eyes. Annoying clangs of plates and utensils on the table caused his head to ache.

Even in his bedroom with the black-out curtains, he had immediately grabbed the sunglasses the moment he awoke and felt the sun. It had come for him! A bright, malicious chase was back on downstairs, as the rays teased him through the open curtain.

"Why are you wearin' those ridiculous shades at the table?" D'Lynn asked, breaking his resentful scowl at the window. Because of her delicate condition, she was forced by Tarva to sit idly while the other woman did all the work. "You are even paler than normal, and why is that bandage on your neck? You look like somebody ... with a hangover! I hope you ain't started drinkin'!"

"The light hurts my eyes. I don't know why," Travis lied. He *knew* why, but he couldn't *say* why. There was an urge to be near D.C., wherever he was. But he was also tired. "I just want to go back to bed and sleep. I don't feel good."

"Did you get in the liquor cabinet last night?" D'Lynn continued, not letting go of her suspicion. "Don't lie to me, boy! I told Mister Lanehart years ago there should be a lock on it. I caught Geoff and one of his friends in there one time, back when they were your age." Then D'Lynn was sad at the thought of Geoffrey. "Poor little Geoff."

The mention of his bastard of a destroyed stepfather made Travis's head hurt worse. "I didn't go in the liquor cabinet," he said. At least that part was true. Unlike many of his other peers, alcohol experimentation had never been an interest of his. "I just feel bad."

"Do you have a fever?" D'Lynn asked. She reached over and touched his forehead with the back of her hand. "Oh my Lord!" she cried. "You're cold as ice!"

Maxine glanced back and forth at them from across the table and looked back down without saying anything.

"You still never told me why there's a bandage taped to your neck," D'Lynn continued. "What's the matter with—"

"I had an animal control officer come out. I even helped him catch that feral cat that was running around outside," Remy said, deflecting, as he entered the dining room. He could hear D'Lynn in the hallway before he arrived. "They got here early. Travis, how do you feel today?"

Remy took a seat at the table and stared hard at Travis to play along.

"A feral cat?" D'Lynn asked.

"Yes, Travis here found it last night. It scratched his neck and bit him when he picked it up. I looked at his neck and treated it," Remy said. "The cat was wild, but it's been taken away."

"The cat *bit* him?" D'Lynn raised her brows. "I've heard of 'em scratchin', but I never heard of a cat bitin' anybody when it attacked. That's why they have claws."

"I guess this was the exception," Remy said, covering his tracks, wondering if he should have come up with a better story. He was more of a dog person and unacquainted with feline behavior.

"Well, his head hurts and he's ice-cold," D'Lynn told Remy. "You need to take another look at him. Gosh, I hope that wild cat didn't give him some disease. They carry 'em sometimes. Travis, maybe you shouldn't go to school today."

"A disease is highly unlikely," Remy said, making it up as he went along. "I'll take a closer look at him after breakfast."

Tarva brought in two more plates and set them down in the center of the table with a thud that made Travis cringe. One plate had fresh biscuits; the other fried sausage patties, with a paper towel underneath to catch the grease.

Tarva and D'Lynn caught wind of what looked to be a hickey on the left side of Remy's neck as he sipped coffee, but they tried not to glare. They were aware of the looks Remy and Flannery had exchanged of late.

"Let me go get some butter and the scrambled eggs," Tarva said. She put on a cheerful big-toothed smile for everyone to cover disappointment over Remy's indiscretions with another woman.

D'Lynn frowned, as she inspected the plate of sausage patties from where she sat. "Tarva, those don't even look all the way done. I see pink."

"Well, I know I—"

"*Oh!*" D'Lynn cried, as her nose turned upward. She pointed to a suspicious patty at the corner of the plate. "That one there looks like it's still bleedin'. Tarva, for goodness sakes!"

Before Tarva could retrieve the plate, Travis, no longer put off by the smell, snatched up the questionable patty and took a quick, giant bite. It dripped red on to his hand as he gobbled up the rest of it in only three bites.

"Ohhh!" D'Lynn moaned, looking as if she could faint or have another heart spell. "*Travis!*"

"I'm hungry," Travis said. He looked up and saw D'Lynn, Tarva, Remy, and Maxine fixed on him. "What?"

"You're probably gonna have worms now," D'Lynn said.

"Oh, that's an old wives' tale," Tarva said, waving away the notion and taking the plate. "I can go cook these some more and get 'em better done."

"Please!" D'Lynn said, irritated. She sighed aloud once Tarva was gone. "I need to get better. I can't keep sittin' around watchin' somebody else do my work. She's a good girl and works hard, but she don't do nothin' the way I would. I love her and all, but that was a half-ass job on those patties." D'Lynn rarely swore and quickly covered her mouth in embarrassment.

"You need to take it easy a little while longer," Remy told her. "This house won't fall apart before you get your strength back."

"The only reason I'm here is because I'm the housekeeper. I'm just livin' here for free when I ain't workin'," D'Lynn said, with a touch of self-pity.

"Oh nonsense, D'Lynn. You've put in many years of faithful service here. You can put your feet up a while longer," said a voice from the doorway.

Clementine LeMonde—or what appeared to be Clementine to all of them—had slipped in through the front door.

D'Lynn discarded her melancholy state for the latest arrival. "Well hey there, hon. Didn't hear you walk in."

"It's time for me to go upstairs and relieve Henry. I wanted to drop in and say hello before I went up to spend the day with Marcus." Clementine's eyes peered around the room, as Conrad tried not to grow too enamored with the likeness of his former self before him. The eyes only paused briefly on Remy before they settled on Travis. "Why Travis, you don't look well."

Travis stared back through the dark shades. Something unsettled him; he looked away. Something about Clementine wasn't the same.

"Well, Travis, don't be rude," D'Lynn said, reaching over and nudging him on the arm. She looked back to where she saw Clementine. "He's not feelin' good this mornin'."

"Oh?" Conrad—as Clementine—replied, keeping a sharp gaze on Travis.

Travis looked up and spoke to Clementine—or whom he believed to be Clementine. "You sound different," he said. "What's the matter with you?"

"*Travis!*" D'Lynn snapped, excited again. She reached back over, this time with a light, scolding slap on his forearm. Then she shifted back to grandmotherly worry. "Oh my gosh, Travis, you are freezin'. Eat and go up to your room. You'll stay home from school and get some rest today."

Conrad was undeterred. "Why are you wearing, um, *wearin'* sunglasses in the house?" he asked, in a sweet feminine voice. *You little bastard.*

"Because the sun is in my eyes," Travis replied sarcastically. No, something wasn't right with her.

"Travis, why don't I have a look at you after you're done eating," Remy suggested. "Maybe we can chat about some other things as well."

Remy knew he had to go back into investigative mode. Even if Flannery had given him another mind-blowing and body-draining night in the basement.

He tried not to think about it, and Flannery was noticeably absent this morning. *I must refocus,* he thought. *Melissa was right. I'm here for Jimmy.*

"Oh my! Not only is there a bandage on Travis's neck, but Doctor Van Buren, is that a *rash* on yours?" Conrad found himself amused. Clementine's hand went to her chest for dramatic effect. Conrad even added a modest giggle, that of an innocent schoolgirl who had heard an off-color joke from one of the bad boys. "Why, Doctor Van Buren, it looks almost like you have a love bite!"

Remy was visibly uncomfortable. "It's just a rash. Maybe an allergic reaction. A wild cat attacked Travis outside last night, and I had to help catch it for animal control this morning. I think I'm allergic to them. I'm not sure," he said, rubbing the spot. He hardly knew Clementine and thought it bold of her to make such a comment.

"Interesting that only one spot on your neck is broken out if an allergic reaction to a cat caused that," Conrad said, pleased to put the doctor on the spot.

Travis stood from the table and moved past Clementine to leave the dining room.

"Wait, and I'll come with—" Remy called after him.

"Don't have time!" Travis called back, already in the foyer and going up the stairs as fast as he could, though he felt weak. He wanted to be away from everyone, including Remy and his accusatory interrogations.

Travis wondered where D.C. was, but somewhere in his mind he already knew he couldn't see him right now. He and D.C. were only casual acquaintances. Why was a groundskeeper on his mind in such a way? Travis remembered something from the woods last night, but nothing else registered about their encounter. He couldn't even remember returning to the house. The next thing he recalled after the woods was sitting on the couch with Remy and Flannery, as Remy checked his pulse and blood pressure.

Travis reached the top of the stairs and the long hallway to his room. It was darker than the rest of the house. Once inside his room with the door shut, his throbbing head and burning eyes settled. *Finally.* He would remain here the rest of the day. Everything would be better by the evening. He wasn't sure why he knew that, but he knew it would be easier once the sun set.

His smartphone buzzed. A text. Maybe it was D.C. *That was ridiculous.* What was up with this fascination with D.C.? All he knew about the guy was that he worked mostly around the stables, sometimes manicured the yard, and was romantically involved with his Uncle Marcus.

That must be it, Travis decided. Marcus was incapacitated and could stay in a stupor forever. D.C. was probably sad and needed a friend. Yes, that's all it was.

The text was from Regan.

Travis set down the phone and ignored it. For some reason, Regan was less important today than yesterday. Maybe it was time to end things. Maybe he didn't want to be in a relationship anymore. He would be eighteen at the end of the month. He would graduate high school in six months. It was time to move on after that.

Travis walked over to the aquarium where Harry the tarantula lazily strolled across a bed of sawdust. Perhaps looking for one of the crickets his master routinely dropped in for him. His eight legs moved in slow succession, as he crept from one side of his small space to the other. Much of the time he was like a furry rock in the aquarium, hours without as much as a twitch. This morning he was more alert than usual.

Travis stared pensively at his exotic pet. *I feel so strange,* he thought. It felt like no other kind of illness he had ever had in his young life. *My head. My eyes.*

He watched Harry's lackadaisical stroll.

I'm still hungry, he thought, realizing what he must do next.

Travis lifted the lid on the aquarium and stuck his hand inside to greet Harry, who obediently lurched forward until he settled in his master's palm.

23

"Stupid, stupid, fucking stupid. All of them," Conrad muttered through Clementine's clenched teeth, as her body reached the top of the stairs.

Conrad thought of Remy at the breakfast table, comfortably immersed with the household. The playfulness was gone; bitterness boiled beneath Clementine's blonde locks.

Remy's look. Remy's sound. Damn it, how Conrad missed that body. Well, not *that* body, but the other half that split and grew alongside Remy in Mrs. Van Buren's womb. The Van Buren gene pool was a blessed one, of that there was no doubt.

Then there was the *reason* he didn't have that body anymore. Fucking punk-ass Travis. What the hell was going on with the little redneck-accented Goth bastard these days? He wanted to walk down to the end of the hallway, burst into the room, and strangle the life out of the little son of a bitch—slowly! Conrad knew he would take great delight when he felt the skinny teenager's pulse fade and then cease forever. Travis's defenses would be down. He would never see such a move coming. Not from a sweet, church pew-warmer like Clementine LeMonde.

Do you know *how wonderful my life was inside that body? How much sex I got?* he would hiss, so only Travis could hear him, as he choked the little bastard to death. *I couldn't walk down the street without women— and even some men—wanting me and hitting on me. Now I hang around this house as some plain Jane that not even a dipshit like Wes Washer wants anything to do with! Not only that, as a* woman, *no less. Oh, and let's not forget I spend most of my days as a woman sitting and staring at your vegetable of an uncle, when I'm not changing his diapers, wiping his ass, or making sure he doesn't fall out of his chair or get a bedsore. Die, you little bastard, die!*

Yes, those would be the last words the punk would hear. Wait! No, not *all* of them.

Conrad loved Marcus. He didn't mind having to look at him or change his diapers or turn him every so often. In sickness and in health, he thought. If he had married his beloved Marcus as he had wanted, then he would care for him the exact same way. He would never leave his bedside. *My Adam who returned to me.*

But if Travis hadn't decapitated Jimmy's body, then Conrad and Marcus would be happy together right now; Marcus wouldn't be in this helpless position. Yes, yes, as soon as he was sure Marcus saw reason, Conrad would start withholding the pills and allow him to return to life. Once Marcus came around they could pick up where they had left off last spring. It might not happen overnight, but Marcus would learn to love him.

Bottom line: it *all* went back to Travis. Conrad found Clementine standing outside Travis's door, but he knew he couldn't allow himself to go into the room. Killing Travis would cause a mess that couldn't be explained away.

I must keep up the ruse ... for now. Play nice with the Laneharts, even remain somewhat civil with that wretched backstabbing bitch Flannery, whom he also wanted to destroy. Stomach a few more evening meals with Reverend Wilkins Washer, whom he despised. He was in constant fear the fat old widower might put the moves on Clementine when they were alone. The elder Washer was difficult to read, and Conrad could never tell what the old windbag was thinking underneath his expanded girth and puffy countenance.

While I'm here ... Conrad remained outside Travis's door. He could *see* through the closed door, into the room.

And just what the hell have we here? Before him—an unusual and grotesque sight!

Travis's sunglasses were gone, and he stuck a—tarantula?—he held on a palm to his mouth. No, *into* his mouth! What was this? Conrad recognized the pet spider Harry that Travis kept. He was fascinated and couldn't take his eyes away from the boy.

Travis squeezed the large, hairy arachnid and moved it into and out of his mouth, with awful slurping sounds all the while. Something oozed out of the large spider. It appeared in a helpless struggle! Almost like Travis had in Conrad's fantasy. But his fantasy hadn't included those crude suckling sounds. What in the hell was Travis doing? *Eating Harry?!* Those god-awful sounds. The *sounds*. A freakish meld of disgust, pleasure, and satiation all in one. It reminded Conrad of ...

He flashed back to Flannery's attack on Tilda Lanehart in the study downstairs last spring. The way Flannery slurped on her sister-in-law at the end of the feeding, when it was well past the point of return.

Then, later that night, Tilda did the same thing to Rochelle Dubois. He had lain eyes on that glorious and monstrous feast as well.

Now, *Travis* behaved in this manner? Was he now one of the undead?

R.I.P., Harry.

Conrad backed Clementine away from the door and down the hallway.

"Oh my," he said aloud, chuckling to himself as he reached the door to Marcus's room. "This is good. This is way, *way* good. I may have to *destroy* the little bastard rather than kill him."

24

"What is a hybrid?" Flannery asked Katarina, in the third-floor lair later that night.

"Why do you ask?" Katarina replied, as she paced the room. She had other things on her mind.

"I'm just curious," Flannery smiled, not wanting to show her hand just yet.

Katarina stopped pacing and faced her. "Something has happened you are not telling me, or you would not ask this."

"I just heard D.C. say something about ..."

"Do *not* lie to me," Katarina snapped. "D.C. has told you nothing. I heard your conversation on the porch last evening. You scolded him about Travis, warned him to stay away from your new love, as well as your brother. You think I was not listening?"

"Wow, did anyone ever tell you eavesdropping is rude?"

"What is it you are up to with the doctor?"

"I am merely causing a distraction to slow him down. Remy's only here to try and find out information about his brother. I'll divert him until I can figure out how to throw him off track and send him away."

"Oh yes, it would cause much trouble for your brother and nephew if he were to find that body. Or find out *where* it is."

"In the woods, I presume, and yes it would."

"But you lie," Katarina continued. "You're developing feelings for him."

"I'm sure you've lied to me about a few things, and I don't have feelings for anybody," Flannery countered, with a smirk. "Remy's just a plaything."

"The whore got her groove back, and now she's in love. It reeks of a bad romance novel. Except the heroine is no longer among the living."

"Speaking of diversions, you've completely changed the subject. On purpose. Tell me, Katarina, *what* is a hybrid?"

Katarina paced the room again.

"*Well ...?*"

Katarina paused yet again and heaved an annoyed sigh. "It is exactly what you think it is. Part human, part vampire."

"How is that even possible? We're dead. We can't reproduce and have babies. How do you come up with a combo?"

"You leave an open wound when you bite someone ..." Katarina cringed as she second-guessed her decision to let Flannery in on a truth.

"So, Travis ...?"

"I am not sure. You would have to keep an eye on him and figure it out. Or perhaps D.C. would know, which is highly doubtful."

"So, you have a hybrid when you leave the wound open for too long. Then what?"

"The hybrid is half-human, half-dead. They can survive without blood, but they still crave it sometimes. They can be triggered into drinking. They still eat and drink as a human. For the *most* part."

"And then...?"

"A hybrid can live a mostly-human life. A hybrid can even have children. But, my little whore friend, the child of a hybrid can *never* be one of us. A hybrid ages half as fast as a human. When a hybrid turns fifty years old, they have the body and appearance of a twenty-five-year-old human. When they are one hundred years old, they appear fifty in human years. And so on. On a hybrid's one hundred fiftieth birthday, they must finally make a choice."

"They look and feel like a seventy-five-year-old human by that point?"

"Yes. They must decide whether to fully die and continue as a vampire, or die a mortal death ... and be gone. If they choose to be a vampire, they revert back to the appearance they had when they first turned hybrid."

"Travis has no choice now but to live to be one hundred and fifty years old?"

"*If* he is a hybrid, yes. But hybrids are also half-mortal. Anything that can kill a human can still kill them. Should an unfortunate accident bring down a hybrid, it is then up to the hybrid's Maker whether to leave them or turn them."

"I'll stake D.C. in his sleep!" Flannery shouted.

"Calm yourself, whore. You toyed with the notion of killing your nephew before D.C. attacked him," Katarina said. "Why do you act as if you suddenly care about Travis? Such a strange show of concern, no?"

"I would've never followed through with killing him," Flannery said. "Plus, he's a Lanehart. He's my family. Not D.C.'s, not yours. *Mine.* I should have a say in what goes on in this house!"

"I told you to calm yourself. Besides, Travis isn't *really* a Lanehart, no? And based on your nephew's dark style, this could be something he enjoys. Think of it this way ... he doesn't have to fully commit."

"This isn't like leasing a car, Katarina, and I don't think he will be happy with this later. One day he'll snap out of this funky little Goth phase of his."

"He can still go to school. He can go out in the daytime, though he will be more sensitive to the light."

"Where is D.C.? There must be a way to reverse all of this."

Katarina gave her usual cackle. "Good luck with that. Would you like a genie and three wishes while he is at it?"

"I blame you for all of this. I want you gone from this house soon. How much longer do you plan to hang around?"

"When I feel it is time," Katarina replied, with a shrug. "You know the terms. What will happen if you try to evict me."

"Yes, you've made it clear. Repeatedly."

"You went to the woods last night?"

"Maybe," Flannery said. If Katarina wouldn't give her a move-out date, then why should she give away anything?

However, as legitimate as the hybrid question was, it had also been Flannery's way to try and find out if Katarina knew who this strange

Scarlett person was.

Then there was the flash-bang and that fleeting wave of light. And more questions. This Scarlett person must be connected to it somehow.

Katarina studied Flannery. "Well, either you did or did not go?"

"I invited you to go. You should've come along. We could've made a girls' night of it."

"Did you run into anyone?" Katarina asked, raising a brow.

Damn it, Flannery thought. She does know. Flannery was starting to know Katarina's gestures and mannerisms all too well. *She's seeing how much rope she can give me to hang myself.* "Why do you ask?"

"Because you are asking about hybrids, and I know you have not spoken to your nephew today. That is why. Somebody else has put you on to this, and I *know* it is not D.C. I did not choose him for his brain!" The Scandinavian accent was always more prominent when Katarina raised her voice.

"So?" Flannery would play this out until she had to cave.

"I assume you ran into someone in the woods who put you on to this hybrid fascination? You were out in the woods to find answers about Travis, but you ran across something else? *Into* someone else?"

"Why do you keep asking these tedious questions when you already know the answers? Good God, were you perched out there on a tree limb? Spying?"

Katarina smiled. "I was not there, but I know you were. And I know you ran into Scarlett."

"Why? Did she tell you?"

"No, stupid whore, *you* just did."

The bitch! And damn my big mouth, Flannery thought. "Okay, fine. Scarlett. Who the hell is she? She looked more Goth than Travis, and she was dressed like she was going to a Halloween party."

Katarina put her nose in the air. "She is no one you should be concerned with. She is like Rochelle Dubois. A little out of control. Perhaps it is time to bring her down a notch."

"Where does she live, and why does she run through the woods in the middle of the night? A weird time and place to get your exercise."

"It is not important."

"I disagree. Is *she* the reason you're hanging around here? Or is she *connected* to the reason? You said you had some big secret about Ten Points to share with me when I found you in the study the other night. Is this Scarlett person somehow related to that?"

"All in good time. There is no need for you to be concerned with this ... for now. I am done answering questions for tonight. One thing at a time. You wanted to know what a hybrid is. Now you know."

"That's not all I want to know."

"That is *all* you will know for now. Patience."

Flannery hated Katarina, but she knew she had no recourse. She left her nemesis on the third floor and went down to the second floor, as Clementine stepped out of Marcus's room.

Someone else she loathed. The two of them eye-locked until they were only feet apart in the hallway.

"Strange to see you come down from the third floor, Flannery. I didn't think anybody used that part of the house anymore." Clementine wore a sly grin and stood with her arms crossed, as if she mimicked Flannery's common stance.

"My comings and goings are none of your concern, Clementine. How is my brother today?"

"He's the same, and there's no need to get all catty, Flannery. I wasn't trying to be nosy."

"Has Doctor Fortier been back this week?" Flannery asked. She was in no mood to let the conversation go longer than necessary; she was still agitated from her chat with Katarina.

"Yes. Everything's the same. No changes. Some of the people at church are including Marcus on the list of people they pray for in their Tuesday prayer group. Reverend Washer won't include him by name on Sundays because of, *well*, you know ..."

Flannery smiled and decided to drag it along after all. "No, I ... *don't* ... know. Please tell me why."

"Well, Flannery, because Marcus is a homosexual and all ..."

"I hope a bolt of lightning comes through the church roof one day and strikes down that fat old goat."

Conrad gave Clementine an expression of surprise and dismay. *Good one, Flannery,* he thought. "Flannery! What a terrible thing to say about a man of God!"

"He's no more a man of God than I am," Flannery replied. "He's a bigot and a hatemonger. I'm surprised Wes is as well-adjusted as he is ... growing up with a Daddy like that."

"I can't believe you wish such bad things on poor Reverend Washer."

"He isn't *poor* Reverend anything, and no, I won't shed a tear if he falls over dead anytime soon."

"That is just a ... hateful ... thing to say. Does it really make you any different than you claim he is?" *Hypocritical bitch.*

"I would like to see my brother now!"

"Well, you can go in there, but sadly, it's the same sight day after day. Speaking of people in your family who aren't well, I wonder if Travis feels any better tonight?"

"You've seen Travis?" Flannery asked. She peered down the hallway toward his closed bedroom door.

"Yes. Something was wrong with him this morning. He was wearing sunglasses at the breakfast table. Odd! D'Lynn kept him home from school." *Then he went into his room and ate a spider like it was a beignet. He may finally have something in common with you besides being a mutual illegitimate bastard.*

"I'll check on Marcus later. I need to see about Travis," Flannery said.

Conrad kept a smile on Clementine's face as Flannery walked away. Then he decided to be playful and throw a nugget her way. "Oh, Flannery?"

She turned back. "What?"

"Do you ever miss Travis's mother? *Tilda?*"

"Pardon?" Clementine wouldn't know about that! Why did she bring up Tilda?

"Oh ... never mind."

Flannery would get to the bottom of that strange exchange later. She reached the end of the hallway and burst into Travis's room without even a knock.

"What the hell," he said, caught off guard. He lay across his bed with a graphic novel. "You can't just barge in here like that. I'm a teenage boy.

What if I had been jackin' off or something?"

"Oh, please!" Flannery closed the door and stood at the foot of his bed. "Now shut the hell up and listen to me! I'm the adult here. You're the child. Look at me!"

"What? Why? No, I don't have to—"

"Do it!" she ordered.

"No," Travis refused, looking back down at the comic book.

Flannery snatched the book from underneath him and tossed it across the room.

Before he could mouth off anymore, she stopped him with a look and began. "I know D.C. attacked you last night, and I know he left a big wound on your neck that he didn't close and Remy treated it. What I didn't know ... damn it."

What I didn't realize was what would end up happening. I'm responsible for this. I engineered the whole attack, she thought, staring at him. It's *my* fault—no one else's!—you've been turned into this.

I didn't know. She knew how to create the undead. She knew nothing of hybrids, not until the encounter with Scarlett. Anger traversed her cold innards. *Damn you, Katarina. You never taught me anything as a Maker should have. I'm sick of your games. I'm sick of this existence night after night for all eternity. My life, all gone. Now half of Travis's. Gone because of you. Who knows what else you will manipulate, whose lives you will destroy, if you remain in this house. You knew what D.C. would do if he attacked Travis. I didn't!*

"I'll fucking destroy Katarina for this," Flannery said, seething, as Travis looked at her strangely.

It was time. The bitch held her hostage. Only someone else had to destroy Katarina. Katarina was her Maker. But Flannery *could* have someone else do the destroying for her.

"What? Katarina? Who's that?" Travis asked.

"Never mind," Flannery said to him. "The less you know, the safer you are."

Flannery turned to leave.

"Wait, where are you goin'? You barged in here like a maniac, and you're not even gonna tell me why?"

"I'll talk to you later," Flannery said. "Something's come up."

"You're such a weirdo," Travis said, rolling off the bed to fetch his graphic novel as she left the room.

Flannery ignored the verbal jab and closed the door. She turned around and nearly ran into Clementine who stood waiting in the hallway.

"What the hell!" Flannery barked, repeating Travis's words a moment earlier. "Are you following me? What is the deal?"

"*Look into my eyes ...*" Their faces were inches apart.

Flannery almost screamed but caught herself in time. She hadn't screamed in years; she wouldn't now. "No way," she said, in a breathless whisper. "You have *got* to be joking ..."

"I know you hate me almost as much as you hate Katarina, but you also know I'm the only one who can help you get rid of her," Conrad said, putting a satisfied smile across Clementine's face.

25

"There's more to this, Conrad. Tell me."

"Shhh! Henry could be back any minute. Don't get into the habit of calling me that." It was Clementine's body and voice, but it was somebody else with whom Flannery had the conversation.

"There's no way I can trust you. The last time we saw each other you were hell bent on having me destroyed. What if I don't want your help?"

"Let's let bygones be bygones ... for now. I'm the *only* choice you have. You can't possibly tell anyone else she's been hiding out in this house the better part of a year. You would be foolish *not* to ask for my help!"

"I would be the frog taking a ride across the water on a scorpion. You'll sting me even if it means drowning both of us. I know you're still pissed I told Tilda what you and Geoff were up to with Bobby. I ruined your big plan. There's no way you would ever help me unless something was in it for you."

"Maybe there is."

Marcus could make them out by shape and the colors of their hair and clothes. They were foggy; everything was foggy. He heard them talk. He understood some words but couldn't understand everything.

He had heard enough.

"I'm not so sure about that," Flannery said.

"That's a gamble you'll have to take with me, I suppose. You do want Katarina gone, don't you?"

"Let's go outside. I'll pretend I'm walking Clementine out for the day.

But, listen, Con—*Clementine!*—Katarina's got a secret about this place, and I have to figure out what it is before you get rid of her."

"Well, well, well. Always trying to uncover somebody else's secret are you, Flannery? How familiar all of this sounds!"

"I think this secret of hers has something to do with somebody in our family named Alexander Lanehart. It was a name on some business card I found inside her vanity. It was a new card, nothing from a long time ago. I've never heard of him. Obviously, I can't ask Marcus about it. Tell me, Conrad, do you know who Alexander Lanehart is?"

"Clementine, damn it, call me *Clementine!* And, no, Alexander Lanehart doesn't ring any bells. I must say I'm flattered by all this newfound trust, Flannery."

"You double-crossed me and let her out of the water ... long before last spring, I've discovered. She's been inside this house for months and God only knows where else before that. I'm putting myself out on a limb. You helped Katarina against me when you let her escape. Again, why turn it all around and help me, Conrad?"

"I won't say it again ... *stop* calling me that!" Clementine's voice growled, the temper fragile as always.

"Okay then, *Clementine,* let me walk you downstairs."

"I have to give Marcus his medication before I leave," the Clementine voice said. "It will only take a moment."

"I don't like the idea of you being alone with him all day."

"You know I would never harm my Adam, and you don't have much of a choice right now, do you? Not if you want my help with Katarina."

"*Adam?* You're still hung up on that delusion?"

Clementine's hand slid something into Marcus's mouth.

Time for this again, Marcus thought groggily. But he had gotten good at it. *Must not swallow. Hold it in place. Under tongue.* The bitter taste of the pill filled his mouth, as he slowly tucked it underneath his tongue.

Clementine's hand was back at his mouth, this time with a bottle of water. The hand forced his mouth open; a splash went in. Marcus let it wash down; he made a gulping noise to indicate he swallowed. He still felt the wet pill in place beneath his tongue. The water hadn't forced it out. Thank God.

"Okay, he has his medicine. Let's go," said the voice that belonged to Clementine but delivered the words of someone else. *Something else.*

Marcus watched them exit the room beneath a cloud, Clementine—or Conrad, rather—behind Flannery.

It was a struggle, but his arm moved upward, with the dexterity of an injured snail, until his hand neared his lips. The tube from the IV drip dangled in front of him, as if he were a marionette, as he dug inside of his half-numb mouth and allowed the wet, saliva-soaked pill to slide out and into his palm. He slowly and carefully lowered his arm down near his thigh.

With a lethargic hand, and careful, clandestine care, he stuffed the pill into the crack between the fabric and the arm of the chair where he had stashed the other two pills from yesterday and that morning. A long and tedious process. It took a full minute; it felt like an hour.

Flannery was forming another alliance with the Devil. All to get rid of someone named Katarina. The name rang a bell. Rusty wheels turned. Marcus struggled to remember.

Katarina. Katarina?

Yes! Katarina. That was the name of Frank Castille's wife. But she had gone missing at the same time as her senator husband nearly six years ago. What did she have to do with all of this? Wasn't she presumed dead? And she knew a secret about Ten Points? What in the bloody hell had gone on in this house that he had missed?

How long have I been out of it? He's drugged me again.

Again. Damn it! Only this time it had lasted much, *much* longer.

Marcus would put a stop to it.

I'm coming back, he thought. Just a few more missed pills ...

He knew what he had to do when he did come back.

26

Wes Washer was anxious and fidgety the next morning when he met Remy at a roadside diner about five miles away from Ten Points. The place smelled of hash browns and grease. Truckers and the working class filled the place as they stopped in for a bite or a cup of coffee. Wes was a regular. Remy saw it as another immersion into southern culture. Nothing bad. Just different.

A heavyset, brunette waitress with acne scars and a bad perm was overly attentive, stopping frequently and refilling their coffee cups whenever they reached the quarter mark. The excessive caffeine worsened Wes's twitchy behavior. Despite his deputy's uniform, he had the demeanor of a meth head. He repeatedly looked up and then down at his coffee cup and back up to Remy.

"So, have you seen Flannery? Does she ever talk about me?" Wes asked, blinking rapidly. He rubbed at the left side of his neck.

"I—I don't think ... You two are friends or something?" Remy said, flustered at the mention of Flannery. He wasn't aware she and Wes knew one another.

"Well, *yeah!*" Wes replied, as if Remy was supposed to know. "We only grew up and went to school together. I mean, we'd probably be married by now if she hadn't run off and tried to make a life for herself in New Orleans."

"New Orleans?"

"Yeah. I mean, you know what happened there? She got mixed up with that senator." Wes shook his head. "She strayed from the path of the Lord. Ended up committin' adultery and it became front-page news."

"How is that?" Remy asked, interest piqued.

"Well, I mean, I'm sure it was even in the newspapers up north in Chicago. The senator and his wife went missin', and then pictures of him and Flannery kissin' in his office came out on the news."

"He and his wife disappeared? Was Flannery a suspect?"

"No. It also came out that Frank Castille had a lot of dealin's with Mafia types. Everybody thinks they buried him in a river somewhere with them cement shoes you always hear about on TV shows."

"I don't understand—"

"You know, the concrete shoes weigh down the body so it don't float back up—"

"No, not that. I mean, how all these people disappear around Flannery, but she never comes under scrutiny by the police. This senator and his wife. Then her brother, his wife, and their son. Am I leaving anybody out?"

Remy made a mental note to go online later and look for whatever he could find out about a Senator Castille and his wife.

"Well, there's your brother. Ain't nobody seen him since Geoffrey, Tilda, and little Bobby went missin'. No offense, Doctor, but your brother and his hangin' around Ten Points was a little shady. If anybody's responsible for Geoffrey and them's disappearin', I'd look at your brother or that Devil-worshippin' Travis Lanehart before I accused Flannery of anything."

"Tell me what happened the morning you went to the house. Don't leave anything out."

"Now *that's* official sheriff's business!" Wes snapped.

"I don't give a shit about sheriff's business," Remy said calmly, working to keep his temper in check. "Tell me anyway. I need to figure out what happened to my brother. I'm tired of roadblocks." Flannery entered his mind again. "And other distractions."

Wes sighed and rubbed the left side of his neck again.

"What's wrong with your neck?" Remy asked. "You keep touching it."

"I don't know," Wes grumbled. He became self-conscious and placed his hand back on the table. "Okay, we got a nine-one-one call last April from little Maxine Lanehart who heard scary noises downstairs and was afraid bad stuff was goin' on. I was still on duty, so the dispatcher sent me to Ten Points to check it out."

"*And?*"

"It didn't turn out to be anything. All I remember is bein' out in the front yard. Then there were some of Geoffrey's clothes and a pair of Bobby's pajamas scattered by the front porch and in the grass."

"Their clothes?"

"Yeah, the only thing we could figure out later was that Geoffrey took off with Tilda and Bobby. They were in such a hurry that they dropped stuff on their way to the car. And there was this weird dust everywhere. All I can remember."

"*All* you can remember? Wes, from the moment you arrived until you left ... *tell me* what happened!"

"I'm tellin' you. All I remember is drivin' up, and the next thing I know, I'm stumblin' around in the front yard of the house. There's this gap in between that I can't remember."

"There's time you can't account for, and that's not *anything?* I really don't understand what you're saying. You have to explain this to me a little more clearly."

"Are you sure Flannery ain't said anything about me ...?" The hand sprang back to his neck.

"Wes, *focus,*" Remy interrupted. "What else? Was my brother anywhere around that morning?"

"No, I never seen him," Wes said. "The last time I saw your brother was when everybody went back to the house the night before, right after Mister Lanehart's funeral. But the night before *that,* well, that was another weird night, too."

"Why? What happened?"

"I had to go to Ten Points and check out a report from Zeke Colson about dead ducks and a raccoon in the front yard."

"Yeah, you told me that the first time we met. And you said Travis did it?"

"Travis is a Devil worshipper! Ain't you been around him enough now to figure that out? He dresses in black, his nose is pierced. He has all those earrings in one ear. He dyes his hair black as night. And he don't like *white* girls."

Remy ignored the racist undertones of the last part. "So you've said."

"I'm tellin' you. You need to be askin' that child of Satan about your brother. I only saw your brother briefly the night I stopped by to ask Geoff about the animals. Your brother was paradin' around the house without a shirt on. Probably tryin' to impress Flannery."

"The shirtless part sounds like my brother," Remy remarked. "He spent years in Hollywood trying to be noticed and become famous." He stopped and wondered why he was telling Wes all of this. "I guess he still wanted an audience wherever he could get one," Remy finished. Saddened, he stared down into his cup of coffee.

"Well, you need to talk to that teenage devil-lover Travis. You've been stayin' there. You've had plenty of opportunity, I'm sure."

Wes squirmed in his seat more. He continued to play with his neck when the waitress returned to refill his coffee cup for the fifth time. Remy held up a hand to cut himself off when she moved the pot toward his cup.

"Yes, Ten Points is an interesting place," Remy said.

"I used to think so," Wes said. Then he leaned in. "But now I think it's a *hell house!*"

"Pardon? A *what?*"

"You heard me," Wes said. "But I wear the armor of the Lord, so I ain't afraid to walk in there if I have to."

"I see," Remy said, in no mood to entertain further rambling. He reached for his wallet. "Thank you for your time. I'm the one who asked you to meet, so I'll get your coffee."

"Why don't you stay and order somethin'?" Wes suggested. "They have really good food here."

"I'm not hungry, but thanks," Remy said, flagging down the waitress.

"Okay then, but tell Flannery I said hi," Wes said, then furiously stroked his neck.

Flannery, Remy thought, as he drove away a few minutes later.

One of the places his brother was spotted in recent years was New Orleans. Flannery spent time there as well. Could there be a connection?

From what Remy had learned thus far, Jimmy called himself 'Conrad' and was friends with Geoffrey Lanehart. There was nothing but New Orleans that connected him to Flannery.

New Orleans was a large city. It could all be a coincidence. Maybe not.

It was still early when Remy arrived back at Ten Points. Travis was outside his own car, carrying a backpack and about to leave for school.

As always, the teenager was dressed in black; he still bore a paler and sickly look. He wore the sunglasses. Remy squinted as he watched the boy from inside the rental car. *Why* hadn't he insisted on a better examination of Travis, taken him to a hospital? Or had he tried and was stopped? *Was it really a feral cat attack?* He was no longer certain.

"How are you feeling, Travis?" Remy asked, when he stepped out of the rental.

Travis was eager to take off in his older-model black Camaro. "Fine," he said, not slowing down, not wanting conversation.

Remy did not care. "Do you have a moment?"

"No, I'm gonna be late," he said, as he opened the car door.

Remy stepped over and put his hand on Travis's arm to stop him. "Then you'll be late," he said.

"You need to fuck off, man," Travis said, jerking his arm away. "That's a Conrad move you just pulled!"

"A *Conrad* move?"

"Oh right, I meant to say *Jimmy*. Because that was his real name, right?"

"Yes," Remy said. "We've put this off long enough. I get the feeling you two interacted while he was here. I get the feeling you didn't like him very much."

"I don't wanna talk about—"

"Tough shit," Remy said. He moved between Travis and the car. "We'll talk about it now, and you'll have to get a tardy mark at school."

"That's what *he* tried to do," Travis said. "Come in this house and take over and boss people around."

"I'm not trying to take over anything or boss anybody. I just want answers, and none of you are very forthcoming. *How* did he try to take over? Tell me! What can you tell me about my brother!" Remy yelled, something he rarely did. He was tired of being nice. He had said in front of the world he would leave no stone unturned when he arrived in Louisiana, and it was about damn time he stuck to his word.

"He wasn't your brother!" Travis yelled back.

Remy flinched as if he had been struck. "What do you mean? Wasn't my brother?"

Whatever color remained in Travis's face, his big mouth had drained. "Um ... You know, he just went by that different name. Pretended to be somebody else. He acted like he didn't wanna be found, man."

"You're not telling me everything," Remy said. "You're backpedaling. I want to know. I *need* to know. What happened before he left here? How did he leave here? Did he indicate where he might go? Travis, please, I've spent seven years without answers. If you can help me, give me any leads to help me find him, I'm begging you. *Please.*"

How did he leave here? Wouldn't you *like to know!* Travis thought, as he stared back at Remy through the dark sunglasses. The doctor's pulsating jugular vein stirred him. He had to ignore it. What was this? *These feelings.* Just as quickly, something told him that Remy was *Flannery's.* Travis couldn't have what was Flannery's.

But how do I know that?

"What?" Remy asked. "You look like you're about to tell me something."

Travis shook off a momentary distraction. "I can't help you. All I know is that your brother was friends with Geoffrey."

"Your stepfather?"

"Well, my legal adoptive Dad, but yes, stepfather is more like it. They were friends. Your brother was gone the day Geoffrey and my Mom and brother went missing. I don't know nothin' else."

"Please, Travis, *think*. Are you sure there's not some little detail, anything you can tell me? It's very important that I—"

"I told you, man!" Travis snarled, angry again. "Now get the hell out of my way so I can leave."

Remy moved aside as Travis got into the car. He started the engine, backed around, and sped away in seconds. Clouds of dust spun up and weaved through the rows of oaks down the Ten Points driveway as the Camaro hauled off into the distance and disappeared. Remy could still hear the car after he couldn't see it any longer.

Remy started for the house as Tarva and Maxine came down the curved steps of the front porch.

"He is bein' a speed demon this mornin'," Tarva said, about Travis. She smiled big for Remy. "What in the world is his hurry? He needs to be more careful."

"I guess he's worried he'll be late for school," Remy said, walking past.

"Well, I better get this one here to school before she's late," Tarva called after him. "Maybe I'll see you later when I come back?"

Remy went inside the house and found D'Lynn seated alone at the dining room table with the newspaper. She looked up and greeted him with a small smile; it dissolved with his solemn glare.

"D'Lynn," he said. "I need to ask you something."

"Yeah?" she asked, both curious and fearful.

"Why doesn't Flannery ever come around during the daytime?"

D'Lynn glanced back at the newspaper, as if she regretted ever smiling at him. "You need to ask her about that."

"But you know the answer?"

She fumbled with the newspaper pages. "I—I, um, you just need to ask her about it. I don't have no definite answers about any of that."

Remy left the dining room and climbed the stairs to his bedroom. He would probably never get the answers he needed here. Maybe it was time to leave. It could all be another dead end in seven years of searching and wondering.

He paused at the top of the stairs. His time with Flannery. In the basement, and in the living room with Travis. Like Wes, there seemed to be gaps of time for which he couldn't account. He recalled a beginning and an end to his latest sexual encounter with Flannery in the basement, but the details in between were foggy. Then a red spot on his neck in the same spot where Travis had puncture wounds. The same spot where Wes kept rubbing his neck at the diner.

"*Vampire.*" For whatever reason, the word slipped off his tongue, but he wasn't sure what it meant. *What did I just say?* Travis's word in the living room when he was delirious.

Remy reached the top of the stairs and slowly walked down the hallway to his bedroom door. Then he saw *it,* as he glanced back toward the staircase to the dormant third floor.

The three small children stood at the foot of the staircase staring at him. Two boys and a girl. Under ten years old; dressed in clothes from what looked to be the nineteenth century.

Remy froze and stared at them for a few seconds, unsure what he saw. He felt the shaky words stumble out of his mouth. "Hello? What are you—?"

He lost his breath before he could finish. The three children said nothing; they turned toward the other set of stairs down to the foyer. A slow and methodical descent stole them from Remy's line of sight.

"Hey ... wait," Remy said, able to talk again. Able to move again. He went to the staircase.

But when he got there, they were gone. He raced down the stairs, turning his head this way and that when he reached the foyer. No sign of children in old clothes from another time anywhere.

"What the hell," he muttered to himself.

He stood in the middle of the foyer, trying to comprehend what he had seen—or if he had really seen anything at all.

27

Percy Stratworth's house reeked of the ammonia of Mozart's piss, even more so than the previous week. Maxine turned up her nose as she walked in, timidly, the dreaded hum of Percy's motorized scooter behind her on the way to the living room. There was the grand piano, in its usual spot. More piles of newspapers had gathered beside a chair since last week.

The four o'clock angle of the sun through a window cast a repulsive shadow in the living room in front of Maxine. Across the wide floor ahead of her, she saw an even heftier Percy, a larger scooter, and the unmistakable shape of the beret on his head. He navigated behind as she went toward the piano. Dust particles swam through the air where the late afternoon sunlight burned through an old beige curtain in dire need of cleaning.

The blue-purple parrot over in the corner squawked loudly in its cage. Maxine thought she might be ill. She clutched her stomach; she wished she could have stayed in the car with Tarva.

"What's the matter, little Miss Lanehart?" came the voice behind her. "Are you not prepared for today?"

Maxine hesitated before she shook her head.

"Cat got your tongue?" Percy asked. A curtailed giggle made Maxine's stomach clench and knot up faster than it usually did when she was around him. "Mozart, give Miss Lanehart her tongue back," he said, to the fat orange cat that almost never left his lap.

Maxine hated the cat and the reek of its piss almost as much as she hated Percy.

"I don't feel good," Maxine said. "Can I call Tarva to come back and get me?"

"Now, Maxine," Percy said, moving the scooter alongside her. "You'll never get better if you don't practice."

"But I—"

"Go have a seat on the bench, Maxine," he said, his tone quiet and serious. Thankfully, he wasn't flashing any yellow teeth. But he stared her down with the bloodshot blue eyes.

Maxine thought again she might throw up but made it to the bench.

Then it happened. She heard the pen fall on to the floor and roll underneath the piano bench, as if he had tossed it.

"Can you be a dear and crawl under there and get that for me, little Miss Lanehart?" he requested, in a sweeter tone.

"Don't you have another pen?" she asked, hardly able to talk.

"No!" he said pointedly. "I *must* have that one. Now please fetch it for me."

With some hesitation, Maxine went down to her knees and started crawling, feeling her skirt move up her legs as she fumbled around underneath the bench. She wanted more than anything not to be there. She wanted to tell, but she was afraid. She didn't know who to tell.

She bumped her head as she crawled backwards from underneath the bench and felt the tears roll out of her eyes. She knew he had taken his phone and camera back out today.

"Now. Let's do something different today, little Miss Lanehart. When you sit back on the bench. Leave your skirt up just the way it is now," he said, his voice monotone, as he gently stroked the big orange cat.

"But I don't—" she said, starting to cry.

"If you don't, well, it won't be good for you, Maxine."

"*Wh—what?*"

"That's right. I'll have to call and tell them to take you away to a foster home. Your uncle is a sick invalid. D'Lynn is too old to be your mother, and Tarva doesn't want any kids to look after. None of them can care for you. I'll have to call and tell the police all about how you need a new place to live. They take little girls like you away all the time."

"No, *please*—" She started to cry more.

"Then *do* what I say. And stop your sniveling. You can't possibly play for me when you have the tears turned on as you do."

She felt a chill as he moved the scooter even closer.

"I have another game we can play today, too, *Maxine* ..." The grin returned, and he was close enough so she could smell his pungent, sour breath.

The squawk of the blue-purple parrot drowned out her quiet sobs.

When Tarva arrived an hour later to pick her up, Maxine slowly and silently climbed into the passenger's seat of the car.

Who can I tell? she thought.

No one. She wasn't sure she would know what to say if she did try to tell anyone. Percy was right. D'Lynn liked Percy. She may not want Maxine in the house if Maxine told her what happened. Tarva's happy disposition made her a difficult confidante for such a horrible secret. Maxine had to figure out a way to get out of her piano lesson next week.

I'll make myself sick. Nobody will make me go if I'm sick.

Or maybe she could just tell D'Lynn and Tarva that she didn't want to take piano lessons anymore. Even if she pretended to be sick next week, there would be all the other Wednesdays after that. Maxine never wanted to play the piano again. If she told D'Lynn and Tarva she didn't want to take lessons anymore, then she wouldn't be lying.

"How was your lesson?" Tarva asked, oblivious as always. "I guess you practice at home on that keyboard you got for Christmas last year?"

Maxine stared out the window and said nothing, but Tarva was in a chatty mood.

"Practice is important," she continued. She smacked on peppermint chewing gum and smiled her usual toothy smile as she casually drove home to Ten Points. Tarva was never in any great hurry about anything. "I just never had no patience or interest to do piano when I was a little girl. My Mama tried to get me to do it, but I wanted to learn how to play a harp instead. Ain't that somethin'? Well, there wasn't nobody around these parts that gave harp lessons, and I suppose I'd've had to go find a harp somewhere to practice durin' the other days. You know, now that I think about it, where on Earth can you go to find a harp in these parts?

It's not like any stores around here have one. You can't just walk in Walmart and find a harp anywhere. I just don't think I know where—"

"Tarva, I'm gonna be sick. Pull over," Maxine interrupted, clutching her stomach again. It was real this time.

Tarva found her misplaced sense of urgency and swerved the car to the side of the road. Maxine opened the door and ran out into a grassy field beside the road and vomited.

"Dear gosh," Tarva said to herself. She turned off the car so she could get out and see about Maxine. "Oh, that poor little darlin'. I hope she ain't got one of those stomach bugs."

As Tarva turned to unfasten her seatbelt, she noticed a small puddle of urine in the leather passenger seat.

Ten minutes later, after Maxine recovered, and Tarva used napkins and sanitary wipes from her purse to clean the car seat, they were on the road again and headed home. Tarva was now as quiet as Maxine. Several times, she turned and looked to the girl and then away. After five more back-and-forth head turns, Tarva finally spoke up. "So, Maxine honey, are you sick ... or is it your nerves?"

Maxine kept her eyes to the passenger window; she said nothing.

Tarva turned and glanced once more and then put her eyes back on the road. She knew the poor child had suffered more loss than many adults. "Is there anything you need to talk about, honey? You know I'm a pretty good listener." She gave a short laugh. "I'm kinda sorta a rambler sometimes and run my mouth and tell my silly stories, I know, but I'll shut up a while and listen if you need to talk about anything."

"I'm just sick," Maxine mumbled.

"Oh okay," Tarva said. They were silent the rest of the way to Ten Points.

Later that night, Maxine awoke from a nightmare with a scream. Within seconds, the beautiful blonde version of Mommy was at her bedside.

Angel Mommy.

"What is it, my little Edela?" she asked, with a gentle but chilly hand on Maxine's arm.

"*He won't stop ...*" she finally blurted out, before she could stop herself. Then she choked and awoke fully, as she realized what she admitted.

Katarina could no longer keep up the sing-song manner. "Tell me who is bothering you. Tell *Moder* now so she can put a stop to all of this! You must tell me. No more *not* telling me. Tell *Moder*, Edela! *Tell Moder now!*" She was firm and forceful with her tone, but it was the only way. She was ready to pick up the girl and rattle it out of her.

If it came to that. Someone had hurt her Edela!

"Mister P—Per—Per—"

"Who? Tell me, my baby," she whispered. She regained a false calm. She took Maxine and held her close.

"H—he made me ..."

"He made you *what?*"

Maxine began crying and pulled to her Mommy. The woman didn't look or sound like Tilda, but Maxine was convinced it had to be a heavenly version of Tilda, and that was why she had the long blonde hair. The voice and the accent were different because maybe people spoke differently Up There. She wasn't sure why Tilda called her *Edela* when she came to visit. It must be a term like 'honey' or "baby' or 'darling' used by people in Heaven. It was all she could figure out. It made perfect sense when Maxine thought of it like that. And now Angel Mommy was the only person she could tell about any of this. If Angel Mommy never came around during the day, then she wasn't real, and she *couldn't* tell D'Lynn or Tarva. And if she didn't tell D'Lynn or Tarva, who were real, then that meant the police wouldn't come and take Maxine away.

The dam finally broke; words poured out of Maxine nonstop for the next five minutes. She told her Mommy who the bad man was, everything he made her do, when it all started, and—when her Mommy asked her—where the bad man lived.

"Please, don't tell D'Lynn and Tarva. Please! He'll tell them to take me away. He said if I told anybody the police would come and take me away," Maxine cried.

A low growl came from Mommy's throat and scared Maxine. It sounded like a large, angry dog about to lunge at a prowler.

"Do not worry anymore, my little Edela," Mommy told her, after the strange and scary sound subsided. "Nobody will come and take you away from me ever again. The bad man will not ever come near you again."

Katarina gave Maxine a kiss on the cheek and stood from the bed and walked toward the door. She turned back to face Maxine before she walked out.

"Moder *promises* you that," Katarina said softly, as she left the room.

Five minutes later, The Cape touched down twenty feet from Percy Stratworth's doorstep.

Katarina walked to the door.

Before she turned the knob to let herself in, she thought of her darling little Edela.

But her mind didn't go back to Maxine's bedroom at Ten Points ... instead, it went somewhere else.

28

Sweden Proper -- 1697

"No! No! You can't do this!" she screamed, as they took the two bodies out of the small farmhouse. It took three of the men from the village to restrain her. The bodies were wrapped in bed sheets. A constable and a doctor who treated all the other sick people in the village carried them out.

When it came to the task of the bloated, stinking corpse of Arfast Gerhardsson, each man grimaced, held his breath, and grabbed an end.

Two other men from the outskirts of the village had broken away and stood outside—far away from the house. Fearful of disease—and other things—they looked to one another in dismay. They were not sure why they had even come since they were not willing to go any closer to the house.

"She's gone mad," one of them, a young farmer, said to the other.

"Dear Providence, how *long* was she in there with them before anyone knew? How many days?"

"Edela! My Edela! Don't take away my Edela!" the screams echoed from inside the house and into the dusk.

Katarina's pleas and shrieks caused the hair to stand and prickle on the other man's arms. He too was a farmer, grayer and older than the other blond man.

"She thinks Arfast and the little girl are still alive," he said, to the younger man.

"She will likely die as well. She could have been inside that house with death around her for days."

"So much tragedy, so many deaths. The rain. It never stopped; we had no crops. Then the illnesses. I am told it is worse in other places. I feel as if the Heavenly Father is trying to tell us all something."

"No disrespect to the Almighty, but I wish He would find another way to tell us. Had my house not been one of thrift ahead of this we would be not be any better off than Gerhardsson and his family. Thanks to God."

"It is a shame the Gerhardssons never had a son."

"There is no need to think of that now. A son would have likely died, too. Arfast was a strong and able man, and now he's wrapped in a bedsheet just like the girl. Almighty, I think I can smell them both from here!"

"The poor child. *Edela,* was it? Yes, that is what Arfast's wife keeps screaming in there. The mad woman must be kept away with the other sick people. I wonder if that is what they will do with her?"

"I am not sure about the woman, but the bodies of Arfast and the child will have to be burned or immediately buried like all the others. I can't imagine anything else."

Both men stared strangely at one another as they shared a thought. They hoped the other men wouldn't deem them cowards for standing dozens of yards away from the house. There was nothing more to be done to save the modest Gerhardsson household. Two other men carried out bodies; several more inside held on to the hysterical woman.

"Edela!"

"She sounds like someone with a devil inside of them. So many mothers have lost children since all this began. They have remained stoic and accepting of God's will. What is wrong with this woman? She did not think this could reach her house, too?"

"She is mad. Not well. Perhaps there is no hope left for her either."

"She will probably die soon enough anyway."

"The constable should burn down the house around her."

"Ernst, that would not be civil or Christian," the older man replied. "You should not say such things."

The younger farmer Ernst waved away the comment. "It might be more merciful."

"I think we have done all we can do here. Did you touch anything?"

"No."

"Good. Neither did I."

As dusk became night, Katarina was left alone inside the house after her pleas for Arfast and Edela—mostly Edela—were never granted.

The constable and the doctor tried to convince her to leave with them, but she refused.

"We have a large space in the village where we are putting the sick and the exposed," the doctor told her.

"I must be here when my Arfast and Edela return," she insisted, an orange glow on her face as she sat and stared into the roaring fireplace. She could not remember who started the fire. Maybe she had.

A late autumn cold snap swept the land, a final deafening blow for the many farmers who first lost their crops—and then their families, before they too perished, and sometimes not in that order.

The rain had stopped, but the barrenness of what it reaped lived on in the ugliness surrounding them. "Very well," said the doctor, knowing nothing would sway Katarina.

The constable agreed. The Gerhardsson house was secluded. If she stayed there, she posed no threat to anyone else.

"I'll be back to check on you over the next few days if I am able," the doctor told her, before he left. But even he wasn't convinced he spoke the truth.

Katarina heard the words but paid no attention. She stared into the fire until it faded to embers. Then the hot orange glow withered away in a slow demise. No one was inside the house anymore. Hours passed; she never moved from the rocking chair. She sat frozen, unable to process what had happened; sometimes she forgot where she was before she drifted back to the chair and the cold wood beneath her.

More time passed, certainly it had, she thought, in her more lucid moments. There was darkness, then daylight, and then night had come again. She never slept. Her body was in the chair, she thought, before she became numb and could no longer feel the chair.

Then came another wave of clarity when she knew she was thirsty and must have water. A bucket from the well outside was on the floor, a few feet away in the dark. The water was dirty, it must be. To drink it could mean she would get sick and die.

The inside of her mouth was parched, her lips chapped; she needed water. Maybe to drink it *would* be to die. Maybe it was best. Or maybe she was already dead.

But she decided she must be alive when she fell from the chair and onto the wooden floor. It felt tracked on; it bore the smell of death. The realization her Edela and Arfast were gone set in again, as her fingers brushed through the dry dirt from the boots. The boots of the men who had come into her home and taken her daughter and husband away. How long ago had it been?

Katarina crawled over to the bucket. Her legs ached from so long in the chair. She couldn't stand and walk. Small splinters from the coarse wooden floor were unnoticed as she pulled herself to the bucket. She finally reached it and drew a dipper full of the water. The foul, rank smell struck before she drank. There *was* nothing else. Now she would wait. She thought she might pray as she waited to fall ill and die as the rest of her life had.

God had dealt her this bad dream she couldn't escape. Or could she? Maybe He would come through and take her; show her mercy at last.

Katarina left the dipper to float in the puddle. She tried to stand; she could not. That was when she heard the noise outside the house.

"Edela," she whispered, her voice hoarse despite the drink of water.

Katarina was weak, but the thought of Edela gave her the push she needed to climb to her feet.

Edela was outside the door. She could walk for Edela.

On wobbly legs, Katarina stumbled in the dark room and fell into the door as she pulled it open. "My Edela!" she cried out, with what little strength remained.

The two men knocked her back down to the floor as they shoved their way in. One of them slammed the door shut behind him.

"Food!" the other yelled at her. A dash of moonlight through the window was all she needed to see they were young and covered in filth.

The one who demanded food had a matted brown beard, wispy hair and rags for clothes. Katarina thought she recognized the other one from the village. He was blond man with a worn but otherwise handsome face. On this night, he was desperate. Pungent odors filled the room once the door was closed and they were confined.

"I—I don't have—" She could barely speak.

"You do!" the one from the village said. He grabbed her by the face and pressed her head into the floor. There was a touch of fear about him, as if he didn't want to do what he did; perhaps a false show of authority to appease his bearded companion.

"Please, I do not. I *need* food. I have nothing," Katarina said through her achy throat. It was even harder to speak with dirty hands pressed on each side of her face between her cheeks and her jaws. She tried to hold her breath as the wave of stink enveloped her.

The bearded one noisily scavenged shelves and makeshift cabinets in the house, knocking things over. Things fell to the floor beside him.

"*Please—*" Katarina pleaded again. She felt the grime of dirty hands on her face.

"Make her stop talking," the bearded one yelled.

"How do I do that?" the blond one replied.

The bearded one continued to knock over things. He gave aggravated curses when he found nothing to eat. He walked over to Katarina and knelt beside the other man. The stench of them together overtook her. She gagged as she struggled to breathe.

"We *make* her," the bearded one replied, pulling up the bottom of her dress.

"Wait. Is this not Arfast Gerhardsson's wife?" the blond man asked quickly, with hesitation.

"Does it matter? I hear he is dead. She is *ours.*"

The blond one refused and backed off a few feet.

"Get over here, or I kill you!" the bearded one barked.

Skittish, he obeyed and slowly returned. Katarina was far too weak to fight back. He held her down, as the bearded one went first.

Katarina screamed and begged, but they were too strong, and there was no more strength. There were two of them. She was only one.

Their dreadful smells and the unspeakable things they did no longer registered after a while. Her head rolled to one side. She felt nothing as she stared into the black, empty fireplace. The fire from before was as dead and gone as her Edela and her Arfast.

Thanks to God, she thought, as she felt what she believed to be his mercy. She passed out before they finished.

29

North of Monroe, Louisiana – November 2015

Katarina released the doorknob as she stood outside the front door of Percy Stratworth's home.

It was much too civil, to do it this way. Why use a door when there were other means?

Inside the house, in the living room, Percy Stratworth relaxed in a musty armchair, where he used a magnifying glass to read a single newspaper page he held in his other hand. A fierce yellow glow from the lamp beside the chair shined down, a spotlight on its master, in his own private corner of an otherwise darkened world. Percy's motorized scooter was parked, beside the rest of the newspaper he had tossed on to the floor next to other ones. Mozart dozed on his lap.

Behind the chair, over in an unseen corner of the room, the blue-purple parrot began squawking loudly in its cage. It made a fuss like one Percy had never heard.

"Polly, shut up, for tarnation's sake," he called, not bothered enough to look away from his reading. The back of the chair was to the birdcage. The slits of Mozart's eyes opened widely at his master's voice, then resettled before they closed again. The neutered feline cared little for anything these days but food and naps.

Had Percy's chair been turned the other way, he would have seen the curtain move in the dark, near a back window, thirty feet behind him, near the birdcage. Polly calmed her panicked squawks. Percy continued reading. Unsteady shakes of the magnifying glass over small print accompanied his efforts. Hand tremors and weak vision were getting the best of him in older age.

Polly remained hushed, but without warning, a melody came from the piano. A dark number Percy vaguely recognized. Played with precision but enough to startle him. He dropped the magnifying glass on the floor, and stumbled out of his seat—no easy feat for a portly man hardly able to walk unaided.

Mozart the cat was jarred awake again by his master's sudden movement. He leapt away with a spooked burst of energy; he scrambled from the room and darted down a hallway.

Percy turned slowly and held on to the scooter as he climbed in. He was disturbed—and confused—by the sight of the young, blonde pale woman in a blue dress. She sat and played his beloved, black grand piano ... quite beautifully but uninvited.

"What—I say, who are you and how did you get in here?"

He moved toward Katarina. The hum of the scooter that so unsettled Maxine was drowned out by a rousing piano version of *Vengeance*.

Percy was impressed but frightened. It also panicked him a bit to see Polly out of her cage and perched on the woman's shoulder. How had this strange, thin, gorgeous woman gotten into his house—his living room—when he was there the entire time?

Katarina was impressed the old pervert had the audacity to come toward her. She gave him a wide smile as she stroked the ivories, never missing a chord. Her blue eyes pierced him as her fingers moved freely and effortlessly.

Moder is about to make the bad man pay, my little Edela.

But first, a chat.

She stopped mid-chord and turned on the bench to face Percy as he reached her. Polly sat idly on Katarina's shoulder.

"Who are you? How did you get in here?" Percy repeated, exacerbated and breathing heavily, though the scooter had done the work for him.

Katarina was delighted to see him unnerved. "Are you not going to be a good maestro and rate my performance?" she asked, with the meek tone of a student seeking a favorable critique.

"That—*that's* not the point!" he shouted. "What are you doing here? Put my Polly back where you found her this instant and get the hell out of here. I'll call the police!"

"No, no. You will not," she said, glancing sideways at the parrot on her shoulder. "Polly will have no more crackers if you touch that phone."

"Where are you from? What is that accent? And why are you playing my piano?" Percy's large jowls trembled, as he shifted his considerable weight in the scooter seat.

"So many questions," Katarina replied. "Let us try to go in order. I am Swedish. English was a, um, difficult language to learn, but I think I have mastered it and eight others quite well. When you have been around as long as I you have to move every so often to make yourself less, what do they say, *conspicuous.* One time back in the nineteen-thirties, I became bored and decided it was also time to master the piano. But enough of my biography. If I go back to the very beginning, it is too much to tell; it could take days. Let us instead talk about *your* piano. I thought it would be nice if it had one last piece before it is destroyed."

"Destroyed?"

Katarina smiled, as she gently set Polly down to perch at the edge of the bench. Then she stood up, reached under the open lid of the grand piano and yanked out a thick steel piano wire as if it were dental floss. One ivory key sank to a limp death, a crooked tooth among an otherwise perfect set.

The walls were thick, and no other houses were close, so only Katarina, Polly, and Mozart—off hiding somewhere—heard Percy's scream.

"Oh my God! *No!*"

"Oh yes," Katarina replied. She placed the long spring wire aside.

"Why did you do that?" he cried, starting to hyperventilate. Percy tried to stand from the scooter, but Katarina held out her hand. Something in the air, something he couldn't see, shoved him back into his seat.

"Why did you hurt my Edela?" Katarina asked, her smile gone. Her plump lips flattened; her mouth was a straight line. She picked up the parrot from the bench.

"*Who?* I don't understand," he squealed, with a helpless look at his damaged piano.

"You do not understand? Well, let us begin by hurting things you care about," she said.

Percy screamed again as Katarina opened her mouth, revealed razor sharp canines, and took off Polly's head in a single slash of a bite. The headless torso of the parrot fell off her palm and on to the brown carpet below where it started to bleed out.

Katarina spit out the severed bird's head into Percy's lap, eliciting a third scream. Her cuspids—her canine teeth—were even longer after decapitating the parrot. The smile was back, the whites of her teeth streaked with some of Polly's blood.

"Too bad the bird never learned to speak," she said, licking more of the blood from around her lips before a lap of her tongue washed the red from her teeth. "Parrots can do that, no?"

"*Oh God, please! What are you...?*"

He quickly hit a knob to turn the scooter around and tried to drive away, but Katarina was on the other side in a flash and blocked him.

"What are you!" he repeated, starting to sob. Katarina smiled again when she saw a large wet spot in the front of his tan trousers.

She crouched over the scooter, her hands on the arms of it so that she was inches from his face. The stench of his piss was strong and satisfying. "I am Katarina Gerhardsson Castille, and *you* have offended me!"

He trembled, his hyperventilation out of control. Beads of frightened sweat dotted his forehead. "C—C—*Castille?* Katarina? The senator's wife? Oh my God, *yes*, the model. But I saw it all in the p—p—paper. I thought you were ...?" His horrified voice trailed off, his breathing so labored he could no longer produce words.

"*Dead?*" she asked, lifting a brow. "Is that what you were about to say? Why yes, Mister Pedophile, I *am!*" she announced, opening her mouth wide and going for his nose.

He screamed in agony as the teeth tore his nose away from his face.

The dark red spilled on the rest of his face and his white shirt. Blood streamed down his large double chin in thick ribbons as he gurgled and began to lose consciousness.

Katarina spit out Percy's nose just as she had with Polly's head. The chewed blob of flesh bounced off his bloody face and landed on the floor beside the scooter.

She went back over to the piano to pick up the wire. "No, no, pedophile. Not yet. Do not go to sleep. There is more."

Percy's slanted eyes widened as he choked and coughed at the sight of her in front of him. She laughed aloud at the sight of an oozing face without a nose. Her teeth were red again.

"I must have you stay awake a moment longer for this last part," she said, moving in, each of her hands on an opposite end of the wire. "*This is for my Edela ...*"

30

Remy typed "Senator Castille" into the search engine, as he sat at his laptop in the guest bedroom at Ten Points. A flurry of news articles and old links with Frank Castille came up. Most of the headlines from the early part of 2010.

No Answers in U.S. Senator's Disappearance.

Sen. Castille and Supermodel Wife Vanish.

Source: Senator's Mob Ties Blamed for Disappearance

The further he went down the list, the wackier the headlines became: *Sen. Castille, Supermodel Wife Abducted by Aliens.*

Finally, bingo—back to the more legitimate stuff Remy searched for: *Photos Reveal Missing Senator and 'Other Woman'.*

Castille Mistress's Privileged North Louisiana Upbringing.

Castille's 'Other Woman' and The Lanehart Dynasty.

'Other Woman' With Senator Before He Vanished?

NOPD: Castille's Mistress Not a Suspect.

The only photo of Flannery that appeared with the links was a generic Castille staff photo of her in business attire. She wore a bright, ambitious, and enthusiastic smile Remy had never seen in person. A dutiful, young career woman working her way up, away from the shadow of her father and his money. The Flannery Remy knew was a blank slate. In this old photo, she looked like a real person. She was ... *alive.*

After Remy read a fourteenth article, studied stock photos of Frank and Katarina Castille, and stared once more at the dated black and white photo of Flannery, he shut off the computer.

There was nothing to tell him if Flannery knew his brother, or if any of the dots connected. He knew most of his search was curiosity.

Then he felt the call.

Remy. Come to me.

Soft and gentle. He stood from his chair at the desk in the guest room but forced himself back into his seat.

No! he said in his mind. What the hell was this?

Remy, the basement. Come to me.

I can't.

Come to me now, *Remy!*

But...

Don't argue. The basement. At once!

Remy felt himself stand to his feet, though he knew it wasn't by his will, and the bedroom door approached. The decision was made for him. He went downstairs, around the corner of the foyer, and into the hallway, where he found the door leading underground.

What Remy failed to see through the cloudy haze, before he went through the door and closed it, was Clementine at the end of the corridor, near the kitchen entrance.

Conrad set down the tray of bottled water and other supplies for Marcus's room upstairs, as he saw Remy disappear. *The basement.* Conrad crept down the hallway and stood outside the door. His eyes—Clementine's eyes—went through the wood, down the old stairs, and pierced the wall of another room deep within the basement for the sight before him. Remy and Flannery kissed passionately; she was already unbuttoning his slacks.

Flannery, you naughty girl, Conrad thought, as he watched. *A naughty girl who's a damn fool to dance with me again.*

Yes, he still desired to see the undead woman destroyed, and her nephew after her. That hadn't changed, but there was no need for her to know it as they plotted together against Katarina. Watching Katarina also turn to dust would be an added perk.

The top of Flannery's negligee was down, and her generous breasts were exposed. Remy's mouth was on them like a starving beast, as Flannery slid off his slacks, putting his well-muscled backside on display for Conrad.

Conrad needed no reminding of what he had once been. He felt ill and was about to spare himself the scene, since Remy's desirable backside blocked the view of Flannery. Before he could walk away, he saw her head come around to Remy's neck, her cuspids as erect as the other man's penis must have been by that point. Conrad's interest returned as he watched her teeth come in for a landing. She was hungry for blood. It looked like sex would wait until the other lust with which she was cursed could be satiated.

Poor Wes Washer. He must be lonely and neglected these days.

Conrad grimaced as Clementine's eyes moved back to Remy's ass, the man turned to the side, and he caught sight of the other doctor's rippling shoulders and chest. How he missed being inside the duplicate of that body. Not for sex with a living corpse such as Flannery, but with anyone else. It had been so long since that itch was scratched, for he would have even settled for Tilda Lanehart right now. *If* he had a desirable body—and a penis—two of the things he missed dearly while masquerading as a dowdy prude of a woman.

Yes, he loved Marcus, but sex was like water. He needed it. So what, if he drank from a different cup now and again?

It wasn't only about the sex. To be looked on with desire and not looked over and forgotten, as Clementine had been all her life. Conrad missed being wanted and turning heads and, yes, being the center of attention when he walked into a room.

I must find a man soon. A desperate, desirable man who needs something and will be willing to bargain anything to get it.

He indeed needed it for a future with Marcus. There was no way in hell Marcus would want to be with Clementine LeMonde—or someone who looked and sounded like she did. Even if Marcus were straight, Clementine wouldn't be good enough for him.

Drink up, bitch, Conrad thought, as he watched Flannery's teeth sink into Remy's neck. *Your days are numbered before I destroy you.*

"Ain't you supposed to be upstairs?" The voice jarred Conrad back to his current reality.

D.C. Cunningham was pale, with dark circles underneath his own dead, hungry eyes. He came across twitchy, even more hungry than Conrad had seen Flannery over the years on her most deprived night.

D.C. also looked quite appealing, Conrad noted. Despite the pasty aura, his lean physique through the sleeveless, half-unbuttoned shirt caught Conrad's eye.

Clementine's smile greeted D.C. as her body and Conrad's attention turned to him.

"Too bad you couldn't have come to me before you allowed Katarina to do this to you," Conrad said. One of Clementine's fingers reached into the open shirt and ran down D.C.'s exposed chest.

D.C.'s own canines were half-erect.

The fool thought he was about to make a meal out of me. Conrad chuckled, but a befuddled D.C. only thought Clementine was amused by him.

"I'm sorry? How the hell do you know about—?" he began. The elongated canines were a contrast to his flustered state.

"I know all kinds of things," Conrad said. "I know Katarina made you what you've become. I *know* you got messy and turned the poor little goth boy into a hybrid. I *know* all about how you kept Marcus's bed warm while he mourned poor, dead Ezekiel. Oh, and he also still mourned the other one before that. I'm sure he told you all about the mysterious disappearance of Landon Smithfield, whom he was practically married to for several years. Do you ever feel paranoid that you'll be the next one struck down by this gay widow curse Marcus carries around? Oh wait, you *are* dead, so I guess it's already happened."

"Clementine, how the hell do you know all this stuff?" D.C. asked.

Conrad moved in closer. "I'll let you in on a little secret." He was inches from D.C.'s ear. "I'm not Clementine," he whispered impishly.

D.C. raised a curious brow. It barely creased his pale forehead. *Young and dumb.* "Who are you then?" he asked.

Clementine's amber eyes transformed into a solid black. D.C. apprehensively backed off a few feet, as Clementine's eyes shimmered as dark pools then went to a fiery, glowing yellow.

"Oh sweet Jesus!" he exclaimed. His canine teeth had retracted back to their normal size. "And to think I almost—"

Clementine's eyes restored themselves. Conrad gave another smile. "To think that you *almost* bit me? Yes, that would have been unfortunate for a young little bloodsucker like you, D.C."

"Um ..."

"And I must say, my dear boy, it's quite sloppy to attack somebody right here in the middle of the downstairs hallway. What if Tarva walked up? D'Lynn? Or even the good Doctor Van Buren who, by the way, is down in the basement naked and bleeding and having the time of his life."

"Oh man, I want to see and drink some of that," D.C. grinned, walking toward the basement door. "That guy is fuckin' hot!"

"Calm down, little vampire fag," Conrad said. He grabbed D.C. by the arm and pulled him back. "Flannery is down there, too."

"Fag is *not* a cool word to use around me ..."

"Oh please. Spare me the P.C. crap. I've probably had more man-on-man action than you could ever dream about."

D.C. stared at Clementine in a new way, as he considered the fact something else was inside her body. "What are you? *Who* are you? Is it a man that's in there?"

"All in good time," Conrad said. He leaned in and gave D.C. a soft kiss on the lips.

"That is gross!" D.C. exclaimed, recoiling and making a disgusted face. "I don't know *who* you are, but it's like Clementine LeMonde just kissed me! *Ew!*"

"Keep your voice down," Conrad said. "I have something I want you to do for me. That kiss was only to satisfy my curiosity—*and* bond us for a little project we're about to collaborate on."

"I belong to Katarina, you know," D.C. said. "And I ain't havin' sex with Clementine, or somebody who's inside her body. Sorry, but it ain't happenin'. Never ever in a million years."

"Don't get your panties in a wad," Conrad said. "This has nothing to do with sex, you half-wit. This is way more important. You may be under Katarina's control, but *Travis* is under *yours*, no?"

"Yeah, that much is true."

"Good. I have something I need you to do for me where young Travis is concerned."

"What do you want me to do?"

D.C. was wary, but Conrad understood and gave him latitude.

A few minutes later, after Conrad had laid out his instructions for D.C., the doorbell rang. Since it was after dark, and Tarva and D'Lynn weren't around, Conrad—as Clementine—took it upon himself to answer the door. It had once been *his* house, after all. One hundred forty-three years of exile as a Ten Points outsider, and it was about goddamn time he answered the door to his own home.

Conrad gave D.C. a sharp look and a hand gesture to make himself scarce before he opened the double doors. D.C. was out of the room by the time Conrad pulled open the doors. He fought hard to avoid a tired groan.

"Sister!" cried a distressed Wilkins Washer. The Reverend's light blue dress shirt was streaked with sweat around the armpits, despite the cold night.

The Reverend held out his arms for a hug, which Conrad granted, begrudgingly. Clementine's eyes rolled once Conrad was in the embrace. The portly old man looked as if he might burst into tears.

"Why, Brother Washer, what's the matter?" Conrad asked, putting on a concerned Clementine voice.

"I just came from Percy Stratworth's house. It's awful. The police are there. An ambulance came, too, but it was too late for that—"

"What do you mean? What happened?" Conrad was genuinely curious.

"Oh, it is like somethin' from the pits of Hell," Reverend Washer lamented, his bloated face pasty and pale.

"Oh my," Conrad tried to hide his enthusiasm for details. This did sound quite titillating. "Did something happen to poor Percy?"

"Yes!" the Reverend replied, trying to find words. "His ... His ... *His head*—oh dear Lord in Heaven!"

"What? Tell me." Conrad was ready to slap the bejesus out of the annoying old man.

"The police found a piano wire wrapped around his neck. Oh, it's the work of the Devil himself."

"A piano wire?" *How fascinating!*

"Yes, yes. His head was almost completely. He was, um, almost decapitated. Neck cut all the way through b-b-by the wire. *Oh!* Blood all over the place. It had to be somebody strong. They think whoever did it used that wire. Poor Percy's head was barely still on him. Oh, dear heavens. *Oh,* my blood pressure! I can't even think about it. Can I sit down? Clementine dear, I need a glass of water. Can you please g-get me a glass of water?"

"Maybe you need some Scotch or brandy." It slipped out before Conrad remembered to whom he spoke.

"Clementine LeMonde! What has got into you, girl! You know I don't touch the Devil's drink."

"Oh, I'm sorry. I know that, Brother Washer. I thought just a little might take the edge off your nerves. I wasn't thinking of anything else."

"Still. You should know better. You know what the Bible says about temptation."

Baptists. "Who would strangle Percy Stratworth with a piano wire?"

"Oh, my dear child, it went way past strangled. And that's not all they did. I've already told you enough to give you nightmares. I just *shouldn't* tell you what else they did!"

Whatever, you old fool. "No, please ... tell me everything."

"Can I please have that water?"

Once Conrad—as Clementine—returned with a glass of water, the Reverend had come around about sharing the rest of the story. "I have to say it out loud to somebody. My sister in Christ D'Lynn's heart ain't gonna be able to handle it, so I can't tell her the bad stuff."

"Tell her *what* bad stuff?" *Tone it down and keep it subtle,* he told himself. He couldn't appear too eager for all the gory details.

"Whoever it was that attacked him ... they either tore off or cut off his nose, too. And also h-h-his ... h-h-his ... *his...* private parts."

Fuck subtlety. Conrad forced a shrill and horrified scream from Clementine for dramatic effect.

"Oh child, I know! See, it's going to cause you to have bad dreams tonight. I shouldn't've told you nothin."

Conrad wrung Clementine's hands and painted her with a

bewildered and shocked expression. "That poor man. Who would do such a thing?"

"Somebody with the Devil inside of 'em!"

Or maybe he had it coming. It sounded like a crime of passion. Or perhaps even one of the vampire variety. He would have to question Flannery and Katarina about this later, he decided. "That is just a horrible thing to imagine! Poor Percy. I hope he didn't suffer much."

"I just don't know how I'm gonna tell D'Lynn about this, with her heart and all. She and Percy were friends, you know."

"Well, you should probably break it to her gently before she hears it somewhere else. Gosh forbid she should see it on the news before somebody can get upstairs to tell her."

"I'll just tell her he died. Let's not tell her the other awful stuff."

"But like I said, it'll be on the news. And in the newspapers. It sounds like a homicide investigation. She'll find out somewhere else if you don't tell her."

Let me tell her, Conrad thought. *Maybe I'll cause the old bitty to have a heart attack and finish her off while the good doctor is downstairs preoccupied with somebody else who's dead.*

"I can tell her if you want me to," Conrad said aloud.

"It's my responsibility, dear child, but maybe you could be there with me when I *do* tell her," the Reverend suggested. "She'll need another woman's understanding when she hears it."

Conrad hated being a woman. "Of course. But I need to look in on Marcus first. Henry and I swapped sitting times tonight, and nobody's up there. Marcus is in his room all by himself."

"I suppose there ain't been any change with Marcus?" It was a surprise to see Reverend Washer express a sliver of concern for Marcus.

"I'm afraid not."

Clementine went up the stairs ahead of Reverend Washer. The Reverend reached the second floor of the house a few seconds after Conrad brought Clementine to a pause in the hallway.

"Wait here, Brother Washer. I'll go in Marcus's room and be right back to go in to see D'Lynn with you."

The Reverend nodded, with no further interest in Marcus's welfare.

A panicked scream came from Clementine after she opened the door and walked into the bedroom, but this time there was no pretending on Conrad's part.

"Sister, what is it?" the Reverend asked. He rushed to the doorway of Marcus's room as quickly as his extra weight could carry him.

Conrad threw up Clementine's hands in dismay and faced the Reverend. Conrad was beside himself. "Marcus isn't here!"

"What do you mean? That makes no sense, child!"

"He somehow got up and walked out of here or somebody took him. *Marcus is gone!*"

31

The next morning Wes Washer and another deputy were back at the house. They questioned everyone they could track down who had any connection to Marcus. A search of the property and the surrounding area during the night yielded no results. There was no evidence of foul play in Marcus's bedroom. It looked as though he had simply unhooked himself from an IV drip and walked away.

Conrad manufactured almost nothing with Clementine, when it came to bemusement and worry. The only time he could get inside Marcus's head was when he slept, and Conrad saw it as another failure, like last spring. This time, Marcus's catatonic state had been no help at all when it came to Conrad wielding influence.

"This ain't your fault," Wes said, patting Clementine's shoulder. "You've beat yourself up about this all night long. It's daylight out there. Go home and get some rest."

"I should have been upstairs with him the entire time, and this wouldn't have happened," Conrad said. *I should have!* he repeated within.

"Well, everything checked out with Henry Jones," said the other deputy, a six-foot-six local boy who went by the nickname of Stretch. "We went to his house. Mister Lanehart ain't there."

"Where is Flannery this mornin'?" Wes asked. "This is an official investigation, and I need *everybody* here! We spoke to her last night, but I need her here *now*," he said roughly, to fatten up any authoritative credibility.

But no one was intimidated by Wes. The mention of Flannery's name from his own mouth caused an erratic twitch of his head. Gently, he stroked the left side of his neck.

"That's what I would like to know as well," Remy said, showing up in the living room. D'Lynn walked in behind him.

Clementine's head turned toward Remy. Conrad would have laughed if he hadn't been so worried over Marcus. Flannery had done a fine job of erasing Remy's memory. The doctor was a little pale but otherwise robust.

"Oh, poor Marcus. You think he was kidnapped?" D'Lynn wondered. "His Daddy, God rest his soul, was always worried some money-hungry criminal would do somethin' like this to one of the family."

"There don't appear to be no signs of any struggle up in the bedroom," Deputy Stretch replied. He looked to be still in his twenties, a bit younger than Wes but already going bald. Despite his youth and towering height, he had the build and beer gut of a former high school jock whose glory days were behind him.

"Even if Marcus was kidnapped, I doubt there would be any struggle," Remy said. "He's been catatonic for more than a week. Somebody could just pick him up and carry him out."

"Who are you?" Deputy Stretch asked, disgruntled a stranger interfered with his conjecture. Remy ignored him.

"*Oh!* First my poor, poor friend Percy Stratworth, and now this whole thing with Marcus," D'Lynn cried, taking a seat in the usual armchair. "I hope none of it's related. I hope some serial killer ain't on the loose."

"There's a forensics team comin' to dust for fingerprints just to be safe," Wes said. "They've been over at Percy's house all night, so they'll probably need coffee when they get here."

"Who do they think killed Percy?" D'Lynn said, ready to burst into tears. "Who would do such a thing?"

"Was Percy Stratworth datin' anybody?" Deputy Stretch asked, with a funny face. He looked like he already knew it was a ridiculous question.

"Why no, I seriously doubt it," D'Lynn said. "Why do you ask?"

"Well, it has all the signs of somethin' a pissed-off woman would do..."

Wes shot Stretch a "shut up!" look, but the other deputy paid no attention.

"What do you mean by that?" D'Lynn asked.

"Well, ma'am," Deputy Stretch continued, ignorant of Wes's eagle glare. "Whoever killed him—please excuse me for bein' blunt, ma'am—whoever it was that killed him either cut off or bit off his ding-a-ling."

"*Ooohhhh!*" D'Lynn bellowed, suddenly faint and slumping in her chair.

"*Stretch!*" Wes yelled. "Why did you have to go and tell her that?"

Remy rushed to D'Lynn's aid and helped her sit back up. "Can somebody please bring a glass of water for her?"

Tarva arrived in the living room just as the request came. "Oh, D'Lynn!" she cried. "Yes, Remy." She rushed over to the bar in the corner of the living room and pulled a cold bottled water from the refrigerator underneath.

"No, it could be bad for her heart," Remy said. "It needs to be room temperature."

As Tarva scurried off to the kitchen, Wes scowled at Stretch like a disapproving parent—or an older, more responsible brother.

Stretch continued to pay Wes no attention, which wasn't uncommon. "Let's get back to Mister Marcus Lanehart," the deputy said. "Does he have any friends—any kind of *special friends*—where he could be hiding?"

"Special friends?" Conrad—as Clementine—asked.

Stretch made a limped-wrist motion with his hand. A grin was at the corner of his mouth. "You know what I mean," he said.

"You're a fucking idiot," Conrad said, but to everyone else it came from Clementine.

"*Ohhh!*" D'Lynn cried out again.

Everyone turned to Clementine with gaped mouths.

"Clementine!" Wes exclaimed. "I've never heard such language from you!"

Conrad brushed an "oops" expression on to Clementine's face. "I couldn't help it. It just slipped out."

"Do you know *who* you're talking to, ma'am?" Deputy Stretch asked Clementine. "I could take you in for that!"

Conrad was ready to kill half the people in the room. "I didn't lay a finger on you. I don't think you can arrest me for calling you a name."

"We'll just see about that," the deputy snorted.

"Let's forget what Clementine said and get back to the matter at hand," Remy said, looking up from where he tended to D'Lynn. "Has every nook and cranny of this house been searched? It's a huge house."

"We didn't go to the third floor," Wes said. "Flannery showed us the basement last night."

Wes's expression changed as he said Flannery's name. The left side of this face twitched again, as if he had a Tourette's tic. He rubbed the left side of this neck once more, then was back to himself.

"Where is Flannery?" Tarva asked, as she returned with a glass of water. "Her brother is missin'. You'd think she would be more worried. You know, when me and my brother were little kids, he disappeared one afternoon. My Mama worried and worried and called everybody far and wide she could think of. People didn't have to worry as much about kidnappers back then, and that was only just about twenty-five or so years ago. Anyway, she was still scared some ol' pervert in a white van grabbed him. Well, it turned out he was just at a friend's house. But still, you should've seen my Mama's face when she thought—"

"Tarva, can you please hand me the glass of water?" Remy cut in. He took it and gave it to D'Lynn. She held it herself and took slow sips.

"As I was saying," Wes continued gruffly, hiding his desperation to rein everyone in. "There is still the third floor to be looked over."

"Nobody's been up there in years," D'Lynn said, as her composure returned.

"Well, Marcus could've wandered up there," Wes said. "It needs to be searched."

Oh hell no. "If it'll help, I can go up there and look around," Conrad said sweetly, in Clementine's voice.

"You won't go up there alone," Wes said. "I'll go with you."

Conrad shook Clementine's head. "Oh, Wes, there's really no need for that. I'll go up there by myself. I feel like I'm partially to blame for this. If I had just been in Marcus's room keeping a closer eye on him none of this would have happened."

"Clementine, I know we're friends and no offense, but this is an official investigation," Wes said, keeping up the tough act. "I can't go with hearsay. I need to see and document the third floor for myself."

I should've snapped your damned neck the night Tilda attacked you last spring, Conrad thought. "Well, if you insist," he replied, as the wheels turned.

But Conrad couldn't figure out a way to stall a third floor-search without raising more suspicion—or blowing his cover. Of course, he wanted to know if Marcus was there, but he wanted to find out on his own when the deputies cleared out.

With some apprehension, Conrad went to the third floor with Wes. Deputy Stretch stayed with the others downstairs.

After they climbed the two sets of stairs, Conrad and Wes stood side-by-side at the edge of the dark, empty third-floor corridor. "It's kind of spooky up here, huh?" Conrad said, meekly, effeminately, and—he *hoped*—effectively.

Wes concurred with a grin. "It smells like dust and loneliness."

Oh God, write a country song, you dipshit. "Well, Wes, all the doors up here are closed. Probably locked. As out of it as Marcus has been, you know he would just be lurking around the hallway in a daze or asleep on the floor if he were up here. Let's go back downstairs. I'm *so* jittery and nervous up here. Plus, the heat doesn't reach up here, and it's cold."

"Then maybe you *should* go back downstairs," Wes suggested. "I need to take my flashlight and look through all these rooms. Dang, there sure are a lot of 'em. Almost as many as the second floor. Why the heck did anybody ever need this many rooms in a house?"

"The Ogdens. There were a lot of us ..."

"Huh? *Us?*"

"Oh gosh, slip of the tongue. There were a lot of members of the Ogden family. My grandpa used to say we may have been descendants on another branch of the tree," Conrad covered. "Anyway, the Ogdens were an extended family ... I hear they had a lot of guests. They were in and out of this house back in the eighteen-hundreds. Many Confederate wives who were friends with the family boarded here during the Civil War. The family thrived up until the Civil War, and Theodore Ogden, Senior..." —Conrad tried not to clench Clementine's jaw as he said his father's name, the bastard— "...loved to be a benefactor. To people he could have power over. He liked to collect on his debts. He liked to put on a front and keep up appearances. If only people had known what kind of man he *really* was."

"Oh wow, Clementine," Wes said, impressed. "I had no idea you knew so much about the history of this place."

The rage stirred, and Conrad couldn't stop. "Oh, but I do!" Clementine turned toward Wes, putting a hand on his arm.

"You seem so passionate about ..."

"Theodore Ogden Senior treated his children, his entire family, like his property. *Not* like people but like his possessions. He called himself 'Ted.' He kept m—*Teddy*—his son, Teddy, *well*, Ted kept Teddy separated from the true love of his life! He tore them apart! All for the sake of appearances ..."

"Clementine, you feel so strong about all this. Why don't you stop this sittin' job of yours and go be a history teacher? It ain't too late to go back and finish college."

"I don't care about going back to school. I just find this place ... *this house*. Well, never mind." *Shut up, Conrad*, he told himself.

"Let's start down the row of doors here," Wes said, turning his attention back to the task. "You stay here with me, and I'll open the door and shine the light in."

They were only two doors away from Katarina's room. Only a few more away from where a machine pumped Jimmy Van Buren's body full of *whatever it was* to keep it preserved for something Katarina had yet to share. Conrad tried to conjure up something for a distraction. Having Clementine become ill would be too contrived. There had to be something else he could do.

The first room was only what was to be expected. Old relics from older days, stored away in an even older room.

The same for the second.

Then, they were at Katarina's door. Conrad knew he had to do something but wasn't sure what.

If we disturb Katarina, there's a chance it could destroy her. I still need answers about the body and whatever this secret is about Ten Points she won't share with Flannery—and I need her help with other things. "I'm sure it's the same in there. Wes, we would know if Marcus is up here. Let's just go back downstairs."

"No, we need to look in all these rooms," Wes insisted. His flashlight was pointed at the doorknob as he fumbled with it.

The door was locked. Conrad felt a sigh escape Clementine's body.

Wes produced a large round silver ring with two dangling skeleton keys. "I got this from D'Lynn last night, when we searched all the other rooms downstairs. One is a master key. Look at this thing ... look how old it is. It's supposed to fit any doors that are locked."

Conrad was in no mood to wax nostalgic over some ancient key he hadn't seen in more than a century. He tried to hide panic. "Is there any need to go to all the trouble? Marcus wouldn't have locked himself inside a room."

"We don't know that," Wes replied. He fit the key into the lock and opened the door.

Damn it, I'm about to have to kill Wes. Clementine's eyes closed, and Conrad was ready to do what was almost done in the living room of Ten Points last spring. It wasn't the thought of taking out Wes quickly and quietly with one swift neck snap that bothered him. He knew he wouldn't be able to explain returning downstairs alone. There would be no plausible way to explain Wes's absence. Katarina was dead to the world. She would be of no help in this situation.

The beam of the flashlight scanned the room. Katarina's white vanity appeared, only it looked like an empty and unused desk. Conrad swore the mirror was even coated with a little dust, for effect.

Then—an old bed from another era in the darkened back corner of the room.

Katarina's current bed.

Empty.

The room was deserted. To the naked eye, it looked as unused as the first two.

Where was she?

They went back into the hallway. Wes closed and locked the door with a slight tremble.

Conrad tried to hide relief from Clementine's face. But he was curious over the blonde bitch's whereabouts. "Something the matter, Wes?"

Wes made a face and rubbed opposite arms with each of his hands. The keys on the ring jangled underneath his fingers. "Just a feelin'. Like the Devil's in here. I feel evil around me."

If you only knew. "I don't feel anything, except the cold air up here. Maybe that's all you feel."

"No, it ain't the cold. I feel that too, but this is different. Let's keep movin'..."

The two following rooms were empty. Then Conrad took another deep breath as they arrived at the next door. Like the one to Katarina's lair, this too was locked. Wes went for the keys again.

"You seem a little anxious about somethin'," Wes said, as he paused.

Let's just get this over with. "I'm not feeling well." Yes, contrived, but maybe it *was* time to stage a floor-vomit episode. No, too dramatic. "You just spooked me with all that talk of evil and the Devil." *Better.*

"I know," Wes said. "A lot of bad things happened in this house over the years. And I know you're worried about Marcus, too."

The door swung open. The beam of Wes's flashlight stabbed the room.

"What?" Conrad whispered in disbelief.

Wes didn't hear it. "Well, there's nothin' in this one at all. I don't guess the Laneharts use this one for storage or nothin'." Wes turned the flashlight back into the hallway.

Empty. The makeshift gurney, the gold machine with its dotted yellow-and-green lights, *Jimmy Van Buren's body.* Not a trace. There was no sign anything had inhabited the room for years.

What are you up to, Katarina? Conrad thought. *Where are you, and where have you taken my old body?*

"Let's hurry up and go through the rest of these rooms," Wes said. "I still feel like evil spirits are up here. I'm tellin' you, no disrespect to D'Lynn, Marcus, or *Flannery*..." —the twitch and the rub of the neck— "...but Ten Points is a Hell House."

"Oh that's nonsense," Conrad said. But his mind was elsewhere. He put it all aside long enough to whip up a schoolgirl voice. "Now stop with all that spooky ol' talk, Mister Silly. Let's look in these other rooms and go back downstairs."

Within minutes, the remaining rooms had all gotten the beam of Wes's flashlight. "Well, let's go downstairs and deliver the bad news," he said. "I thought for sure we might find him somewhere up here."

Conrad felt Clementine's cheeks flush, but he controlled his anger.

Marcus. Katarina. Jimmy Van Buren's corpse. All missing from the house.

Conrad would get answers. And he would find all of them.

32

Regan Johnston parked her older-model Nissan Sentra in the Ten Points driveway that evening. She stopped and stood outside the house and looked up to the window of Travis's bedroom. She wasn't sure if showing up was worth the effort. Travis's aloof behavior and distance of the last few days only told her one thing. He wanted to end things and couldn't find the proper way to tell her.

She had decided to show up unannounced at Ten Points. She would face the truth no matter how much it might hurt.

Regan was quiet and a trifle timid at times, but she could speak her mind and stand up for herself in an instant, if her hand was forced. Even the enduring patience of a petite and mild-mannered seventeen year old had a threshold. Travis's short behavior and one-word text message replies had all but broken it.

Regan rang the doorbell and stood aside, as she waited for someone to come to the door. Her relationship with Travis had been challenging enough the past eighteen months. Their parents disapproved of a black girl and a white boy dating, so there was that. Even after Geoffrey and Tilda vanished, she and Travis still faced the objections of her mother.

Tarva answered the door. It was just past dusk, and the sun was gone for the day. "Well, hey there, Regan. I guess you're here to see Travis. Gosh, there's been a lot goin' on in this house today."

"Yeah? What's up?" Regan asked. She could hear voices from the living room.

"Oh Lord, you didn't hear?" Tarva replied. She hated to be the bearer of bad news, at least when it affected her. "Well, Marcus ain't been seen since last night. It's gettin' on close to twenty-four hours. It's like he came out of that coma or whatever it was and just walked off the property. Nobody's found him yet. And I guess you heard about Percy Stratworth? D'Lynn was already upset about that, and now this thing with Marcus has got her even more worked up."

"Who's Percy Stratworth?" Regan answered, with a shrug.

"He was Maxine's piano teacher. They found him dead in his house! We haven't been able to tell Maxine yet. We're still tryin' to figure out how to do it without scarin' or upsettin' her."

"Oh, that's terrible," Regan said. "I hope Marcus is okay. I suppose Travis is out lookin' for him?"

"The last time anybody saw Travis he was headin' toward the woods. Lord, I hope Marcus didn't wander out there somewhere. It's been cold at night."

Regan pulled her jacket more securely around her. "I'm feelin' a chill now," she said. "But I'll go out there and look for him."

"It's dark out there, hon. Why don't you just come sit in here and wait for him? Those woods get kinda spooky-lookin' at night. You couldn't pay me to go down there. You know, it's probably my Uncle Billy's fault I'm scared of the woods at night. When I was a little girl he used to tell me these scary stories about this monster called Two Toes that lived out in the swamp, in those woods we had near our place. Two Toes roamed around the woods at night lookin' for little girls to eat. Ain't that somethin' to tell a little kid? Well, anyway, Uncle Billy finally—"

"So how long ago did Travis leave?" Regan interrupted, in no mood for Tarva's rambling.

Tarva was disappointed Regan didn't want to hear the rest of her story. "Oh ... about twenty minutes ago or so."

"Well, I guess I better go look for him," she said, turning to leave.

"Wait," Tarva called after her. "You need a flashlight before you go out there. I wish you'd just stay in here with us, but you're bein' persistent, so let me get you a flashlight."

Once she had the flashlight, Regan took off across the clearing and tried to forget about Tarva's ridiculous Two Toes story. She could see the dark shapes of the trees off in the distance, underneath the moonlight. The woods were indeed menacing and mysterious, if you were in that frame of mind. Who needed a tall tale about a swamp monster infused with that?

Regan forced her a shift in her thoughts. She went over what she would say to Travis when she found him. Maybe it was better to have the conversation away from the house.

Regan neared the trees. She thought about Tarva's silly tale again. She felt as creeped out as she had when she was a little girl and caught *The Exorcist* playing on cable one weekend. She was a frightened eight year old all over again. She didn't want to go into the woods alone, but her determination to find Travis won out.

Regan's flashlight cut through ahead of her. The woods were empty. The cold air silenced the crickets and other nocturnal noise-makers. There was only the hoot of a stubborn owl off in the distance, holding its ground for the season. If Travis was around, he was deeply entrenched.

"Travis?" she called out, not too loud. When no answer came, she realized it would take more than a low whisper. *"Travis!"*

She waited a few seconds. Nothing. Maybe he wasn't there.

Regan sniffed around, as an odor caught her attention inside the edge of the forest. A sweet smell, kind of like incense, only different. It was almost like a cigarette, only fruitier and less obnoxious than tobacco smoke.

Regan's hands trembled as she scanned the trees with the flashlight. She wasn't sure if it was from being cold or scared, or both.

Then the light caught the face about ten yards away. She screamed and dropped the flashlight.

Regan thought at first it was Travis, but the husky voice was that of a girl or woman. "Oh, for the love of God! Another damn flashlight in my face?" it bellowed.

Regan picked up the flashlight and shined it back on an eerily-familiar face. "Travis?" she asked, even though it wasn't him. But the girl *looked* like him.

She had short dyed-black hair like Travis's and black clothes, only she wore black lipstick. She was maybe late teens or early twenties; it was hard to tell. She smoked what looked to be an electronic cigarette. A light on the end of it glowed red as she took a lazy drag while casually perched on a tree stump.

"You people have *really* got to chill it with the lights in my eyes, man," the Goth girl said.

Her black lacy top looked Victorian, but she wore a mini-skirt and black fishnet stockings that caused Regan to wince and look twice.

"What's the matter? Forgot how to talk?" she asked Regan. "Lookin' for somebody?"

"Who the hell are you?" Regan finally asked. Out of courtesy, she turned the flashlight away but kept a glow around them so they could see one another. Regan stepped closer to the strange girl. "And why are you out here in these woods alone ... smoking? I'm looking for Travis."

"Vaping. Not smoking. Do people even still smoke real cigarettes?" Goth girl grinned. She reached into a small backpack at her side—also black. She pulled out a cigarette case. "I got extras. Wanna join me, man?" she asked, cracking open the case and revealing more of her strange, skinny e-cigs. They weren't white but as black as her clothing and lipstick.

"Thanks, but I don't smoke cigarettes," Regan said.

"Well, like I said, it's vaping, not smoking. These are 'sick sticks'. They're not real cigarettes. And not sick, like they'll make you get sick and die. Sick as in they're *sick,* man!" she said, with an obnoxious but obliging laugh. "But that's cool."

"You still didn't tell me who you are," Regan said. She was closer but kept a cautious space between them.

"I'm Scarlett. And yeah, my hair used to be red to match my name, but I hated my hair, so that's why it's black now. But I get a question for a question. Who are you?"

"I'm Regan. I need to find Travis. Have you seen him? Do you *know* him?"

Then an ugly thought popped into Regan's head.

What if Travis was cheating on her with another girl—*this* girl? This Scarlett person looked to be his type—and certainly the type he would feel at home hanging out with. They even looked alike. Enough to be related. Scarlett was pale, with a skinny build and the same sharp blue eyes.

"I haven't run into anybody tonight, man. But maybe I know him. What does he look like?"

Regan shrugged. "What does he look like ...?" *Um, like you!*

"Look, Regan. In the last couple of weeks, I've had some skinny pale guy dressed all in black with hair like mine shine a light in my eyes. I had some other pale bitch with wavy long hair and mean green eyes wanna throw down and try to kick my ass. Now I've got you shining your light on me askin' random questions. You're the only three people I've run into out here. That are *from here,* anyway."

"From here?"

Scarlett gave a sheepish grin as if she had said too much. "Never mind. I guess the answer to your other question is no, I ain't seen anybody named Travis tonight. And why is a pretty girl like you out here all by yourself anyway?" Scarlett's grin curled salaciously and took another shape as she took a drag off her sick stick. The blue eyes wandered up and down Regan.

Regan returned a nervous laugh. Nope, this Scarlett person wasn't interested in Travis—or *anyone's* boyfriend, for that matter. "Okay, well, nice to meet you, Scarlett. I'll head back to the house now. If you see Travis, tell him to—"

A bright flash of red-orange-white light from deeper in the woods jarred Regan's attention away and almost made her drop the flashlight again.

"What the hell is that?" Regan asked, frightened again. "It looked like a flare, but it went out!"

"Shit," Scarlett said, sliding her sick stick back into the case with the others. When she stood from the tree stump Regan noticed she wore dark running shoes. Shoes that noticeably mismatched the rest of her ensemble. "Well, Regan, I hate to keep this short, but I *must* go ..."

"What?" Regan asked. "Go where? What was that?"

"There's no time. You need to go back where you came from. *Now!*" Scarlett warned her. She slid her arms through her backpack-purse and reattached it to her body.

"Huh?"

"*Go*, Regan! Get the hell out of here!"

Scarlett took off sprinting. "Nice meetin' ya, but do what I say. Go back to where you came from and get out of these woods! It won't be safe in a minute!" Her voice and footsteps trailed off into the distance.

Scarlett hoped Regan heeded her advice, but there was no time. She moved quickly through the darkened woods, ducking hanging branches just in time as trees zoomed by her. The one thing she enjoyed about being a hybrid was her gift of enhanced night vision. It came in handy when the abundance of trees shielded the forest from most of the moonlight.

And tonight, the trees guarded a full moon.

Even the full moon didn't provide much guiding light, and, despite her skilled sight, Scarlett didn't always see everything in time. Out of nowhere, a hand grabbed hold of her. Then two hands had her by the shoulders, pinned against a tree. The cold bark of the pine tree poked at her back, forbidding any escape.

"Well, well, if it is not the little hybrid dyke out again where she does not belong."

Had she been without her enhanced vision, Scarlett would have recognized the thick Scandinavian accent anywhere.

"Let me go, man!" she growled, struggling against Katarina's firm grip.

"I have her. She is over here!" Katarina yelled out into the forest.

"Oh God, *really?*" Scarlett sighed. "Are you out here with *him?* You better not let that fucker put his paws on me, man."

"I am no man, and you are in no position to tell me what to do, junior lesbo. Before he gets here I want you to tell me. *Who* from the house did you run into tonight? I could hear you talking with someone."

"Hmmm .... wouldn't you like to know, Goldilocks ..."

"Do not play games with me," Katarina warned her. "You already made Flannery more suspicious than I need her to be. Thankfully, Travis is too preoccupied with his newfound hybrid identity to care about you."

A look of concern swept Scarlett's face. "The skinny pale kid? Is that who this Travis person is? *Who* attacked him? *Why?*"

"Again, that is no concern of yours," Katarina said, just as footsteps and the crunch of dead leaves and twigs were heard nearby.

"Oh my, what have we here?" His sarcastic and condescending tone caused Scarlett to roll her eyes.

The silhouette of the slim frame with a walking stick, the tall felt top hat, the long elegant jacket, and the large pair of goggles around the eyes were unmistakable from a short distance away.

"Shit," Scarlett muttered. "Really?"

The man walked closer so that he was more visible. He wore a large smile. A fairly young and handsome face that never hid conniving thoughts well—even when infrared goggles covered dancing blue eyes.

"You always wander so far away from home," he said. He used the elegant black walking stick for pompous show rather than assistance with any disability. "Why do you have to be such a little rebel?"

"Take her back where she belongs before someone else sees her and everything is ruined," Katarina ordered him. "I will see you tomorrow."

The man in the top hat turned to Katarina. "Our little party has to end so soon? What a *chore* this evening was! But well worth it, I might add."

"We did what we agreed to do," Katarina told him. "Our task is complete for the moment. We will wait until tomorrow night and then discuss what is to come."

"Well, yes, there is so much more to come," he said, with a delighted smirk. "But the full moon is *tonight*. How do I know it will be back tomorrow?"

"Tomorrow," Katarina repeated, ready to leave. "There are *other* ways ... if the moon changes."

Scarlett was curious but knew they would only talk in code while she was around.

"You vampires and your inconvenient schedules," he remarked, with a smarmy tone and arrogant grin. "How will I ever get my beauty rest when I always have to meet up with you at ungodly hours?"

"If you want your little project to go smoothly, you must," Katarina said, unamused. "*But* ... I could always fix it so that night time is permanently more convenient for you."

"Oh snap!" he replied, with a fey, short laugh.

"Blah blah blah. Can we just *go?*" a huffy Scarlett asked the man, as Katarina released her grip.

He gave a sharp nod and then turned back to Katarina. "Okay, fine. I'll see you tomorrow night. Eight o'clock sharp."

Katarina returned an icy stare. "Do not come back into the house at Ten Points unless I specifically extend an invitation," she told him. Her tone was no-nonsense as usual, but he wasn't swayed. "Tonight was risky. You were almost seen."

"You *still* haven't told Flannery about me?" he asked Katarina, who ignored the question.

"I have to see Conrad about something," she said instead.

"You better keep that *thing* away from me," he hissed, using the walking stick for gesture. His breeziness had dissipated. The sour reaction caused Katarina to smile.

"Hey man, I really wanna see that house sometime," Scarlett said, of Ten Points.

"You *have* seen it," the man said, the walking stick pointed back at the ground. A cooler grin resurfaced as he faced Scarlett.

"Well, not *that* one ..." Scarlett began.

"It's the same!" he replied tersely. The discussion was over—and that was that. "Let's go."

He led Scarlett away but turned back to Katarina. "See you tomorrow, Katty Kat," he said, with a flourish of a farewell wave.

Katarina kept a straight face. "Yes, Alexander," she said. "We will meet again tomorrow."

33

"Travis, I went to the woods and looked for you. I thought you were there, but I couldn't find you."

Travis was sprawled across his bed, reading another graphic novel when Regan walked into his room without an invitation.

He looked up at her, shrugged, and then back down.

"What is the matter with you?" she asked, upset. "Why all this distance? You've barely given me the time of day lately. What is it?"

Travis closed the book, looked at Regan again, and then stood from the bed. He walked over but kept a good foot of distance between them.

"I don't love you anymore," he said calmly. "I think it's time to go our separate ways."

Regan looked like she had been slapped. "What? I—I don't understand. Since when? What the hell is going on with you?"

"I just told you," Travis said, a chill in his voice. "Now please leave me alone."

"I went traipsin' through some damn field and walked half a mile in these shoes with a flashlight in the dark lookin' for you in those scary-ass woods, and *this* is all I get when I *do* find you?"

"I've been back at the house for a while now. You should've looked up here before you went to all the trouble," Travis said. He picked up the book up from the bed and replaced it on a shelf.

Regan stood paralyzed. "What is with the attitude? Are you for fuckin' real right now?"

He walked back over to her. "Sometimes people change, Regan, and they grow apart. I've changed. I'm sure you will too at some point and see that this is for the best."

"Why didn't you tell me all this before? At school?"

"I was trying to think of the right time and place. This ain't really it, but you kinda cornered me, so I guess now is as good a time as any."

Regan turned her back to him. She faced the door so he couldn't see the tears. "Wow, you're a real asshole, Travis," she said, her voice low.

"We're graduating soon. I'll be eighteen in just a couple of weeks. It's time to focus on other things."

She shook her head and couldn't find words.

"You were fun while you were around. But now our fun has ended."

Regan spun around and slapped him across the face as hard as she could. Tears streamed down her cheeks; rage was in her dark eyes. "I was *fun?* That's all? Go to hell, you son of a bitch!"

Travis hardly reacted to the slap and only stood there with a stony glare.

Regan walked out of the room so he wouldn't have the benefit of seeing her cry. She slammed the door as hard as she could on the way out. She wanted Travis's head between it and the doorframe.

She went down the stairs, as quick as she could, wiped her eyes, and prayed she could duck out of the house unnoticed. Luckily, she made it to the foyer and out the front door before anyone saw her.

Outside, Regan went down the front steps toward her car as fast as she could. Then she paused near Travis's Camaro.

Regan's car keys rattled in angry hands. Before she could control her emotions, she pulled one of the keys up like a weapon and went down the side of Travis's car, leaving a long silver line of a scratch in the dark paint.

It wasn't enough. Over by the house, a rake was propped against the corner of the front porch, left behind by one of the daytime groundskeepers. Regan went and grabbed it and was back at Travis's car in two seconds.

With angry force, she smashed out one of the headlights with the handle end of the rake. The crunched sound wasn't enough to quench the fire. Furious exhales of cold fog piped from her nose and mouth.

Between bitter huffs, Regan took out the other headlight. Then she moved to the windshield and gave a hard punch with the wooden handle. She left a spider-web crack in the glass on her second try.

She heaved and cried as she surveyed the damage, but that wasn't why she sobbed. *Damn you, Travis! Damn you!*

There would be consequences. She would be in trouble. She might even face criminal charges. She would worry about it later.

Regan threw down the rake and walked to her own car.

"Vandalism. Tsk tsk," came the voice, a few yards away in the dark.

She gasped and looked up and around before she could open her car door.

A blonde woman Regan had never seen emerged from the shadows, over near one of the oak trees. She came closer. "Do you always have a habit of breaking other people's things?" she asked, in a heavy accent Regan couldn't place.

"I—I don't know who you are. I'm leaving." She sniffled, as she fumbled to unlock her car door.

"Not so fast," said the blonde woman, coming closer. "I would like a word with you. *Regan,* is it?"

Regan stopped her struggle with the car keys and glanced up at her. "How do you know my name? I've never seen you before."

The blonde was only about five feet away. "But I have seen you many times at this house. Perhaps it is time we became better acquainted. Were you in the woods tonight?"

"How do you know that?"

"That does not matter. What did Scarlett tell you?"

"I don't know what you're talkin' about."

"Don't lie to me," Katarina snapped at her. "Do *not* lie to me. I can see it on your face. What did Scarlett tell you?"

"This is too weird. Do you even belong here? You sound like you're from another place. I'm callin' the police."

"Do you think that is a good idea? They will likely arrest you when they discover you did such damage to your boyfriend's car."

Regan pulled out her smartphone anyway, but Katarina quickly snatched it away.

"Hey lady, give that back ..."

Regan's eyes widened in horror before she could get the sentence out. Katarina opened her mouth and revealed large white canine teeth.

There was no time to scream. Katarina was fast.

34

Travis felt an intrinsic shift and shut off his iPod.

Regan.

What had just happened a few minutes ago? Vaguely, he recalled Regan in his room. Then she left all upset. Bit by bit, their conversation trickled back.

"Oh my God!" he exclaimed. He jumped off his bed and rushed out of the room.

He had to find Regan. It had only been a few minutes. Maybe there was still time to catch her. There must be a way to make her understand he didn't mean what he had said. He wasn't in *control.* How could he make her understand it wasn't him—that he wasn't responsible for his own words?

Travis heard voices up the second stairway to the third floor as he neared the other end of the hallway. One of which was familiar.

D.C. Cunningham.

Another shift.

Yes, D.C.! D.C. was in his room just a few minutes before Regan arrived. *D.C. had told him to do something.*

But Travis had no recollection of anything D.C. told him. He was drawn toward the sound of D.C.'s voice at the top of the second staircase. Ever since that strange encounter in the woods, he wanted to be wherever D.C. was. An atypical attraction he could not explain.

Travis forgot about downstairs. He turned the corner and creeped up the second staircase to the third floor.

"We have to be careful," he heard D.C. say. D.C. was with somebody in the third-floor hallway, not far from the edge of the stairs.

"Yes, I know. She told me not to come back to the house unless she extended an invitation," said another man, whose voice Travis didn't recognize. "Good thing it's a full moon outside, and she couldn't see me come in."

Travis paused three-quarters of the way up the stairs, out of sight so he could hear what was said.

"Well, I invited you, and I'm a branch of Katarina," D.C. said loudly, with a laugh. "Here, let's go in this room over here. Nobody'll see us in there."

"Let's keep it down," the other voice said, quieter, more discreet. "I've done a lot for her, but I still don't need her pissed off at me."

"Where is she anyway?" D.C. asked, so loudly that the other man shushed him again. Travis wasn't sure of whom or what they spoke.

Travis tiptoed the rest of the way up the stairs to the third floor just as the first door on right side of the hallway closed gently.

"Here, I'll light a candle," he could barely hear the other man say.

"We don't need that," D.C. replied, muffled but still too audible for discretion.

"We *do*. I want to see this," the other man said, with a short snicker.

What the hell was going on? Travis edged his way closer to the door. D.C. was his master. D.C. wouldn't mind if he invited himself inside the room. D.C. would be happy he desired to be around him.

He hasn't summoned me. I shouldn't, Travis's internal voice said.

But reason argued. *Of course, I should. It's D.C. He will be grateful that I'm so devoted.*

Why was there a dialogue with himself? Where did the other voice come from? Thinking no more of it, Travis placed his hand on the doorknob and gently turned it. He pushed open the door, gentle again, and was confused at the sight before him.

D.C. was slouched in an old armchair, head back and lightly moaning, pants down around his ankles. Another man was down on his knees, hunched over between D.C.'s spread legs. The back of a man's head bobbed up and down into some unseen crevice of the chair, at

D.C.'s crotch.

D.C.'s usual sleeveless button-up shirt was wide open. Travis could see the other man was still wearing a long, old-fashioned-looking jacket. A tall dark top hat, a pair of goggles, and black walking stick with a golden handle were on the floor beside the chair.

As Travis realized D.C. was receiving a blowjob from the other man, an embarrassed look washed over his face. He knew he had to slowly back out of the room and quietly close the door before they knew they were caught.

But a tired crack of the old floor beneath Travis's feet caused both the men to disengage as if one of them was on fire and look in Travis's direction.

The stranger with D.C. had dark blond hair and blue eyes. He jumped to his feet, with the startled expression of someone with something to lose. Travis was more confused by the familiarity of the stranger's face. He was an odd mix of Marcus and Geoffrey Lanehart.

"What the hell are you doing in here?" the stranger demanded, moving toward him.

D.C. gave Travis a bewildered stare. He quickly pulled his pants up, tucked his rather large and erect penis inside as best as he could, and pushed himself out of the chair and to his feet.

"Shit," Travis said, as he backed faster into the hallway. The strange man got closer.

"Shit!" D.C. repeated, panic in his eyes. "Travis, now you just need to go back downstairs ..."

"D.C. you better find a way to erase his memory *right now,*" the strange—but familiar—man ordered. Travis's eyes stayed on the face. The angry, disapproving scowl was eerily reminiscent of his stepfather Geoffrey. Whoever he was, he looked as if he could be Geoffrey's and Marcus's ... *brother?* But they never had a brother, only a sister.

"Oh my God, you look so much like ..." Travis finally said it aloud. "But I don't get it..."

"Shut up. You don't need to *get* anything," the man said sternly, even closer. He looked young, early-to-mid-thirties at the oldest.

"Stay the hell away from me, man," Travis said. He stumbled

backwards down the hallway, afraid to turn away and make a run for it. "I don't know who you are, but I don't care if you guys came up here to fool around. I mind my own business, so it's cool. I ain't gonna tell anybody what I saw if that's what you're worried about."

Travis knew the edge of the staircase was behind him. He caught his footing just in time.

"Alexander, just leave him be. I can handle it," D.C. said, from near the doorway.

Alexander looked over his shoulder at D.C. "You dumb fucker. Why did you have to go and say my name in front of the kid?"

"Alexander? It's cool! I don't know any Alex—" Travis began, but it was too late.

All it took was a swift shove from Alexander Lanehart to send Travis tumbling down the stairs.

The ceiling and the floor spun in circles as Travis fell down the long row of stairs. There were rolls, impromptu somersaults, and the jagged crooks of the steps jabbed and poked. One bang of his head and everything went black as the landing rose to greet him.

Travis hit the landing at the second floor with a thud that could be heard from where the other two men were.

"Oops," Alexander said, with a Cheshire grin.

"Is he dead?" D.C. said, as he ran to Alexander's side.

"Who knows, but it certainly takes care of his memory if he is," Alexander replied. "He was already *half*-dead anyway."

It was impossible to tell how badly hurt a sprawled-out Travis was down below. "Oh holy fuck, how am I gonna explain this?" D.C. muttered, quieter for the first time of the night.

Alexander reapplied the pair of goggles and then his top hat. He gave D.C. a playful strike on the rear with his walking stick. "Not my problem, Dwight Charles. You'll figure it out. But first, please see me out of this obnoxious house before Katarina knows I sneaked in here without her permission."

35

"I'm fine. I'm strong enough to leave here. I *need* to get back to Ten Points," Marcus insisted.

Flannery and Izzy stared at him with some skepticism and shook their heads in unison.

"Thank you for letting me stay here at your house, Izzy," Marcus said. "I guess it was a better idea than Zeke's house."

"Oh please, of course it was," Flannery said. "Zeke's house is the second place they searched after Ten Points. I brought you a change of clothes without anybody seeing me carry them out. I left them in a chair out on the porch when you're ready to get rid of those pajamas."

Marcus had escaped Ten Points the prior evening, just after dusk. After waking in the basement at Ten Points, Flannery checked in on Marcus, who was alone. That was when he revealed he was alert—and that Conrad had drugged him. Flannery used her influence over Henry to have him sneak Marcus out of the house. Thankfully, Flannery successfully distracted Conrad while Henry drove a woozy but conscious Marcus to Izzy's house.

Despite his concerns over Flannery's newest alliance with Conrad against Katarina, Marcus allowed her to help him. He wasn't sure if he trusted her, but there was no other option. He knew Flannery would keep an eye on the safety of everyone else in the house as he regained his strength.

In other developments, a cab driver had gotten a bite from Flannery and the fare of a lifetime by driving Maxine to their Aunt Hattie's house one hundred miles away in Shreveport.

Now Marcus was determined to return to Ten Points and do battle, but neither of the women would hear of it.

"Rest here just another day. I can cook for you. You need to eat!" Izzy said to Marcus. She wagged a scolding finger as if he were a five-year-old child.

"We may not have another day," Marcus said, looking to Flannery. "I'm only here to regroup and strategize. I have a couple of people I need to kill!"

"Careful," Flannery said. "You could still face charges for what you did to Remy."

"And I feel horrible about that. Thank God he's okay. But the others would be justifiable homicide."

"It's already been proven that we can't kill Conrad," Flannery said. "You would only kill Clementine instead. If Conrad hasn't killed her already. And I wish I would've never told you about Katarina."

"You let me in on *that* secret by accident. I was able to hear one of your little powwows with Conrad in my bedroom."

"Well, I also told you those things about the Swedish bitch last night," Izzy said to Marcus, with a guilty expression for Flannery. "Excuse my language, y'all."

"Flannery, I wish you would have told me about Katarina when you first knew she was in the house," Marcus said. "I could've helped you get rid of her. She's responsible for what's happened to you. She has no power over me."

"There's more," Izzy said dreadfully.

"*More?*" Flannery and Marcus asked at the same time.

Marcus was weak but managed to stand from Izzy's sofa. "Izzy, what else is there? Please, I need to know."

"Katarina. She's been spendin' time with Maxine."

"Damn it! I hope she doesn't know how to find her at Aunt Hattie's house. They would both be in danger. We have *got* to go back to Ten Points. Now!" Marcus's hazel eyes were on fire, alert for the first time in days.

"She won't hurt Maxine," Izzy continued. She squinted her eyes, as she dug within and wandered in her mind. "She somehow confuses Maxine with the daughter she lost centuries ago."

Izzy also knew about Percy Stratworth's murder and why Katarina killed him. Marcus was already out for blood. He would only be further agitated if told his niece had been the target of a pedophile.

"She's a three hundred and forty-year-old monster," Marcus said. "I don't want her around Maxine, period. I don't care if she's Mary Fucking Poppins. I don't want her around anybody in my family. Even if Maxine's not in any danger, this Katarina *thing* will kill Aunt Hattie if she figures it out where to find Maxine."

"There was the scrap of paper and the card she kept in the drawer upstairs," Flannery said. "Katarina told me what 'vampire' meant, but I still haven't figured out who Alexander Lanehart is—or if he's anybody at all. I'm working on it. And I hate to say it, but—"

"I've never heard of any Alexander Lanehart in our family, and I hope you're not about to tell me you've asked that son of a bitch Conrad to help you find out who he is," Marcus said, moving closer to Flannery. "It's bad enough you're using him to help you destroy Katarina. He wanted *you* destroyed the last time he was at Ten Points, or have you forgotten that? What makes you think he isn't working with Katarina ... playing you both? It's a good thing I don't hit women, Flannery, or I would slap some sense into you."

"One of us needs to ..." Izzy said, her eyes wandering.

"I didn't have a choice!" Flannery yelled at them. "My back was up against the wall. Plus, we've got this D.C. and Travis mess. It's a cluster fuck over at Ten Points right now!" she continued, then demurred. "Oh, sorry, Mother."

"Make that *three* people to kill. D.C. is going down for what he did to Travis," Marcus said. "I'll send that little redneck bastard straight to hell when I see him again."

"Well, it's—it's not really *all* D.C.'s fault," Flannery stammered. Fearing Marcus's reaction to the next part, Izzy turned away.

"What?" Marcus asked. "How can this shit storm get any thicker?" He was too angry to watch his manners anymore and apologize to Izzy for all the profanity inside her home.

"Look, there's something I need to tell you, Marcus. I need you to keep an open mind and not get angry ..." Flannery began.

Izzy shook her head at her daughter and tried to prevent the next blow. "Gettin' worked up ain't good for you right now," she said, turning back to Marcus. "You're just gettin' able to walk and talk again."

"I'm a big boy. Flannery, tell me. *Now,*" he demanded.

"D.C. is under Katarina's control. She's the one who attacked and turned him." She paused. After a nervous beat, she continued. "I told Katarina to have D.C. attack Travis. I didn't know what would happen ..." It was better to get it all out.

"Flannery, *why?* Oh my God ..."

"Travis knew the secret. I thought if D.C. wielded some influence he could erase Travis's memory of my—my secret."

Marcus turned away. "I know your secret." He looked back to her, his temper gone. The disgust and rage on his face frightened her. "I've known your goddamned secret these last months! I may not have said anything out loud and I may not have wanted to know, but I *know!* Why didn't you just have him attack every-fucking-one of us in the house? Or leave that bitch boarder to just kill us and turn us all in what you all are. You're a thoughtless, selfish *thing* that's not even a real person anymore. I've never been more disappointed in you than I am right now."

"Don't say that," Flannery said, cowering from him.

"No, it's the truth. When everybody judged you for the whole Frank Castille thing, I didn't because you were human and humans make mistakes. But this—this—*this* is unconscionable! You're not even a human anymore, so *how* could you do the right thing? You're nobody ... you're ... *nothing.*"

"Marcus, maybe we can fix it. We don't know if ..."

"Travis could be permanently affected," Marcus said quietly. But he looked like he might explode again at any second. "D.C. was too stupid to realize what he would do. This is on *you,* Flannery."

"I didn't realize it either. Marcus—"

"Get the hell out of my sight, or I'll crawl out of this damn house and go home on my own!" Marcus shouted at Flannery so loudly that even Izzy jumped. "I just want to be away from you. *You're a monster!* You're not my sister! Not anymore! You're some shell of a thing that used to be her, but you're *not* her! I hate you right now, Flannery! I hate you for what you've done to this family!"

Flannery face fell as Marcus's words destroyed her. It was the most human she had felt in nearly six years—even more human than when Izzy revealed they were mother and daughter months earlier. That revelation had brought her some sense of joy and understanding of who she was and why Maximilian had hated her. Marcus's would have torn her heart out, had she still felt it. But they still struck and hurt somewhere.

Flannery walked out to the porch. Izzy looked to Marcus with a mix of pity and disapproval before going after her daughter.

"He's upset. He didn't mean any of that. He'll calm down and be okay later," Izzy assured her, once they were outside. She placed a tender hand on Flannery's arm. "Just let him settle down."

"But he's right," Flannery said. "Everything he said is true. I'm not what I used to be."

"You're still my daughter," Izzy said, stroking her arm. "And I still love you, no matter what's happened or what you've done."

Without any warning, Flannery grabbed Izzy in an embrace. She surprised even herself. Izzy held tightly to Flannery.

It's the last time you'll ever see her.

The voice came from another place, a whisper into Izzy's ear through the light breeze across the front porch. She knew nobody heard it but her. She felt the tears well as another tuft of soft wind brought it again.

It's the last time you'll ever see her.

Izzy pulled away and put on a smile for Flannery. She nodded toward a couple of old wooden rockers. "Let's just sit out here for a while longer. We can let Marcus settle down, and you don't have to leave right now. Just stay a while longer," Izzy pleaded. *It's the last time you'll ever see her.* This was really happening. This was it. "Please don't go just yet. Let's sit here on the porch a while."

"I have to go," Flannery said. "Goodbye ... Mother."

Izzy felt the back of her throat swell but refused to let her daughter see her cry. "Please. Let me look at you." She ran her hands through

Flannery's long, curly hair and touched her face.

"I'm glad we found each other," Flannery said. "I just wish it would've been sooner."

Izzy's chin trembled, but she continued to fight it. "I treasure what time we've had," she managed to say before her voice could break.

Flannery pulled away. She walked down the rickety wooden steps and into the yard. "Promise me you'll get these steps fixed before you fall and hurt yourself one day."

Izzy nodded but struggled with words.

"Why don't you just move out of this house?" Flannery asked. "Marcus would make a place for you at Ten Points."

"I like it here," Izzy said, with the last bit of composure she could muster.

Flannery turned in the yard and looked back once more. She gave Izzy a smile and a wave, then turned and took off.

Izzy managed to hold it together until she saw The Cape ascend into the night sky off in the distance. That was when she finally allowed herself to cry.

It's the last time you'll ever see her.

36

"Flannery Lanehart is a vampire," the voice whispered, into the ear of a sleeping Reverend Wilkins Washer.

"Mmmm," the Reverend mumbled, with a stir.

The bedroom of the parsonage was dark. Conrad—as Clementine—knelt by the Reverend's bedside and fed the old man's subconscious.

Conrad put a hand in the air to cast sleep over the Reverend so he wouldn't wake and find Clementine in his home.

Then he was back at the Reverend's bedside and in his ear. "Flannery has been attacking your son Wes and drinking his blood."

The Reverend tossed a bit more and murmured an unintelligible response.

"Flannery is also the one who killed Percy Stratworth," Conrad lied. "She needed his blood ... Flannery Lanehart is a vampire *and* a tool of Satan."

"Satan!" the Reverend called out. His girth rumbled underneath the covers but he failed to wake.

Conrad smiled. "Yes, that's correct," he cooed, in the soft, sweet voice of Clementine. "It is indeed Satan. Flannery Lanehart *is* Satan. She *must* be destroyed."

Once he was confident the sleeping Reverend was properly fed, Conrad quietly slipped from the bedroom and out the front door of the Reverend's home.

Katarina greeted him out in front of the quaint brick parsonage. She offered a cool nod of approval when the look on Clementine's face told her everything she needed to know.

"He will go after Flannery now?" Katarina asked Conrad.

"Yes, and he won't even realize what led him to it. He'll only know what must be done," Conrad said.

"That will teach her to double-cross me," Katarina said. "Doing it this way is much more, what do they say ... *pragmatic*. Of course, what the old preacher has in store for her isn't even the *real* surprise that awaits the two-faced whore."

"Well, now that I've scratched your back, my dear, it's time for you to return the favor."

"Yes, there is our disorderly friend D.C. that must be dealt with. You will get what you want, and once again I will also get something."

"I wish I could say that I'll miss being Clementine, but I won't. I'm ready to be a man again."

"She is still alive? Clementine?"

"She made a deal with me so she could have Wes Washer as her husband. Flannery upset her so badly the night Clementine and Reverend Washer were at Ten Points, the night Marcus stabbed Remy Van Buren. Clementine was willing to do anything to get back at Flannery after that humiliating scene. That's where I came in. Poor Clementine. But given her job, and Marcus's stay at a mental hospital, it all worked out perfectly for me."

"But you left Clementine LeMonde alive? You were not so merciful with Jimmy Van Buren."

"Jimmy was much more fun to inhabit. I couldn't give it up. Until that punk bastard Travis forced it."

Katarina was intrigued by Conrad's treachery, but she had her own plans for him. She was grateful her thoughts were inaccessible to him. "And D.C. has done with Travis as you asked him to do?"

"Yes, thank you for loaning his will over to me. And in case I forget later, thank you again for what's next. The next part of our plan will be quite ... *delicious*."

And that's only part of what's to come. There is also what's in store for you, demon bastard. "Be that as it may, our dealings are complete after that. I do not stay allied with those I cannot trust," Katarina said, leaving it at that.

"You're so optimistic ever to trust anyone at all."

Katarina laughed but not because anything he said amused her. "Well then, let us go, demon. I will return to Ten Points by air. *You?*"

A final smile from Conrad crossed Clementine's face. "I think I will as well," he said.

A few minutes later, when they were both gone, a confused and groggy Clementine LeMonde came to in the dewy, frigid grass in Reverend Wilkins Washer's front yard.

She shivered as she sat up. Though her teeth chattered, they were hers to chatter once again.

"*Where am I?*" Clementine mumbled, wrapping her arms around her trembling body, though it brought no warmth.

Suddenly, she knew she had been asleep a long, long time.

37

Katarina found D.C. alone, kneeling over an unconscious Travis at the bottom of the third-floor staircase. Helpless, D.C. looked up, unsure what to do. "I think I killed him. The rest of the way," he said.

Katarina shrugged, uninterested, as she took a glance at Travis sprawled out on the floor. "You didn't turn him?" she said. "That is what you do when the heartbeat stops. If you want him reanimated." *Idiot.*

"I don't know if there *is* a heartbeat," D.C. said. "I can't find it. And I'm afraid somebody's gonna walk up any second. Buddy fired me, so I'm not even supposed to be on the property."

Katarina rolled her eyes and knelt beside him. She put her ear to Travis's chest. "Oh," she said, with a flat expression. She detected a faint pulse, but he didn't have to know that.

"*What?*" D.C. asked, his earlier panic returning.

"He's completely dead," Katarina fibbed, rising to her feet. She gave D.C. a fake pout.

"Oh my God! I have to *turn* him?"

"Or you can let him stay dead and be buried like most other humans," Katarina said. "Or, in his case, buried as a dead half-human."

"It's bad enough that I've turned him into this hybrid thing. I don't know if I can turn him the rest of the way. He has school. He has to be out in the daytime."

"You're *so* considerate."

Her sarcasm went over his head as he carried on. "There've been so many weird things goin' on around here. I just don't know what to do."

"Yes, it has not been boring at Ten Points this past year ..."

"I just don't know." D.C. repeated, as he stared at what he believed to be Travis's lifeless body. "I wish I hadn't snuck Alexander in he—" His eyes widened as he realized his big-mouthed mistake and quickly shut up.

Katarina moved closer to him. "Please finish. You sneaked Alexander in where? Here?"

D.C. returned a sheepish grin. "He kinda propositioned me. I wanted to see if it was still possible to ... well, you know."

Katarina looked on him with disgust. "Sex is overrated and a waste of time," she said. "And *very* human at that ..."

"It's different for a man," D.C. said. "You wouldn't understand."

"I understand men are fucking pigs," Katarina shot back. An angry twist of her face brought her memories of depravity. "I was attacked and raped by two men who came to pillage my house after the bodies of my Arfast and Edela were carried away. They had no feelings. They were filthy animals. *Pigs!*"

She was almost embarrassed, uncertain why she allowed herself to blurt out such things to D.C. Katarina never revealed anything about her past life with anyone, much less an underling such as the one before her.

"But I dealt with them later," she added, a smile surfacing, as her mind took an excursion.

She was wrapped in a thick shawl. It covered the top of her head, but she was still cold. Blood still ran from between her legs.

She didn't know if she closed the door when she stumbled from her modest home. Or the *house.* It was no longer a home.

Katarina wobbled her way through the freezing woods on injured and aching legs. She knew she must get away from the house. It stunk of her two attackers, and there was the pungent bite of death before they arrived. She had taken off with little protection from the cold; she wore a flimsy pair of last year's shoes.

The sharp air and mist in the forest hit her on the surface. Her skin prickled underneath her thin shawl and rag of a dress. She had felt so little the past few days; the cold made her feel. There was a strange solace in the agony and tangibility of it.

The mist, in some small way, helped wash off death and the mark of the two animals. Her legs hurt from days in the chair, the rape that followed; her sex ached underneath the crust of her blood. Her jaw trembled, her teeth chattered.

It was dark in the woods; the bright red-orange-white light farther away brought her back to her senses and shoved the wet and cold to the background.

She stood planted underneath the elements, convinced after a moment it was her imagination. Or maybe not. Could it be?

Edela.

Katarina moved in the direction of large flash, gone amongst the trees and into the darkened sky. It was from Heaven, from Above; it must be! The Almighty and the angels would smile upon her. It was time to go Home. To be with them.

"Edela ... Arfast ... Edela," she said, stumbling through the thickets of small trees, her voice cracked, hoarse, and deflated. She let the mist go into her mouth, as she inhaled and exhaled through it. She trudged through leaves and twigs and paid no attention to the wear on wet, bruised, bloody feet inside rotting shoes.

Katarina could barely see ahead into the dark. She was disoriented; she lost even more direction. She no longer knew from where the light had come. Yes, she convinced herself, again, it was a hallucination, nothing real.

Then—a faint noise off in the distance. Or maybe it too was only in her mind. Icy mist blew at her.

Katarina stopped again. There *were* sounds of footsteps. Someone running. Furious footsteps. Someone came for her. Perhaps someone from the village who would demand to know why she was out wandering when she had been ordered to stay in her house.

Or *maybe* it was one of the two men—or someone else—who would violate her again.

She wanted to turn and run away. She was too weak. She could never outrun whatever it was. The footsteps were too heavy. Too noisy for Edela; too menacing for Arfast.

"No, please," she pleaded, inaudible, unable to change whatever might happen. She couldn't see anything around her.

Then the brute force of the hands came out of nowhere. They reached out and shoved her to the wet and frozen forest floor.

Katarina screamed with what was left inside her, but she wasn't sure why she bothered. She resigned herself to the fact she was to be attacked and raped again. She prayed it finished her this time.

"Who are you?" the voice of a man demanded. His accent was different. Katarina had never been out of Sweden; she couldn't place it.

"Please, I am the wife of Arfast Gerhardsson."

She kept her head turned; fearful eyes squeezed shut as he pinned her down to the ground.

"What did you see? To whom did you speak?" he asked, rattling her.

"The light?" she coughed out, then clammed up. "I saw n-nothing else. I s-saw no one." *Please, kill me, please...*

"Do not lie to me, woman," he said. "To whom did you speak?"

"No one. Please ..."

"No one came from the light? Are you sure of that?"

"Yes, please ..."

"Very blonde. A pretty lady. Where is your husband?"

"He—He—*He's* ... dead."

"Open your eyes. *Do it!*"

"I want my Edela," she cried, slowly opening her eyes. Her hazy stare appeased him.

He looked like a Spaniard, with thick curly light brown hair and an olive complexion with brown, almond-shaped eyes. What she had heard of how Spaniards looked anyway. Despite being in the middle of the frosty woods on a frigid night, he looked clean and his face was freshly shaven. His force greatly outweighed his modest build.

"Beautiful," he said, looking down on her. She saw a hint of a smile.

"Please let me. I must ..." *Die.*

"Your husband is dead, you say?"

Katarina began to shake uncontrollably and turned her head away again.

"If he is dead as you say, he has no claim on you any longer. You will come with me to *Tres Puntos* at once," he said.

"I do not understand," she said.

"*Tio Poäng.*" The smile began to fade. "I will make you understand," he said. His mouth opened, and his canine teeth were twice their previous size.

"Oh my blessed God ...!"

"I am Demetrio," he said. "And you are *mine!*"

She was too weak to fight. He sank his teeth into her. There was a sharp pain, but she could feel. Soon, it gave way to a state of rest and relief. An escape from the last days of despair; weeks of illness and worry and fear. She surrendered. It was time to go; she let herself go.

I will now go to be with my Edela and my Arfast, she thought, her final mortal thought.

Then Katarina Gerhardsson died.

She wasn't sure how much time had passed when her eyes opened and took in the night sky above her. The air was dry, but stars and other worlds twinkled a greeting amidst the black above her.

There was no heaven, no Arfast. No Edela. *There was no God.*

But there was this. She was on another plane, and it was better than where she had ever been.

There was suckling. Her lips. Her teeth. They were latched to something. As her eyes considered the sky, they moved to where she fed on Demetrio's wrist. It was slashed, and she drank from the wound ... was it *his blood?* It felt natural, normal. It made her strong; it awoke her. She could see the shapes of the stars, the colors, and then past the stars. There was more beyond that. There were thoughts and knowledge she had never possessed. Unlike all things from before, her husband, her Edela, her body, nobody could take this away.

"There, there," Demetrio said to her in a coddling manner, as if she were a newborn. "Easy easy. Too much, too soon. There is time for it all. More time than you realize."

He cradled her in his arms and looked down on her with adoration that hadn't been there when they first met. With love, he brushed small but firm hands across her forehead and hair.

Katarina's body was new and no longer ached. There was no more lonely or scared or cold or wet. The weather and the elements of the forest were of no consequence to her. Since Demetrio forbade her more of his wrist, she methodically licked the rest of the blood from around her lips. She refused to spare a drop. She stared into the dark eyes. She was *his*. She wanted to be *his*.

Her Master.

"You will now go with me. To my Tres Puntos. Your Tio Poäng," Demetrio said.

"Is that a village? You must explain," Katarina said. Her voice was strong again. There was no effort with her words.

He laughed and smiled, and tenderly brushed her cheek with the back of his hand. "I *must?* I think I will very much enjoy your company," he said, then threw his head back and laughed again.

Katarina sat up but refused to leave Demetrio's arms. She wanted to be near him. She *needed* him. "Where is this place you speak of?"

"Three Points is a place," he said. "There are ten such places in all the world. They are mine. One day you shall understand. I shall teach you all I know. You will be *mine*."

Katarina wanted to see and to understand, but first, *first,* she wanted more blood. A stolen glance at Demetrio's quickly-healed wrist told her he would oblige her no more of his.

"Before we go to this Three Points you speak of," she said, drawing even closer to Demetrio, running a finger through one of his dark brown curls, "may we stop by my village? There are two men there I would like to bid a farewell."

"*You dealt with who? Who did you deal with?*" D.C.'s twang brought Katarina back to Ten Points.

Tio Poäng. The thought of Demetrio made her smile.

Katarina came to her senses and refused any further romantic indulgence in front of a curious D.C. She shook off days past and took on a sober face. "Never mind. It is none of your concern. But I will deal with Alexander later for his disobedience."

"I hope I didn't get him in any trouble," D.C. said. "You know, sometimes *I just wish ...*"

Katarina came closer to D.C. Her plan for Conrad would be easier to accomplish than she thought. "Sometimes you wish *what,* little vampire fag?"

"That this'd never happened. I want to be a human again."

"Hmmm." Katarina looked away with a grin and then her eyes were back on him. "What if I told you there was a way? A way for you to *feel* human again ..."

"Well, I'd be human again only to go to prison for killin' somebody," D.C. said, nodding to an unconscious Travis, whom he believed dead.

"No, no, perhaps this method we use to make you *feel* human can also resurrect little Travis?" she said to him, with a smile. "Then everyone wins, no?"

"What is the *method?*" D.C. asked, skepticism on his face.

"Well, since you did Conrad's bidding like I asked and helped drive a wedge between Travis and Regan and led her to *me*, I think you deserve a reward." *D.C. was so gullible.*

"Oh cool okay," D.C. said. He smiled, embracing the idea of a prize. "What's the reward?"

Katarina could feel Conrad's presence circling them, as the hallway grew warmer. "You sell your soul to Conrad and *his* Master."

"Oh, I don't know," D.C. said. "That would mean I'll go to Hell when I *for real* die?"

"Come now, D.C.," Katarina said, putting a maternal hand on his shoulder. "Hell will be like one big gay circuit party. Lots of hot young men. All for you. All for eternity. You like the sound of that, no?"

D.C.'s smile widened. His baby blue eyes did a dance. "Like in *Doctor Remy* hot, or what?"

"Way, *way* hotter than Doctor Remy," Katarina promised, her own eyes narrowed. Men were indeed pigs. "They will make Doctor Remy look like, what do they call it, a cow patty ... you like, yes?"

"I do miss my old life," D.C. said. "And it would be nice to eat some of D'Lynn's fried chicken. And see the sunlight. Maybe I could even talk Buddy into givin' me my job back."

Katarina shrugged and played along. She couldn't see or hear Conrad but could feel his frustration and impatience, through the mugginess of the hallway.

"*Yes?*" she said, motioning with a hand gesture for an answer.

"Okay, it's a deal," D.C. sighed.

His loud exhale was interrupted by a jolt of his body. A spasm shot through D.C. His face contorted as if he were in a violent seizure.

He was.

After a few seconds, he ceased shaking, and, following heaves and deep breaths, D.C.—or what appeared to be D.C.—settled and looked over to Katarina.

"I'm a man again," Conrad said, relieved and smiling widely. He glared down at Travis on the floor. "And what about him?"

"What about *D.C.?*" Katarina asked. "I gave you latitude. What did you do?"

"D.C. just walked in past the doorman at that circuit party you promised him," Conrad smiled. "At least I hope that's what happened, but who the hell really knows," he added, with an impish smirk he could never quite pull off as Clementine. "No pun intended, of course."

"If D.C. is destroyed and his hold over Travis no longer exists, that means Travis is fully human again and no longer a hybrid," Katarina reminded Conrad.

"That's the only part of this I *don't* like," Conrad replied, new loathsome eyes on the sleeping boy. "I would've preferred the little son of a bitch to be fully turned. Watching him eat Harry the tarantula was amusing. I looked forward to more of those kinds of moments. I will still take care of him for good. One day."

"Well, I have taken care of Regan, so his return to humanity won't be a happy one," Katarina said. "Just as you asked, demon."

"Where is Regan?" Conrad asked, with a concern for the girl Katarina did not understand. "What have you done with her?"

Katarina's eyes wandered mischievously and then back to Conrad. "Just know that she is around."

"What does *that* mean?"

"It *means* I have plans for her. It is nothing for you to worry about."

"*Don't* do anymore harm to her," Conrad warned. Katarina wasn't sure why he made the request. Why was Regan's well-being important to him? "I know I wanted you to *turn* her. Use her however you like but don't do anything else to physically hurt her. If you agree to keep Regan safe, I will play along with whatever it is you are up to."

"Thank you for your help with the Flannery problem," Katarina said. She was curious about his odd Regan request but wouldn't inquire any further, not for now. "I threatened to kill everyone in this house if Flannery crossed me, but feeding the Reverend's ear may turn out to be a more favorable alternative."

Travis stirred on the floor.

"Put on your best D.C. imitation and carry the skinny kid to his room. Pick him up off the floor, demon. You're a man now."

"And then?" Conrad asked.

"D.C.'s hold is broken so Travis will not remember anything from this evening," Katarina said.

"I will put young Travis to bed. My score will be settled with him another day. For now, it's time to watch Flannery go down."

"Watch whatever I do to her from afar," Katarina told Conrad. "As I said earlier, our alliance is over. I want no more to do with you, demon."

As she walked away from him, Conrad ran his fingers inside D.C.'s shirt, proudly rubbing at his new body.

We're not finished, bitch, Conrad thought. *You only think we are.*

Katarina walked away with a victorious smile. Conrad was a fool. He had just possessed a body dead for days. *A vampire.* Had he not done his homework? Did he not realize he too was doomed as well?

38

"Where is Travis?" Remy Van Buren asked, in the living room of Ten Points.

Thunder rattled the house, as a rainstorm moved in from nowhere, but no one paid it any mind. It was Louisiana, and storms crept up at odd times.

Flannery, D'Lynn, Tarva, and Wes Washer were all seated at various places around the living room. Flannery and Wes, in two of the leather armchairs; D'Lynn and Tarva, on the sofa.

Flannery noticed Remy wouldn't look in her direction. He had called a meeting; she knew his mood was no-nonsense.

"I told him he needed to be here," Tarva said. "Regan stopped by and went up to his room about an hour ago. Maybe I should go check on him?"

"You should probably knock first," Flannery said.

"Can you please go see about him?" Remy said. "I'll keep this as brief as possible. I know it's late."

"What is this about?" Flannery asked, wishing he would give her eye contact. She would be able to read him, know what he planned to say, and steer him in another direction—if warranted.

"Let's wait until Tarva and Travis are here," Remy replied, staring nowhere.

They sat in uncomfortable silence a few more minutes, isolated inside the warm living room from the chill and spill of late-autumn rain, audible through a shuttered window.

Tarva returned, with a look of concern. "Travis is alone and asleep," she said. "He mumbled for me to 'eff off' and rolled on his side when I tried to wake him. I'm sure he didn't know it was me when he said that."

"Sounds like Travis," Flannery said. She was pleased to hear some things hadn't changed since D.C.'s attack.

"Oh, that boy has been through a lot, but I *will* hold him down and wash his mouth out with a bar of soap one of these days," D'Lynn said.

"Travis and I have spoken more than once, and we never get anywhere," Remy said. "We can have this meeting without him."

"Why are we here?" Wes asked, twitching every time he looked across the room at Flannery. "This has more to do with your brother?"

"Yes," Remy said. "I'm heading to New Orleans tomorrow and then back to Chicago after that."

"What?" D'Lynn asked immediately, disappointed. "You've been such a help here in the house since my heart spell."

"And I was happy to help you," Remy replied, "but with all due respect, my purpose here was never to be anyone's resident doctor." His eyes went to Flannery and quickly away again. "Nor was I here for any *other* reason," he added. "I lost focus, and now I need answers. I *must* have answers!"

"We've told you everything we know," Wes said.

"I believe *you* have, Wes, but I don't think everybody has. I need to know what my brother did here, with whom, and why he was calling himself Conrad."

"You would have to ask *him* that," Flannery said coldly.

Remy was leaving. *Fine.* Flannery wasn't sure how else to distract him. He would find fewer answers in New Orleans than he had at Ten Points, or the Monroe area. Conrad hadn't exactly left a paper trail of receipts and documents in his years of roaming the world. He had taken great care *not* to do so. Remy would hit roadblock after roadblock. Then he would be forced home to Chicago, head down, tail between his legs. *Good!* Flannery thought. But it bugged her to think she might not want him to leave.

She had to stop thinking like a human.

Flannery noticed Wes's eyes on her, his unusual tics and twitches.

She would have to pay him visits again once Remy was gone.

"I never really saw this Conrad fella," Tarva said. "I was awful busy with D'Lynn in the kitchen that weekend. I didn't come out here much where the guests were."

"He was a business associate of my brother's. That's all I know," Flannery said, sticking with her original story. D'Lynn knew there was more to it than that but didn't let on otherwise.

"Then I guess I leave with little more than I already knew when I arrived here," Remy said, accepting defeat.

From the foyer, one of the large front double doors creaked open, brought a new distraction, and turned up the volume of the rainstorm outside. Everyone was caught off guard, though they couldn't see past the living room doorway to the unexpected guest. The noise of heavy rain faded as the door closed again. Then came the wet and squeaky click-clacks of hard-soled shoes across the marble floor. Whoever it was came for them.

Tarva gave D'Lynn a shrug as everyone turned to see who would be next to walk into the living room.

"This meeting is adjourned, I guess," Remy said, less interested and turning back to the group. "I'll probably never know what happened to my brother. I'll be on my way in the morning. Part of me feels like coming here was a colossal waste of time."

"No, it wasn't," Marcus said, appearing in the living room. Everyone but Flannery burst with sighs of joy, relief, awe. Marcus was freshly shaven, showered, and dressed in the white button-down dress shirt, tan jacket, slacks, and black loafers his sister had left at Izzy's house. He looked more like someone off to church than a homecoming.

"Oh, it's a miracle!" D'Lynn called out to everyone, with a smile. "Praise Jesus!"

Flannery looked up at her brother and then away again. He seemed to have regained even more strength since tearing into her only an hour earlier at Izzy's house.

Marcus favored D'Lynn with a smile and a nod. He quickly motioned for D'Lynn, Tarva, and Wes to retake their seats when they stood to greet him.

Marcus turned back to Remy. "You coming here wasn't a waste of time. I have the answers you need about your brother."

Remy wore an incredulous expression. "Where have you been? How are you feeling?"

Marcus shook his head. "Never mind about me. I know words can't make up for what I did to you in the study, but I hope one day you'll find some way to forgive me. For now, the only way I can try to make amends for what I did to you is to tell you the truth."

"Then tell me the truth," Remy said.

"Marcus, you haven't been well. Maybe—" Flannery began.

"*No,*" Marcus said, with a sharp turn to his sister. "This has to end. Tonight. No more secrets. No more hiding the truth."

"What ... *secrets?*" Remy asked.

"Your brother Jimmy. He was here. He was possessed by a demon. Or maybe a spirit. An evil spirit. I don't know what to call him ... except for *Conrad.* The last seven years of his life ... Conrad lived inside your brother's body. He came here, and he made a deal with my brother Geoffrey ..." Marcus turned to Wes. "I need you to take a statement. This will probably incriminate me. I don't care. I'll do this without a lawyer here."

"*Marcus!*" Flannery insisted. He ignored her.

"Um, okay," Wes said, fumbling for a small notepad from his front pocket. He was still in full uniform after coming off a shift.

"This is incredible," D'Lynn murmured to a petrified Tarva. "I never heard of such. A *demon?*"

"Yes, D'Lynn, it's true," Marcus said, then turned back to Remy. "Last spring ... well, probably way before that ... the family finances were in a jam. Geoff wanted that fixed. But Geoff wanted more than that. Daddy was still alive at the time, but Geoff wanted control of the property, the businesses. He wanted better assurance *he* remained the sole heir, even though Flannery and I were disowned and out of the family. He somehow came into contact with Conrad, maybe through his lawyer James Ruffin? I'm not sure how Geoff met Conrad. I guess we'll never know. Conrad promised him all the wealth he could imagine *if* Geoff promised to hand over Ten Points—and Bobby."

"Oh my Heavens!" D'Lynn exclaimed, starting to cry. Tarva patted and tried to calm and shush her.

"*A demonic possession?*" Remy asked, a half-smile. "How is this incriminating? It sounds a little ridiculous, don't you think?"

"A year ago I wouldn't have believed it either. I'm not a religious person. But I swear on the lives of everybody I care about in this house that what I'm telling you is what I believe to be the truth," Marcus said.

"It all sounds ludicrous," Remy said, feeling the need to sit in one of the other empty chairs. "If this is your way of trying to cover up something else, then I'll—"

"I'm *not*. Conrad has a stake in Ten Points. He was born and died here." Marcus took a deep breath. Of course it sounded crazy! "Conrad is the spirit of Theodore Ogden Junior."

Remy gave a short, disbelieving laugh.

"Who is that?" Tarva asked.

Marcus knew he had to ignore Remy's skepticism and continue. "His father, Theodore Senior—he went by 'Ted'—built the original house and later, *this* house. The original house burned to the ground in the year 1821. Ted Senior was the original master of Ten Points. He spent the next eight years building *this* house. Then Conrad—or *Teddy*, as he was called in those days—inherited it. Conrad killed himself in the study, back in the year 1872. He thought the love of his life, his cousin Adam, had died of the flu. Teddy's three children and wife died that winter, but there was some kind of mix-up. Teddy thought Adam died, too. That was what sent him over the edge. He killed himself before he could be told Adam was still alive. Teddy loved Adam more than his own wife or kids."

"Those three kids I saw in the hallway ..." Remy exhaled quietly, a serious expression back on his face.

"You've seen them, *too?*" Tarva gasped, then went quiet.

"I've seen 'em before but not in a long time," D'Lynn said, still sniffling over the Geoff and Bobby revelation. "I also had staff quit over the years, claimin' they saw ghosts. One young woman who used to help me with the cookin' snuck up to the third floor one time and ran downstairs screamin' and carryin' on. She told us Ted Senior came after her. She even said she touched him, and he felt like a real person. Mister

Lanehart fired her after that, for breakin' rules and goin' to the third floor. He called her a crazy blankety-blank, cut her a severance check, and made her leave."

"Good ole Dad," Flannery muttered.

Marcus stayed silent about his own experience with another mysterious ghost child. He continued. "Conrad knew Jimmy Van Buren's body would eventually grow old. He planned to possess and take over Bobby when Bobby came of age."

D'Lynn shook her head and grabbed a tissue from a side table.

Tarva shrugged. "But *why?*"

"Bobby was mentally challenged. Geoff didn't want the burden. Conrad would have pretended to be Bobby. I guess a version of Bobby who finally developed normally, who knows. Geoff planned to take Tilda and go away so they wouldn't come under suspicion. Bobby, or *Conrad*, would have gained control of the estate."

"Geoff and Tilda would come under suspicion for *what?*" Wes asked, looking up as he jotted notes.

Flannery, uneasy, made a slight turn in her seat.

"Of being the living dead," Marcus announced, after another deep breath. He knew no other way to say it. Better to rip off the bandage. Better not to sugar-coat it.

"Oh, come on!" Remy replied, slamming a hand down on the arm of his chair. He was on his feet. *"The living dead?"*

"It sounds incredible, but it's true," Marcus said. "Geoff and Tilda were already dead. It happened the weekend I came home for Dad's funeral. Tilda turned Bobby into one of them to keep Conrad from her son. Conrad went crazy with rage and destroyed Tilda. She turned into dust in this very room. I never believed in such things, but I saw it. *I did!* I was here when it happened!"

D'Lynn started bawling, and Tarva had to put her arms around her for consolation. Remy refused to sit back down and paced the room, trying to process but unable to accept what he heard.

Remy wasn't the only one. With a raised brow, Wes set down the note pad. "I don't mean no disrespect, Marcus," he said, "but this sounds way too hokey and crazy. I can't put none of this in a report. There's not even no evidence to prove it."

"Wes, you were there when the rest of it happened," Marcus said. "Bobby tried to attack you and chased you outside to the front yard. Geoff went after him to try and stop him. It was dawn, and the sun came up. Geoff ran out of time. He burned up and exploded into a pile of dust on the front porch. Bobby did the same thing when he chased you around the yard. That was why you found their clothes but no bodies."

D'Lynn cried loudly. Tarva sobbed alongside her. Flannery sat motionless and expressionless. Waiting to be exposed, Marcus assumed, as he looked at her. His eyes went back to the others before she caught him. He was still angry over her revelation about Travis and couldn't entertain the idea of a one-on-one conversation with her.

"There's that time gap," Wes said, looking to Remy. "Remember, I told you there was a chunk of time I couldn't remember from that day."

Flannery broke her mannequin pose and quietly stared down at her hands in her lap.

"*How* did Geoff and Tilda and Bobby become one of those things ... those livin' dead creatures?" D'Lynn asked, red-eyed and clutching the tissue tightly in her hands between sobs.

Marcus shook his head and looked away. As angry as he was with Flannery, he couldn't betray her.

She saved him the trouble. "Because of me," Flannery said, breaking her silence. Her eyes remained on her hands. She was so stiff in the chair that only her mouth moved. *"It's all because of me."*

39

"Marcus has told them everything about you," Katarina whispered to Conrad. Her cold hand rested on his shoulder as they listened from the second floor at the top of the stairs.

"Yes, my dear, I have ears. I heard it all at the same time you did," he replied.

"Now the whore is down there revealing herself to them. What will she say? I have power over her. She cannot tell them of me."

"Well, if Marcus knows, he can sing them a song about you. You have no power over him."

"What about you? They now know who you are."

"They will only think I'm D.C.," he corrected, with a grin. "Unlike you, I'm very good at disguises."

Dead *disguises. Just wait and see what happens to* you *in the next few days, demon bastard.* "The doctor finds the story too incredible. He may be our only chance."

"Don't be ridiculous," Conrad told Katarina. "He's desperate to know what happened to his brother. After Flannery is done he will believe everything. I should have destroyed her long ago."

"You should have been a better nurse and made sure Marcus Lanehart was properly taking his dope."

"Once I have control of Ten Points and Marcus again, Katarina, you will need to find a new place to hide. Only it will be from *me* this time. After I deal Flannery and Travis, *you're* next." Conrad smiled and gave Katarina a peck on an icy cheek.

She knew differently but kept her hand low. He could do nothing to make her play it this early. "You think I am so stupid to know you weren't conspiring with Flannery and me against the other?" Katarina asked, wiping away Conrad's kiss. "I always have a plan." *Just wait and see, demon.* "You are a fool to keep chasing after your precious Marcus. What is it about him that is so special?"

"He is the reincarnation of my Adam," Conrad said. He stared at her as if she should understand.

His unwavering belief in such nonsense made it hard for her not to chuckle back at him. "You do not know that. You should forget Marcus. Go on a singles site with this new body and identity. For lack of a better phrase, there are other fish in the sea. Don't you like the women as well? Double your chances."

"You closed yourself off from that kind of thing long ago. You cannot possibly understand. Marcus *is* Adam."

"My Arfast is gone forever. He cannot be replaced. My husband will not ever come back to me in some reincarnation, as you call it."

Conrad narrowed his eyes. "Oh no? Well, my dear, you certainly seem to think your *daughter* has."

"You do *not* speak of my Edela ever, demon," she hissed, as the eyes flared. "*Ever.*"

"You and your precious Edela may be split apart forevermore when Flannery finishes her last speech ever down there. What will you do to prevent that?"

Katarina peered around the corner and down to the foyer toward the living room. "There are other ways out of this house. I will take Edela and go into the night. I know *where* to go."

"You mean Maxine. You'll take *Maxine* and go into the night ..."

"Shut up, demon."

"You know, Katarina, all could be forgiven when the Laneharts find out how you protected Maxine from Percy the pedophile. They may even let you stay here and be a live-in nanny. Hell, you would probably be up for a community service award. But you would still have *me* to worry about, of course."

"I will take her and leave this house," Katarina replied, unamused.

"Enjoy your little mother-daughter fantasy with Maxine while you can, bitch, because I meant what I said. Once Flannery and Travis are gone, I'm coming for you."

"I am not certain why you think you have a score to settle with me, demon," Katarina said, unafraid. "I have done nothing to you. I even kept your secret when you did your drag number as Clementine."

"But you took Jimmy Van Buren's body away and didn't tell me. Where is Jimmy?"

"Nowhere you will ever find him."

Conrad batted his eyes mockingly. "Pretty please, with sugar on top...?"

"Why is it so important? You will never be able to inhabit that body ever again. Who knows if it could ever be useful to you anyway. It has stitches and scars. It is flawed and ugly. Why would you want it?"

"Why would *Alexander Lanehart* want it? I already know he has it. And you're a fool if you think I don't know where he took it. *What* are his plans?"

"I did not ask him," Katarina said, with a shrug. "But we both know you're not able to touch what Alexander holds. Now that you have *D.C.'s* body." *And you won't touch anything else for much longer.*

"Damn you both," Conrad said, the smile now only clenched teeth.

"It is time for me to leave. Flannery cannot expose me, but her brother can. I do not intend to wait around."

"Will you leave a forwarding address?" Conrad asked, with one last stare. "I *do* have to eventually destroy you one day and all."

Katarina ignored the jab. "I left something outside in the yard for the whore. If you see her before she finds it, tell her it is from *me*."

"Oh yes, the surprise you mentioned when we dumped Clementine off at the parsonage. I hope you got Flannery something good. The holidays are around the corner."

Katarina gave him a smile. "My gifts are always good. And this one is the kind that keeps on giving, as they say."

Conrad turned to eavesdrop downstairs once more, as Katarina walked away. He listened in as Flannery confessed to the others.

Stupid, he thought, as he turned his attention to Flannery. *You've just signed your own permanent death warrant. You better pray one of them destroys you first.*

Then a sudden scream from the other end of the hallway. *"Edela!"*

The shriek pierced the second floor. Everyone went quiet downstairs as Katarina's loud wail traveled throughout the rest of the large house.

Katarina flew down the hallway from Maxine's bedroom in a panic. "My Edela! *My Edela is gone!*"

Conrad was gone, too. Marcus, Remy, and Flannery raced to the top of the stairs and were face-to-face with Katarina.

"Like hearing a super loud rat trap snap shut," Marcus said to Katarina. "I'm glad I got home in time to see you take the bait. Did you *really* think I would leave Maxine alone anywhere in this house after I found out about you?"

"Where is my Edela?" Katarina cried, her blue eyes jumping from Marcus to Flannery to Remy.

"She's the hell away from you, that's where," Marcus replied. "And my niece's name is Maxine, you dead bitch."

40

"Stay here, ladies," Wes said, as D'Lynn and Tarva stayed on the sofa and held tight to one another.

A flash of lightning outside caused the lights of the house to flicker, but no one noticed.

"What was Flannery sayin'?" Tarva asked, looking strangely at D'Lynn. "She's a vampire? *That's* what it's called? And she turned Tilda into one?"

"Oh, Reverend Washer is right. The Devil's found his way into this house," D'Lynn said, pulling another tissue from a nearby box.

"I'm goin' up the stairs to see what the ruckus is," Wes told them.

"Yeah, you're the one with a gun. You shoulda been the first one up there!" Tarva snapped at him.

Wes sprang up the stairs, where Marcus, Remy, and Flannery faced down a blonde woman in a blue business suit in the hallway.

"You turned my sister into a monster, and I swear to God I'll destroy you if it's the last thing I ever do," Marcus said to her.

"Where is my Edela?" Katarina repeated. She appeared helpless and outnumbered, at least to Wes or any other stranger. "Bring her to me!"

"I've already told you her name is Maxine!" Marcus said. "She's not your daughter ... she never was!"

"Who is this?" Wes asked.

"Katarina," Marcus said, not taking his eyes off her. "The one who's responsible for what Flannery's become."

"I'm standing right here," Flannery said. She hated when people spoke of her as if she weren't in the room. "I know you're mad at me for what I did to Travis, Marcus, but I'm standing right *here!*"

Marcus ignored her. A heavy roll of thunder outside rattled the house.

"How do we get her out of here?" Remy asked. "Does she know where my brother is?"

"I don't know," Marcus said. He moved toward her, but Katarina bared her fangs and hissed loudly at him.

"What the hell," Remy muttered, stepping back.

"Oh dear Lord," Wes mumbled, reaching for his gun.

"Marcus, don't go any closer to her," Flannery warned. "She can take you down in one strike."

Wes stood back with a hand on his revolver and radioed for backup.

"What the hell will that accomplish?" Marcus asked, staring over his shoulder at Wes. "You can't cuff her or take her to jail, and I doubt a taser or a bullet will work."

"Me and Stretch can at least get everybody else out of this house," Wes said. "This *hell house!* Where's Travis?"

"Tarva said he was in his room when she came in earlier," Flannery said. "Don't you remember?"

"What are you doing?" Remy asked, as Flannery moved closer to Katarina.

"We're the same," Flannery said, at Katarina's side. "She and I can talk this out. Everybody else ... go downstairs."

"No way," Marcus said. "This won't be negotiated. Not while I'm here. There's only *one* way to end this."

"So, whore, you're on my side now, yes?" Katarina said, staring at Flannery and back to the others. "You are done plotting with Conrad to destroy me?"

"Conrad?" Remy asked. His dark eyes widened with strange hope. "My brother *is* still around? *Where is he?*"

"He's not here," Flannery said, fast and dismissive. "Now *go!*"

"Wait, wait," Katarina said, regaining her composure after the Edela panic. She wagged a finger at the three men. "You told them everything else, Flannery? Yes, Doctor Remy, your brother has recently been in this house. But not as you would like to think about."

"What does that mean?" Remy demanded, moving toward her. Another hiss and flash of Katarina's canines kept him back.

"You did not get to the part about what Travis did to Jimmy Van Buren?" Katarina asked. Amused eyes volleyed between Flannery and Marcus.

"No. *Don't*," Flannery insisted to her foe.

"Give me my Edela, and then I won't!" Katarina said, ready for an exchange.

"You'll never see Maxine again," Marcus said. "I don't care what kind of threats or blackmail you try. You'll have to kill me first."

"Travis," Katarina said, a smile forming as she looked back to Remy. "He took a sword and ..."

The front door swung open downstairs. The sounds of rain filled the house again; its smell whooshed upstairs. The strong wind from outside trailed through the foyer and caused the door to crash into the wall.

"Where is she?" a familiar voice bellowed, from the foyer below. "I demand to see Flannery Lanehart *now!*"

"Daddy," Wes said to himself. He peered down the staircase. "What on Earth?"

"Brother Washer, *please!*" Clementine cried out, rain-soaked, as she rushed in behind Reverend Washer. She tugged at the shoulder of his saturated jacket, unable to calm the blustery Wilkins Washer, who shook her away like a perturbed wet dog.

"Flannery Lanehart!" he angrily called out. *"Show yourself, devil woman!"*

"Reverend Washer, what in the world?" Tarva exclaimed, rushing into the foyer from the living room.

Upstairs, Wes turned to the others in the hallway. "I'm not sure what's goin' on down there," he said. "My Daddy is havin' a fit about somethin.'"

"And he has *Conrad* with him," Flannery said.

"*Conrad*," Remy said, stepping back and staring blindly down the stairs. "Where is he? I don't see him. *My brother?*"

Katarina grabbed Flannery's arm. "No, it is not Con—"

"Let go of me," Flannery said, taking her arm back.

"But you do not understand ..." Katarina began.

"I understand more than you think I do," Flannery said to her. "I don't have the power to end this, but Marcus and everybody else does. I won't do a damn thing to stop them either."

Katarina backed off. "I knew you would forsake me, whore. As soon as the old troll downstairs is done spewing, exposing you, and the coast is clear, you will find my final gift to you outside of this house."

"Your *final* gift?" Flannery asked. "Does that mean you're going away for good?"

"One of us is," Katarina replied cryptically.

"Wes, will you go see what your Dad wants with Flannery?" Marcus asked. "He's carrying on like a madman."

"Now I don't think I need to leave y'all alone up here!" Wes argued.

"I've got this. Go!" Marcus ordered, and Wes quickly obliged.

"You said Conrad is downstairs?" Remy asked. His head went in ten different directions. He turned and ran past Wes down the stairs.

"He thinks Conrad is downstairs in Jimmy's body," Flannery said.

"He doesn't realize Conrad is disguised as Clementine. Neither does the Reverend," Marcus said, shaking his head.

Katarina giggled. Soon it became mad laughter. The more her eyes ping-ponged between Marcus and Flannery, the more she carried on with her jovial fit. Flannery had never seen such amusement from Katarina, not even the night she was drunk on the homeless man's booze-tainted blood.

"Conrad downstairs? You are fools," Katarina finally said, as the laughing subsided.

Another gust of wind shot up the stairs, burning Marcus's nostrils with the dead of autumn. Katarina looked past Marcus and Flannery, and then she was back on Flannery.

"Don't forget my parting gift to you, whore," Katarina said. In a flash, she transformed into The Cape. A black mass blew past, over their heads and down the stairs. Another wave of thunder shook the house as The Cape collided head on with the wind in a loud bang, and Katarina made her escape out the front door.

Remy was in the foyer. He saw it fly out the door. *The thing I saw in Wes's driveway the first night I was here.* His confusion compounded.

The double doors of the great house slammed shut behind Katarina. D'Lynn rushed into the foyer behind Tarva, where Wes, Clementine, and the Reverend assembled.

"What in the world was that?" D'Lynn said, beside herself. "It sounded like a gunshot inside the house! I saw some big shadow and then the doors slammed so loud!"

"I saw it ... *again,*" Remy said.

Marcus and Flannery rushed down the stairs to the others.

"She's gone," Marcus said. "She got away."

"There she is!" Reverend Washer exclaimed. He pointed a finger of condemnation at Flannery. "The Devil incarnate herself! There she is!"

Flannery stood still; she said nothing. She lingered on the bottom step and motionlessly looked down on the Reverend as the harangue rolled off his tongue.

"Jezebel! She's also a killer! She *murdered* Percy Stratworth in cold blood! Like a harlot spit out of Hell by Satan! Wes, arrest this woman at once!"

"I can't," Wes said. He twitched and rubbed the left side of his neck.

"Can't we all just go sit down and talk and be rational about all this?" D'Lynn asked, tugging at the Reverend's jacket sleeve. "Please."

"No, D'Lynn, you can't reason with the Devil!" Reverend Washer clamored. He moved away from D'Lynn.

"Oh shut the hell up!" Marcus said to him. "Leave my sister alone! The one we should all be worried about just flew out of here to God knows where!" Marcus looked past Reverend Washer to Clementine. "And the other one we need to worry about is standing right behind you, you old hatemonger."

"You won't speak to me that way, sodomite! You and your whore sister—"

"Get the hell out of my house now, you nasty old bigot, before I physically throw you out of here!" Marcus went for the Reverend, who backed away a step. "I won't have a hateful fanatic like you in this house ever again! Now *leave!*"

"God wants me here!" the Reverend yelled back, standing in a puddle he tracked in.

"No, *He* does not! *Go!* And take *Conrad* with you!" Marcus shouted.

"Conrad? *Where* is Conrad?" Remy demanded to know. He was near tears in his aggravation. "I don't see my brother!"

"Conrad is in Clementine's body," Marcus said, calmer. The words drew a plethora of expressions and reactions. "He drugged me for days. Pretending to be her. I would have been back to my senses a long time ago if it weren't for my sitter over there feeding me pills twice a day."

"That is a lie! You are makin' up a lie to protect your murderer of a sister!" the Reverend blasted, unrelenting.

"Daddy, calm down," Wes said to Reverend Washer. "I think Marcus might be tellin' the truth."

"*You* as well?" The Reverend wore betrayal on his puffy face as he looked scornfully on his son. His jowls were beet-red. "My own flesh and blood? Sleep with dogs and you wake up with fleas, son! See what happens when you spend time with a sodomite and a whore!"

Marcus grabbed the old man by the arm. "*That's it!* You are out of here! You better never show your face on this property again, old goat, or I'll have you arrested for trespassing!"

"I'm an old man and a servant of God!" the Reverend hollered. "How dare you put your hands on me this way!"

"I don't give a damn how old you are," Marcus said, as he pulled him to the door. The Reverend's boots squeaked across the wet marble floor. "I want you out of this house."

"Wait!" Clementine called out, as Marcus made it to the door with Washer Senior. "I'm not Conrad. I swear! I'm *not!* I came to a while ago. It's me. I swear, it's me, it really is!"

"I don't know what to believe anymore," Tarva said to D'Lynn, who started to cry again.

"Where is my brother?" Remy continued, exasperated. "For God's sake, will somebody please tell me where the hell my brother is!"

"*Your brother's dead. I killed him.*" It came from the top of the stairs.

Everyone's heads turned as Travis slowly came down the staircase.

Once he reached the bottom, he moved past the others and stood before Remy.

"He was trying to choke Uncle Marcus to death, and that's when I cut off his head with a sword. Your brother's gone. I'm sorry," Travis said to Remy.

41

"No!" Marcus let go of the Reverend and rushed to Travis's side to face Remy. "Your brother was gone long before he ever came into this house. Conrad was the one who killed him, *not* Travis."

"I killed the body," Travis said. "I have to take responsibility for what I did, Uncle Marcus. I'm sorry, Doctor Van Buren."

Remy turned and walked across the room, the color drained from his face. He shook his head as he tried to comprehend Travis's story. "I—I don't. I—" Remy struggled for words.

"Oh my goodness," D'Lynn said, with a sniffle. Tarva put an arm around her. "I need to go sit down. I can't take all this!"

"Where's the body now?" Wes asked. "I have to radio the department. We need the remains for evidence."

Marcus's mouth went dry. "It was—I buried it in the woods. Near a tree about fifty yards into the woods out to the east of the property. If you take anybody in, Wes, take me. I'm the one who got rid of the body."

"I helped you," Travis said. "You'll have to arrest me, too, Wes."

"Let's stick with one thing at a time. Stretch is on his way and should be here soon. I'll need y'all to take us to where the body is buried. It's comin' down out there, so I sure hope he has tarps with him."

"Well, I *can't* take you where the body is," Travis said. "I don't know where the body is ... it's gone. Somebody took it. I went and tried to dig it up last week, and it ain't there anymore."

"Oh my God," Remy wailed. He sank into a seat on the floor in the corner of the foyer as he cried. *"Jimmy...!"*

"What do you mean it's gone?" Wes asked. "Why did you want to dig it up, Travis? For one of them there Satanic rituals of yours?"

"Wes, don't be ridiculous," Marcus said.

"I'm not a Devil worshipper, you dumb fuck!" Travis shouted at Wes. "I went to make sure it was still there because Doctor Van Buren was here askin' questions, and I got nervous!"

"Who could've moved the body?" Wes asked, looking to Marcus.

"I didn't move the body," Marcus said. "It's the first I've heard of this."

"Who else knew about it?" Wes continued, in full interrogation mode.

"No one." Marcus lowered his voice and peered to the living room, where Tarva had taken D'Lynn to sit. "D'Lynn saw what happened that morning, after the fact," he whispered. "But she's blocked it out of her memory. She saw the body and the head on the living room floor and fainted. She never remembered after she woke up."

"So, you, Travis, and D'Lynn. Nobody else?" Wes asked.

"No. Except Geoff and Bobby, but they're dead and gone. D'Lynn can't dig up and move a body. I don't understand how it can be missing. Somebody else must have seen us bury it out there."

"Katarina," Flannery said, still frozen at the foot of the stairs. "It has to be her. She was inside the house all last spring, and nobody ever knew. She must have seen them bury it."

"What would Katarina want with a body?" Marcus asked, staring at Wes. He was still having trouble meeting his sister's eyes.

"Son, you are right! This *is* a hell house!" the Reverend shouted to Wes. "I can't take it anymore," he grumbled, walking out the door into the rainy night.

"Good riddance! Don't ever show your face here again!" Marcus shouted after him. He turned back to Wes. "You'll have to arrest me. I tampered with evidence and hid a body. Leave Travis out of this. *I* killed Jimmy Van Buren."

"Maybe we should ask Conrad what he knows," Flannery suggested, her emerald eyes fixed on Clementine. "Tell them."

Clementine looked to the ceiling and trembled. "I swear to God, I didn't mean it! I only needed a favor! He was charming. Oh God up above, forgive me, I shouldn't have done it, but I—"

"What is she talking about?" Marcus asked. "I think it really *is* Clementine."

"Well, *who else* would it be?" Wes asked.

"I told you. Conrad is inside her! Or *was*," Marcus said.

Clementine stopped praying and ran over to them. "I'm so ashamed! I just wanted *you*, Wes!" She started to cry. "How many years has it been since high school? Seventeen? Eighteen? And all this time, *all this time*, you've wasted all your hopes and wishes on Flannery over there. I come to your house, I bake you cookies for work, I sit by you at church ... and *she* comes back to town, and you're like a puppy. Chasing after her all over again! What about *me*, Wes? *What about me?*" Clementine backed away, more hysterical. "I had had enough! I only did what was left to do. And *he* came to me. *He* told me he could make you love me! The night they took Marcus away, after I left here, after Flannery was so mean to me ... *he* appeared to me. *He* told me he could make *you* love me, and that he could also help me make Flannery pay! So I did it! I took him up on that offer he made me. I didn't care if he was of the Devil. I was *so* mad at the way she talked to me in here that night!"

Clementine turned to face Flannery. "I hate you! I hate you! *I hate you!* I hope you rot in Hell, you spoiled rich ... bitch! You always thought you were better than me and all the other girls at school! *I hate you!*"

Clementine then ran out the front door, leaving it slung open. The sounds of the rain floated back in, this time a calmer breeze accompanied the echoed splatter past the porch outside.

Before anyone could say anything else, a terrible scream came from Clementine out front.

"What now?" Marcus asked, as they all ran to the front porch.

"Oh dear God! *Daddy!*" Wes cried. He quickly went down the steps into the driveway, where Clementine was hunched in the rain over an unconscious Reverend Washer.

"What happened to him?" Marcus asked, following Wes. Cold drops of rain stabbed at his head and face.

Travis and Flannery stayed back. Remy stumbled to the doorway, emotional and sniffling.

"His neck!" Clementine screamed, as Marcus reached them.

Marcus immediately knew what was wrong when he saw the puncture wounds on the left side of Reverend Washer's neck.

"He's got a pulse, but it don't feel strong," Wes said, with a sad face, as he looked back to the house. "Doctor Van Buren! I need you out here! Please help my Daddy!"

Remy snapped to his senses and rushed down the steps to where they were. "Move back," he said. "Let me have a look. Somebody hold their jacket over us so he doesn't get wetter than he already is."

Marcus turned and stared toward the porch at Flannery. Not knowing what to make of his expression, she came down the steps and closer to them.

"Is the wound closed?" she asked Marcus, through the rain.

"*What?*" he replied, confused, and barely able to hear her.

"The puncture wounds. He'll end up like Travis if the wound isn't closed soon."

"Who cares," Marcus said, turning back to the old man with a disgusted look.

"He's a hateful bigot, Marcus, yes. But be the better man here. *Always* be the better man." She went over to Remy. "Move away," she told him. "I can fix this."

Without questioning her, Remy obliged. He, Wes, and Clementine stepped back as Flannery knelt beside the Reverend. She put her index and middle fingers to his throat.

"Oh my God. What the hell," Remy said, with a loud exhale, when he saw the bright yellow light emanate from Flannery's fingers. "What is she doing? What *is* she?"

"She told us earlier," Wes said, with a shaky voice. "And I guess it's true."

After a few seconds, Flannery stood. "He should be okay," she said. "I'm not sure if it was Katarina, or who did this to him."

"Oh my gosh, I can't believe this is happenin'. Flannery, thank you for savin' my Daddy's life!" Wes said, back over at his father's side.

Flannery nodded and stood back. She took a few steps backward toward one of the oak trees, as Remy, Wes, and Clementine huddled over Reverend Washer. Marcus was off on the other side of all of them.

Marcus looked across the way at Flannery and gave her a small smile. She nodded and returned a fuller smile to her brother. Their eyes locked for a moment.

I love you, big brother, Marcus heard her say to him, though she was yards away, and her lips never moved.

Then alarm struck Marcus's face; he saw the figure come from around the large oak tree behind Flannery.

Marcus tried to yell out a warning. Flannery shook her head in bewilderment at his change of expression, and that's when she felt the sharp pain between her shoulder blades. She wasn't sure what had just happened.

What? Did somebody hit me? Why does it hurt?

"*Surprise,* bitch!" Regan hissed in Flannery's ear, from behind. She drove the dagger the rest of the way in. It pierced Flannery's heart and came out the other side of her.

Flannery's emerald green eyes widened one last time as she stared down at the silver end of the blade protruding from her chest.

She weakly turned her eyes. Regan wore a large smile and bore long canines. The rain washed a last bit of Reverend Washer's blood off Regan's dark face. She pulled the dagger out as quickly as she had shoved it in. She held on to it as she circled around. Flannery caught a glimpse of the familiar, emblazoned letter 'D' on the weapon, as it slipped from Regan's hands and to the ground, making a tiny bounce before it settled in a puddle.

Katarina's parting gift.

"*No!*" Marcus and Travis shouted at the same time. Flannery saw them run toward her. It was slow motion; her vision faded. Marcus's face was twisted, angry, and bereaved. Through her fluttering eyes, she saw her brother speed up as he reached out and caught her. They went to the ground together, as she collapsed into his arms.

Travis took off in another direction after Regan, who shot off toward the woods in a blur.

"Oh God, no, stay with me," Marcus cried, cradling Flannery on the soggy ground. As desperate as he was, he knew begging for help would do no good.

Wes and Remy ran to them. Clementine helped a conscious Wilkins Washer to his feet.

"Flannery?" Wes said pitifully, as he looked down at a sobbing Marcus. Remy stood stunned beside him. He also knew it was hopeless.

Marcus clutched Flannery tightly to him. *His words.* The last words he said to her at Izzy's house. They were burned into his memory. Marcus found himself burdened with yet another regret.

"I didn't mean it. I'm sorry. Oh God, don't leave me. I love you, Flannery," Marcus sobbed, holding her face next to his, as he gave her kisses up and down her cheek. The heavy rain was merciless as it washed them. *"I didn't mean it..."*

Flannery's hand made one last shaky effort as it went up and brushed Marcus's wet hair. Then it vanished along with the rest of her, as she disintegrated in his arms.

Marcus was left huddled on the ground, crying out loudly to the heavens as his arms were draped with his sister's soggy and empty clothes.

Remy stood back, suddenly free from a bondage he hadn't consciously known was there. It was liberating, and he couldn't understand why relief, a calm—an enlightenment!—swept over him, if Flannery and Jimmy were indeed dead and forever gone.

He would never be able to explain any of this to anyone.

He grew sad again.

Jimmy, Remy thought, as he turned away from the others and looked back at the great house of Ten Points. Then he started to cry again.

42

Travis ran across the clearing, catching glimpses and shadows, but unable to see Regan clearly. The rain slacked off away from the house, but it still came down hard enough to slow him and obstruct his view in the night. Just when he thought he lost her, he saw a figure several dozen yards away move into the woods.

Or was it a large Cape he saw fly into the woods? Everything had happened so fast in the past few minutes. It was too difficult to process or make sense of anything anymore.

I'll never find her in there, he thought, as he stopped at the edge of the forest.

Regan. She was one of the living dead now. Since when? Before or after she was in his room? Was he responsible? How would he ever explain this to her mother? What would he do when he *did* find her? Destroy her? Try to understand her?

He *couldn't* understand her. Not anymore.

Flannery. His Aunt Flannery. She could be mean at times, yes, but she was family. In her own strange way she had loved him and was remorseful for what she allowed D.C. to do to him. Now she was gone. Regan destroyed somebody in his family.

Travis now understood what D.C. had done to him. He also knew there was another shift earlier in the evening. He felt normal. His enhanced night vision was gone. He felt no urges or longings to be near D.C. *What had happened?*

"Regan!" he called out. "Where are you? Regan!"

No answer. She hid from him. Ashamed of what she did?

No, she wasn't ashamed of anything because this wasn't Regan. Regan would have never stabbed somebody through the heart. This murderous, running, flying thing was something new—not the Regan he had known; the girl to whom he had given eighteen months of his life and heart.

Whatever she was, she was lying in wait, plotting an attack as he went into the forest and considered how to comb the woods.

"Regan, I know you're in here ... somewhere. Come out. Face me. Let's talk about this!"

He crept through a maze of trees and tried to avoid hitting brush, branches, or twigs to draw attention. It was hard to see. The trees shielded forest innards from moonlight. There wasn't even a breeze anymore. Trees shook off droplets of rain, and outside that, no other sounds were heard. Droplets hit the forest floor in uneven patterns.

"I know I said some bad stuff to you earlier, Regan. I didn't mean it. I want to talk about it. Can we talk about it?"

He grew more frightened as he went farther. Part of him—no, make that *most* of him—wanted to turn around and go back to the house. Katarina and Conrad could also be out here somewhere. *Or* was Conrad really Clementine, as they said back at the house?

Flannery. Tilda. Bobby. Zeke. And even Geoff and Maximilian. Why did there always have to be so much loss around him?

"Travis," called the voice, deeper into the woods. *"Come find me, Travis."*

Just like the nightmare he had about Conrad. Only this was someone he loved. Or *had* loved. "Regan? Where are you?" he called back. He tried to sound unafraid.

"I'll tell you when you're gettin' warm, silly boy," it said, followed by a short giggle. *"Right now you're cold. Freezing cold."*

"I'm not in the mood to play some messed-up version of hide and seek," Travis said, his voice shaking. "Just come out and show yourself to me, Regan!"

He moved forward and efforted light steps instead of trudges. She could announce herself with an attack from any direction at any moment. He blindly relied on her love for him—if there was any left—to keep him from potential harm.

Maybe she was pissed over what he had said to her earlier. Coldly, he had dismissed her from his room, as if he fired her from a job.

"Regan, please, I take back those awful words earlier. I want to talk. I swear I didn't mean it," he said, in a sweeter tone. He wasn't convinced she would buy it, but he had to try.

Please God, please keep me safe out here. It was his first prayer in a long time, though he had plenty of doubts whether prayer worked—or if there really could be a God.

"*A little warmer,*" it said. The voice was closer.

A chill ran through him. What would she do when he did find her? He doubted highly that she would sit quietly and listen with reason as he pleaded for forgiveness.

Which would only be a trick to smoke her out of the woods, he decided. She would have to be destroyed. Quietly and quickly. He couldn't allow her to live like this. She was already dead. It wasn't the *real* Regan.

"Regan, I—"

The bright red-orange-white flash of light blinded and jarred Travis into a new fear as it illuminated the entire forest with a light booming sound. The final, white part of it slowly fizzled and died down. He could still see a faint glow ahead.

What the hell is it, and where did it come from? he thought, as he walked toward the residual light. That was when he saw it. The old stones where a well once existed on the property. Now covered with a cement cap.

A cap that was slightly ajar as if it had been moved recently. A kaleidoscope of bright red, orange, and white danced through the cracks seductively ... as it ushered Travis toward it.

He remembered the old well in the woods from when he was a boy. Maximilian warned him never to go near it. Maximilian told him ghosts of slaves from Ten Points' days gone by lived in the well, along with other monsters.

Anything to keep a small boy away from a dangerous and remote area. Or was it such a tall tale?

Travis walked to the cap and tried to look inside through the crack. It was like trying to peek through a slightly ajar curtain from outside a window. *Like at Doctor Colson's house last spring, when I watched Geoffrey move in for an attack.* Travis couldn't get a clear view of what was inside. He would have to remove the concrete lid—if he could manage to do so.

To his surprise, it felt as if the lid weighed no more than eighty or ninety pounds. Travis wasn't the strongest guy, but with some effort and a few grunts, he slid the circular piece of concrete further off the top of the well. With one final shove, it fell off and landed on the ground.

The height of the stones around the well came only to his knees. He was cautious when he bent to peer inside.

A multi-colored glow that matched the flash of light he had seen through the forest emanated from what looked to be a pool of water deep below.

He carefully leaned over the edge a little more for a closer inspection. The flashes of white were so bright he squinted as they hurt his eyes. Then the voice was behind him.

"Hot!"

He stood up straight and spun around to face Regan. She had crept up. She smiled, canines still elongated.

"R—Regan," Travis stammered, unable to move. Or run. "What happened to you?"

"What do you mean *what happened?*" she asked, with a giggle. "Don't you like me this way, Travis?"

"I never said I wanted you to change anything," he said nervously. He wasn't sure what answer would be satisfactory.

"Well now, D.C.'s spell on you may be broken, but we can get you right back to where you were—and then some," she said.

"Wh—what?"

"If you really love me, if you really want to make it up to me like you say you do, then you'll come over to my side."

"Your side?"

Regan lost the smile and looked on him with impudence. "Why do you keep answerin' everything I say with a question? I know you're not dumb, Travis."

"Not dumb. Just *numb*."

"I attacked Reverend Washer because I was hungry," Regan said, licking her lips. "But I knew it would also bring your Aunt Flannery outside. I knew I could destroy her and prove my loyalty to Katarina. It was for *her*. I'll be a much better servant to Katarina than your ungrateful bitch of an aunt ever was. I mean, I proved it when I destroyed your aunt! I can also teach *you* how to serve *me*, Travis."

Travis regained his ability to move and backed off a step. "No, I can't let you do that."

Regan was unwilling to take anymore rejection. "Come with me, Travis. Nobody wants it at first, but then when you have it you wonder why you didn't cross over sooner. It's so ... *divine*." She moved closer. "What little blood I got from the Reverend wasn't enough. I need *more*. We can do this the easy way ... or the hard way, Travis."

"I said *no!*" he argued, losing his footing. He almost went over the side of the well. He reached down and caught himself on a piece of old stone in time.

"That could've been bad," she said. "Of course, you would probably like to see what's down there."

"I'm okay up here," he said, losing his breath. He wasn't sure anymore how to coax her from the woods.

"If you won't obey me up here, then I think you need a closer look down there," Regan said, giving him a strong shove and sending him in.

Travis took a free fall but caught a jagged stone on the way down. He held to it with all the strength he could muster. His breaths were loud, fast, and panicked as he dangled at least twenty feet above the multi-colored glow below him. It was shiny.

Shiny like water.

Or shiny like *glass*.

Was it fiery and hot below, or did something else propel those flashes of red-orange-white light? He felt no rise of heat.

All he had in front of him was a murky stone wall. His aching hands started to slip from the jagged stone to which he so desperately clung.

Regan stared down from solid ground ten feet above. "Regan, please. Okay. Just let me out of here. *Please.* Why did you push me?"

"Because I was *told* to push you. Just now. I wanted a drink, but Katarina told me to wait. I can hear her voice inside me. It's so beautiful. *She's* so beautiful. Don't worry, Travis. You won't be alone for long."

"*Wh—what?*" he said, struggling with words as he struggled to hold on.

"I have to make a wish first," she said. Regan dropped what appeared to be a penny down to the bottom.

There was no splash. Travis was too petrified to look down. He heard a *ping!* from below. As if the copper penny had hit glass or a hard surface instead of landing in a pool of water.

What the hell was down there?

The errant stone gave way under Travis's weight. It broke free from its foundation like a gigantic loose tooth. Travis screamed out as he went down again, this time fast, with nothing to reach and grab.

The glistening, bright bottom of the well came for him. He prepared for a painful thud that would break his fall—and at least one of his legs.

Instead, the membrane shattered into dozens of pieces as Travis and the errant stone that fell away with him crashed into and went through it.

It was then that Travis passed through to the other side.

Conrad

By the time Katarina ran down the upstairs hallway shrieking and carrying on for *her Edela,* Conrad had stashed himself away in one of the second-floor guest bedrooms. He stood inside the darkened room, where he overheard the exchange between Katrina, Marcus, Flannery, and Remy—and, later, Wes—in the hallway.

Thankfully Katarina's focus was off Conrad. Her madness turned to her fantasy child and the others who confronted her when her panic revealed her whereabouts inside the fifty-seven-room mansion.

Then there was the commotion downstairs, as Reverend Wilkins Washer stormed into the foyer with the wind and rain, demanding a showdown with Flannery. The voices in the hallway moved downstairs, and Katarina vanished sometime during all of this.

Conrad strained to hear whether Flannery would give Old Goat Washer what he wanted when it came to a face-to-face. The old man carried on as if he had a wooden stake and hammer, ready to rid the world of the embodiment of evil—the label he had branded upon Flannery.

Thanks to me, Conrad thought, happy to have exposed her, as he kept a curious ear close to the door.

Before things could grow more titillating, a stoic Marcus—ever-protective of his dead sister—threw the Reverend out of the house. From upstairs, it sounded as if physical force may have even been involved.

Moments later, Clementine LeMonde's scream came from the front yard near the driveway. Having possessed her body for days, Conrad knew the loud wail. He ran to the window, threw back the curtain and peeked outside. The room was dark enough. No one outside in the night and the rain would see him peer down from a second-story window.

Out near one of the oak trees, everyone was hunched over the Reverend. A heart attack or stroke? Surely, Marcus hadn't hurt or upset the old man *that* much?

As Flannery moved in and put her fingers to the Reverend's neck, Conrad nodded. Ah yes, he had been attacked by someone else. *Something else.* Not Flannery. Katarina? *Or...?*

The Reverend regained consciousness. With Clementine's help, he slowly sat up as the rain fell on them.

Flannery backed away toward an oak tree, and that was when Conrad saw the figure—Regan!—emerge. She stabbed Flannery through the back. *Through the heart.* Conrad could see the silver blade come out the other side.

Ah, so *that* was Katarina's final surprise for Flannery. Now the queen vampire bitch would pay double, for robbing Conrad of the opportunity to dispose of Flannery himself. He could take no satisfaction in any of this if it was devoid of his hand.

Marcus cried out a *No!* that caused Conrad to flinch. Marcus ran toward his sister and yelled her name. He quickly took her into his arms as they collapsed on to the ground.

My Marcus, Conrad thought. As joyous as it was to think of Flannery forever gone—and as bitter as it also made him that *he* was denied the opportunity to annihilate the insubordinate traitor of a former comrade—he couldn't bear to see his Marcus, his *Adam,* so overcome.

Conrad moved his eyes away from Marcus. He saw Travis take off into the darkness toward the woods. Travis chased after Regan, who took off in a streak as if she had been released from a sling-shot. He wasn't sure, but Conrad *thought* he saw the girl transform into a large Cape-like apparition once she reached the clearing.

Travis had better not hurt Regan. Or the skinny bastard would pay double. No one but Conrad knew his reasons for wanting to protect the girl. *No one at the house anyway.*

Conrad left the window. Yes, he was sorely disappointed that Flannery was gone, and he had no role in it. Yet, there was glee over her demise. Was there a word for such an odd, mixed feeling? Bittersweet was too gentle and kind. *Damn you, Katarina,* he thought.

Conrad's thoughts were forced elsewhere when the cold, dead hand reached out and grasped his shoulder.

He let out a small yelp as he spun around. The goings-on outside were no longer relevant. No matter how dark the room, the fierce, stern blue eyes of the sandy-haired man staring back at him were unmistakable.

"Daddy?" Conrad asked. He shook his head in disbelief and backed away a few steps.

"You've been a *very* naughty boy, son," Theodore Ogden Senior frowned, half-sprouted canines visible as he spoke.

Travis

The bright red, orange, and blinding white hues of the vortex melded, separated, and blended again as Travis passed through at a breakneck pace. Like a vacuum, it pulled him forward. He was aware of the wide space around him, unsure if it was a tunnel. Colors surrounded him as he flew against his will, where to he did not know.

Then he heard the voice. It was soft, low, but omnipresent, as if some deity whispered in his ear. He could only make out words and phrases here and there as everything else flew past him.

Ten Points...1817. Tenth of the Ten Points. Nine came before it.

He turned and twisted every which way; there was no control over anything—or how fast he flew.

He tried to listen to the voice, but the sounds of wind and the whirl as he sped forward drowned out some of the data fed to him.

Theodore Ogden Senior begat Theodore Ogden Junior...1834.

Travis wasn't sure where The Whisper came from, or if it was the voice of a man or a woman. It sounded almost like a machine. Was he inside a computer?

Theodore Ogden Junior married Isabella...1862. Begat Mary Ann...1863, died 1872...Horace, born 1864, died 1872...Martha, born 1867, died 1872. Theodore Ogden Junior, born 1834, died 1872.

Then there were more names; more dates. It continued down the family line. Every time a name was recited, the red, orange, and white would rotate so that one of the three colors dominated. A new color for each name. When it was time for the white, the light so bright and blinding that Travis squeezed his eyes shut.

Only bits and pieces of The Whisper remained audible. But Travis thought he heard incorrect information here and there. Some of the names and dates began to go off track from what he knew to be true.

Maximilian had known the family history well and always enjoyed telling the stories of past generations.

The Whisper eventually made it down the line to Maximilian.

Maximilian Lanehart. Born 1942.

Maximilian and Jessica begat Geoffrey Lanehart. Born 1973.

Maximilian and Jessica begat Marcus Lanehart. Born 1978.

Maximilan and Jessica begat—it was inaudible but Travis was certain it wasn't Flannery's name he heard—*born 1980.*

The Whisper went high and low. A louder gust in his ear made it more difficult to hear anything else. He never heard Flannery's name, Bobby's name, Maxine's name, or his own name. Why the hell not?

Am I dead? he wondered. *Is it the voice of God I hear? Am I going to the afterlife? Is this what happens when you die?*

The three colors started to fade; the vortex grew darker. Travis went from being pulled horizontally. He felt an upward tug; he rose and no longer flew. Straight up a tunnel, as if he were in an elevator.

He realized he was inside the well again, as he was shot out the top—propelled like a cannonball, as the well rejected and purged him.

Travis landed hard on the grass a few feet away.

This was no longer in the woods. The well was now, *somehow*, only about fifty yards from the house.

But the house of Ten Points was different. It had always been white.

Now it was more an *off*-white.

He pulled himself to his feet, then stumbled and fell from dizziness.

"I can't walk," he said, coughing. He crawled through the grass, a duller color from what he guessed were the recent November night freezes. It was wet with dew; there were no signs of rain from the night before. The morning was cool but sunny.

"How can it be morning already?" he muttered aloud, though no one was there. It felt as if only five or so minutes had passed since Regan's shove.

A loud motorized noise came from overhead. It sounded a lawn mower. In the sky. But when Travis looked up, he saw a chrome-colored ... *what the hell* ... a chrome-colored bicycle with a propeller.

An odd combination of a bicycle and a helicopter, about one

hundred feet up in the air. Travis could still see its pilot pedal at a rapid pace, perhaps to keep the motor or engine alive?

A sharp whistle from the ground came from over near the house.

"He's gonna crash and break his neck," Travis heard a familiar voice exclaim loudly, with a laugh that must have been from where the whistle came. "Damn fool."

Travis was still too dizzy to stand and walk. He kept crawling for the house. The house that didn't look quite the same.

Then something else caught his eye.

A tarantula crawled toward him across the grass; it came from the direction of the house.

It couldn't be.

"Harry?" he asked. *Or Harry's ghost.*

Oh Harry, I was out of my mind. I didn't mean what I did to you, boy.

Travis gained a clearer picture as the giant spider got closer. It wasn't furry and menacing; it was shiny and metallic. A robot spider the size of a human hand. A child's toy?

"Hello," it said to Travis in an electronic, monotone voice, once it was an inch from his face. The eight legs of metal stopped moving and parked themselves at his nose. "What is your name?"

"What the fuck," Travis mumbled. He must be dead.

"I do not recognize 'whatthefuck,'" the robot spider said. Then a small red light on top of its golden thorax started to flash and beep. Loudly, out of control.

"What the hell? We got a trespasser?" Travis heard the whistling man off in the distance, up where the house was. Yes, the same familiar voice from before that had whistled and laughed.

The robotic spider was some kind of alarm system? It was too perplexing.

"It's okay," Travis heard another voice call out, to the other person at the house. This one, the husky sound of a female. "He's my boy. I got it, man."

The flashing light on the robotic spider was shut off from afar as Travis saw a familiar figure approach. Goth girl from the woods. Short black hair. Black lacy top, this one not-so-Victorian, and the same hooped mini-skirt. She wore long black stockings and had already applied black lipstick for the morning.

She narrowed her eyes as she reached him; he wasn't sure what to expect.

"You again?" he coughed out, as he sat up. "What's up with the house? And why is it mornin' already?"

"The name is Scarlett, and shut the hell up, man. Don't say another word. Why are you crawlin' around on the ground, and how the hell did you get here?"

She reached down and took his hand and pulled him to his feet.

"Here?" Travis asked. He brushed wet grass off his own dark clothes and stared into her eyes. Eyes that strangely and eerily matched his own. "I live here," he said.

"Um, okay," she said, with a sarcastic smile. "I'll take you to the house, but I'm grounded right now, so you better keep it down, man."

"Why are you grounded? And why are you taking me to my own house?" he asked, still dizzy and unsteady on his feet.

"Be quiet!" Scarlett said to him, as they reached the main yard. She grabbed his arm and steadied him. "Just keep it down, or they'll all think you're crazy or high. And for the love of God, man, walk normal and quit stumblin' around."

"What the fuck are you talking about?" he shouted.

"Cool it, man. *Now,*" she said, raising a painted black eyebrow and sticking her index finger in his face.

"Who are you?" he asked. "I see you in the woods ... *once* ... and you suddenly think you live at Ten Points?"

"I told you. I'm Scarlett. And I *do* live here. You'll see."

"But I don't underst—"

"Shhh," she quieted him, for the third time. She let go of his arm. "We're gonna walk in there and pretend like you're my friend from school."

"You still go to school?" Travis asked. "You look too old."

"I'm eighteen at the end of the month. I'm a senior. *Old?* Whatever, man."

When they reached the porch, Travis paused. *"D.C.?"*

The whistling man from earlier was D.C. Cunningham standing off in the front yard. But he was dressed oddly. In a long, blue swashbuckler jacket, and white shirt with ruffles in the front. He pointed to the strange flying invention in the sky and spoke to another man whose back was turned to Travis and Scarlett.

The other man near D.C. also wore a long-sleeved white shirt and a dark blue tapestry vest. He held what looked to be a cup of coffee. Travis could only see the back of his head.

"Why is D.C. dressed that way?" Travis asked, as they approached. "That other man, too. And what is that thing in the sky they're watching?"

"*Be quiet,*" Scarlett repeated, lightly slapping him on the arm.

D.C. was still too loud for a private conversation, no matter what his dress. "Geoff Lanehart and his flying toy. That fool just ain't right!" he exclaimed, with another raucous laugh.

Geoff? Travis squinted and looked to the sky. He could see a tiny figure of a man pedal furiously and happily wave down to the others on the ground.

Then the man with the vest turned to D.C. Travis let out a cry of a gasp. "I never thought he'd get that thing off the ground, to be honest," the familiar man in the vest said to D.C.

"*Zeke!*" Travis ran to the vested man and hugged him tightly. Zeke Colson almost dropped his cup of coffee from the surprise. Travis felt tears well in his eyes as he clutched on to someone he was certain he would never see again. "Zeke, you're alive! Oh my God, I can't believe it's you, man."

"Whoa, buddy!" Zeke laughed nervously, taken aback by the strange kid who appeared out of nowhere and grabbed him. He turned to Scarlett. "Who is this?" he asked her, pulling away and staring at Travis.

"Oh look, Zeke, you got a new friend," D.C. teased, with a laugh. "Scarlett, who's this friend of yours? Have y'all been hangin' out and smokin' the funny stuff this mornin'?"

"He bumped his head and isn't feelin' good. We were about to go to school, but he fell and hurt himself," she said. She gave Travis a 'shut up and play along' glare.

Zeke pulled Travis toward him and studied his eyes. "His pupils look normal," he said. "Maybe we should take him in the house for a closer look. I'm better with animals, but we can see if he's okay."

"Zeke, I can't believe it's you," Travis repeated, with a disbelieving smile. "It's *really* you!"

The front double doors of the house opened, and Travis's confusion grew.

"What's going on out here?" Marcus asked, stepping on to the porch. He was dressed in an elegant gray frock coat, vest, and pants. Like a character from a Dickens novel.

"Uncle Marcus?" Travis asked, as Zeke led him up the curved granite steps of the front porch.

Marcus smiled and stared at Zeke. "Did he call me *uncle?*"

"Scarlett says he fell and hit his head," Zeke said. "He's some school friend of hers. Let's take him inside the house and have a look at him."

"Good luck," Marcus said. "The Queen Bee just made her entrance downstairs."

"Oh jeez, it's too early to have to deal with her," Zeke said. He turned and motioned for Travis to follow him. "Come on inside our home. What's your name, kid?"

"I'm Travis," he replied, the blue eyes back and forth between Zeke and Marcus. "You both know *who* I am! Oh my God, what the hell is happening?"

"Shut up," Scarlett growled, from behind. She gave him a poke in the shoulder with her finger.

"Your friend may be hurt," Zeke told her. "Be a little nicer there, Scarlett."

"We just heard about more attacks last night," Marcus said to Zeke, as they passed through the threshold of the front door. "That vampire that's been on the loose. *Katarina,* they call her. She's been picking off more people. She showed up again during the night. Nobody knows where she comes from. I doubt she's working alone. The sheriff's office may put everybody under a curfew tonight."

Scarlett looked the other way and feigned ignorance.

"Vampires," Zeke said, with a disgusted grunt. "They're multiplying like cockroaches. Something's got to be done."

"You've let yourself get too riled by those town hall meetings and curfews," Marcus said. He shook his head and put a loving arm around Zeke.

"It wouldn't hurt you to be a little *more* riled about it," Zeke said.

Marcus laughed and shook his head again. "You're the political one of us, and it'll be under control soon. I won't let any of this dictate my life. Let's take this guy inside and make sure he isn't badly hurt."

All them stepped into the foyer. It was the same, Travis saw.

Why wasn't everybody else the same? he thought. And the *clothes*.

"Yes, I understand. Thank you, sheriff. I'll tell my husband and stepchildren about the curfew." Another familiar voice drifted to the foyer from the living room, only it was more formal, a tad stilted. Travis heard a landline phone hang up.

Then *she* walked into the foyer from the living room. The face was the same, but it looked a bit tighter, and bore make-up. The dark brown hair was perfectly coifed and colored, to cover any grays. But much of it was hidden underneath a burgundy-colored headdress. The slimmer figure was enveloped by a matching Elizabethan-style dress. At her collar was an extravagant necklace with rubies and other jewels.

Instead of her usual warm and grandmotherly demeanor, the older woman stared down her nose at Travis with disdain. "Who is this?" she asked.

"*D'Lynn* it's me!" Travis said. "Why are you wearing that dress? And since when do you have a husband and stepkids?"

She moved back a step and scoffed in insult. "I do *not* know who you are, but while you're in *my* house, young man, you will show some decorum and address me as *Mrs. Lanehart!*" D'Lynn said, with a scowl.

"He's a friend of Scarlett's. We found him outside," Zeke explained.

D'Lynn gave Scarlett a contemptuous glare. "I'm not surprised he's a friend of *hers*," the older woman said.

Steps came down the hallway. Travis's eyes grew wide again. *Grandpa?*

"D'Lynn, dear, what are you carrying on about in here? I could hear you from the study," Maximilian Lanehart said, walking to her side. He nodded and greeted Marcus and Zeke with a smile. "Good morning, son and my favorite son-in-law."

Zeke gave a laugh. "I'm your *only* son-in-law, old man."

Maximilian returned the laugh and gave Zeke a playful jab on the arm. Maximilian offered Travis a more welcoming expression than D'Lynn had. "Who have we here?" the old man asked, kindly and warmly.

"I just spoke with the sheriff on the phone. There will most definitely be a curfew tonight. More vampires!" D'Lynn said, ignoring her husband's question. She gave Travis a suspicious glare. "I hope this isn't some child of *Demetrio* in our house."

Scarlett's nervous eyes hit different parts of the room.

"*Demetrio?*" Travis asked.

"You can't be serious, D'Lynn," Marcus said to his stepmother, with a laugh. "This boy was outside in the daylight. Who believes some silly old legend about a handsome Spaniard roaming the woods and turning widows and virgins into vampires? *Demetrio?* Please."

"Well, all the vampires had to come from somewhere," D'Lynn argued. "And legend is somewhat based in fact most of the time. At least in my opinion."

"You are getting yourself a little worked up this morning, my love bug," Maximilian said to his wife.

"Do *not* call me an insect, and enough with all of this," D'Lynn said, in a haughty manner Travis had never seen from her. "I need my morning tea. I must have it at once! Where is that woman?"

"My mother is probably in the kitchen," Scarlett said, to D'Lynn.

"Well, dear, if you aren't in any hurry to get to school, maybe you can go light a fire underneath her to bring my tea," D'Lynn suggested.

"Comin', comin'!" came another voice, as it carried from down the hallway.

Travis's jaw dropped when the servant in the drab black-and-white maid's uniform appeared in the foyer with a silver tray.

"I'm sorry, Mrs. Lanehart, I had trouble with the pilot light on the stove, and it took a while to boil the water," Tilda said. She set down the tray and rushed timidly to D'Lynn with a cup and a saucer.

"*Mom?*" Travis croaked out, feeling faint again.

Tilda smiled at him strangely. "Huh?"

"No, man," Scarlett said, staring at Travis. "She's not your Mom. She's *my* Mom."

"Oh my God," Travis said. "Where am I?"

None of this can be real. Half these people are dead. This must be a dream.

He knew he had to wake up. He bit the inside of his lip. He felt it. And he was still there with all of them.

"*Well, who have we here?*"

Alexander Lanehart came down the stairs, buttoning a sleeve on the familiar tan long jacket. His dark blond hair was combed perfectly. The top hat and goggles were absent, but the walking stick was propped under his arm as he tended to his sleeve. He wore a smile that belied warmth as he looked directly at Travis.

"Oh shit, it's *way* too early for him," Scarlett said under her breath.

"You," Travis said, narrowing his eyes, as they locked with Alexander's.

"Yes, *me,*" Alexander said, the smile wider as he reached the bottom of the stairs. He held the golden-handled stick firmly in his hand and planted it beside him on the bottom step. "Welcome to *Nine* Points, Travis. I see you've met my family."

View other Black Rose Writing titles at www.blackrosewriting.com/books

and use promo code PRINT to receive a 20% discount when purchasing.